RETURN TO LEMURIA

Richard Gradner

Copyright © 2014 Richard Gradner

Second edition 2016

All rights reserved.

ISBN-13: 978-0-620-62265-3

www.richardgradner.com

https://www.facebook.com/richardgradnerauthor

About The Book

Billy Bayer has just alerted the mysterious descendants of an ancient civilisation. A civilisation that claim responsibility for every major historical event.

Billy is taken prisoner by the Lemurians after conspiring against his mob-boss. He is taught how to tap into his extra-sensory abilities and his life changes forever. This newfound power gives Billy the courage to confront his captors and challenge their age-old ideals. Together with his crew of loyal companions, he devises a plan to thwart the organisation's very existence.

But how can one man stand up to a 12,000-year old prophecy that predicts adversity for all mankind? The answer, it seems, is hidden deep in the Brazilian Amazonia with anthropologist Dr David Steel, who, together with the FUNAI Foundation, is on a mission to save the endangered tribes from persecution. It's his research that appears to contain the key to the survival of the human species.

When you finish reading this book, please consider posting a review on Amazon and/or Goodreads. Thank you.

About The Author

Richard Gradner is a Director at Mustard, a Creative and Digital agency based in Cape Town. He was the first Red Bull Marketing Director in South Africa and has a passion for brands and branding. Richard trained and taught Kung Fu and Tai Chi for over 12 years and currently runs his own massage therapy practice called GLVTE. He has a deep connection to all things spiritual and maintains a healthy mind and body through the daily practice of Power Yoga. He is also an international, bestselling author of fantasy novels, Return to Lemuria, Unicorn, Servant of Memory and Acoustic Alchemy, all available on Amazon.com. To find out more, please visit richardgradner.com.

Dedicated to Adéle, my wife, my soulmate.

PROLOGUE

New York, 16 November, 1888

Jemima Gadson considered herself a woman of worth. Her daddy was one of New York City's most prominent architects and was in high demand for his special talents. She was proudly married to James Gadson, a decorated Lieutenant General in the U.S. Army. James helped coordinate the fundraising effort for the construction of the Statue of Liberty in 1886, spearheaded by close friend and owner of the New York World newspaper, Joseph Pulitzer. It was no surprise that the Gadson's became very popular amongst New York's high society as a result.

Close friend and confidant, Peggity Lipman, was over for tea. Peggity's curly blond hair framed the friendliest smile. She recently moved to the New York area with her family and met Jemima at one of the Liberty fundraisers. They hit it off right away.

Jemima was sporting her new, pale-blue, box-pleated skirt. The latest fashion was a very narrow skirt, tied tightly behind the thighs which made walking quite difficult. She twisted her hips in an attempt to relieve the pressure, while she bent over the stove to remove the teapot of rapidly boiling water.

Jemima's long brown hair was tied up into a bun, yet she instinctively brushed her free hand past her face to wipe away some imaginary strands.

"They say that she was the first Russian woman to acquire U.S. citizenship," said Jemima nonchalantly, as she walked into the living room with a tray of tea and biscuits. The smell of hot tea and freshly baked goodies reminded Peggity of her mother's kitchen in Louisiana.

"Oh, really? I'm so excited to meet her. Tell me more!" said Peggity in that typical, high-pitched, southern drawl.

Jemima sat down across from Peggity and began pouring the tea. "You know that when I first met her, she grabbed my hand and twisted it around to read my palm? She told me that I was a selfish lover with an enthusiasm for life, and I was to stop allowing myself to be manipulated by my mother."

"And? Was she right?" Peggity shifted forward to the edge of her chair in anticipation.

"Spot on! I often find it hard to give in to James when we're having a debate because I feel that it'll make me appear weak. And then it dawned on me - my mother really does force me to do things that I never really feel like doing."

"Oh. Wow," said Peggity. "That's incredible. She sounds truly amazing."

"Yes. Such an inspiration." Jemima sighed. "You know, that she started the Theosophical Society over fifteen years ago already?"

"Really?"

"Yes. Her teachings and philosophies make so much sense. I've never been clearer about who I am and my true purpose in this world." Jemima gazed reflectively out of the window.

"Oh, golly!" exclaimed Peggity, as she glanced at the clock on the mantelpiece. "It's four o'clock. We'd betta get goin'." She took an extra large sip of tea, placed her teacup down on the tray and then stood up to straighten her dress.

"Oh, yes, yes, of course," agreed Jemima. "The Met is on Fifth Avenue, just a few blocks away. It shouldn't take us too long to get there."

The Metropolitan Museum of Art was busy. Over one hundred people gathered in the Medieval Hall. Peggity and Jemima pushed their way to the front of the crowd, who were all waiting eagerly in front of an empty podium for their speaker to emerge. The prattling died down and turned to applause as soon as she arrived. Helena Petrovna Blavatsky stepped up to the podium to welcome her supporters with a warm smile and open arms. She was small in stature but had a presence about her that was larger than life, which was partly due to her traditional Russian attire, consisting of a black petticoat, framed by a heavy, metal skirt. Her eyes seemed to bore right through the crowd as she looked out from beyond the wooden pedestal. Madame Blavatsky, as she came to be known, was born of Russian nobility and came to America in 1873. She spent most of her time promoting Eastern teachings and occult concepts through the Theosophical Society.

"Friends." Her Russian accent was thick and heavy. "Welcome to the Metropolitan Museum and the launch of my new book, *The Secret Doctrine.*"

Applause and cheers erupted from the gathering of onlookers. Peggity squeezed Jemina's hand in excitement.

"I would like to introduce you to a brief summary of the magnificent learnings that I have been fortunate to acquire during my travels to India and Tibet, without which, this work would not have been possible." Helena scanned the crowd, drawing her listeners in like bees to honey. "We begin, as all beginnings do, with the creation of the world which occurred within seven epochs made up of seven days and seven nights. Mankind was given his own days and nights, contained within them a finite beginning and a finite end, emerging at birth into the light of his own day and departing at death into the darkness of his own night. Seven epochs also spanned humanity, the first of which was known as the Polarian root race. This epoch came into being 150 million years ago as a terrestrial race of spiritual beings, leaving no physical trace of their existence. They were ethereal and angel-like, described by the Aztecs as colossal, dark-skinned giants."

There were murmurs from the crowd. Helena continued.

"The second root race was called the Hyperboreans. They lived near the North Pole, in the Land of the Eternal Sun. They were also etheric beings, leading spiritual lives with very little physical dependency. After a global cataclysm, the third root race, the Lemurians, emerged. They were the first root race to have physical bodies, although they were still considered a highly evolved spiritual race of man, with advanced psychic abilities. They experienced the mind and its awakening into a more physical existence, which included the formation of the sexes. They inhabited a continent called Lemuria that existed in the Pacific Ocean, between what is now America, Australia and the Orient. This vast continent was ravaged by volcanic and seismic activity and sank into the depths of the sea over 12,000 years ago, never to be seen again." Madame Blavatsky looked directly at Peggity.

"Oh me, oh my," exclaimed Peggity. Her face went hot.

"The Atlanteans were the fourth root race. They came into existence towards the end of Lemurian epoch. They possessed advanced technological prowess and lived on the continent of Atlantis, which was destroyed due to the abuse of their psychic powers. The Atlanteans were the ancestors of the fifth root race, the Aryans, the present-day epoch of terrestrial humanity. There are two epochs of humanity yet to come, the next one being the sixth root, often referred to as the New Age or Age of Aquarius. The seventh root race will only appear in a few millennium when humanity reverts to a purely spiritual existence."

"Ohh," Jemima turned to look at Peggity who was fanning her face. She looked completely flustered. "This is just too much for me, Jemima. I must have a copy of that there book. I do believe that it will *completely* change my life."

Part 1

They who dream by day are cognisant
of many things which escape those
who dream only by night.

- Edgar Allan Poe

CHAPTER ONE

Flight

Continent of Lemuria, 10,448 BCE

T'was the dawn of a new day. High upon the mountain peak, Mala embraced the morning with a wondrous delight. Her sea-green eyes were closed, yet they could see. The energy that was Gaia beneath her flowed, connecting with her life force, a magnetic energy so powerful, pulling and twisting with every breath she inhaled and every breath she expelled. Her breathing, emphatic as it was, finally became an instinctive reflex, as the forces that flowed around her, caused her connection to merge into a singularity of purpose. Connected she was. Free she became. The corners of her mouth lifted until a magnificent smile spread across her beautiful face. The sensation expanded, flowing through her body, until her entire being beamed in a magnificent, radiant glow of fiery delight. Warm rays, an extension of the sun's reach, clipped over the horizon, expanding and then swallowing her into a harmony of energy that was truly golden. The fiery glow erupted, as she held fast like a celestial comet on an exploratory journey of self-discovery. She traversed the island, crisscrossing its length and breadth in a matter of moments, observing the transition from night into day as the planet woke from its nocturnal inertia.

Mala rode the currents, as they bristled across the mystical divide, exploding into a sea of colour, spreading out and across the landscape until the infection spread as far as the eye could see. The sun's warmth resulted in a response from the flowers and trees, a gentle hum, that caused an ever so slight distortion in the flow. And then it settled. A chill rose up the base of her neck as she reached the ocean, diving in, on the back of a sunbeam, quickly reaching the coral in the shallow waters. The response, immense as it was, caused her to become one with the huge organism, identifying with its responsive shimmer and caressing the colourful sea life it contained. She shifted her gaze up, burst from the ocean and into the magnificent sun in all its glory, the source of power for her tribe and all life on the planet.

Mala, Mala.

It came to her, a breeze at first, rippling across the expansiveness that was the ocean, tugging at her heartstrings, teasing and testing. It was a calling from Shaia, her mother, Queen of the Lumni tribe and Sovereign of the Seven Kingdoms of Lemuria, a telepathic signature in a frequency that only she recognised, summoning her back to the valley. The calling increased in intensity, as she reluctantly released her connection to the harmony of energy and retreated back into her physical body on the mountaintop. The time had come once more for Mala to join her family in the morning ceremony - a series of chanting mantras acknowledging the powers of nature and the universal life-force that kept all living things bound together on the planet. But it was far more than that. It was a powerful, metaphysical union of the tribe, a spiritual experience that transcended time and space, transporting them on a journey across multiple dimensions and distant galaxies. It was Mala's recent encounter but on a far grander scale. The daily practice each morning was a union of the tribe honed into one powerful force of energy that rushed forth like an unstoppable torrent, arcing into the heavens in praise of the Creator and all his designs.

Bounding down the mountainside, charged with radiant, sun

energy, Mala was excited to share her latest experience with the rest of her family. Her footsteps barely touched the ground as she skipped into the ceremony space, an oval, well-worn patch of ground in the centre of the tribal village. She glided into place next to her mother who looked down and gave her a warm, reassuring smile, her green-grey sparkling eyes, a reflection of Mala's own. Looking down at her feet, she made sure that they were firmly rooted into the ground before reaching out to grab hold of her mother's right hand. At sixteen summers, Mala was the youngest of three siblings. Her two older brothers were twins, but they looked so apart that it was hard to believe they were related. To Mala's right, was her fair-headed brother Cuthru, a sympathetic and easy-going character. His natural desire to do better for others, made him well liked amongst the Lumni, and it was no surprise to see him often winning the annual talent event at the Lumniart Festival held each year of the sun on Baybol Beach. Mala smiled as she looked up at him. To the right of Cuthru was Asbeth. He was dark, fierce and intense. His chiselled features enhanced his regal stature and his natural arrogance only added to his reputation as a merciless, hot-tempered character. To the left of her mother, solid as a rock, was her father, King Andor. He looked quite regal, in his thick, tan-hide cloak and matching, long, bushy beard. The rest of the Lumni tribe of 180 members was beginning to assemble in a circle around a long, marble-hewn pillar, with a pyramid-shaped apex and a series of petroglyphs carved into its base. Not a word was spoken, as the final participants stepped into place. Mala glanced around the circle to watch everyone closing his or her eyes. She followed suit. The preparation sequence was always the most uncomfortable.

You've done this before. Relax. Everyone else is going through the same experience. Let go. Only then will it become easier.

With her eyes closed, she remembered her training with Groth, helping her connect her core to the collective. Groth was a seasoned light master, skilled in the art of light weaving and the natural arts. He was a short, stocky man with a bald head, white goatee and twinkly pale-blue eyes. His kindness and patience could tame a reptile.

"Mala you must let go of your desire to be," Groth would say. "This is what is holding you back. The only way to connect is to let go."

"But I'm *trying*. I really am!" squealed Mala in consternation.

"Ahh, but that's the catch" responded Groth with a friendly grin. "You're trying too hard. You have to stop trying, only then will you find your way."

"Stop trying? But if I stop trying, then how can I progress? How can I ever hope to find my way?"

Groth smiled patiently. "Hold my hand, child and close your eyes."

Clasping her tiny hand in his, Mala closed her eyes. Groth's probing thoughts found hers. The anxious feeling of frustration slowly but surely began to dissipate, and Mala found herself drifting in space. Serene. Timeless. Calming. A flicker of light in the distance grew into a solid beam that edged closer until it washed over her and connected to her core.

"Can you feel it? Can you feel the connection?" Groth's soothing voice echoed inside the open space he had created as a preparation ground for the connection he had initiated between them, and it was then and there that Mala learnt how to stop trying, let go and find her way.

It was this same feeling she experienced now, as she connected to her tribe. Beams of light washed over her in lavish abundance, a myriad of souls all connecting with her core and hers with theirs, to form a blinding column of solid energy that expanded and illuminated as one consciousness within the immaterial. The stone column in the centre of the circle was visible as a shimmering obelisk of dark matter, designed as an anchor, used to draw the group consciousness back to Gaia at the end of the ceremony. A collected surge of determination push-pulled the consciousness up and away from the circle, leaving a wispy trail of ethereal sparks in its wake. The cosmos lit up in expectation as the tribe traversed the expanse of time and space, gathering and absorbing energy from the shards of creation and then expelling it across the sky. A painter immersed in his work. Sliding his brush across a canvas sea of colour and inspiration. Back and forth they glided exploring the far reaches of the universe. Mala felt a tug-tug-tugging as the tribe doubled-back towards the firm foundation of the obelisk, a glowing beacon in an ocean of chaos, guiding them home from their distant voyage.

CHAPTER TWO

Vision

Mala sat inside the dining area of the royal quarters. She was famished. She wolfed down some fruit, before breaking out into a monologue of her morning experience on the mountaintop. "Mother, it was amazing! I felt the coral move. It was so big. And the fish! They were swimming everywhere…"

Shaia smiled, watching her daughter narrating her animated story enthusiastically. "Wonderful, Mala, wonderful! I'm *so* proud of your progress. Well done my child!" Mala's face beamed with pride. Her aura glowed. "Your brother Cuthru is waiting for you in the training area. Please go and see him, he has something exciting to show you."

Mala jumped up and skipped over to the training area, just behind her living quarters. She found Cuthru, holding the cutest little ball of fluffy, brown fur. Two large, round eyes stared out from inside his cupped hands.

"For you, my beautiful sister. She reminds me of your charm and character."

Mala looked at Cuthru as tears welled up in her eyes. She ran forward and jumped up to hug her brother fiercely, his familiar, woody scent permeating her senses, enveloping and comforting. "Oh, thank you Cuthru! I love you so."

Cuthru acknowledged her gratitude by responding with a hug in return that made Mala smile from ear to ear. Mala's smile

17

turned her aura a deep, radiant orange. She reluctantly released her grip and carefully picked up the baby monkey from her brother's arms, staring soundlessly back into its eyes.

"His name is Ketu, Mama," announced Mala, as she presented her new pet to her mother. "Cuthru said he rescued him from a pair of wild cats that killed the rest of his family deep in the jungle. He told me that he and some warriors were hunting and came across the cats chasing down the monkeys."

The Queen smiled as she watched Mala feed Ketu some of her fruit. "He is so beautiful Mala; I know that you're going to take good care of him."

Queen Shaia was an attractive woman. She had strong, high cheekbones and long, dark brown hair that she had twisted into a plait around her head. A green-and-blue-dyed piece of fabric that matched her eyes was woven into the plait. Her soft gown billowed and flowed around her slender frame, giving her a regal appearance that befitted her title as Monarch of the Seven Lands.

With less than five days to go before the twins' eighteenth birthdays, Shaia still had much to prepare. It was the first time in generations that twin boys in the royal family made ascension together. A single ascension involved an arduous, two-day journey from the village to Mount Vexus and back. It included an initiation ritual that lasted all through the night, followed by a ceremony of eating, dancing and celebration. The journey to the volcanic crater was the physical test, while the initiation ritual was the spiritual part of the trial. A double ascension meant that it would take almost twice as long to complete, as only one male was permitted to ascend at a time. The great ascension was a generations-old tradition that was part of a male's initiation into adulthood. Females undertook a similar ritual but also spent time studying with the High Priestess. The ascension was never about competing with anyone but oneself, never giving up, pushing through the pain and self-torture, moving forward with the faith of all those who went before. It was the ultimate test, the culmination of years of training, study and dedication. And

18

for Cuthru and Asbeth, as royal subjects, the burden was particularly   onerous.

The Queen glided across the dining area, with the grace and charm of a dragonfly, skimming across a pond filled with beautiful lilies glistening in the morning sunlight. "Hotha!" She called for the Lady of the Baths.

"Yes, your Highness?"

"Please prepare the inner chamber for Cuthru and Asbeth's return from their initiation rituals." The bath salts and sensual oils that were used to soothe and cleanse the boys from their physical endurance and spiritual awakening, had to be sourced and placed in this chamber, along with Mariaka spirits – a powerful brew from the Mariaka tree, used to revitalise and replenish the graduates' spent energy from their powerful ordeal.

"Yes, of course, your Highness. It shall be done."

The Lumni tribe lived at a time where everyone and everything was equal and in abundance. Peace reigned, as it had since the beginning of creation. It was a time before the great sin of modern man, a time long forgotten in the annals of history; before the great books of antiquity were compiled by the sages of our known past. The Lemurians possessed a profound ability that connected them to the living forces of nature. They were aware of their purpose on Gaia and lived it to the fullest, each and every day. It was a simple task, yet proportionally immense in its cause. It was loved and honoured for its veracity yet feared and humbled for its infinite power and omnipotence. It was the duty and burden bestowed upon each and every living Lemurian to share the goodness of the Creator, to reveal the forces of energy that were infused into the planet, fuelling the perpetual cycle of life on Gaia.

King Andor was such a man. He shared his love for his people with passion and zeal. There was nothing more rewarding than witnessing his citizens prosper under his rule. The King stood, deep in thought, on his balcony and looked down onto the village below. The view was nothing short of remarkable. The royal quarters were positioned on the highest hill overlooking the village with the tops of the trees in the forest below reaching almost up to the ramparts. Over to the west, the cool, blue ocean, lapped at the edge of the continent like a thirsty pup, tasting the soft sea sand on the distant shore. Over to the east, loomed the great Mount Vexus, sheathed in a puffy grey cloud. A monstrous, slumbering giant, hunched beneath a warm coat of fleece.

King Andor was endowed with the ability to see into the future, and the one that he saw now was troubling. His eyes saw beyond the palpable, the familiar and into an uncertain event that came to him in hazy bursts of sepia. This was one of those times that he preferred to label his gift as a curse. Prophecy came with responsibility, and, as King, he was responsible for not just his family, but also the seven kingdoms and its loyal subjects. It was several months ago that he began having a series of disturbing visions. He woke up late one night shouting incoherently and covered in sweat.

"What is it my King?" said Shaia, startled awake by the King's outburst.

"It's nothing. Just a bad dream. Go back to sleep."

The King, however, remained awake for the rest of the night, too distressed by his vivid revelation to even consider the luxury of sleep. Each time he closed his eyes, he saw death and destruction. A cataclysmic event striking the land without warning, causing widespread devastation. The visions began to increase in frequency, building in strength with each showing. He knew that this was a sign that it was becoming increasingly more likely for his visions to transpire. He also knew that the more focus he placed on understanding and deciphering them, the sooner they would come to fruition. The trick was to do nothing, to focus on not seeing, and then, in so doing, he could bide his time and somehow contemplate a way to save his people. Either way, he had to focus on the fact that there was a ray of hope, a chance of survival for the Lemurians. King

Andor resolved to call a meeting with his closest advisors, share his vision with them and put a contingency plan in place to save his people from impending doom.

CHAPTER THREE

Twins

Cuthru loved spending time with his younger sister. She provided him with the sense of freedom that he often longed for, especially after a long, hard day with Groth, whose training had taken its toll on the young prince. His muscles ached, and his head throbbed constantly. He longed for the time where he could just relax in a soothing hot spring mountain bath with not a worry in the world. Just a few days to go and it would all be over. With his Ascension complete, he would be recognised as a true member of the tribe, a warrior, a mature light-bringer. This was the intention he set for himself, before the start of the infamous tribal ritual.

Cuthru laughed as he watched Mala play with Ketu. "Mala you're going to tire each other out if you don't have a break."

"No, I won't." retorted Mala in-between a dive-roll. "This is too much fun!" The back of Cuthru's head began to tingle from his father's probing, beckoning him to report to his chambers. He turned to say goodbye to Mala, but she was so wrapped up in her playful tumbles with the monkey that she was completely oblivious to his departure.

The King sat relaxing on a suede divan in the audience area of his chambers, his calm demeanour disguising his inner turmoil. Cuthru anticipated something far more heartening than the unexpected feeling of foreboding that overcame him when

22

he stepped into the room. A brief flicker of acknowledgement passed between them and then the King placed his fingertips onto Cuthru's temples. With their eyes closed and the connection made, the King initiated the transfer of knowledge. Tears streamed unaided from Cuthru's eyes as he was thrown into a maelstrom of fiery images, that sought to tear the flesh from his bones. It was as if the scenes he experienced were real. His body felt the pain from the scorching flames, his nostrils filled with the stench of burning flesh and his ears rang from the cacophony of defenceless screams. Cuthru turned back to look through a rolling tunnel of smoke and fire, which began to obliterate everything in its path. At the other end of the tunnel, quite a distance from his position, a band of fleeing Lumniites appeared to have harrowingly escaped the hungry flames licking at their heels. He was at the core of the anomaly, the eye of the storm. The sounds of devastation around him resounded in his ears like the muted bellows from a stricken sea creature beneath the deep, dark depths of the ocean. Time stood still, as the finest detail became etched into his memory, giving him what seemed like ages, but were, in fact, moments of time, to take in his surroundings with absolute awe and reverence. And then as soon as it started, it was over.

Releasing his touch, The King sank slowly into his seat like a defeated warrior in battle. Cuthru remained still for a few moments longer, gently rocking back onto his heels, his eyes closed and his head throbbing with the overload of discordant information coursing through his mind. At last, he opened his eyes and slowly sat down next to his father. The shocking imagery left an indelible mark behind - a cold, stark reality that tore into Cuthru's soul like a sharp, merciless blade, cutting into the prey of its unfortunate victim.

"How much time do we have left?" Cuthru feared the answer to his question and immediately felt regret for having asked this of his father.

There was an uncomfortable silence before King Andor's mighty torso lifted up with a great big breath and then out again in a melancholic sigh. "Days my son, days..." King Andor took in another big breath. "For weeks I ignored the signs, the visions, refusing to believe their authenticity. But the elders confirmed them time and again. I have always believed we had more than a slight chance of saving ourselves, relying on my gift once more to deliver us from the danger you have seen in my visions. But the convergence of far too many probabilities has led me to the same conclusion each and every time – that we are all doomed."

Turning to look at his father, Cuthru felt the tables turn for the first time in his life. His father was a rock, a solid, stalwart mountain of a man that always held everything together. Right now, though, Cuthru felt as if the burden of responsibility had shifted onto his shoulders. He was overwhelmed by the weight of it and immediately felt anxious and quite afraid.

The King gripped Cuthru firmly by the shoulders and looked deep into his sea-green eyes. "Cuthru, my son. The fate of our people rests with you. The time will come when the land will tremble, and the sky will rain fire. You have seen a light at the end of the tunnel, a light of safety and salvation. It is *you* who must lead the way. It is *you* who must save us all. I cannot say when this event will occur. All I can tell you is that you must be prepared. Turn your face to the sun my child and the shadows shall fall and whither behind you. "

Taking a deep breath, Cuthru gritted his teeth and gazed back into his father's eyes. He had a mission to fulfil; a duty passed down to him by the King. "Father," he whispered in a soft breath like he was speaking for the very first time, taking the very first step towards his new destiny and carrying the burden of so many across a chasm so wide that his lips quivered in fear and trepidation. "I will do your bidding. I will bear the beacon of light and guide us all to safety. I will fulfil your vision and save us from the impending fire and destruction, for I am your son, Prince Cuthru of the Lumniites and the Seven Kingdoms of Lemuria".

Asbeth had progressed quickly through his levels of training with Groth, but his temper still flared out of control from time to time, which stymied his advancements in the finer arts. If it weren't for his training, he would have been an insolent adolescent, full of brazen remarks and temper tantrums. He attracted like-minded, mischievous acquaintances in his youth, which caused much consternation for both his parents and the royal ministers.

"Asbeth! Come here at once!" The King's voice boomed through the royal chambers causing a pair of doves to explode through the passageways. Asbeth was just seven summers old when he broke the Vase of Fordin, an ancient relic, shaped by King Andor's ancestor aeons ago. The vase was a solid piece, designed to hold fiery, liquid earth from Mount Vexus. The King was most distraught. A group of three uneasy looking young boys stood in front of the enraged King, their faces downcast.

"It wasn't me!" squealed Asbeth. "He did it!" Asbeth pointed to a scrawny looking boy who clapped his hands over his ears and scrunched himself up, curling his head into his chest in fear and dread.

"What's your name boy? What do you have to say for yourself? Does my son speak the truth?" The King's baritone voice seemed to send a quiver through the boy as he spoke. It looked like he was going to curl up into a ball and hunker away like a frightened tortoise. There was a minuscule nod of his head in disclosure.

Asbeth beamed. "You see? It wasn't me. It wasn't me!"

Each time a prank was unleashed, it was Asbeth who led the fray and each time they were apprehended, his friends covered for him. He became known as the Renegade Prince, cunning and daring like a fox on the hunt. He was highly competitive which put a lot of strain on his relationship with his brother Cuthru, and being a twin, made it all the more so. Cuthru always received the accolades by winning almost all of the challenges and tests they had to go through together while growing up.

Their encounters became exceptionally heated, leading up to the Ascension Ritual, so much so, that Asbeth had purposefully ignored Cuthru, following their last disagreement.

Asbeth sat cross-legged, hovering above his meditation mat in his chambers, eyes closed, connected to his breath, focusing on refining his levitation technique. By the age of fourteen, disciples completed their levitation training and by eighteen, they were expected to maintain levitation for no less than 100 breaths. Asbeth completed his session and slowly lowered himself down onto his mat. Fine rivulets of perspiration trickled down his face, neck and back from the exertion. He swept his long dark hair away from his face and tied it back behind his head as he glided up to a standing position. With his eyes still closed, and his hands in prayer position against his sternum, he slowly lifted his head up off his chest, opening his third eye to look beyond his chamber and into a parallel world. Asbeth was not interested in paying tribute to the on-going, creative forces present in the world. He believed that his purpose was destined for something different, something greater. He spent most of his time exploring beyond the permitted zone, leaving the confines of the tribe and exploring the realm of chaos and disorder.

Soon after Asbeth's twelfth summer, he began testing the limits of the spiritual realm, privately advancing, questioning and probing. With every visit into the ether, Asbeth returned changed in some way. His experience gave him a sense of freedom, release and more importantly, power. He gained much but also began to lose himself to the chaos, the madness, until it tipped the balance and consumed him. In his mind's eye, he approached the edge of the "safe" zone and subtly slipped through its perimeter.

The first time he attempted this so long ago, it felt like a magnet was holding him back as he forced his way through a surreal grid-like matrix and into a multi-dimensional landscape of shifting colour. Try as he might, he couldn't make sense of the disordered terrain and became lost as time slipped by like a

26

fast-flowing river. He began to panic as disorientation turned to despair. Groth's voice came to him, a calming, soothing sound and his mind turned to a pebble falling silently through a thick body of water. He concentrated hard and followed the pebble as it sank deep into the depths of the body of water that surrounded him. He found himself transported back into the safe zone. He opened his eyes, drenched in sweat, to find Groth cradling him like a baby, with deep concern mirrored in his pale-blue eyes.

It took Asbeth a while to attempt the expedition again but this time, he was prepared. He wore a red crystal orb from the Isle of Atlor around his neck that helped him focus his intent. The crystal gave him the courage to journey beyond the confines of his limitations. It worked much like the marble pillar in the tribe's ceremony area, by acting as a beacon to guide the user home. Now, as Asbeth glided through and into the all too familiar shambolic milieu, he felt a sense of acquaintance with the raw power that coursed around his being. He allowed it to flow over and through him like a strong oceanic current washing him away and into its icy grip. With each ebb and flow, he let go some more, succumbing, relinquishing. There was an incessant buzzing sound that vibrated down to his very core, a pulsating hum that carried him out and into the furthest reaches of the ever-expanding universe of space and time.

CHAPTER FOUR

Ascension

Beating drums woke the twins from their fitful slumber. The portentous day had come. The first trial in the Ascension ritual awaited - the gruelling journey to Mount Vexus. The King stood before his two sons. They looked at him expectantly.

"The two of you will journey together to the volcano, but only one of you will ascend at a time, so as to allow the full powers of the mountain to work their enchantment properly on each of you. The passage will take two full days and nights. Stay alert and focused because it will require all of your strength to endure this ordeal."

The Ascension ritual was an ancient rite of passage, a ceremonious acceptance of responsibility, an obligation to both the individual and the tribe. Cuthru had drawn the longer straw and so would remain at the base of the mountain through the evening of the first day, while Asbeth continued towards Vexus alone.

The first rays of sunlight sliced through the jungle and into the enclave. Smoke billowed up and out from the fire pit like a white dragon, rippling and weaving through the crisp morning air, chasing after an energy trail from a long forgotten tribal crusade. The Lumniites gathered in the early morning dawn, preparing themselves for the twin's departure into adulthood. The tribe was covered in ceremonial paint, multi-coloured

28

stripes and magical garments that transformed them into a rainbow of splendorous colour. The rhythmic beating echoed through the valley, mixing with a plethora of voices, a harmonious blend of sounds, transforming the scene into a vibrant, energetic concord.

The muscular frames of the twin youths as they stepped out and into the crowd of gathering onlookers, cast stretched-out shadow-strips on the hard-packed ground behind them, shooting out and into the trees like long-tipped spears ready for the hunt. The ceremonial, ululating melody that came from the depths of the tribal enclave became monotonous, droning out the sounds of the forest as it blended into the *boom, boom, boom* of the drums. The beat enraptured the young princes. They swayed in unison, shifting left to right, in perfect balance, waiting, watching. They began to move forward, toward the great stone pillar, thickly as if through mud. The King and Queen stood resolutely on either side, hands stretched out, eyes closed, casting their blessings over their sons as they trudged by methodically. The tribe created an opening in their midst, allowing the boys to pass through and out, into the jungle beyond, to begin their destined journeys together.

The Ascension rules were unerringly clear. The only sustenance that was permitted for the two-day journey was some fruit and water. Participants were also allowed to carry a weapon of choice, usually a spear, as well as some protective armour or a shield. There were a variety of dangerous, wild animals, often impolitely disturbed along the path, which were prone to attacking unsuspecting travellers on their expeditions, so one had to take the necessary precautions before embarking. For the first few hours, the brothers walked resolutely, side by side, each in their thoughts, contemplating the challenge that lay ahead. The sound of their footsteps, crunching on the gravel turned to a soft *pat-pat-pat-pat* as the terrain changed to long, flowing green grass, interrupted intermittently by mounds of volcanic rock, overgrown with shrubbery and more tall grass - the remains of some long forgotten earthly discharge. After briefly stopping to drink some refreshing water from a nearby stream, and to eat some juicy red berries from the trees alongside the riverbank, the boys continued along their fateful path, occasionally looking ahead to view the volcanic peak, as it grew closer and closer with each and every step.

Dusk began to settle in at the end of the first day, as the twins arrived at base camp at the foot of the infamous Mount Vexus. The colossal, rugged mountain was steeped in history. Legend had it that a seed was planted in Gaia's core at the time of creation that helped spread the life force needed to feed the planet and its inhabitants. There were a number of volcanic peaks that were formed during this process that were designed to act as vents, spewing forth the by-product of the creative process. Towards the end of this process, most of these vents dried up and naturally sealed, while others, like Vexus, remained open, a constant reminder of the Creator, His architecture and omnipotence. The Lumniites had learnt how to tap into the raw, primitive energy that flowed inside the volcanic peak and convert it into a life-sustaining primal force that gave them the ability to enhance their natural powers, live longer inside their physical bodies and heighten their supernatural, cerebral abilities tenfold. This was part of the Ascension Ritual, the access to adulthood and the activation of the primary energy field within each and every living human being.

Cuthru lay down to rest. He closed his eyes and was immediately drawn to the powerful energy deep inside the Earth's core. It blazoned across his inner vision, burning a fiery path deep into the very fibre of his being. He focused his mind, invoked his inner breath and began to disconnect from the magnetic force that tugged and pulled him into its turbulent depths. His years of training triggered an instinctive rhythmic discourse, a kind of prayer that he repeated to himself, willing him into a fitful slumber.

Dark, grey clouds of ash and smoke rose from inside the crater as Asbeth hiked up the Eastern side of the mountain, away from his brother. The first few stars appeared in the evening sky, just as he arrived at a fissure in the Mountain's seemingly impenetrable exterior. This was the entry point, the doorway to the beginning of a new life, a new existence. Waves of excitement flowed through his body, as Abeth stepped through the crack and onto a narrow path that led him deep, down and into the bowels of the giant volcano. With every passing hour, the heat around him intensified, until the sweat ran down his body and dripped off his fingertips, landing on the packed, dry, earth beneath his feet. Asbeth rounded a corner, where the path began to widen out into a naturally formed oasis, partially surrounded by a river of thick, molten lava, seething and sluggishly flowing, a monster consuming the very earth in its relentless path. A soft, rumbling sound echoed through the cavernous chamber, while strong, sulphurous fumes clogged the arid air.

Drenched in sweat and dirt, Asbeth removed his spear from his back, before kneeling on the hot, baked ground in the centre of the oasis. He closed his eyes, shifted his consciousness out of his body and dived headfirst into the raging energy surrounding him. This was what he had been waiting for, what he had prepared for all these years - the training, the exploring, the venturing beyond his comfort zone and into the chaos beyond. He felt powerful waves of energy wash right through him. He revelled in the magnificence of the power that it brought him, the selfless feeling of wanting more, of letting go to get more. It was the same as it has always been, but different. The energy was raw and pure, cleansing and purgative. It was far denser than the energy of the universe. It was rooted in the core of Gaia. Asbeth became one with the energy as he traversed its denseness, explored its complexity, probing, interrogating. He pushed hard to reach the source of the energy, the foundation of its being, its existence. He searched for answers that he knew were hidden deep in the bowels of the fiery depths of molten earth. The craving for knowledge and power consumed him. It engulfed his soul and swallowed it whole. Asbeth was no longer Asbeth. He was a servant of energy, a single entity, directed at reaching its destination, absorbing yet relinquishing. The persistent arc of raw energy continued on its journey towards the source, delving deeper, penetrating, disclosing.

Abruptly and unexpectedly, the singularity that was Asbeth encountered a barrier, a force field, which prevented him from probing any further. He pushed against a wall of thick jelly, impervious to his attempt. He drew on his final reserves of energy and gave a single, final thrust. Back on the oasis of dry earth, the physical body that was Asbeth, shuddered and then crumpled to the ground. He relinquished the last of his strength to penetrate the invulnerable barrier and failed.

His energy depleted, Asbeth drifted silently and serenely beyond the jelly-wall, a solitary jellyfish, drifting unfettered and aimless in the deep, blue sea. A conscious glimmer of discovery rippled through the jellyfish. He allowed his consciousness to adapt, to let go. He dropped his defences and probed the barrier, feeling and learning. The jellyfish shifted, changed and became like the jelly and then eased forward and became one with the wall, merging into the soft resistance that had abruptly become compliant and acquiescent. The new substance gradually became one with its surroundings. There was no resistance, yet there was also no purpose. The energy deep within the Earth's core swirled and swam through a sea of hot lava. The consciousness that was Asbeth returned to its source, reconnecting with the body that lay in the chamber deep inside the volcano. Asbeth opened his eyes and lay still, not moving for a long, long time.

Asbeth was changed. He had ascended but not in the way that was intended. His expedition had taken him on a different path, guided by his selfish desire to attain more. He had lost part of himself to the madness that he had been journeying into all these years. What had returned from the abyss was only a part of him, together with a kind of psychosis, a fanatical, crazed, carnal desire. His eyes burned with volcanic fire, reflecting a wild, harsh energy.

The sun rose from beneath the horizon, as Asbeth stepped

out from within the bowels of the rumbling mountain of fire. He passed Cuthru, watching him, as he prepared to make his ascent, glancing briefly into his brother's green eyes. Cuthru winced as his brother's aura washed over and through him, a wild, jagged energy that was disturbingly malicious in origin. There was an angry fire in his eyes and a chilling image of his father's vision suddenly came to life. Asbeth stopped and turned back to gaze at Cuthru. His voice was different - guttural and serrated like a rusted blade.

"My brother, I have become more powerful than you can ever imagine. I have been charged with a new destiny, a purpose. I am leaving this land, this prison. I have already sent word to my minions of my ascension, and they now wait in anticipation for my return. Perhaps we will meet again in this life but for now, I am travelling very far from here." Asbeth spoke down to his brother like he was nothing but a speck of mere existence. "Mark my words little brother, I will rise to rule this world and all will bow before me." And with that, Asbeth turned and was gone.

CHAPTER FIVE

Escape

Hunched over and deep in thought, Cuthru began his climb up the side of the mountain, his troubling thoughts plaguing every beat of his heart. As soon as he entered the mountain's crevice, however, his head began to clear, allowing him to focus on his trek down into the bowels of the Earth. The path was narrow, yet safely constructed aeons ago, traversed by hundreds of thousands of initiates before him. Cuthru unexpectedly lost his footing when the ground beneath him shuddered. He looked up with a furrowed brow, as some loose earth fell from above, raining down on him like a mid-morning shower. He continued along the path as it twisted down, curving this way and that like an insidious serpent, intent on leading him astray. The air became increasingly humid and acrid, the deeper Cuthru ventured. At last, drenched in perspiration, he reached his destination, the heat from the molten river around him, singeing his throat with every laboured breath. He stripped down to his loin skin, lay down on his leather tunic and closed his eyes. The tumult in the volcanic chamber slowed down to a whisper, as he focused on opening his third eye to the raging energy flowing around him, allowing it to take him away on a current of fiery belligerence. Cuthru was not afraid. His regular training with Groth had given him the courage to complete Ascension with ease, having practised the ritual many times before.

34

Just be and you will become. Groth's voice was calming, gentle. Cuthru let go of ego, of self, to become one with his surroundings, one with nature and all living things.

Asbeth was already at the edge of the forest. His followers gathered in a small band around a softly burning fire. He approached them with an earnest look in his eyes. "My disciples, I'm so pleased to see you."

"Asbeth, my lord," said a young devotee. "We are ready to do your bidding."

News of the Ascension reached his cohorts, instructing them to immediately grab their most treasured possessions, before embarking on an indefinite expedition into the wilderness. It was the way in which Asbeth's message was delivered that most compelled them to act. Usually, extrasensory powers transmitting a message resulted in what felt like a probing, gentle nudge followed by a trickle of information. This time, it came without warning and then burnt the same message into each of their minds like the river of molten earth beneath Mount Vexus. Asbeth left his tribe a boy and returned a man, more powerful than even his father, the King. The tribe members that he had hand-picked were in awe of the young prince, this usurper, who had taken command and displayed the use of his raw, unmitigated power, instructing them to act beyond a reasonable doubt.

Asbeth and his followers uncovered several wooden sailing vessels, hidden behind the trees at the water's edge. The Lemurian ships were used for fishing in the waters around the island and were equipped with the necessary fishing gear and provisions for several days at sea. They pushed them out, one at a time, before clambering on board, ready to set sail.

"Come, my people, we must leave this land if we are to survive another day. Let us depart this place and allow the seas of change to carry us towards our combined destinies!"

The energy beneath the volcano was pure and powerful. It

swirled and spun in multiple directions, pulling Cuthru this way and that. He succumbed to the ebb and flow and became one with the turmoil, allowing himself to wrap around the willful current, like a porpoise, swimming through the great oceans of the world. He smiled from within, as he tamed the wild, fire-beast, guiding it through the cavernous sea of lava, spraying flame-foam around him, as he arced and spun through its fiery depths. He felt elated and charged with a new reserve of energy that coursed through his body like a powerful, molten current. He was on fire.

Another earthly shudder, this time far stronger, threw Cuthru off course, until he was forced to return gradually to his body waiting in limbo on the surface. Slowly and with concentration, Cuthru opened his eyes, just as a pocketful of sand and stone dropped from the roof above and onto his forehead. He rose to his feet, dusted himself off and looked around the cavern. Stalagmite shards and small rocks were shifting and sliding down into the molten river below as it gurgled and spluttered unusually more frequently than before. Cuthru grabbed his meagre belongings, took a swig of water from his leather pouch and began the return journey to the surface. His Ascension had brought him instantly heightened senses, which allowed him to witness the vibration of all living things around him. The rocks shimmered in a rainbow of colour as if they were alive. They whispered to each other in anticipation of something immense about to transpire.

Just as he stepped up and out through the fissure on Mount Vexus, a mighty boom sounded that forced him to his knees. The next sound that followed was even more deafening. Cuthru cupped his hands over his ears, as the volcano began to erupt in a roar of red anger and yellow fury. He looked up to the horizon, his now heightened senses allowing him to see with the eyes of an eagle, many leagues away. A group of Lumniites was escaping the clutches of the fire tendrils on the beach at the other end of the island. *Asbeth*. He watched through a compressed corridor of fire and knew that it was his father's vision come to life. He was going to perish while his brother would live to fulfil his destiny and that of the tribe.

Cuthru ran down and away from the spewing, one-eyed monster, as chunks of burning earth rained down all around him. It was too little too late as he watched in horror while the Earth ignited and exploded around him like a ravaging beast, injured in the hunt, frenzied and wild with pain and anguish. A giant flaming ball of fire came down so hard and fast that he did not see it in time, and became flattened beneath its full, bone-crushing force.

Asbeth and his team gazed back at the devastation from the safety of the ocean, witnessing the complete and utter destruction of their people. Columns of molten earth were blasted high into the air, forests burnt intensely and mountains moved implausibly across a landscape in complete havoc. The island continued to erupt and explode, totally destroying the Lemurians and all semblance of life, before sinking below the depths of the vast ocean, all within what seemed like the blink of an eye.

Asbeth smiled maliciously, his eyes flickering across the ravaging landscape before him, taking in its annihilation with a cruel delight. This was his destiny, and he revelled silently in its culmination, like a newborn baby into a world of its own choosing.

Part 2

Stone walls do not a prison make,
Nor iron bars a cage;
Minds innocent and quiet take
That for an hermitage

- Richard Lovelace

CHAPTER SIX

The Deal

New York, Present Day.

New York's Legacy hotel was situated in the heart of Greenwich Village. It was a top-class, boutique establishment, complete with nature-inspired digital screens in the toilets, a rooftop bar and swimming pool, as well as a basement lounge with VIP booths for private occasions.

Jimmy 'The Germ' approached the hotel on foot. His Levi jeans, flat-soled sneakers and black leather jacket had seen better days. His gaunt face and scrawny frame added very little credence to his character as he stepped through the hotel's revolving door. He popped out the other side and almost into a middle-aged, African American doorman, who looked Jimmy up and down distastefully.

"Good evenin' young man. Are you lost? How can I be of assistance?"

"Hiya doin? Just visiting a friend from outta town, is all. Thanks for your help, but I know where da go."

Jimmy hustled over to the elevator as quickly as he dared. *Ping!* The doors opened, and he stepped inside. He pushed number five, turned and gazed into the mirror at the rear. He licked his palm and wiped his hand across his forehead a couple of times, straightening out his greasy, unkempt hair. *Ping!* The elevator groaned and then shuddered to a halt. The doors opened. He stepped out, turned right and walked briskly to the end of the corridor. The rap of his knuckles on the solid oak door echoed eerily down the passage. He peered left, as if to follow the echo and then turned back to glimpse a shadow pass across the glass-domed peephole, all the while shifting his weight restlessly from side to side.

Yes, it's me, Jimmy. Open the fucking door, dammit.

The sound of the latch clicked loudly in the lock, and the door opened.

Holy crap.

Jimmy's knees buckled. The most exquisite redheaded creature stood on the other side. Blood rushed to his face, and his head spun. He couldn't help but gaze wistfully at her cleavage, behind a white, low-cut sleeveless, tank top.

"Hi, I'm Foxy." She smiled. Jimmy just stared at her extended hand. Her dark brown eyes swallowed him into their chocolate depths.

Of course, you are.

Time slowed to a trickle. His muscles froze. He opened his mouth to speak, but his vocal cords refused to cooperate. The *thump, thump* of blood through his body, was loud in his ears. He continued to stare at her hand as she slowly lowered it.

"Why don't you come inside?"

Jimmy's heart pounded against his sternum, trying in vain to tear itself out. He stole a quick glance back down the passage again, before taking a big step across the threshold as if he was crossing a chasm.

"Please, make yourself at home while I get the cash."

Home. Jimmy's heart ached. He had never really had a home. He was an orphan for as long as he could remember, raised on the streets by the unscrupulous, trained in the art of survival. He walked over to the lounge area but not before turning his head to stare at Foxy, as she disappeared down the passage, her high-cut, blue denim shorts hugging her curves as she walked away. Jimmy sat warily down on the couch. *Sweaty palms.* He wiped them across his worn-out jeans.

"Who the hell are you?"

Jimmy looked up at an imposing figure in a long black coat. His long, matted dreadlocks, stirred like a nest of snakes as he spoke. His accent sounded peculiar. Jimmy couldn't quite place it. "Um, name's er, Jimmy," he stammered. *Where'd this fucker come from? And why's he wearing shades in the middle of the night?*

"Who let you in? Foxy!" shouted the man in black.

"What is it Kaimi? I'm coming." Foxy walked back into the room with a white envelope in her hands. "Stop interfering. That's all you do. All the time. Why can't you just leave me the fuck alone?"

Kaimi dropped his voice to a menacing whisper. "I told you that if I catch you on that shit again, there's going to be trouble and it ain't gonna be pleasant."

Foxy took a step backwards. "This is *my* money and *my* shit!"

Jimmy stood up. "Listen, I was asked to make a delivery. If dis is a bad time…"

"You sit the fuck down!" Foxy glared at him from across the room.

Jimmy's eyes widened like apertures as he slowly sat down again. "OK. OK. Let's just get dis over with. I wanna get outta here already."

Kaimi turned to Foxy. "I told you before; you're not doing this shit anymore. We had a deal."

"Fuck you and your bullshit," she said angrily. "I'm sick and tired of your deals." She side-stepped Kaimi and moved swiftly towards Jimmy. He jumped up, off the couch as Foxy approached. She thrust the unmarked envelope towards him. "Here. Three-K, right? You might wanna count it."

Reaching into his inside jacket pocket, Jimmy pulled out the bag of crack. A strange buzzing sounded in his ears, followed by a fluctuation in air pressure as if he was sitting in an aeroplane coming in to land. He looked up at the scene in front of him. *What da fuck is going on?*

Crouched down on one knee, Kaimi's fingertips touched the

41

ground like a sprinter at his starting blocks.

"Oh no, you don't!" Foxy pulled out a silver gun and spun around to face him. "Don't do it. I'm warning you!"

Kaimi stared at the two of them from behind his crimson shades. The air pressure increased and then Jimmy's ears popped. It was as if Kaimi was sucking the very air out of the room. And then it came without warning - a powerful force that lifted both Jimmy and Foxy up into the air and back into the wall at the other end of the room. Jimmy hit the side of his head against a big black vase as he came down. The last thing he remembered was a cacophony of whispering voices and the refraction of light from a red crystal, piercing his head like needles.

Special Agent Felix Brody was alerted to Jimmy's arrest when he was booked in by the NYPD and then shipped off, under custody, to New York Presbyterian Hospital. Jimmy was commonly referred to as a snitch - an informer, that kept Brody updated as to the inner dealings of New York's criminal elite. Brody approached the officer sitting outside Ward 5B on the second floor. He jumped up in surprise when Brody pulled out his badge and flashed it in his face. "Morning, officer. How's the patient doing?"

The cop leant forward and squinted at Brody's badge before straightening up. "Err, Agent Brody, Sir, um, yeah. I believe the perp is in a stable condition."

Brody nodded briefly at the officer, pushed open the door and stepped into the room. The hydraulic damper inside the door closer, caused the door to shut gracefully behind him with a click, as he consciously approached a motionless Jimmy. He glanced up and around the room to see if there were any other patients sharing the space but the two other beds alongside Jimmy were empty. He pulled the only available wooden chair towards the bed and sat down, leaning forward and into Jimmy's face. "Jimmy, Jimmy."

Increasing both the tension and the pitch in his voice, Brody tried to get a response out of the unmoving figure. Jimmy stirred, grimaced and then twisted his head slowly from side to side, eliciting a rough groan. He screwed up his gaunt face in agony. Long, greasy hair stuck to his forehead. Seaweed on a rock at low tide.

"Jimmy, it's me, Brody. Felix Brody, remember?" He gripped Jimmy by his shoulders and gave him a brisk shake. "What the hell happened to you?"

This time, Jimmy slowly opened his eyes. "Uhhh, Brody."

"Yes, it's me, I'm here."

"What? Where?" Lifting his head off the pillow, Jimmy looked around the room. He dropped it back down and let out a heavy sigh.

"You're in the hospital, Jimmy. You're all right now. I need to know what happened, Jimmy. Talk to me. *Please.*"

Blinking slowly, Jimmy took a deep breath. "It was Saturday night. Got a call. Dunno who it was from. No caller I.D." He took another breath, shifted on the bed and squeezed up his face in pain. He closed his eyes, released his breath and relaxed again. "All she said was to come to room 505, Legacy Hotel. And to bring some blow."

"Why did you go, Jimmy, if you didn't know who it was?" asked Brody.

Jimmy coughed. "Coz room 505 is *my* room. I always arrange hotel deals in room 505. So, I guessed dat whoever it was, must know me…" Jimmy watched Brody raise his eyebrows. "Well, I didn't know dem, if dat's wot you tinkin'."

"OK. So tell me about Foxy. Did you kill her?"

"What!? No! She's dead?"

"Yeah, she was found lying right next to you in the hotel room. Cause of death unknown."

He coughed again. "Shit. Fuck."

"What?"

"Dare was dis other guy, wit dis crystal."

"What!? You mean to tell me that you're back on the meth?"

"No, boss. I mean he had dis red crystal. He was waving it in

43

my face." Jimmy was in a trance-like stupor, revisiting a scene that Brody wasn't sure was an actual event or just one of his flashbacks.

"So who was this *other* guy, Jimmy? And what's with this crystal? Where is it and why was he waving it in your face? Be straight with me, Jimmy."

"I dunno who he was, but he definitely roughed up Foxy. He had deez red, shiny shades and wore a long, black coat. Can't remember much more dan dat, except he got inside my head and calmed me down. Made me forget…"

"OK," continued Brody. "So what about the blow? Where'd you get it?"

"Dare's dis new supplier dat operates from Howland Hook." Jimmy shifted his scrawny frame in the bed, grimacing from the pain. He twisted his head from side to side, scanning the room apprehensively.

Brody scribbled inside his notebook. "Yeah, continue."

"It's deez two guys. I meet dem once a month. Same time, same place. And we do da deal, da exchange… you know? Troo da windows. Nobody gets out."

"Good, Jimmy. You've done good."

Howland Hook was a container port facility situated in northwestern Staten Island. Brody dispatched a team to stake out the harbour area. It seemed that Jimmy was right. Several unidentified exchanges were recorded from an unmarked vehicle, a black Buick Regal that was parked alongside the offices of the Nefaro shipping line. Before they knew it, the two suspects were being handcuffed and shoved into the back of an agency-issued Chrysler, their noses still white from their mid-morning fix.

CHAPTER SEVEN

Billy

The monotonous hum of the bumper-to-bumper traffic drowned out the sounds of the twittering birds and buzzing bees. A slithering, serpentine leviathan, advancing on the city, eager to devour its very contents. A shiny, black limo turned gracefully into Fifth Avenue. It's only passenger, a well-groomed, astute-looking gentleman, gazed thoughtfully out of the window, as the sun rose stoically into the dawn of a new day Central Park sailed quietly by, as Billy Bayer watched the early morning joggers, the rough looking vagrants and the pin-stripe-suit Wall Street traders glued to their mobiles. Anxious addicts. Pulling back from his hiatus, he reached up to flip open the vanity mirror from the roof of the vehicle for a quick inspection. Piercing brown eyes regarded him pensively.

Looking good, Bill.

He turned to his laptop. A scrolling banner moved across the home page of the Van Nest Park website. Van Nest Park was nearby Billy's family home. It was where he spent most of his youth while his mother worked long hours in a busy deli in the city. His time spent in the park, and the fun he had there with his friends while growing up, was ingrained into his memory. He often imagined himself as the King of Van Nest, a fantasyland in which he ruled austerely over his loyal subjects. Billy was one of the park's benefactors and had, over the past ten years, invested more than 100,000 hard-earned dollars in its maintenance. He was also responsible for the design and development of the park's website that was taking unreasonably long to complete. He scrolled down the page, looking for the new donations button that still wasn't there.

Damn! What's wrong with these fucking idiots?

He called Jeremy at Five-Six-Seven Web Design Studio. He counted seven rings. His blood began to boil. A female voice finally answered.

"Five-six-seven, can I help you?"

Billy restrained his anger and responded, tight-lipped. "Jeremy, please."

"I'm sorry, but Jeremy's not in. Can I take a message?"

Billy's face went hot. He envisioned throttling Jeremy until he choked. "Just tell him Billy called and he's *really* pissed." *Click.*

Closing his eyes, Billy sank back into the limo's comfy head-cushion. He remembered wearing his favourite, charcoal-coloured Hugo Boss suit when he first met the New York City mayor in the late nineties. After hitting it off together, they donated a sizeable sum of money to the upkeep of Van Nest Park. That was his first business relation with a politician and Viktor Kadezi, one of New York's most notorious gangsters, noticed. It was at a political rally that Viktor approached Billy and purposefully knocked his drink from his right hand. Billy instinctively shot out his left to catch the falling glass but not before spilling half of it on the floor.

"I'm sorry," said Viktor, in a strong, Eastern-European accent. "My mistake."

Billy jovially replied, "no problem. I'll just get another."

"No. Wait. Let me get it. What're you drinking?" Viktor's eyebrows pushed his forehead up into a crease of lines beneath his bald head. "In fact, why don't you join me at the bar?"

Billy gave Viktor a quick once-over, taking in his grey and white pinstriped suit. His golden cuff links sparkled in the light of the chandelier and his cerise shirt balanced the ensemble perfectly. Billy replied nonchalantly. "Sure. Of course." And right there and then, a new friendship was established.

That was almost fifteen years ago. A lot had happened in fifteen years. Billy was now in charge of a healthy operation that included money laundering, drugs and prostitution. His agreement with Viktor included a substantial share of the profit with every transaction rendered. Today was 'payday' as Viktor liked to call it. The day when all of his operators paid him his share of the takings for the previous month's work. Billy snapped his laptop shut as the limo turned right into East 128th Street. He stepped out of the vehicle, soon after it pulled over at an abandoned garage repair shop.

"Thanks, Gerard. I'll see you at half-past."

Billy made an involuntary check on his Glock, an Austrian-manufactured, .380 military-calibre, low-recoil model of pistol, before proceeding towards the derelict structure ahead. A hidden camera with integrated DNA signature scanning technology recognised Billy and released the lock on a rusted sliding door. The door rolled open just far enough to allow him inside, and then rolled back to click closed behind him again. He stepped forward a few feet and onto an unassuming, corroded, metal, corrugated disc, around four feet in diameter. He waited a few moments before the disc vibrated softly and sank with a hum into a concealed chamber, fifteen feet underground. He stepped off the disc and placed his left eye over a scanning device attached to the wall. There was an electronic, whirring sound, a beep and then a loud click. A thick, steel door swung open to reveal a large reception area, where he was greeted by solid muscle inside a black tailor-made suit. Billy handed his firearm over to the over-sized sentry before he was allowed into Viktor's office.

"Billy my boy!" Viktor smiled a wide, toothy grin and swung his right-hand around to smack into Billy's with a loud, stinging *crack*.

"Hi Viktor," said Billy impassively.

"So my friend, what can you tell me? How's business?" Billy was stifled by a strong waft of sandalwood from Viktor's cologne. A 24-carat, gold link-chain swung loosely around his neck, as he leant over his desk to peer disparagingly at Billy.

"Business is good. We're up this month by just over nineteen percent."

"Ha, Ha! Excellent my friend, excellent. You know what I say? Good things come to those who work their asses off and never give up!" Viktor loved churning out clichés. They pumped up his already overinflated ego the more outrageous they sounded.

Viktor rolled onto his heels and flipped open the cedar-wood humidor on his desk. He pulled out a long, roasted cigar and guillotined the end off, before warming it with a butane lighter, rolling it slowly through the burning flame. Made in Honduras, with a blend of the finest tobacco, the Churchill began to release notes of leather, chocolate and spice that tickled Billy's nostrils. The aroma brought with it a feeling that he was being seduced by a first-class whore, pulling him into her smoky, sweet-smelling embrace. A puff of smoke enveloped his face, his throat burned and the spell was broken. He waved the smoke away only to find Viktor pushing a short glass of scotch into his hand. The ice clinked against the sides of the glass. He lifted it up to his lips and savoured the smooth, chilled liquor as it rolled down the back of his throat.

Billy smiled sardonically. Viktor had two kinds of friends - the type, like Billy that owed him something, and the other type that he wanted something from. Everyone else got in his way. And if you got in Viktor Kadezi's way, you disappeared in a hurry. Billy sat down on the hard, high-back chair in front of the mahogany desk and took another sip of scotch. "So boss, when we gonna move that shipment? It's been over two weeks already."

"Patience my friend, patience. That scum Brody is still interrogating my boys, but he won't get anything out of them. I'm going to take care of things so that we can continue with our business and then he can go and suck the sweat from his mama's armpits that piece-of-shit-motherfucker!"

48

The FBI office, situated at 26 Federal Plaza, just across from Thomas Paine Park, was busy as usual. Special Agent Felix Brody was staring at what looked like a golden sheriff's badge hanging on the wall in a box-frame at the back of his office. It was a Medal of Valour that he had received for being part of the team that finally found and killed Osama Bin Laden. He was awarded the Medal by the President of the United States and attended a prestigious ceremony with his team to receive it. It was his proudest moment. His wife and two children by his side made it all the more fulfilling.

Looking down involuntarily at his suit, Brody made sure it was in immaculate condition. He was a perfectionist. He ironed his tie every morning and polished his shoes with a toothbrush. He owned ten white shirts and five black suits so that he wouldn't have to waste time and energy deciding what to wear each day. An idea that he had put into practice since he read that Einstein followed the same routine.

He marched down the Eastern corridor to the fourth-floor interrogation room on the other end of the building. He was running out of time before his prisoners had to be transported to the East Jersey State Prison to await trial. The Prison, a maximum-security institution, sporting a large, prominent dome and imposing metal gates, was home to some of the country's most notorious inmates.

"So tell me..." Brody glanced at the file in front of him. "Mr Hector Martinez." Brody pronounced his name with emphasis, slowly mouthing out the words like an English teacher. "Who do you work for?"

Silence.

"Hmm. It says here that you're from Puerto Rico and wanted by the authorities there. How about we just deport you? Right now!"

Martinez squirmed in his seat. "I want a lawyer," was all that came out.

Brody continued as if Martinez hadn't said a word in reply,

his voice calm and composed. "It's just a matter of time until we find what we're looking for. You see, it's like this: the longer you choose to be uncooperative, the harder it'll be for you to climb out of the pit you're digging for yourself."

Martinez was silent. Brody watched a bead of sweat roll down past his temple. "We caught you and your chum red-handed or should I say white-nosed? Two kee's of coke means that you'll get time, and a repeat offence means no parole." Brody paused for effect. "Unless... unless you tell me where you got the blow. Come on, Martinez, let's do a deal. You help me out and I give you a break. Huh?"

The atmosphere was tense and the silence deafening. "Fuck you. I want my lawyer." Martinez spat on the floor.

Smiling wryly, Brody flipped open the folder on the table. "OK. Let's look at the facts, shall we? It says here that the Nefaro Shipping Company operates a fleet of container ships that travel all over the world, including destinations like Cuba, Brazil, China, South Africa, Europe and the USA." He looked up at Martinez. There was no reaction. "It seems your company doesn't operate the obvious cocaine-related trade route - South America and the US, so the next best bet has to be China. Hector?"

Silence.

"OK. Martinez, two can play this game. I'm going to fetch Bruno. Don't move a muscle; I'll be right back."

Brody proceeded to make his way across to the holding cell at the other end of the passage. He was alarmed to find the door standing slightly ajar. He reached for his standard issue firearm and stepped inside, his finger on the trigger, weapon pointed down and close to his chest. His heart dropped into the pit of his stomach. Bruno lay motionless on the floor. A steady pool of blood was beginning to form around his head. This was a fresh kill, not more than a couple of minutes old. The assailant had evidently used a silencer to muffle the sound of the blasts and was probably still in the building. Brody stepped hastily out of the cell and instinctively slammed his hand into a panic button, setting off the alarm, triggering a full lockdown. *Skreeeee!*

No one is leaving this building in a hurry.

He ran back to check on Martinez. His instincts told him to expect the worst. Martinez lay facedown on the interrogation desk. He blinked as he watched another pool of blood ooze out of Martinez's head and onto the floor. Brody's sixth sense tingled. His FBI training kicked into gear. He scanned the immediate area with hawk-eyes, looking for the faintest clue. He intuitively stepped into the offender's shoes and glanced warily around, trying to imagine where he would go. Brody headed for the nearest exit and passed an open window on the way. He stopped and quickly doubled back. Dangling from the window ledge was an abseil rope, with a multiple twisted, polyester core.

"Dammit!" He rammed his fist into the wall, bruising his knuckles in the process. The pain fuelled his anger even more. He grimaced. *One step forward, two steps back.*

CHAPTER EIGHT

Danse

Swish, swish, slash. Ting, tang!

The fencing blades sliced through the air in a blur, and then connected, sending a reverberating quiver down the arms of each of the practitioners as they attacked and parried across the hardwood floor. Both fighters wore a white, form-fitting jacket, plastic underarm protectors, breeches, suspenders, long white socks and flat-soled shoes. The ensemble was complete with a special mask and bib to protect the face and neck. The combatants circled each other - a pair of gazelle, gracefully looking for an opportunity to engage. One of the opponents thrust forward, quickly moving the point of the blade down in a semi-circle - a deliberate attack. The other fighter twisted the sword into a circle, using a counter movement to catch the opponent's sword tip, flicking it defensively away. Back and forth the gazelle glided around the training area, engaging in a dance-like, prancing exchange, horns interlocking for a moment before twisting out to begin again. It was difficult to distinguish between the pair of fighters as they shifted and turned across the sparring area. One figure appeared more lithe and agile than the other but the fine, mesh-covered fencing masks hid every facial feature and the fighting garments concealed every bodily shape and curve.

Billy had to concentrate hard. His opponent was quick and

responsive. It took just one miscalculation, and he was vulnerable to being struck. It took him months to learn to anticipate his adversary's every move, to connect with the flow of energy, the attacks and feigned strikes. Fencing is a sport but also a form of martial art, where the sword or foil becomes an extension of the fighter's arm, cutting through the air in flowing, thrusting movements. The fencing practitioner hones his focus and energy, learning to anticipate the slightest shift in his opponent's movements, always looking for the smallest opening or opportunity, while at the same time, remaining guarded and alert in his defence. The biggest challenge is the ability to find stillness and become relaxed, yet remain vigilant. A successful balance between these abilities produces the very best fencers.

Billy nimbly dodged a thrust, followed by a riposte – a return attack. His opponent stepped back and then twisted quickly around to the left in a strong slashing motion. Billy anticipated this with a downward slash-block. At the last minute, the other fencer feigned the low cut and twisted the blade up, around and down to connect it with Billy's upper right shoulder. Billy staggered back a step. His opponent seized the opportunity and pounced like a cat, up and onto his chest, toppling him over, their combined weight crashing them down and onto the floor.

"Uhhh." Billy landed with a thump and a wheeze and his very breath crushed out of his chest. He opened his right hand and let go of his blade in defeat. It clattered to the ground noisily Billy was pinned to the floor by his opponent's knees pressing uncomfortably into his shoulder-pits. He was winded from the ordeal and struggled to catch his breath. His opponent reached a free hand back to pull her mask up and off. Long, flowing, auburn hair bounced out to reveal a strikingly attractive face with sensual, strawberry coloured lips and sparkling, hazelnut eyes.

"Hahahaaaa!" Her delightful laughter cut through the tension like the jingle of a thousand bells. She hopped off Billy's chest and reached out a hand to help him up. Billy hoisted himself up and onto his feet. He tore his mask off and threw it to the ground.

"Well done Kee. You did it again."

"Yeah," she replied, breathing hard. "You owe me a romantic dinner, loser." She grinned.

Kisha gripped Billy's head with both hands, thrusting her body forward and into his, their mouths connecting and exploding in fiery passion. Tongues plunging. Hands groping. Billy gripped her tighter until his body throbbed and ached to be a part of her, inside of her. He closed his eyes, and his head erupted in a searing fountain of desire as he savoured the rousing, climactic experience.

"Mmmmhh, aaaaahh." Kisha moaned out loudly as she writhed against Billy like a wild Medusa, fervently clawing at his garb, pulling it off, piece by piece. The passionate couple dropped to their knees, toppling over and onto the floor in visceral pleasure.

CHAPTER NINE

Coup d'etat

"James! Make it another double. On the rocks."

The Soho Supper club was busy. Billy gazed through the thick haze of smoke that hung over the establishment. And then, he spotted her. A cabaret dancer, injecting passion and fire into her moves. Wild. Carefree. Living for the show, her life. He was captivated.

"Who's the new girl?" Billy lifted his chin in the direction of the stage.

"Oh, that's Kisha," replied James without turning around.

Billy watched her move to the music. A sleek, black panther in a mini-dress and diamante-encrusted stilettos. Billy felt his groin stir in response. He had to meet her, just to say hello. "OK. Listen. I need you to deliver a bottle of champagne to her changing room."

"Sure thing, sir."

He regularly returned to watch Kisha dance around the room, exuding confidence and pure emotion into her moves. He delivered the same gift each and every time.

On the fourth visit, following her show, Kisha came out to sit next to Billy at his table. "OK. You have my attention. What do you want?" She was direct, poised and self-assured.

Smiling, he gazed into her mesmerising, dark, brown eyes. "Just to talk. You know, to get to know you a little."

"Bullshit. I know your type. You've just got one thing on your mind."

"So what if I have?" Billy decided to play her game. The direct approach seemed to work. Kisha smiled and stood up. She turned to walk away but then beckoned to Billy with her finger. She continued towards her changing room. Billy felt himself move forward involuntarily, his feet lifting themselves up, forward and then down, one in front of the other. A powerful magnet, pulling him towards its source. Before he knew it, he was sitting in a chair in her changing room, while she rode him like a bucking bronco at a Texas rodeo.

Their relationship grew out of lust. They became partners in a wild journey of energy and adventure. Over time, they grew close and then Billy made a conscious decision to introduce Kisha to his world of treachery and corruption, where they developed quite a reputation in the crime circles of New York. They moved into a penthouse apartment in the Laureate together - a twenty-story luxury condominium, located on the corner of 76th Street and Broadway, in the heart of Manhattan's Upper West Side. The Laureate featured a classic pre-war design, with a granite and limestone base and characteristic Juliet balconies. Their apartment included large, energy efficient, sound-attenuated windows and a state-of-the-art, home automation system; that was even capable of programming macros designed to turn on the TV, boot up the computers or run the air-conditioning system.

Billy stood on his corner balcony, deep in thought, looking out and onto the Hudson River. The sun sank languidly into the horizon - the end of another busy summer day in the Big Apple. The sun shined its warmth on his face. He closed his eyes and savoured the moment. Kisha had just returned from her afternoon run through Central Park. She stepped onto the balcony next to Billy to gaze out and watch the dusk roll in. Rivulets of sweat ran down her neck, and her wet vest clung to her muscular frame, accentuating the curve of her breasts and the tone of her abdomen. "I'm gonna jump in the shower.

Won't be a moment."

For the past couple of weeks, the couple had spent, this time, each evening, meeting on the balcony to strategise and plan Project Coup d'état, an ingenious plot to overthrow Viktor's little empire. Billy was tired of being bullied around by the greedy Serbian and dreamt of the time when he could put him out of his misery. It hadn't been easy all these years, being Viktor's 'boy', constantly ordered around to do his dirty work. Viktor had no remorse for those that got in his way and then treated those closest to him like dirt. He was a repulsive character who reminded Billy of an avaricious troll, smashing and devouring everything in sight. He was simply designed with no conscience - an abomination that had to be eliminated.

Kisha's all too familiar floral signature tickled Billy's nostrils. He turned around to find her standing behind him, her wet hair tied back loosely. A dark-blue, Japanese silk kimono hung loosely over her slender frame. He became instantly aroused, drawn to the low cross of the gown over her partially exposed cleavage. He moved towards her, carefully licked his lips and then placed them over hers in a soft, wet kiss. He slipped his tongue tenderly into her mouth, and she rolled her tongue against his like she was gently sucking on a piece of soft chocolate. He visualised the two of them naked, making passionate love underneath a blanket of stars on the balcony. No. He used a reserve of self-control to pull himself away from his lustful desires.

Billy smiled. "I'm sorry. It's just that I cannot afford to be distracted right now."

He had more important work to do. The love-making had to wait, at least until after the mission. Billy had to be in control Now more than ever. He craved the protection that it gave him from his feelings. His messed up feelings. Billy was an only child, raised in the Bronx when it was still a pretty rough neighbourhood. He was bullied at school, but he could hold his own. It was at home where he first experienced oppression, and it came in the form of his Uncle Harry, a short-tempered, surly character on his mother's side of the family who was inebriated most of the time. Uncle Harry ended up relocating into the spare room of their house after his ugly divorce cost him everything he owned. Billy clearly remembered the conversation his parents were having that fateful night. He watched through a slit in their bedroom door as his father raised his voice.

"I said no! I don't want him here. He's a drunk and a slob."

"But he's my brother! He's family and has nowhere to go! Please, Matthew, I'm begging you. Just for a couple of months until he gets back up on his feet."

A couple of months turned into a year of hell. Billy was seven years old and had just returned home from school when his uncle stumbled into his room and locked the door, from the inside. The abuse continued until one day he snapped. All he remembered was screaming himself hoarse. He lost his voice for three days and cried himself to sleep for weeks after that. Everything else was a blur. Ever since then, he knew that he could never lose control again. Not like that. Ever.

Billy had been waiting for years for the right moment to arrive, and now it had finally come. His ship was coming in. Literally. Billy was probably Viktor's most trusted operative. Well, thought Billy to himself, trust was not the right adjective. Viktor trusted no one. Billy was, rather, the one person that Viktor would least expect to double-cross him. He was, in fact, best positioned to take advantage of Viktor because he was so entrenched in his affairs. He received at least one call a day from the mob-boss who checked in with him to make sure that his latest operation was running smoothly.

Billy was mostly responsible for building Viktor's fortune over the years. He had opened so many doors for him; he had lost count. Billy valued his relationships. People naturally liked him and trusted him – a rare characteristic to have in this industry. He spent valuable time every day visiting his clients and colleagues, even if it was just to shoot the breeze. Viktor on the other hand, due to his treacherous temperament, very seldom ventured far from his bunker. The mistake that Viktor unwittingly made was to place Billy in this client-facing position. Billy would be silly not to strengthen the relationships that he made on Viktor's behalf, for his personal gain.

Billy and Kisha studied the plan. They had been through it dozens of times. "OK. This is the last time we are running through this before we put it in motion tomorrow at noon," said Billy.

Project Coup d'état was primed and ready, and nothing was going to stand in its way. The first step was to draw the rabbit out of its hole. Viktor would not step away from his compound willingly. There had to be a large enough motive for him to do so. Billy spent time in Belgrade, Viktor's hometown in Serbia, getting to know the city, its attractions and of course its people. He developed quite a fondness for the city. His favourite place was the Nikola Tesla Museum and its display of Tesla's interactive exhibits. The very last exhibit summed it all up for him, with the funerary mask of Tesla's face and the quotation of the American inventor E. Armstrong right next to it: "The World, I think, will wait a long time for Nikola Tesla's equal in achievement and imagination." The other great place he visited was the majestic Serbian Fortress, which was founded by Celtics in the third century. The fortress consisted of ancient turrets, towers and bridges overlooking the Danube and Sava rivers.

Viktor's family lived in Barajevo, a rural municipality of Belgrade, with a population of around 25,000. Viktor's father owned a small Orchard farm, and his mother was a potter, giving pottery classes to a few locals from her garage twice a week. Viktor was an only child, so when Billy arrived to visit them, they were overjoyed to hear that their son was alive and well and living in New York City. As to be expected, Viktor cut ties with his family years ago, when he left his hometown to seek his fortune in the great United States of America. His parents couldn't have called him even they wanted to.

The ungrateful prick. What goes around comes around, and boy is it coming!

CHAPTER TEN

Setup

Turkish Airlines, Boeing 777 from Belgrade, touched down at JFK International at 10.55am. It was seven minutes earlier than expected, but Viktor was there. How could he miss a visit from his parents that he had not seen for over a quarter of a century? Billy had booked Viktor's parents in at the five-star, Million Hotel in Crosby Street, Soho. The hotel had a modern look and feel, with magnificent floor-to-ceiling windows and a great view overlooking the city. Clive "The Jive" Gibson was the concierge at the Million, and one of Billy's oldest clients. He used to be a liquor rep in the city and, as a result, was well connected to the New York nightlife. He threw regular parties around town where he moved a serious amount of dope. Nowadays, the parties were less frequent but far more exclusive. From the rooftops of some of the tallest buildings in New York to luxury yacht parties on the Hudson River, Clive entertained stars like Paris Hilton, Colin Farrell and the late Amy Winehouse.

Clive welcomed Viktor and his parents as they arrived from the airport to check into the hotel. "Good morning Mr and Mrs Kadezi. My Name is Clive. Welcome to the Million. We are here to make your stay as comfortable as possible." He handed Viktor's father a little black electronic device with a small, red rubber button. "Please push this button if you need anything – a taxi, a restaurant booking or anything else. The device will send me an instant message, alerting me to call you." The electronic transmitter was also fitted with a GPS tracking device, linked directly to Billy's desktop at his office. Billy scheduled a week-long itinerary for Viktor and his parents that would take them to strategic locations all over the city. Everything was going according to plan.

Traditional container pallets are made of wood, but Viktor chose the more modern, plastic pallet instead. Plastic pallets offered far more benefits than the wooden variety, including easy sanitation, durability and non-splintering, which made them more environmentally-friendly as a result. Viktor was no environmentalist. He couldn't even spell the word. The real benefit for Viktor was the fact that the plastic pallets he used, were injection moulded, which meant that the three base strips of each pallet were hollow – perfect for smuggling purposes. Stuffed into the hundreds of pallets currently sitting in his African curio warehouse, was around one tonne's worth of cocaine with a street value of over US$300 million. The pallets were filled in Santiago, Cuba. Cuban Tobacco was packed on top of the pallets and exported to Cape Town. The Tobacco was unpacked and replaced with African curios and then shipped to New York. Finally, the curios, together with the pallets were unpacked and delivered to a warehouse, at 622 Communipaw Avenue, in Jersey City.

Part of Billy's plan was to 'borrow' some of this stash without Viktor finding out. Like Viktor, he didn't want to expose the ingenious cocaine trade route. It was far too valuable. Billy planned to take over operations once Viktor was out of the way, so the clandestine nature of this job was of utmost importance. He was counting on the fact that Viktor was too pre-occupied with entertaining his parents to be concerned with anything else right now. With Viktor's eye off the ball, Billy was free to operate and operate he did. He arranged for the security team covering the warehouse to be replaced with his own. A crew of guys that were paid handsomely to do what they were told, no questions asked. These were pros, handpicked from a group of ex-mercenaries, designed to kill, or die trying.

The security camera system was a little more complicated because Viktor kept close tabs on all movements in and out of the warehouse. Billy decided to enlist the services of none other than Carl Finnegan, an electronics expert from Ireland. His mop of unkempt, red hair, matched a pointed goatee, and his sparkly green eyes hinted at a wryly, mischievous character that reminded Billy of a Leprechaun.

"Good day sir, top of the morning to ya!"

"Hello, Finn, good to hear your voice. What's the status?"

"Well, sir, I've identified where the security cameras are positioned around the warehouse and just finished tapping into the feed to supply an uninterrupted loop of pre-recorded footage. My team is ready. On your signal, sir."

"Go for it. Let's do this."

Finn barked some commands into his receiver. A short while later, a black, unmarked pickup pulled up outside the delivery entrance of the African curio warehouse. Towards the rear of the stockpile of African sculptures inside the building, two men moved away a stack of boxes to reveal two blue, plastic pallets. They turned the pallets upside down and opened their specially constructed compartments, to reveal the smuggled dope wrapped up tightly inside. The pallets were replaced, and the goods packed back on top of them. The black pickup was loaded before speeding off into the night. Finnegan radioed Billy back shortly afterwards. "Sir, I've just disconnected the feed from the security network. Mission accomplished." Finn watched as the frame jumped once and then stabilised. Billy smiled as his phone vibrated with a message confirming the success of the heist. So far so good.

On the Upper East Side of town, about a block from Central Park, and on a recommendation from Clive 'The Jive', Viktor sat having dinner with his parents at Cicco Palamos Italian restaurant. "Bring me the Grilled fillet mignon with portobello mushrooms," snapped Viktor to the waiter. His father ordered the roasted rack of baby lamb with rosemary potatoes and his mother, a fillet of pan-fried organic salmon, with a fennel and dill sauce. Viktor was in his element. "You know, that Billy is such a stand-up guy - how he went out of his way to find the two of you and bring you over here to see me. I'd forgotten how much I missed you guys after all these years."

Viktor's memories of his hometown in Serbia came flooding back to him now as he sat looking into his mother's eyes. He ran away from home in search of the dream that he was now living, and it didn't include his parents. This never really bothered Viktor because he lived his life in the moment, always looking ahead. He had a simple philosophy. If it doesn't serve you, move forward and never look back for there are only ghosts. His parents had taken care of him until they had nothing left to give, so he walked away from home and into the United States of America, the land of freedom and opportunity. It was this attitude that got him where he was today. His cold, callous, arrogance was just enough to serve him as he waded through the dense, swampland that was the crime-riddled underbelly of New York City.

The black pickup began a long and tedious journey all over the city. In the back, three men sat weighing the coke and distributing it into small, transparent plastic bags. Up front, the driver and his accomplice plotted their course through the streets of Manhattan, making deliveries to a long list of Viktor's closest personal friends and acquaintances all over town. It took all night and most of the dark hours of the morning to distribute almost 50 kilos of cocaine eventually. Each visit was the same. Together with each lucky packet, a card was inserted that read: *With Compliments, VK.*

03h23. A *rap-tap-tap* on his door woke Brody with a start. He rolled out of bed in one fluid motion, pulling his Glock 22 out from under his pillow, ready to fire. He crouched down low next to his bed and whispered softly into the dark. "One, two, three, four, five." He darted to the edge of his bedroom door, then across the hallway and alongside the front door. He crouched down low to peer underneath the door and heard what sounded like a Chevy truck speed away. He ventured forward to peer through the door's spyglass. There was dead silence and no movement in sight. He carefully opened the door to find a small plastic packet lying on the front doormat; that contained what looked like around twenty grammes of blow and a mysterious black card. He opened his laptop and accessed the encrypted FBI database, searching for clues to the bizarre delivery.

VK. Brody's search brought up dozens of results from companies such as Visual Kaleidoscope, a production company whose owner was bust several years prior, for growing a marijuana plantation in the basement of his home, to Vladimir Korkachov, a Russian drug mule, caught carrying seventeen condom-bullets of cocaine in his stomach. There were other names and details, which he would have to get his team on first thing in the morning. The problem was, there was absolutely no way he was going back to bed. Brody closed his laptop and started his morning exercise routine consisting of five repetitions of sit-ups and push-ups, followed by bag punching for twenty minutes. After a quick cup of coffee and a bowl of muesli, he made his way to the office.

After another two hours of digging, Brody had narrowed the search down to a few other prospects but nothing as intriguing as Viktor Kadezi, a well-known mobster in the New York area. Viktor had come close to being bust many times, but each time he ended up on trial, he was cleared on some technicality. It was as if he owned the judicial system like it was working for him. Brody stared at his monitor.

Hmm. Seems that Kadezi all but disappeared after his last indictment. But why the hell would he deliver a bag of cocaine with a compliments card to my personal address? Makes absolutely no sense.

Brody smiled as he strode over to the forensics lab in the heart of the FBI headquarters, pondering over the television series, CSI New York, that glammed up the whole investigative function of the NYPD, as it followed a team of forensic technicians revealing unusual deaths and other crimes in the New York area.

The lab was headed up by Doctor Felicity Halden, an intelligent, redheaded feline from the UK. She had a strong British accent that gave Brody a warm fuzzy feeling when she spoke.

"Felix." Halden dipped her head slightly as Brody stepped into the lab, acknowledging his presence. Halden had only recently transferred to the FBI offices from MI6, Britain's secret service organisation. Brody had taken an instant liking to the spirited, young doctor and they had recently started dating, off the record. Personal relations were not tolerated in the working environment at the FBI, hence the strictly business affiliation during office hours.

"Felicity, I'd like you to please take a look at this." Brody handed Halden the black business card and the packet of cocaine powder. "It was delivered to my house at three-thirty this morning."

"Delivered?" questioned Halden, puzzled. "What do you mean?"

"That's *exactly* what I mean," replied Brody. "There was a knock at my front door early this morning. I heard what sounded like a truck pulling off in a hurry and then I found this."

"Hmm. Interesting. Perhaps it was an invitation from an old fling?" Felicity's words rolled off her tongue in that delicious accent. Brody's skin tingled.

"Very funny Halden. Very funny." Brody caught a whiff of her floral signature, as he moved past her to switch on the Carl Zeiss, confocal, laser-scanning microscope. He resisted the urge to reach out and touch her. Halden examined the black card and then inserted it into the machine for a much closer inspection. Brody found himself holding his breath while she examined the evidence. She adjusted the microscope, twisting the knobs and dials.

"Very interesting. Come and have a look at this." Billy brushed slowly past Halden as he stepped over to the microscope before gazing through the apparatus. He had to blink twice before his vision cleared fully, to reveal a tiny list of what appeared to be names in alphabetical order.

"What the hell? The police commissioner? Judge Marks? Vanessa Peoples? I wonder what the common thread that binds these people together is?" He looked up, seemingly trying to draw the answers out of the ceiling. Halden continued to examine the card for any further possible clues.

"I'm picking up a few fingerprints, but nothing conclusive enough."

"Thanks, Halden. Good job. Please extract those names and send me the list? I'm going to get my team to investigate further. Ah yes, one more thing."

"Yes, what is it?"

"Please examine the coke as well and let me know what you find?" Brody stepped out of the lab, but not before turning back to steal a wink at Felicity.

CHAPTER ELEVEN

Viktor

"Finn? Just checking in."

Carl Finnegan's Irish accent was heavy. "All good, boss. Kadezi knows nothing. I tapped into his mobile phone account and rerouted all calls through a high-tech system that only I can monitor. So, basically, I have circumvented the messages and calls from his super-surprised customers and friends that received their little gifts last night. Right now, only calls from you are cleared to connect to Viktor. As soon as Viktor tries to connect to any numbers in his phone book, the call will reroute directly to the recipient's voice mailbox."

"Love your work Finn."

Viktor was so busy with the itinerary that Billy had put together for him and his parents that he had precious little time even to be concerned with his phone or calling anyone besides Billy to check on his plans and bookings.

"Kadezi's hanging out with his folks at the Empire State, followed by Ground Zero and finally a cruise to the Statue of Liberty and Staten Island."

"Great! Please keep me updated with Brody's progress. I need to know where we can help him along the way."

"Sure thing boss."

Billy's plan was to lead Brody directly to Viktor. It started with the micro-list on the business card, naming Kadezi's closest friends, colleagues and business associates, a bunch of corrupt businesspeople, cops and politicians, all as greedy and insatiable as Viktor. Brody was slowly putting the puzzle pieces together that would place Viktor Kadezi in the centre of the mix. Brody had already found several more cards and bags of cocaine after apprehending a few of the individuals on the list. Halden had also just delivered the report on the cocaine Brody had asked her to analyse, and it confirmed that it was the same batch that his team had found on the two perps at the Nefaro Shipping Company. Further investigations linked the thugs directly to Kadezi. "Felicity, I'd like you to please take a look at this." Brody handed Halden the black business card and the packet of cocaine powder. "It was delivered to my house at three-thirty this morning."

"Delivered?" questioned Halden, puzzled. "What do you mean?"

"That's *exactly* what I mean," replied Brody. "There was a knock at my front door early this morning. I heard what sounded like a truck pulling off in a hurry and then I found this."

"Hmm. Interesting. Perhaps it was an invitation from an old fling?" Felicity's words rolled off her tongue in that delicious accent. Brody's skin tingled.

"Very funny Halden. Very funny." Brody caught a whiff of her floral signature, as he moved past her to switch on the Carl Zeiss, confocal, laser-scanning microscope. He resisted the urge to reach out and touch her. Halden examined the black card and then inserted it into the machine for a much closer inspection. Brody found himself holding his breath while she examined the evidence. She adjusted the microscope, twisting the knobs and dials.

"Very interesting. Come and have a look at this." Billy brushed slowly past Halden as he stepped over to the microscope before gazing through the apparatus. He had to blink twice before his vision cleared fully, to reveal a tiny list of what appeared to be names in alphabetical order.

"What the hell? The police commissioner? Judge Marks? Vanessa Peoples? I wonder what the common thread that binds these people together is?" He looked up, seemingly trying to draw the answers out of the ceiling. Halden continued to examine the card for any further possible clues.

"I'm picking up a few fingerprints, but nothing conclusive enough."

"Thanks, Halden. Good job. Please extract those names and send me the list? I'm going to get my team to investigate further. Ah yes, one more thing."

"Yes, what is it?"

"Please examine the coke as well and let me know what you find?" Brody stepped out of the lab, but not before turning back to steal a wink at Felicity.

Viktor dropped his folks off at the Million Hotel, before heading off to his favourite haunt, The Hedron, a sleazy downtown strip joint where he was treated as a very special guest. Viktor hadn't been to The Hedron in quite some time. Each visit cost him well over 5,000 dollars, and this one was no different. He went straight to his private booth on arrival and spent several hours satisfying his carnal desires. Brody and his team arrived at the venue on a tip-off. No more than two hours later, Viktor came stumbling out of the club with a girl on either arm. He was singing what sounded like the Serbian anthem but completely out of key. Brody stepped out of his car and walked up to the staggering trio. "Viktor Kedazi. I'm Special Agent Felix Brody, FBI. You are under arrest for illegal possession and distribution of narcotics. Please come with me."

Brody pulled out a pair of stainless steel handcuffs and reached forward to clamp Viktor's wrists. Instinctively, Viktor snapped out of his inebriated state, hastily shoved the two scantily clad strippers onto Brody, turned and fled down the street. Brody half-caught the girls as he toppled heavily to the ground. He managed to pull out his firearm and fire off two shots in Viktor's direction as he sprinted away. He pushed the two girls out of the way, jumped up and gave chase. Viktor ducked down the alley behind the club, yanked open the kitchen entrance and dashed inside. Brody followed closely behind, signalling for his team to follow him in. He reached the entrance and paused for a moment, listening intently to Viktor's movements inside. He turned and stepped into the kitchen only to see Viktor enter the club on the other side of the room. Brody spoke quickly into his receiver.

"He's in the club. Mat, Terence, Mickey, take the front. The rest of you, follow me."

He slowly pushed through the double doors and peeked inside. There was complete pandemonium. Topless girls were running around screaming while customers were either lying on the ground or making a run for the exit. Viktor had grabbed the closest victim he could find. She was a young, semi-naked, Eastern-European girl. He had his left arm around her neck, while the other held a gun that was pointed dangerously at the side of her head. Viktor was shouting and swearing in Serbian, warning others to keep away from him.

Brody shouted, trying to make himself heard above the commotion in the room. "Kadezi! There's nowhere to go. Let the girl go. Nobody has to get hurt!"

"Bullshit!" Viktor shouted back. "I'm walking out of here, and she's coming with me!"

"C'mon Kadezi. Let's make a deal! Let her go and come with us. We can talk this through!" Brody was biding time, trying to get him to rationalise his position.

"Talk to this!"

Viktor pulled the girl aside and opened fire in Brody's direction. Brody ducked behind a table as a barrage of bullets rained over his head. He had to time this perfectly. He counted the shots fired from Viktor's weapon.

Two more and he'll be outta ammo. Brody moved. He rolled out from behind the table just as Viktor fired his last shot, aimed and pulled the trigger. Viktor was still holding the girl in one hand, but he had to open up to fire his gun. It seemed as if everything turned to slow motion, from the *booka, booka* sound of Brody's gun, to the *thwack, thwack* of bullets hitting their mark. A bullet tore through Kadezi's left collarbone, sending him back into a spiralling twist, while another entered the top right area of his forehead, forcing its way through bone and then into the soft, fleshy part of his brain. The back of his head exploded in a messy chunk into the mirror behind him. Viktor Kadezi crumpled to the floor. The wide-eyed stripper, her face splattered with blood, broke the silence that followed, with a terrified scream. The Serbian bulldog had finally been put to rest.

CHAPTER TWELVE

Providence

The first-class air hostess on board Air Canada flight 1755 smiled before escorting Billy and Kisha to their seats. "Good afternoon and welcome aboard Air Canada."

"Afternoon," Billy smiled in return. "Thank you."

Billy and Kisha were on their way to Cuba. For over fifty years, The US has had an embargo against Cuba, as a result of Cuba not transitioning to democracy and improving human rights. The embargo included restrictions on travel between the US and Cuba, hence the multi-city trip via Canada from New York. Billy was eager to meet with the Cuban Tea merchants, as well as their cocaine supplier on the island. He hadn't seen either of them for years and needed to re-establish their relationships now that he had stepped into Viktor's shoes. An odd looking gentleman travelling alone and dressed in a long black coat also stepped onto the flight. He looked around the cabin, spotted Billy and Kisha, smiled contentedly, and settled down into his seat.

After landing at the Havana Jose Marti International Airport, Billy and Kisha jumped into a cab and headed off to the Santa Isabel, a 5-star colonial style hotel located in the most beautiful area of the Old Town of Havana. Billy left Kisha sipping a Mojito by the pool, climbed into a cab and headed off into the Cuban jungle. Halfway through the uncomfortable ride, the cab driver began to pull over. "Hey! What're you doing?" said Billy in earnest as two men jumped into the car either side of him. The last thing he saw before blacking out was the cab driver's red, reflective sunglasses and his long, braided hair.

The darkness was stifling. Billy felt battered. His body ached in so many places. The heavy fabric bag thrown over his head and secured around his neck constricted his breathing. He sat on a hard, wooden chair and only realised that he was crudely tied to it when he tried to move his hands and found them limp, heavy and completely numb from the deeply bound cord that was twisted roughly around his wrists. After he had regained consciousness, Billy sat for what must have been hours, struggling to fathom how and why he had arrived in this predicament. He had come to several conclusions. One: There was no way that Viktor could be behind this. Billy was always ten steps ahead of him. Two: He was flying from Toronto to Havana when Viktor was apprehended and only booked his flight a few hours previously. Whoever had tracked him to Cuba had already been watching him for some time and either followed him all the way from New York, or arranged someone to apprehend him after he landed, or both. Three: Then there was the situation that he now found himself in. He was alive, which meant that his captors wanted something from him. Otherwise, he probably would be lying undiscovered at the bottom of a six-foot hole somewhere in the jungles of Cuba, rotting and decaying along with earthworms and flesh-eating maggots.

Billy was cautious. He made sure he covered his tracks but in this crazy game, he knew that he couldn't trust anyone. He sifted through all the people he knew in his head, struggling to find motive or purpose. Perhaps in his rapid climb to the top, others looking for the same success blinded him. These and many more questions plagued Billy as he contemplated his uncertain fate.

Rough hands tugged at the bindings around his neck, and the

bag was jerked off his head. The pitch black was replaced with a blinding white light that seared into the back of his head. He screwed up his eyes in pain as he felt the heat from the bright, radiant light pierce his very core. He opened his mouth and let out a wailing bellow of agony. Perspiration rolled down his face as the suffocating space under the bag was replaced by a fresh intake of air into his lungs. He sucked in a deep, invigorating breath, shook his head and expelled the air once more. He dropped his head, his chin resting against his chest as he gradually regained his composure. The light was still too bright to open his eyes, so he just kept them closed. He screamed again, this time, louder than before as an intensely penetrating, high-pitched, ringing sound inside his head threatened to render him unconscious once more.

The ringing abruptly changed to a dull hum, pulsing heavily through his entire body. An uncomfortable weight pressed down on top of him until he buckled under the immense pressure. He fought just to breathe. His lungs burned from the incredible effort. As he sat there, eyes closed and body completely immobilised, he began to sense another entity enter his space. Not physically but mentally. There was another 'someone' inside his head, reading his thoughts, scanning his mind and sensing his emotional state.

How was this possible? How could someone be reading my thoughts? Am I hallucinating? Is this real?

A myriad of conflicting thoughts, challenging the veritable, swished around Billy's head like a yacht in a storm, lost in the current. Down he fell, pitching and rolling into a giant trough, that turned into a whirlpool of swirling, vortex energy, sucking him in, deeper and deeper until his head spun so violently that he passed out again.

Billy opened his eyes to a soft, warm light, bathing him in its radiance, soothing him with its tender embrace. His bonds were gone and so too was his pain. There was a soft haze around the room that seemed to permeate each and every crevice, shifting through the air like a fine sea mist. He looked down and found himself lying in a comfortable, king-size bed, wearing pale blue, silk pyjamas and covered with a soft, white, lavender-scented, duck-down duvet. A mermaid glided into the room from an unseen entrance and came to stand next him. She had long, straight white hair and soft, plum-coloured lips that parted into a gorgeous smile. She leant towards him, opened her mouth and out darted a serpent-like tongue that continued to extend out and wrap itself gradually around his neck. Although his hands were loose, try as he might, he could not move them. They remained glued magically to his sides beneath the covers. The girl's eyes began to shift and change in colour, from a deep brown to a dark, bottomless black and then to a fiery red. *Hissssss!* A guttural seething rasp began to vibrate from the thing's lungs and out through its mouth as the writhing tongue began to tighten its grip on Billy's throat, suffocating him in the process. He could see her tail whip fervently from side to side as the rest of her body began to morph and twist, mutating into a fully scaled beast, intent on devouring its helpless prey. Billy, struggling now to breathe, watched the walls around him begin to melt into each other becoming a blazing, fiery furnace. Smoke poured into his lungs with every painful gasp for air, burning him from the inside out.

The blinding light was back. Billy lifted his chin off of his chest, his hands still bound behind him. His shoulders ached from the prolonged strain of having them pulled back for so long. He realised that the vivid and intense, nightmarish dreams that he had been having could only have been the result of a drug that his captors had been feeding him.

"Well, well, well. If it isn't the enigmatic Billy Bayer." The voice was strong and deep, with a mixture of accents that was hard to identify. Billy picked up a trace of Spanish or Italian behind the mostly American accent. Squinting as he looked up, Billy tried to see beyond the glare to where the voice was coming from.

His throat was parched, and his voice jagged as he spoke. "Who are you? What do you want?"

"The question is not what I want, Billy. The question is what do you want? Is it wealth? Control? Power?" The voice was cynical, mocking.

"What do you mean?" Instinctively, Billy's defences intensified. Billy could almost hear his captor smile behind the bright light.

"Billy, Billy, Billy. We know everything." There was an unusually long pause. "We know all about Viktor, your plans, Kisha."

Billy tensed in his seat. "If you…"

"Don't worry, Billy, we are only interested in you right now. We are interested in your future, your destiny, and we are going to help you get what you want. All that you have to do is cooperate with us, while we teach you the path to Providence." Billy's mind was racing, his head spinning. He closed his eyes and tried to piece things together but the psychological torture and physical strain over the last several hours had drained him of his ability to think straight.

The path to providence? What the hell was he talking about?

All that Billy knew was that he was the captive in this whole mess and that the only way to find out what was going on was to cooperate. When the time was right, he would somehow plan his escape from this madness. "OK. What do you want me to do?"

"First, let's get you cleaned up. Then the training begins."

CHAPTER THIRTEEN

Sortie

Kisha was having the time of her life. The unrelenting Cuban sun baked down as she sipped on her second Santa Isobel Mojito. She savoured the mix of flavours - a good balance of white rum, sugar and lime. The combination of crushed ice and soda bubbles tickled her palate, while the crisp flavour of fresh mint reminded her of the time she was with Billy in Mykonos enjoying a zucchini, mint and yoghurt dip at Bouzouki Restaurant, overlooking the magnificent marina and lagoon. Just as her Prada's slipped a little down the bridge of her nose, she spotted a Greek-looking hunk of a man, in checked, blue and white, tight Vilebrequin trunks. He stood up off his lounger and walked languidly towards the pool. Kisha kept her head facing forward, narrowed her eyes to slits and gazed wistfully to the right to watch him, her dark shades concealing her scrutinising, flawlessly. She smiled imperceptibly, keeping an eye on her man as he reached the pool and took a well-controlled dive into the water, disappearing beneath its sparkling surface.

Ahh, the life.

Kisha took a deep breath and closed her eyes to the sound of seagulls squawking faintly overhead. By the time she woke from her afternoon slumber, her throat was parched from the beating sun and the island rum. She ordered a still mineral water and then pulled out her phone to check the time. 3:55pm. She

Instagrammed a magnificent shot of the swimming pool, with the ocean beyond, glistening like a bed of diamonds in the hot summer sun. *#cuba #summerlovin #mojito #paradise.* She flipped to her contacts and then tapped out a quick SMS to Billy.

>Hi babe, loving it here by the pool! See you for dinner at 7! xxx

She stood up, off the lounger and made her way back to her room for a cool shower, before an incredible, hot-stone massage in the spa. Her skin tingled. She got dressed for dinner and then checked her phone once again.

Hmm. Still no word from Billy. That's odd.

She tried calling him, but it didn't ring. Instead, there was that silent interval that preceded voice mail, and then Billy's recorded voice began playing. Kisha killed the call. At seven thirty, she made her way down to the restaurant and ordered dinner. She tried calling again but to no avail. She began to worry and then thought of calling Finn.

"OK, Miss Kisha. I've run a trace on his mobile, and I'm picking up that it's in Barbados."

"But that must be more than three thousand miles away!" Kisha was flabbergasted.

"Just over two and a half to be precise Miss K," replied Finn, matter-of-factly.

"Shit. I know something bad has happened. We have to go and get him!" wailed Kisha. *"Please!"*

"Just give me a bit more time to pinpoint his exact coordinates…"

Kisha heard Finn on the other side of the line, typing furiously into his keyboard. And then the typing abruptly stopped. "Shit. Fuck."

"What? What happened?" Kisha's started to panic.

"The signal is gone," replied Finn flatly.

"What do you mean gone?"

"I mean it's gone, disappeared. I'll keep trying to find it, but I'm afraid we're gonna have to move to plan B. I'll give Josiah a call."

Billy found Josiah Ligman while at a charity dinner in

Washington DC. He was this imposing brute of a figure standing resolutely at the entrance in a black tuxedo, welcoming guests as they arrived. Billy watched the doorman move his tree trunk of a neck, his muscles protesting under the tailor-made suit. Despite his size, there was something comforting about his presence. Billy approached him. He seemed even larger close-up. His bald, black head shined in the fluorescent light. He smiled to reveal pearly white teeth. "Good evening sir, how may I be of assistance?" A deep baritone voice matched his powerful physique.

"Good evening. I'm Billy." With some trepidation, Billy held out his right hand. He mentally prepared himself for the grip he expected to receive. His entire arm tensed in anticipation.

"Josiah. Josiah Ligman." Billy closed his eyes for a split second as Josiah grabbed his hand to shake it. Instead of a bone-crushing squeeze, Josiah gave Billy a firm, yet relaxed handshake. With Josiah's enormous hand in his own, Billy got a good feel for the size and weight of the rest of the towering doorman as he shook his hand up and down a few times. This was one fella that he wouldn't like to get on the wrong side of. Billy looked up at the hulk of a man.

"How would you like to work for me?"

Josiah smiled that big white, toothy smile. "Make me an offer." And from that day on, Josiah was on Billy's payroll. It was seldom that Billy made such a quick decision about someone, but he was a great judge of character and this time he knew he was spot on.

Josiah trained at Criss Cross, a cross-fit training gym in the city. He was performing floor slams with a thirty-pound sandball, a kind of soft medicine ball filled with sand yet far more versatile. Extending the sand-ball over his head with both hands in a triple extension, he squeezed his abs as tight as he could and then forcefully threw the sand-ball to the ground in a whip-like motion, working his core to its fullest extent. He walked over to the sand-ball for another repetition when his phone rang.

"Josiah, it's me, Finn. The boss is in trouble and needs your help."

"Hey, Finn. What kinda trouble?" replied Josiah, concern in his voice.

"Just meet me at the warehouse in an hour. Pack an overnight bag and bring some toys. We're going to Barbados."

Finn put down the phone and proceeded to call Maria Aleksey, a KGB operative who defected to the US with Billy's assistance, nine years prior. Amongst her peers, she was considered one of the most dangerous of snipers in the field. Soon after Billy arranged for her Green Card, he recruited her to work for him, frequently partnering with Josiah on a variety of missions and assignments. Maria was a tall, tough woman who kind of reminded Finn of Lara Croft, with her long, straight dark hair tied up behind her head and her dark brown leather boots with matching, loosely fitted waistcoat. She had that typical Russian, high, cheek-boned face, with dark, striking features.

"Hello, Finn," Maria answered the call, her deep, rolling Russian accent making its way through the receiver like a Black Mamba writhing through the long, dry grass of the Savannah.

"Meet me at the warehouse in an hour; we're going to Barbados. Bring Tessa." *Click*.

Maria had always given her guns names. She felt more comfortable with them when she did so. She even sang softly to her weapons, coaxing them into position, before taking aim. Tessa was her Soviet-produced semi-automatic Dragunov Sniper Rifle. The Dragunov self-loading rifle was named model of the year in 1963 and today is still considered the standard squad support weapon of Eastern European countries. Finn, Maria and Josiah assembled at the African curio warehouse at 622 Communipaw Avenue in Jersey City. After a flurry of quick greetings, the trio sat down in the office to talk through the P.O.A.

"OK, guys. This is the story," began Finn in earnest. The other two leant in to listen. "Billy is somewhere in Barbados. We don't have an accurate location on him yet, but we know he is in the south-east quadrant, probably somewhere near the capital, Bridgetown. This was where his mobile phone signal was last recorded before disappearing. We don't have any further intel as yet, but we do know that he must've been kidnapped because Barbados was definitely not his destination of choice. This is a rescue mission. We go in, find Billy and get him out. A plane will drop the two of you over the island, and I'll be waiting with a boat in a hidden cove nearby to take you out. Any further questions?"

Josiah raised his hand. "Yeah. What we got to eat, I'm ravenous?"

"OK, you buncha wackos. Anything else?"

"I just got one thing to say," piped up Maria. "It takes something like forty-two muscles to pull your face into a frown and only four to pull the trigger of a decent sniper rifle. So, let's do this!"

CHAPTER FOURTEEN

Kaimi

Billy looked around. He was in a fortress. His escort, a young guard in a black, unbranded military uniform, marched him down a long, windowless corridor and into a restroom with toilets and showers. The shower was warm and the blue soap smelt like industrial dishwashing liquid. Billy closed his eyes as the water ran over his face. He shifted slightly under the flow, positioning his head directly under the shower nozzle until his ears filled with water, fully blocking out the ambient sound around him. The gushing sound of water pounded forcefully around him like a waterfall, cleansing and refreshing every molecule in his aching body. His mind drifted as he thought about Kisha, hoping that she was OK and not too concerned about his sudden disappearance.

Billy found a pair of loose, cream drawstring pants, matching shirt and flat-soled canvas loafers folded neatly nearby the shower. He discarded his dishevelled clothes and pulled on the fresh set and then followed the guard down a corridor and into a mess hall where he noticed other people wearing similar attire and helping themselves to food from a self-service area.

"Please grab a tray and help yourself to food and drink," said the guard in a solemn voice.

Billy was already starting to feel stronger as the appetising food replaced the gnawing feeling in his belly. The young guard was waiting patiently for him once again, as he stepped out of the canteen. It was only then that he realised there were guards stationed at almost every corner and that getting out of the complex was going to be far tougher than he initially envisaged. His situation seemed to be improving, though, so he decided to stick it out to see what was going to be thrown at him next. The guard led Billy into another room that branched off to the left of the main corridor. The lights in this room were switched off, leaving the soft light from the passage to illuminate the dark corners and shadowed crooks of the ceiling above. Billy could just make out the outline of a table and chairs ahead of him. He looked around only to find that the guard had mysteriously disappeared. Moving forward, he sat down at the table and noticed the outline of a figure sitting at the other end. The voice that came from the figure sounded calm and composed.

"Billy. Welcome to the first part of your training. My name is Kaimi, your guide and teacher."

As Billy's eyes adjusted to the darkness, Kaimi's features became more distinguishable. His long, dark, braided hair was somehow familiar, but Billy couldn't quite place it. "Why are we sitting in the dark?" asked Billy.

"I have an aversion to the light." From the sound of his accent, Billy guessed he was from Hawaii or somewhere in the Caribbean.

"So what exactly are you training me to do?" Billy had so many questions, but he held himself back for fear of sounding too zealous.

"I know that you have many questions, and soon you will have plenty more, but the question which I'm sure is plaguing your mind most is - why am I here? Why have you been so abruptly snatched away from your comfort zone?" Billy nodded. "We've been watching you, Billy, for a while now, waiting for you to make your move."

"What move?"

"Last night's move. The one where you arranged to get rid of Viktor." A chill shot down Billy's spine.

"This is why we have brought you in. You see, Viktor worked for us. So naturally we have been very interested in your um, how should I put it, progress?"

Billy shifted apprehensively in his seat. "So what you are saying is, I now work for you?"

"Very astute, Billy. Yes. You now work for us."

"OK, so what is it I *do* for you exactly?"

"That's why you are sitting in that seat, Billy - to learn the answer to that question and so many more like it. What I am about to tell you will be hard to believe. In time, you will understand and in time you will believe because belief comes from understanding."

What the fuck? This is crazy. Who is this guy and what the hell am I doing here?

Kaimi leant across the table, into the light and for the first time, Billy noticed a pair of red-lensed glasses on his face. And then it struck him like a bolt of lightning - the taxi driver! Kaimi smiled knowingly. "Don't worry Billy; I'm not here to hurt you. We're on your side. We call ourselves Lemurians, descendants of the lost continent. Lemuria or Mu as it is also known is the ancient motherland of man. It existed as a landmass in the Pacific Ocean and was swallowed up by the Earth itself, over 12,000 years ago." Kaimi looked up and then closed his eyes. Billy blinked. In the wan light, he thought he saw Kaimi shimmer. "It was a rich land, full of promise and potential, with a King who ruled over seven golden cities and millions of loyal subjects. These people possessed a connection to the life force that surrounds us with such vigour that they lived an almost ethereal existence."

OK. This guy is really crazy. Where does he get this shit from? I mean, how does he expect me to believe this crap? What kinda bullshit is this?

Kaimi slowly lowered his head and stared at Billy again, his eyes shifting as if he were in some kind of trance. "So you're wondering why I'm telling you this bullshit story?"

How did he do that thing? It's like he knows what I'm thinking!

"Because it's not bullshit. There's evidence. And yes, scientific proof."Billy found Josiah Ligman while at a charity dinner in Washington DC. He was this imposing brute of a figure standing resolutely at the entrance in a black tuxedo, welcoming guests as they arrived. Billy watched the doorman move his tree trunk of a neck, his muscles protesting under the tailor-made suit. Despite his size, there was something comforting about his presence. Billy approached him. He seemed even larger close-up. His bald, black head shined in the fluorescent light. He smiled to reveal pearly white teeth. "Good evening sir, how may I be of assistance?" A deep baritone voice matched his powerful physique.

"Good evening. I'm Billy." With some trepidation, Billy held out his right hand. He mentally prepared himself for the grip he expected to receive. His entire arm tensed in anticipation.

"Josiah. Josiah Ligman." Billy closed his eyes for a split second as Josiah grabbed his hand to shake it. Instead of a bone-crushing squeeze, Josiah gave Billy a firm, yet relaxed handshake. With Josiah's enormous hand in his own, Billy got a good feel for the size and weight of the rest of the towering doorman as he shook his hand up and down a few times. This was one fella that he wouldn't like to get on the wrong side of. Billy looked up at the hulk of a man.

"How would you like to work for me?"

Josiah smiled that big white, toothy smile. "Make me an offer." And from that day on, Josiah was on Billy's payroll. It was seldom that Billy made such a quick decision about someone, but he was a great judge of character and this time he knew he was spot on.

Josiah trained at Criss Cross, a cross-fit training gym in the city. He was performing floor slams with a thirty-pound sand-ball, a kind of soft medicine ball filled with sand yet far more versatile. Extending the sand-ball over his head with both hands in a triple extension, he squeezed his abs as tight as he could and then forcefully threw the sand-ball to the ground in a whip-like motion, working his core to its fullest extent. He walked over to the sand-ball for another repetition when his phone rang.

"Josiah, it's me, Finn. The boss is in trouble and needs your help."

"Hey, Finn. What kinda trouble?" replied Josiah, concern in his voice.

"Just meet me at the warehouse in an hour. Pack an overnight bag and bring some toys. We're going to Barbados."

Finn put down the phone and proceeded to call Maria Aleksey, a KGB operative who defected to the US with Billy's assistance, nine years prior. Amongst her peers, she was considered one of the most dangerous of snipers in the field. Soon after Billy arranged for her Green Card, he recruited her to work for him, frequently partnering with Josiah on a variety of missions and assignments. Maria was a tall, tough woman who kind of reminded Finn of Lara Croft, with her long, straight dark hair tied up behind her head and her dark brown leather boots with matching, loosely fitted waistcoat. She had that typical Russian, high, cheek-boned face, with dark, striking features.

"Hello, Finn," Maria answered the call, her deep, rolling Russian accent making its way through the receiver like a Black Mamba writhing through the long, dry grass of the Savannah.

"Meet me at the warehouse in an hour; we're going to Barbados. Bring Tessa." *Click.*

Maria had always given her guns names. She felt more comfortable with them when she did so. She even sang softly to her weapons, coaxing them into position, before taking aim. Tessa was her Soviet-produced semi-automatic Dragunov Sniper Rifle. The Dragunov self-loading rifle was named model of the year in 1963 and today is still considered the standard squad support weapon of Eastern European countries. Finn, Maria and Josiah assembled at the African curio warehouse at 622 Communipaw Avenue in Jersey City. After a flurry of quick greetings, the trio sat down in the office to talk through the P.O.A.

"OK, guys. This is the story," began Finn in earnest. The

other two leant in to listen. "Billy is somewhere in Barbados. We don't have an accurate location on him yet, but we know he is in the south-east quadrant, probably somewhere near the capital, Bridgetown. This was where his mobile phone signal was last recorded before disappearing. We don't have any further intel as yet, but we do know that he must've been kidnapped because Barbados was definitely not his destination of choice. This is a rescue mission. We go in, find Billy and get him out. A plane will drop the two of you over the island, and I'll be waiting with a boat in a hidden cove nearby to take you out. Any further questions?"

Josiah raised his hand. "Yeah. What we got to eat, I'm ravenous?"

"OK, you buncha wackos. Anything else?"

"I just got one thing to say," piped up Maria. "It takes something like forty-two muscles to pull your face into a frown and only four to pull the trigger of a decent sniper rifle. So, let's do this!"

CHAPTER FIFTEEN

Touchdown

Josiah shuffled his feet on the dusty warehouse floor as Finn and Maria checked their kit.

"Right, let's run through the plan once more," said Finn. "When we reach Barbados, you're gonna wait for my signal before making the jump. Your exit point will be over Dash Valley. After you touch down, make your way west, towards Bridgetown."

"That's the capital, right?" enquired Maria.

"Affirmative. I'll continue to Grantley Adams airport and then to Oistins Bay to pick up the boat. From there, I'll cruise over to Off the Hook Fishing Charters, where I've arranged for the boat to be moored. Let's synchronise our watches. All things being equal, I'll see you at The Bridgetown Inn in five hours and forty-three minutes."

Josiah's deep voice boomed inside the dark, stuffy warehouse. "Sure thing Finn. Sounds good. Have you located Billy yet?"

"Negative." Finn's voice was cold as iron. "Been trying all day. I'm certain we'll get a fix on him when we get to the island."

The Beechcraft King Air gained altitude as it soared above the clouds en route to Barbados. Josiah and Maria were doing final checks on their parachutes while Finn began to sing softly to himself. Josiah closed his eyes and Mariah slowly turned the corners of her mouth up into a smile as Finn's sweet Irish voice cut through the drone of the engine with a verse by John Masefield.

I must go down to the seas again, to the lonely sea and the sky,
And all I ask is a tall ship and a star to steer her by;
And the wheel's kick and the wind's song and the white sail's shaking,
And a grey mist on the sea's face and a grey dawn breaking.

Finn's voice trailed off as he gazed out of the window at the puffy, white, cotton wool clouds below, bobbing along in the breeze. The crew flew in complete silence the rest of the journey, the steady drone of the engines drowning out any desire to converse further with each other. Soon after they reached the island, Finn turned back to look at Maria and Josiah. "Ten minutes to jump point. Get into position."

Maria made sure the specially designed canister for her sniper rifle was securely fastened to her back. She triple checked all the knots, straps and fasteners before settling into place, closest to the door. Josiah checked his weapons and his chute and then sat down next to Maria. The plane gradually began to drop in altitude. Finn signalled to the pilot who gave him the thumbs up. He reached forward to slide the side door open and then turned to Maria.

"Ready? Three, two, one, Go! Josiah. Go, Go, Go!"

The pair jumped from the plane, skydiving briefly before pulling their chutes and landing safely in an abandoned field. Finn touched down at Grantley Adams, hopped into a cab and made his way to Oistins Bay and then on to Barbados. The Bridgetown Inn was a small, homely residence. Finn was busy checking in when Josiah and Maria stepped through the door. He glanced at his watch and yawned, his mouth gaping wide.

"You're late. Have you two been rolling in the hay again?"

Maria looked over the top of her glasses at Finn. "Yeah, it was really kinky. At least we're getting some."

Finn smiled and winked at Maria. "Go and get cleaned up and then meet me in my room, number 402. We got work to do."

Finn had rigged up his portable GPS surveillance device in the hotel room. It connected via satellite, to the local mobile phone network, tracing the last known location of Billy's telephone on the island. After around ten minutes, a red light started flashing on the front panel of the device. Finn started punching at his laptop keyboard. His screen flashed once, twice and then a satellite image of the Earth materialised, with a pulsing orange dot in the centre. After a few more taps on the keyboard, the image of the Earth began to enlarge until it took over the entire screen. The continents grew until the kidney-shaped island of Barbados came into view. The zooming imagery slowed down as the resolution began to enhance, the orange dot now a slightly larger pin on the map. "OK. Looks like this is around three miles from here." Finn's fingers flew over the keyboard, opening up several browser windows, all gathering information about the environment surrounding the target area. "It seems that the last signal from Billy's phone came from here." Finn pointed at his screen, indicating a static Google street-view image of a diner on the corner of Harbour View and Junction Roads, on the outskirts of Bridgetown. It looked like a typical American diner with a stainless steel, neon, mahogany, and chrome finish. The kind of design that would have looked cutting-edge in the 40's and now came across really retro. The neon sign read Denny's Diner. Maria slid her fingers over the trackpad, rotating the view on the screen.

"Looks like a motel on the other side of the street, around three floors. We'll make our way to this location and onto the roof where I'll set up Tessa for surveillance. Once we have more of a fix on the target, Josiah can go in."

Josiah nodded his head in approval. "Sounds good to me."

"I don't have any eyes on this location, so I'm relying on you two to keep me informed as to what's going on." Finn was persistent.

"Sure thing. Will radio you once we reach our destination," replied Maria.

Maria's right eye was pressed into the sight on top of the Dragunov, as she scanned the perimeter from the rooftop of the three-story building, looking for signs of anything untoward. Josiah spoke into his radio. "Finn, we've scanned the perimeter, and everything appears to be clear." There was a soft hissing and then Finn's voice came back.

"OK. Go down there for a closer inspection."

"Wait!" Maria's husky voice interrupted the conversation. "I see something. The guy sitting outside the diner - his shoes are wrong."

Josiah spoke back into his radio. "Finn, I think we've found something. I'll report back shortly. Out."

Josiah headed down to street level. He stood across the road, casually looking at the beggar outside the shop. He was wearing torn, worn out jeans and a filthy, brown blazer with one sleeve. His head hung heavy on his chest, long, matted hair covering most of his face. He held out a red and blue baseball cap, collecting a few meagre coins and the odd note from passers-by. Maria was right. His shoes were odd. They didn't match the rest of his dishevelled outfit. He wore black leather cowboy boots and they looked brand, spanking new.

Josiah sauntered nonchalantly across the road, coming to stand in front of the bedraggled man. He thrust his cap out towards Josiah, making a series of incoherent grunts. Josiah pulled out some loose change and turned towards the beggar. He noticed an unusual mark on the inside of the man's wrist. It was a spiral tattoo. In the centre of the spiral was what looked like an eye. Josiah blinked and then frowned. He could have sworn that the eye moved. He opened his hand to let the coins fall into the cap and then quickly grabbed the man's wrist with his other hand so that he could examine the tattoo more closely. There was a sudden flurry of movement. The man was on his feet, the barrel of a Kahr PM9 shoved into the side of Josiah's ribs. The Kahr was a small pistol, easily concealed due to its size.

Whizz, thwack! The man crumpled. Maria's bullet pierced the beggar's blazer in the centre of his chest, and Josiah turned to catch him as he fell. He carefully placed the limp figure up against the diner's window in a seated position; cap pulled down over his face as if he were sleeping. He pulled out his phone, snapped a photo of the tattoo on the dead man's wrist and then did a quick search of his blazer. All he found was a plastic key-card with another strange symbol on one side and a magnetic strip on the other.

Josiah crossed back over the road, stepped into the hotel and radioed Finn. "We found a suspect, and we were forced to take him down."

"What the fuck!? I told you guys to keep a low profile!" Josiah felt the phone grow hot. He instinctively pulled it away from his ear.

"Chill. There were no witnesses. We'll come back tonight to dispose of the body. We've picked up some very interesting evidence. See you back at the hotel."

Finn Googled the photo of the tattoo, searching for its etymology, while Josiah studied the other image on the plastic key card. "It says here that the spiral represents an energy force while the eye could be a number of things, the creator, the sun, all-seeing eye, etcetera, etcetera." Finn continued scanning the web. "Ahh... What have we here? The spiral and eye pictured together represent a brotherhood belonging to an ancient civilisation that existed thousands of years ago. It says here that the Brotherhood itself is a myth and that the lost civilisation is just a theory that has never been proven to have ever existed."

"Very interesting," said Maria "but what has this to do with Billy, I wonder?"

"It goes on to say that this civilisation lived on a continent called Mu that disappeared beneath the Pacific Ocean over 12,000 years ago."

Josiah handed Finn the key-card. "Here, check this out."

Finn scanned the image on the key-card with his phone, blue-toothed it to his laptop and then loaded it into Google. The image was simply a circle with a dot inside it, a square around the circle and then another circle around the square. The results that came back from Google weren't very conclusive. Finn decided to try something else. He typed, *Mu ancient symbols meaning*. He clicked on 'images' and then scanned through the results. There were dozens of different petroglyphs and rock engravings, depicting a variety of symbols and illustrations. He flipped back to the web results. "Here, listen to this. Over 2,000 Mexican stone tablets were found by an archaeologist in the 1920's that mysteriously went missing en route to the U.S. The tablets depicted over 2,000 symbols that allegedly told the story of the lost civilisation on the continent of Lemuria or Mu, their belief system and many more unsolved secrets. All that's left of these tablets are a few hand-drawn facsimiles." Finn delved deeper and found a document that dissected each symbol and offered an explanation for its significance. He looked for circles in squares and found a plausible explanation. "The inner circle represents the Creator - a never-ending circle of energy, while the dot inside it is Lemuria. The square outside of the first circle is the physical world and the circle outside of that one, represents the spiritual. OK. It seems that we are dealing with some kind of cult here. A very old," Finn raised his arms and quoted the air with his fingers. "And potentially dangerous brotherhood of fanatics intent on possibly starting a revolution. Why they chose to abduct Billy and what they have done with him is a mystery we are going to get to the bottom of people!" The others nodded in agreement. "I want the two of you back at that diner, searching for the electronic door that this key opens." He flashed the key-card in the air. "And don't forget to dispose of that body!"

Josiah pushed the weighted body bag over the side of the boat and into the ocean. It sank rapidly, protesting with a series of gurgling bubbles on its way down to the ocean floor. He looked up at the moonbeams as they danced across the ocean like millions of tiny fairies at play. The bubbles slowed down and then stopped altogether, the evidence hidden beneath the watery depths.

Maria turned on the PC in the office of the diner. It made a whirring sound and then a beep. The monitor sprang to life with a fizzle.

Ah crap, it's asking for a password.

She turned off the computer, proceeded to open the casing and remove the hard-drive.

Finn is gonna have to crack this back at the hotel.

She continued to rummage around the office, looking for any further evidence that would help them locate Billy. She began searching for the mysterious electronic door that the key-card probably opened but to no avail - the office was clean.

Maria and Josiah sat next to Finn as he scanned the hard-drive. "Looks like spreadsheets and other info for the diner. No hidden folders or files. What the?" Finn jumped up in his seat as the screen repeatedly flashed and then went dark. The same symbol on the card flashed once on the screen and then it went black again. "Shit. It's dead." He checked the power, trying to turn his laptop on and off. "My machine is fried! Whatever was on that hard drive has infected my laptop and somehow killed it. Damnation!"

Josiah stood up and folded his arms. "Well, at least we now know that there's definitely a connection between the bum on the street and the diner."

"Yeah, I bet that whoever owns that diner, has taken Billy. Bunch of fanatical bastards!" Maria punched her fist into her palm with a smack. She stood up and paced around the room, running the evidence and the series of events through her mind, trying to come up with a plan, a strategy.

"OK. Let's stop and think about this." Finn lifted his hands. "Let's review what we know. Billy has been kidnapped, more than likely by a group of delusional cultists that believe in a lost continent. They obviously want something from him, so let's try and find out what that something is, don't you think? Then we can plan our next move."

"Perhaps they're after money and power," said Josiah. "After all, that beggar did carry a gun, and he was quick to use it, probably to protect his identity."

"I think you're right there, Jo," said Maria approvingly. "The bum in the street was protecting something all right, otherwise, why would he have been stationed where he was, heavily disguised and concealing a weapon?"

"OK. So it's settled then. It's back to the diner for the two of you. There has to be more evidence. Check the perimeter of the structure and find me that fucking door!"

CHAPTER SIXTEEN

Telepathy

Billy had a restless night's sleep, plagued by troubling dreams that woke him with a start every couple of hours. The next morning, try as he might, he could barely remember them. He gazed at his reflection in the mirror. His eyes lost their focus, as the memory of experiencing vertigo from standing on top of a hill overlooking a cold, barren land, came back to haunt him. He closed his eyes and shook his head to dissipate the dream-tendrils.

After a filling breakfast, the young guard stationed outside his chambers led Billy to a room filled with huge stone carvings of figurines and strange-looking animals. A series of stone tablets hung on the wall followed by dozens of bookshelves filled with tomes of books. Kaimi was sitting at a round table in the middle of the room and beckoned for Billy to take a seat across from him. "Good morning Billy, did you sleep well?" Kaimi smiled warmly.

"Actually no," replied Billy. "Bad dreams."

"Oh no, that's too bad. Here, drink this." Kaimi pushed a glass filled with a green liquid towards him. "It'll make you feel better."

Billy picked up the glass and smelled it's contents. "What is it?"

"It's a naturally blended herbal tonic designed to refresh your mind and give you a bit of a boost. It contains Ginkgo Biloba."

Billy sipped it gingerly. "Hmmm. Tastes kinda like apple juice."

"Now, I am going to show you something. Don't be alarmed. Just try and relax. Close your eyes and start focusing on your breathing. Now slow it down. Gradually. That's it. Concentrate only on your breathing. Empty your mind. Release all your anxiety, your stress and your worries. Allow someone you love to come into your mind and open your heart."

Billy concentrated hard and then tried to relax as much as he could, focusing on taking deep breaths of air. A girl was dancing, spinning and then leaping into the air. She turned and twisted her graceful body, her green dress flowing around her. It was Kisha and she was smiling. Billy smiled back and felt a warmth move down his spine. Then what came next started as a tingling, a pins-and-needles sensation in the back of his head, that turned into a pressured pulsing, a gently throbbing heartbeat.

Billy, it's me, Kaimi.

Billy felt Kaimi's voice inside his head. Billy tried to communicate, but he felt like a deaf mute that couldn't even hear himself shout.

You're trying too hard. Take a deep breath and relax.

Billy remembered Kisha. He watched her glide through the air, smiling down at him as she danced. He took a deep breath and a long, drawn-out sigh.

That's better, now don't try and talk to me, rather just think it. Your thoughts become your words.

How's that possible?

I'm reading your thoughts and allowing you to read mine. I am inside your head, but you are not inside mine. This skill takes time to develop.

Let me guess. You're gonna teach me?

That's correct. This is just the first step in your training.

Billy felt Kaimi leave, so he opened his eyes. He was at a loss for words. He couldn't believe what just happened. Kaimi smiled.

"I told you before that I'm a direct descendant of the Lemurian people. I'm also a Kupua - a Hawaiian Shaman - fluent in the secret traditions of my people. This foundation of knowledge helped me to connect to the mind-reading ability that I now possess, which was fully realised with the assistance of the Supreme Master. I live my life by a set of principles called Huna, inherited from my ancestors. They are as follows: One. The world is what you think. Two. There are no limits. Three. Energy flows where attention goes. Four. Now is the moment of power. Five. To love is to be happy. Six. All power comes from within. And seven. Effectiveness is the measure of truth."

Kaimi's eyes were closed. His had his palms pressed together in prayer position at his sternum as he recited the seven principles of Huna. Billy watched Kaimi with reverence. His level of concentration was so intense that Billy could almost feel the air around him vibrate and hum like a supercharged conductor exhibiting a powerful field of raw, unmitigated energy.

Billy spent the rest of the day with Kaimi, learning to become familiar with his probing, penetrative mind-reading abilities. Kaimi massaged the dormant, inactive regions of Billy's brain responsible for telepathy and extra-sensory ability, bringing them to life for the very first time. He gradually improved in his capabilities, finding it one of the most stimulating things he had ever done in his life.

Still feeling surprisingly energetic and light-headed, Billy retired to his quarters. He couldn't sleep. Instead, he lay in his bed, gazing up at the ceiling, his mind alert to a new, profound sense of awareness. He witnessed a vibrant network of metallic lines, spiralling in and out of each other like shifting grains of sand in a barren desert. He was going through a metamorphosis, a caterpillar transforming into a butterfly, awakening, tearing through its chrysalis, reborn into a world of beauty and wonder.

CHAPTER SEVENTEEN

Denny's

Josiah and Maria strolled casually into the diner and sat down at a table closest to the office. A waitress soon arrived, an island native.

"Good morning and welcome to Denny's Diner. Can I get you two some coffee?"

Maria thought she was in London when she heard the waitress's accent. The primary language on Barbados is Bayan, but this is only spoken socially. English, the second language is far more prolific, due to the centuries-old British occupation on the island.

Maria looked at the waitress's name badge and responded with a smile. "Morning Jackie. Yes, please. Two coffees. One black and the other, cappuccino."

"Anything else?"

"Nope. That's it, thank you."

Jackie smiled, turned and headed off to the kitchen to place the order. Josiah singled out the manager, a scrawny, ginger-haired, geeky-looking character with freckles all over his face He wore a green, short-sleeved Polo shirt and matching baseball cap, embroidered with the diner's logo in the centre.

"Archie doesn't look like our man." Josiah tilted his head in the manager's direction. "My guess is that the connection is through one of his staff which is going to make it a tough investigation. I mean maybe he, or she, isn't even here right now. Let's do a quick scan of the diner to see if there's any unusual activity taking place or if there are any suspicious-looking staff."

"Hang on. I've an idea. Let's approach this differently. How about we pose as representatives of a television documentary channel on food or something?" Maria was getting excited as she spoke. "We can tell Archie, that we need to do a small, five-minute interview with each of his staff, as part of the background to the story. What do you think, man?" Mariah slapped the side of Josiah's thick bicep in encouragement.

"Sounds like it could work," replied Josiah enthusiastically. "We'll need to arrange some basic camera recording equipment."

"Carl Finnigan, you're the man!" Maria gave Finn a big hug. "I don't believe it! How the fuck did you arrange a Sony digital, shoulder-mounted camera, a clipboard and even business cards, in like no time at all!?

Finn's cheeks turned as red as his hair as he shrugged his shoulders. "I guess I'm a resourceful kinda guy."

"This is great, Finn," beamed Josiah.

"OK. You're Mary Gibson, the producer and Jo is Jack Smith, the camera man."

"Cool. I'm ready. Let's do this!" said Josiah in his *I love Barbados* baseball cap turned back-to-front and one of those reporter's sleeveless jackets with about a dozen pockets. Maria wore a black, fitted jacket with a matching knee-high, pencil skirt and a pair of rimless glasses.

"You guys really look the part, if I may say so myself," retorted Finn with a great big grin on his face. "Go 'n get 'em troopers!"

Hugging the Perspex clipboard to her chest, Maria walked back into the diner with Josiah in tow. She approached the ginger-haired manager, pulled out her business card and introduced herself with a sexy smile. "Good morning. Mary

Gibson, from the Food Network."

The manager took the card. "Um. Hi, Saul Pilltree. How can I help?"

"This is Jack Smith, my cameraman."

Josiah smiled and extended his hand. "Hi bro, how do you do?"

"We're in the middle of a documentary entitled, Foods of the World and would really like to interview you and your staff. Your diner will get valuable publicity on satellite television. We won't take long and can position ourselves in the corner over there." Maria pointed to the far end of the diner, an unoccupied space closest to the toilets. "We'll need say five minutes or so per staff member if it's not too much of an inconvenience?"

Saul looked around the shop. He counted seven patrons. "OK. You can interview them one at a time, but no longer than five minutes, please. I have two waitresses and one waiter on duty with another one coming in at eleven."

"Great. Thank you. Do you mind if we start with you?"

"Uh, OK. I guess…"

Hoisting the camera onto his shoulder, Josiah began recording. Maria held up the microphone and looked into the camera as she spoke. "Here we are at the very popular Denny's Diner in Bridgetown on the island of Barbados. Saul Pilltree. the manager is here to tell us a little about the Diner's history and its interesting menu." She turned towards Saul, pointing the microphone towards him. "Saul. Tell us a little about this fascinating Diner, its history and the kind of food that you serve here."

Saul looked into the camera and smiled nervously. "Sure, Mary. Um, Denny's diner was opened in 1992 by Denny Harrington and changed ownership in 2003. We serve a variety of dishes from our very popular Denny's 100% beef burger to our signature steak and eggs, flapjacks, and handmade milkshakes."

"Thank you Saul, just one last question. What's your most popular dish?"

"Definitely Denny's Ultimate Fried Breakfast, that comes with two slices of bacon, two beef sausages, two poached or fried, extra-large eggs, chips, hash browns, beans, tomatoes, mushrooms and toast. It's a favourite amongst our locals."

Josiah and Maria continued to interview the rest of the staff, asking them simple questions about the diner and the food they serve their patrons, all the while looking for clues that would expose them as more than just simple waiters or waitresses. The first to be interviewed was Jackie, the waitress that served them earlier. She was outgoing and engaging. Maria didn't really find anything suspicious or untoward about her, or any of the others questioned.

It was 10.55 when another waitress walked in. At first glance, she looked like any of the other staff in her green, branded apparel. She was also definitely a local, with olive-coloured skin and dark, brown eyes. Maria watched as Saul approached her and pointed in their direction, obviously explaining the reason for their presence. She looked up at Maria, their eyes met and instantly she knew that this was their mark. Even from across the room, Maria immediately sensed a cautious and far more wary disposition from this waitress than any of the others. It was more than just a naturally guarded reaction to being interviewed.

This waitress is definitely hiding something.

"Hi. I'm Dorothy." The waitress held out her right hand to shake Maria's, accompanied by a friendly smile from ear to ear.

Maria returned the handshake and for split second, she froze. There was a tattoo on the inside of her wrist. "Hi Dorothy, I'm Mary and this is Jack. We're filming a documentary entitled Foods of the World and we'd like to ask you a few questions, if you don't mind?"

Dorothy smiled. "Sure, no problem, I'll do my best to assist."

Maria looked down again to have a closer look at the tattoo but Dorothy had placed her right hand, palm down on her belly. She held onto her right wrist, hiding it from sight.

"OK Dorothy, so how long have you been working at

102

Denny's?"

"Um… about thix months or so." Her accent was definitely local and she had a slight lisp as she spoke.

"And what's your favourite dish on the menu?"

Dorothy turned her head to gaze across the diner. "I'd thay the hot meatloaf sandwich with tomato and mozzarella. It's really tasty and our customers like it too."

It was then that a blue, crystal pendent around Dorothy's neck caught Maria's eye. Ordinarily she wouldn't have looked twice but the crystal was unusually shaped and really quite beautiful. She reached out towards it. "Wow that's an exquisite looking crystal necklace. Where'd you get it?"

Dorothy instinctively brought her hand up to protect the crystal and then took a step backwards. She stuttered in reply. "I, I got it at, at… the market in town." She lowered her hand, rolling it open to reveal the tattoo on her wrist for a split second once more. It was definitely the same design as the one on the beggar's arm in the street. She was undeniably another member of the cult. Maria turned to look at the camera and signalled for Josiah to stop filming. She turned back to Dorothy with a smile.

"Thank you Dorothy for your contribution to our documentary."

"It's my pleasure ma'am," she responded abruptly, turned and went quickly back to work.

Maria turned to Josiah and checked over his shoulder to see that they were out of earshot. "She's the next link in our investigation. We're gonna have to keep an eye on her, follow her home and trace her every move."

Josiah responded in a whisper. "Yeah, she has to lead us to Billy, or at least a clue as to where he's been taken. Wait here and keep an eye on her, I gotta go take a slash."

After relieving himself in the urinal, Josiah buttoned up his jeans and washed his hands. The drier had what looked like a credit card swiping mechanism attached to its side. Josiah stared at it as he was drying his hands, frowned and then pulled out the key-card. He checked that he was holding it correctly with the digital strip on the right-hand, side before swiping it through the slot. Nothing happened. Josiah was about to walk away when he thought of swiping again for good measure. This time, there was a loud click and the whole machine shifted forward with a shudder. Josiah waited.

That's weird.

He put his hand on the drier and gave it a pull. The entire front panel opened to reveal a digital touch-screen behind it. A series of indecipherable symbols flashed on the screen. Josiah pulled out his phone and snapped a photo, before closing the drier with a click. He walked back into the diner.

"Maria, you won't believe it, I found the door that the key-card opens. It's actually the drier in the men's toilet."

"Huh? What do you mean the drier?"

"There's a card panel attached to the hand-drier that opens up the front to reveal a digital touch-screen behind it. Look here." Josiah showed Maria the picture he took.

"Holy crap Jo, we're gonna have to get Finn to take a look at this. Don't touch that panel until we know what those symbols mean."

"Of course, that's why I took the photo. I'm sending it to Finn now, asking him to work out what it says."

Josiah tapped out a series of commands on his smartphone while Maria kept an eye on Dorothy, who remained oblivious to their true identities, as she went about her work in the diner.

CHAPTER EIGHTEEN

Clues

Kisha was getting agitated. Finn wasn't answering his phone, and he promised he'd keep her in the loop. Clearly, the news wasn't good, but surely it couldn't be bad either?

No news is good news.

She was trying to stay positive. She tried him again. This time, the phone went straight to voicemail.

"Hi, I'm clearly very busy. Leave a message or send me an SMS." Beep.

She killed the call. Damn! She switched on her tablet and started looking for flights to Barbados from Havana. She couldn't find any direct flights. The quickest routeing was via Jamaica. She booked the first available flight and started packing her bags.

The José Martí International Airport in Havana was about ten miles from the hotel. The cab pulled up outside terminal five, the official terminal for Aero Caribbean Airways, providing domestic and international flights around the Caribbean. Kisha paid the cab driver twenty Cuban Pesos for the one-way trip, before climbing on board the flight to Barbados via Jamaica. She settled down to read her latest novel, a twisted love story about a twenty-something lawyer and her client, a corrupt, Scandinavian business person involved in a sustainable energy project, that was causing more harm than good to the environment.

Kisha pushed her key-card into room 211 of the Sauvignon Hotel in Bridgetown and collapsed on the queen-size bed. She tried calling Finn again, but she just got directed to his voicemail. She sent him a text as well as an email, letting him know that she was in town.

"Hello. Room service?"

"Good evening ma'am. How can we help you?"

"I'd like to order an Italian salad, the line-fish and a double gin and tonic."

"Certainly ma'am. That will take around twenty minutes."

"Thank you." *Click.*

She ran a hot bath, stripped out of her clothes and stepped daintily into the tub. Her dancer's body was near perfect and in absolute proportion, from her soft, round breasts and pink, perky nipples to her flat, chiselled stomach and curvaceous bottom. The muscles in her long, defined legs, rippled ever so slightly as she entered the water. Bubbles caressed her lithe form as she sunk below the surface. She closed her eyes and images of Billy came to mind. She focused on all the good times they had together, hoping and praying that he was still alive. Tears of worry and heartache rolled down her cheeks, but she held her resolve, staying positive, mentally and emotionally. She closed her eyes and allowed the heat to melt it all away. She just finished tying her white cotton bathrobe around her waist, when there was a knock at the door.

"Room service!"

The food was filling, although a little bland, but she didn't complain. She was famished and needed to replenish her energy. She checked her phone to see if Finn had responded. Nothing. She downloaded her email and scanned through her in-box. Her heart skipped a beat. There was a mail from Finn.

Hello, Miss Kisha. Apologies for the delay in response but all of my electronics are on the fritz. I am sitting at an Internet cafe in Bridgetown writing this mail to you. Meet me at the Bridgetown Inn, room 402 at 4 pm.

She checked the time. That was in twenty minutes. She finished off the rest of her meal, threw on some jeans and a vest and called for a cab.

There was a loud knock at the door.

"Must be Miss Kisha," said Finn. "Please open for her."

Maria had a quick peek through the peephole before opening the door. "Kisha!" Maria kissed her three times on her cheeks.

"Maria! How are you? It's been too long."

"I'm great, how are you?"

"Guess I'm OK. Just so worried about Billy, you know." Kisha's face sank.

"Yeah, I know, but we've been making headway here - Finn, Jo and myself."

"Hello Miss Kisha," replied Finn. "You look well, considering."

He walked up to Kisha and gave her a reassuring hug.

"Yeah, I've been worried sick actually. That's why I came. What's wrong with your phone, Finn? I've been trying to reach you for days."

Finn's body language betrayed his mood. "It's a long story but a computer virus fried my laptop, which created some kind of chain reaction that also short-circuited my phone that was plugged into it. I'm collecting new equipment first thing in the morning. I've just come back from the internet cafe where I was researching the meaning of a bunch of symbols to crack the code to a digital combination lock that we discovered this morning."

"Oh. OK. And what are the results?"

"Well, the symbols relate to a bunch of petroglyphs that were found in the 1920's. We found a total of twelve symbols, and I managed to decipher eight of them. I'm sure I can decipher the rest based on the ones that I found. It's kinda like a language with symbols. You have to break down the symbols into simpler images to decode their meaning." Finn walked over to his desk where he had placed a printed page from the Internet cafe containing a variety of spirals, circles and squiggly lines. "So, this circle in the diagram represents the infinite life-giving energy of the Creator. These spirals represent the primary forces at work that keep the creative process flowing on the planet, and these squiggly lines are the pathways of the primary forces emanating from the Creator. Now, if I can just get the sequence right, I'll be able to crack the code." Finn scratched his head, deep in thought.

Kisha turned to Josiah and pointed. "Jo, what's that you're holding?"

"What? This? It's a key-card. I found it on a suspicious cult member."

Kisha took the card from Josiah and examined it carefully. "Hmm, looks like you guys missed something here."

All three of them uttered, *what?* At almost the same time. The word echoed around the room in layers like they were standing in a cave.

"Well, if you turn the card horizontally and look at the edge, there are a series of stripes running across it in a pattern. It's really tiny 'cos the card is so thin, but you can make them out if you look carefully enough."

Finn pulled out his spectacles. "Here, let me see."

Kisha handed over the card to Finn who squinted his eyes into slits to see along the card's edge.

"You're right," he replied. "It's like some kinda barcode." He closed his eyes, deep in thought. "That's it! We have four lines close to one another, then a small gap followed by two lines, then three, then another three. That's a ratio of 4-2-3-3, the sum of which is twelve."

"Looks like the number twelve matches the number of images that I counted on the screen behind the hand-drier," said Josiah. "What else can we corroborate?"

"I think I've got it!" responded Kisha excitedly. "How about we tap the fourth image across on the panel, then the second one after that, then the third after that and finally the third?"

"Yeah, that could work," said Finn. "Let's give it a try. But we need at least two more options in case it doesn't."

"Cool, we'll think of the best possible solutions. One of them has to work!" Maria threw her arms into the air as she said this, feeling as frustrated as everyone else in the room.

"OK people," said Finn. "This is how it's gonna go. Miss K will head down to the diner later this evening to see if she can crack the box with all the options that we're gonna give her."

Kisha looked at Finn like a wide-eyed goldfish.

"No one will recognise you," said Finn. "Just step into the men's, swipe this key card through the slot on the side of the hand-drier and the box will pop open to reveal a digital panel. This is your queue to call me on the receiver. I will guide you through the sequence, and we should have the panel cracked in no time at all."

Kisha took a deep breath as she approached the diner. She had a quick look around, scanning the perimeter for anything unusual before stepping casually inside. She sat down at the nearest table. Within a few moments, a smiling waiter approached her. "Good evening and welcome to Denny's. Can I get you something to drink?"

Kisha looked up and smiled back. "Hi. Can I get a coffee, please? Black." As soon as the waiter turned towards the kitchen, Kisha stood up and made her way over to the toilets. She slipped into the men's, closed the door and moved over to the hand-drier. She pulled out the key card and swiped it through the side slot. The machine lurched forward. She gave it a pull, and it opened to reveal the digital panel. Kisha whispered urgently into her radio.

"Finn? I'm ready."

"OK, let's try that first sequence." Finn's voice sounded distant.

Kisha carefully punched out the sequence on the screen. There was a dull beep.

"Nope, not working."

"OK let's try in the opposite direction this time."

Kisha punched in the sequence in reverse. Another dull beep.

"Still nothing."

Kisha studied the key-card once more, scrutinising the uneven, barcoded lines on its edge. Holding the card between her thumb and forefinger, on the opposite side to the stripes, she swiped the card from left to right across the screen and over the twelve digital symbols on display. A green light flicked on from inside the device, illuminating the display. She stepped back and the light went out. She waited a moment, but nothing happened. She lifted her radio to her ear. There was a whirring sound that grew louder and then disappeared just as quickly. She turned her head, straining to listen to the peculiar sound. The ground beneath her feet began vibrating softly, followed by a slight shudder. She watched as the walls dropped rapidly away. Her stomach wrenched up into her chest, making her gag uncomfortably. She looked up at the ceiling of the toilets above that had already become a small square of light, as the elevator floor dropped rapidly beneath the diner and into the Earth hundreds of feet below.

CHAPTER NINETEEN

Domination

Kaimi was inside Billy's head again. He couldn't hear him, which was odd because he was talking. There was no sound, no voice or whisper but rather a feeling, a sense of acknowledgement. He knew that it was Kaimi because he had an intuitive sense of recognition that was hard to explain. Like seeing a colour and instantly knowing that colour by its name, or smelling something and identifying the smell with an object like a flower, some perfume or food. A steady flow of information seeped into his head like a sponge drawing water, filling itself up with every moment that passed.

Relax Billy. Breathe. The effective transfer of communication is more conducive to a relaxed and focused state, free from anxiety and tension.

Billy was anxious and also a little afraid. He still felt like a prisoner with an uncertain fate, kidnapped and brought, against his will, to a clandestine, underground fortress. And being exposed to supernatural powers of the mind, with the guidance of an extraordinary Kupua, was something that he would never have believed possible, until now. The surreal scenes played out before him like a predetermined script from a science fiction movie.

It'll take a few months of hard work and dedication to master this skill. But, with my assistance, you will develop your talent in no time at all. Everyone has this talent lying dormant inside of them. It's just like

111

receiving the instruction manual and then being taught how to use it, learning how to nurture the seed, making it grow into a powerful field of constant energy. Once you have access to this energy, you will become fierce and formidable.

Kaimi led Billy into a room filled with rubber balls.

Watch and learn.

Kaimi placed his hands on his hips, widened his stance and turned his feet out slightly. He bent his knees and sat down in a low squat, closed his eyes and became as still as a statue. Billy watched the gradual rise and fall of Kaimi's chest - the only evidence that he was still alive. What happened next caused the hairs on the back of Billy's neck to rise. His eyes widened, as the multi-coloured balls began to move.

This has to be some kind of trick, an illusion.

Deep down, he knew that it wasn't. This was the real deal. More balls started moving, rolling around in a clockwise direction, gaining momentum, spinning faster and faster, crashing into each other and some even started bouncing off the walls. The balls continued to swirl round and round and then magically began to rise off the floor, one at a time at first, then dozens more, the faster they turned. It was like watching a mini tornado, twisting and turning; a rainbow blur of colour that began to whip up a wind of its own, spinning and gyrating impossibly through the air. Kaimi just sat there in his low stance, his eyes still closed and his face turned up towards the balls as they spun like he was basking in their glow. He threw his arms up forcibly into the air. The balls immediately stopped and then hovered in mid-air, frozen in time. Billy's jaw dropped. He was gob-smacked. Kaimi brought his arms down, shooting them rapidly away from his sides, fingers outstretched, pointing towards the floor. The balls came crashing down together, bounced hard and then flew back up into the air, shooting off in a multitude of directions, a maelstrom of disconnected circles of colour, hitting the walls, the roof and then back down to the floor again. The tumult continued a while longer, slowing down as the balls lost momentum until at last, they came to rest all over the room, a few still rolling around from the animated eruption.

Kaimi slowly straightened his legs, bringing his palms together in a silent prayer for a few moments before turning around to walk gradually over to where Billy was standing. He smiled as he looked at Billy, who was still standing with his mouth agape in astonishment.

"Let me take you through today's first lesson," said Kaimi, his hands on Billy's shoulders, shaking him gently so that he rocked back on his heels. "You can do this. Anybody can." Kaimi turned and waved his arm back and over the colourful field of rubber behind him as he spoke. "All it takes is for me to show you how."

"But I don't understand. Surely this kind of ability is genetically acquired at birth? How are you just taught them?"

Kaimi twisted his mouth into an infuriatingly, knowledgeable smirk as if he was waiting his whole life to answer Billy's feeble question. Billy felt uncomfortable and out of place. He looked away and found himself staring at the hundreds of rubbery balls in the room.

"Billy Bayer. You don't quite know who we are, do you?" Kaimi's rhetorical question came at him like a dart. "We have access to knowledge and power way beyond your scope of awareness, so I forgive you for your naivety. I do, however, have some valuable advice for you, Billy. Be patient because patience is the master of perseverance and perseverance is the path to knowledge and wisdom. Follow this advice and you will learn these abilities as I teach them to you. Question not the source of this knowledge only know that it is ancient knowledge passed down over many centuries, from generation to generation. You have witnessed the result of this power that we have subjugated and continue to exploit. This is who we are and who you will become. This is why you are here. You are being initiated into the tribe of Lemuria and will become one with her people and her ways. Rejoice in this reward that we bestow upon you now. There are not many who have the opportunity to be trained in the art of light weaving."

Kaimi threw his head back, shaking out his braids. His eyes lit up as he looked at Billy. "The rubber balls before you represent life on this planet, a vast array of colourful elements forever moving, changing and reinventing themselves. The spinning force of the balls together creates a ripple effect that permeates the very nature that surrounds us, whipping up a rotating bundle of energy that grows and expands the same way that H_2O moves through its various states. This energy spreads, bringing life to the inanimate and vitality to the crestfallen." Kaimi moved his hands about as he illustrated his point, adding gusto and enthusiasm to his explanation.

"This is known to the modern world as telekinesis, a metaphysical power of the mind used to move physical objects from a distance. In the land of Lemuria, this mental super-power was part of everyday existence. In the physical sense, it was like being able to perform the ability to run, following the capacity to walk. The Lemurians of old lived on a higher plane of existence. They naturally tapped into this and a host of other psychic abilities, bending the rules of science and nature as we know it, manipulating time and space and advancing exponentially forward. They were an advanced race on every level and we are grateful to be here today to benefit from these super-humans who once ruled the Earth." Kaimi finished his soliloquy, dramatically emphasising his point towards the end, throwing his hands up into the sky and his head back once more, his braids slicing the air with a light *swoosh* for added effect.

Kaimi moved his hands onto Billy's head, closed his eyes and constricted his face in a ball of concentration. Billy was up close. He could see a solitary sweat droplet form on the bridge of his nose. He watched it trickle down and then abruptly stop. In fact, everything stopped. It was if time stood still, yet he could move, albeit in slow motion. He blinked slowly, so slowly that he was not sure if he opened his eyes again after closing them. This was partly because what he saw next, was a very different scene from just a moment ago. Kaimi was no longer in front of him. Instead, all he saw was just a soft yellow glow of light around him. He turned his head from left to right, and a faint mist was disturbed in the process. He watched as the misty particles shifted and glided past, brushing his face with their dampness, like some invisible ghost, searching forlornly for its final resting place. There was a muteness about this place that was uncanny, yet familiar. Billy looked down. The mist was so thick that he couldn't see past his waistline.

Billy, you are inside your own mind. You must learn to let go, to release your grip on the physical world. Close your eyes again and imagine that you are a bird, soaring high above your clouds of uncertainty, far from the shackles of your doubt and unease. Cast yourself free Billy and experience what it is to be truly alive.

He closed his eyes and imagined he was an eagle, soaring high above a sparkling ocean, reflecting the sun that was also shining on his back. He looked down and marvelled at the magnificence of flight as he glided effortlessly through the sky, flexing his wings and twisting in-between the currents that buffeted his aerodynamic frame. He heard a flapping sound like a flag in the wind and turned his head to find another bird right next to him. It was big, black and majestic; its beady eyes fixed on his. As he looked into the other bird's eyes, he recognised something familiar.

Kaimi's voice pushed through the vision and into his mind. *Yes, Billy, you're doing it. You're expanding your consciousness. Only you alone can do this Billy. C'mon, keep on going!*

Billy climbed higher, beating his wings as hard as he could. He pushed against the icy cold air repeating the motion, again and again, straining upwards and forwards to grab hold of more air, pulling and tugging at it and then thrusting it behind him as he flew. The anxious feeling in his gut turned into confidence, as he soared higher and embraced the freedom of flight like he was borne unto it. Billy's head was buzzing as he opened his eyes to hundreds of tiny stars twinkling in his periphery vision.

"Billy, you OK?" Kaimi was sitting next to him; concern

etched onto his face.

"Yes. I'm fine. A little lightheaded, but fine, thanks."

"Great! Please fetch one of the balls. Any ball. Place it on the table over here." Kaimi gently touched the table with his right hand.

Billy picked up a soft, blue ball from the collection on the floor and placed it on the table in front of Kaimi. "OK, now I want you to stare at the ball for as long as you can without blinking. When you feel that you're gonna blink, close your eyes." Sitting down, Billy sat down and placed his palms in his lap and turned to look at the ball in front of him. "Try and empty your mind of all thoughts and focus only on the ball. Imagine that you have microscopic vision, and you're able to see inside the ball, into the molecules that make up the very fabric of the ball itself." Kaimi dropped his voice to a whisper, as Billy stared at the round, blue shape in front of him. After a while, his eyes began to burn. The ball filled his vision as he focused all his attention on it, clearing his mind of every other thought. His eyes began to fill with tears as he strained to keep them open.

How long had it been?

The agony was unbearable. He needed to close his eyes. Any longer and the tears would cloud his vision and then he would be forced to shut them in any event. As soon as he closed his eyes, Kaimi was there, inside his head.

The ball is still there Billy. Can you see it?

Billy nodded his head ever so slightly in affirmation. The circular outline of the ball seared into his vision.

OK good. Now, listen carefully. The ball is a collection of molecules all bound together and vibrating at a very high frequency to form the shape that you see in front of you. Even though the ball appears to be a solid, physical object, it is really, like all things in physicality, moving energy. Now with this in mind, what you have to do is identify the energy signature of the ball and then interact with it. I know that this might sound foreign to you right now, but you must do as I say. Keep concentrating on the ball but this time, focus on the vibrating particles of energy that make up the

116

ball. Connect with these particles of moving energy and then cause them to move even faster.

With his eyes closed, Billy could still 'see' the round object that he had been staring at for so long. It shimmered as if it were alive. With his attention focused on it even more directly, a tingling vibration tickled his eyelids. He saw stars again at the edge of his vision, causing his eyeballs to shift and move around incessantly until his eyeball became the ball. He watched it roll around in his eye socket, jerking this way and that until he subdued the twitching. As soon as he gained control of his roaming eyeball, he knew that he could manipulate the energy of the blue ball on the table. It was like cracking a Sudoku puzzle – one line of numbers unlocked the formula of another. He pushed into the vibrating vision of the ball with his mind's eye, connecting to the now familiar energy that made up each and every rubber molecule. He raised the ball's vibrational energy simply by connecting to it and then making it so. He soon realised that it was all about focus followed by control, so he shifted into this unfamiliar environment to prove to himself that it could be done. At the same time, he was excited about his acquisition of power and the exciting consequences that followed. Kaimi was right – he was truly blessed to be chosen to receive this training and these extraordinary powers.

OK, good, good, Billy. I see that you have made the connection. Well done. Now make the ball move.

He couldn't make out facial features when Kaimi communicated to him this way, but he could feel the insistence in Kaimi's voice as it bounced around inside his cranium. Billy willed the ball to move, but nothing happened. He pictured the ball as his eyeball and then shifted his focus there. His eyeball shifted to the right and so did the ball (he thought). He opened his eyes and saw the ball rolling slowly across the table. A wave of elation washed over him that sent a ripple of goose bumps up his arms and down the nape of his neck. He did it. He moved the ball with his mind. Billy looked up at Kaimi and grinned from ear to ear.

Kaimi smiled. "Well done Billy. Now all it takes is lots of practice and then soon you'll be spinning balls like I did."

CHAPTER TWENTY

Trapped

The room was dark. So dark that she couldn't see her hand in front of her face. She looked up, but the speck of light inside the diner toilets had vanished. Her ears pricked, as a high-pitched whining sound pierced the silence. It grew in intensity until it became unbearable. She slammed her hands over her ears and scrunched up her eyes in agony. The sound grew so loud that there was nothing else inside her head but the searing pain that threatened to disconnect her from consciousness. She crumpled to the floor as her body's defence mechanism triggered a total shutdown. The sound ended abruptly. Several pairs of hands lifted her from the ground and carried her away.

Kisha opened her eyes to a dull, throbbing headache. Everything was blurred. She rubbed her eyes vigorously and then slowly opened them again. The scene before her cleared. She was lying in a comfortable bed in a small, windowless room with grey walls. There was a single chair in the corner and a small toilet and basin on the far side of the room. An abstract painting hung next to the bed that reminded her of the setting sun against a backdrop of pink, fluffy clouds on the Hudson River. She dragged herself over to the basin, retched and then collapsed back onto the bed.

What the fuck is going on? Where the hell am I?

These questions and more plagued her mind as she

contemplated her fate. The door opened, and a young guard dressed in military attire walked in with a tray of food and drink. He placed the tray on a low table in front of the chair and hastily stepped out the room.

"Wait!" Kisha shouted as she bounded out of bed, running over to the door after the young officer. She grabbed the handle and pulled it down. It was locked. Kisha banged her fists on the door in frustration. "Open this door you fucking pricks! Let me out! What the hell do you want from me?!" Her voice echoed around the room, falling on deaf ears. She stood there for a moment longer, staring at the door in consternation, willing it to open but to no avail. "Billeeeee!" She knew he was here. Maybe, just maybe he would hear her and come rushing to save her. Her mind swirled. He was probably locked up just as she was, while their captors took control of his empire.

Come on Kisha. Stay positive. Think. You're still alive. There's a good chance you'll make it outta here.

"Kisha? Kisha?!" Finn shouted into the receiver in frustration. His cries were received with a loud hiss. She was gone. "What the fuck is going on? How could she have just disappeared?"

"Maybe there's some kind of frequency jam?" Josiah shrugged his shoulders and lifted his hands.

"Could be something serious," said Maria. "Let's go check it out. C'mon Jo."

Josiah and Maria stepped inside the busy diner. Maria looked around for Dorothy, the suspicious waitress that they interviewed earlier, but there was no sign of her. Josiah walked over to the men's toilet with Maria in tow. The door was locked. Josiah planted his feet firmly on the ground, dug his shoulder into the door and pushed. His leg muscles rippled into action. He took in a deep breath, grunted it out and heaved. The door gave way, and he stumbled inside. He walked up to the hand-drier and gave it a solid punch on its side. The cover dropped forward and down to reveal the digital panel. The strange symbols flashed across the screen as before. Maria looked around the room. There was no sign of Kisha. She was gone, together with the radio and anything else she was carrying. Where the hell did she go?

There was one window above the urinal, but it was far too narrow for anyone to fit through. This was a most peculiar mystery.

"Finn." The radio hissed.

"Where is she?" Finn sounded livid.

Josiah replied. "There's no trace of her. The door was locked from the inside, but there was no one here after we bashed it down. This is starting to get really weird."

"That waitress. What's her name?"

"Dorothy."

"Yes, Dorothy. Where is she?"

"Dunno."

"She is our only link to all of this. Find her and we find Kisha and Billy. Well, what the fuck you waiting for? She's not gonna just appear out of thin air. Start looking!"

CHAPTER TWENTY-ONE

Belias

He was flying again but this time, he was being hunted. He was trying to lose his pursuers as he flew close to the mountain range but he could still hear the rustle of their feathers in the cool night air, each time he banked left or right. Ghostly, white wisps of cloud came into view. He punched through their shapes, breaking them apart like soap bubbles, as he fled from his assailants. A loud screech shattered the otherwise silent night, and a large shape dropped down from above. He twisted left, lifting his right wing to avoid the strike but he was too late. Iron-clad talons slashed across his face and connected with his shoulder, digging through flesh and bone, ripping and tearing as they found their mark. He felt his wing go numb as he dropped into an uncontrollable spiral, falling from the sky, down towards the ground below.

Billy woke with a start. He sat straight up in bed. His pillow was drenched in sweat, and his entire right arm was numb with pain. He climbed out of bed and walked over to the basin to splash some water on his face. He switched on the bathroom light and looked in the mirror. He was shocked to see a long red welt on the side of his cheek. He touched it gingerly. It stung like it was fresh. He splashed more water on his face, dabbed it dry with a towel, turned off the light and went back to bed, flipping over the damp cushion in the process. He slept uninterrupted and dreamless until his body clock woke him again in what felt like morning, beneath sombre, fluorescent light. After a filling breakfast, Billy went to meet Kaimi in the ballroom for his next round of training. He made no mention of the dream, but Kaimi sensed his unease and naturally saw the red scratch across his cheek.

"Rough night?"

"Yeah. Rough."

"It's your heightened awareness. It's opening up your defences, making you vulnerable to attack. Today I will teach you how to prevent this from happening, how to strengthen your resolve. But first, let's practice." Kaimi began teaching Billy how to sense the presence of more than one ball on the table. To speed up the process, he guided Billy through the first few steps by entering his mind and expanding his consciousness. At first, he struggled to connect to the energy signature of both balls at the same time. He stood across a chasm that he didn't know how to cross. A bridge appeared, and he stepped cautiously onto it. He knew that the bridge was a manifestation of Kaimi projecting his will, showing him the way. Billy crossed the divide and found himself on the other side, faced with the next obstacle. He could sense both balls, their round shapes and vibrating energy particles but as soon as he tried to get them to move, they blurred into one fuzzy sphere of energy, and he lost control.

Focus, Billy, focus.

Kaimi was there again, catching Billy as he fell, lifting him up to face the balls again. This time, the fuzzy silhouettes of the balls sharpened and solidified. Billy could sense the micro-particles of the balls shifting and rotating at super-high speeds, colliding into one another, yet maintaining their positions to preserve their overall shapes. Kaimi gently nudged the back of his mind, casting his will, targeting the vibrational energy of each ball, and then pushed. He felt an odd, magnetic pull as he pushed, a strange force repelling off each ball. The balls moved, and he moved with them. He opened his eyes and watched the balls roll off the table and onto the floor below. The expectant thud of the balls on the floor didn't materialise. Billy jumped up and darted around the side of the table. The balls were hovering just off the floor as if they were riding on a cushion of air. They rotated slightly as they hovered, before gradually rising back onto the table. Kaimi stared at the balls, concentrating intently for another moment before looking across at Billy, a broad, toothy grin spread across his face.

"Wow. Impressive." Billy's mouth was agape in awe. "I felt another kind of magnetic energy as I pushed the balls this time. Was that you?" Billy frowned as he posed the question.

Kaimi smiled again. "No. That was you. I've been waiting for this sign to arrive."

"What do you mean?"

"What you felt was the magnetic force we call gravity. Every physical thing on this planet has mass. Whether it's a feather, a rock or even a human being, the greater the mass of each object, the greater its gravitational pull. It stands to reason. When you pushed the balls, they repelled with their equivalent gravitational force. When the force you exert exceeds the mass of the object you are trying to move, there is always an equal and opposite reaction."

Billy scratched his head. "OK. I think I follow you, but what is pushing back? What is that magnetic force I felt?"

Kaimi continued, his hands moving, animating his explanation. "Think of a tree. It's attached to the Earth by its roots. Without these roots, the tree would fall over and die. Every other physical object on this planet is also attached to the Earth, but its roots are invisible. Think of these invisible roots as the connection between the vibrational energy of each object on the planet and the gravity-energy flowing out from deep within the Earth. When we push against an object, the force and effort we use to make it move flows into the object, out via the gravity-energy connection and down, into the Earth. This surge of energy flowing in the opposite direction to the gravity-energy causes the object to dislodge itself from its current position. The current of energy flowing from the person projecting it, is often brief and sudden, and as soon as it wanes, there is a reverse reaction as the energy shoots back up from the Earth to re-establish its invisible connection with the object above it. This magnetic surge is what you felt. Understand?"

Billy nodded his head in confirmation. "Yep. Makes kinda sense. Just a lot to grasp, you know?"

Kaimi responded with a nod. "This is why I wanted you to experience it first-hand. It's far more plausible once you feel this energy field yourself." Billy was in awe of this newfound knowledge. He felt like a kid in physics class. Kaimi continued. "The Earth was created with an invisible web of light lines called the gravitational, magnetic grid. Some call it the crystalline matrix. These lines of light radiate from intersections on the planet's surface, linking with the web network surrounding other planets. Even Plato spoke of this interplanetary grid that maintains the Earth in its gravitational field around the Sun. The ancient Lemurians traversed these lines of energy like big wave surfers, connecting to all life on the planet. They even used the electromagnetic grid to travel to other planets in our solar system and beyond."

Billy sat down, hard. This was all way over his head. "But what are you... the Lemurians, got to do with all this? And what's my role in the scheme of things?"

"Let's discuss this in more detail later. First, I'm going to take you through some defence training. Since I unlocked the telekinetic ability in your brain, you have become vulnerable to attack. Even though some of these attacks may take place in a dream-state, they can cross over into the physical world, inflicting mortal damage to your body while you sleep, hence the fresh mark on the side of your face. As you grow into your natural abilities, so too will the intensity of such attacks which is why we cannot delay in employing this defensive training technique." Billy instinctively reached up to touch the welt on his cheek as Kaimi spoke, his mind drifting to the lucid dream he experienced in the middle of the night. "I'm going to go inside your mind again but this time, I'm going to release a trigger that will activate your body's natural defence system, each time that your life is threatened. Once this trigger has been activated, your defence system will be able to sense the start of an attack automatically before it happens. You will then be able to block the attack instinctively."

Billy grinned. "Ha! Just like Spiderman's spidey sense!"

Kaimi smiled and then moved closer to Billy, placing one hand on his temple above his right cheekbone and the other over his solar plexus. "Now, close your eyes and focus on your breath. In and out, in and out." Billy closed his eyes and took several long, deep breaths. He felt Kaimi tickling his mind for a brief moment and then it was over. "There, it's done. The alarm is set."

He felt a high-pitched ringing in his eardrums; that sent a shock wave through his entire body. He slapped his hands over his ears and squeezed his eyes shut in pain. A moment later the ringing stopped. He opened his eyes and wiped away tears that had run down his cheeks. His back began to warm up rapidly, and there was another, strange tingling inside his head.

Kaimi rose from his seat, bowed his head to his chest and muttered, "your Eminence." Billy slowly turned around and encountered a hooded figure in a red velvet gown that appeared to be floating in mid-air.

"Billy Bayer." The voice that came from beneath the cloak was strong and distinct. Billy recognised the voice. His throat constricted. He was anxious. It was like a bad dream had surfaced from his sub-conscious, come to haunt him in the real world. He remembered the voice taunting him, while he sat on the hard, wooden chair in the cold, wet dungeon. Billy struggled to see the face beneath the hooded cloak. He felt a sense of power and authority surround the shrouded figure.

"I trust that Kaimi has been taking care of your needs?" The question was more of a rhetorical statement. Billy didn't answer. "My name is Belias Stongrathen, leader of the Lemurian people in this Aquarian age." Belias lifted his hands to his hood and threw it back. He had white, wavy, shoulder-length hair that framed a clean-shaven, chiselled face with high cheekbones. His dark eyes were set deep in his skull giving him both a striking and macabre look at the same time. A chill ran up Billy's spine. Belias lifted his right hand, signalling for Billy and Kaimi to take a seat. He glided over to the head of the table.

Billy felt that he should say something. Words involuntarily blurted out of his mouth. "Um, thank you for your hospitality." Belias looked at Billy with a piercing, hypnotic stare, blatantly ignoring his words of gratitude. Billy struggled to look away.

"I believe that you have a few questions?" Again that rhetorical line of inquiry. "I'm sure that Kaimi has explained a few things already. I'm here to fill in the gaps." Belias maintained his glare. Billy blinked. "When Asbeth the omnipotent, our Lemurian forefather, escaped the obliteration of the Motherland, he seeded the rest of the planet with his supernatural powers, spreading his great knowledge and rebuilding his empire. The Lemurian race was succeeded by his offspring who were taught the secrets of Lemuria by Asbeth himself. The Lemurian Kingdom has remained clandestine ever since - controlling the world's superpowers from behind secret, underground locations like this one. The Mayans, the Egyptians, the Incas, the Roman Empire, politicians, the Mob, prostitution, drug cartels - you name it, we've been instrumental in the rise and fall of all of this and more. We control world events, the Pope, your president and many others in power around the world. We are the masters of destiny, the prophets of the New Age and the harbingers of war. Nothing escapes our attention. We are invincible. We are supreme."

Billy's mind was racing. *He's a fucking madman, a crazed, evil tyrant, vying for world domination. If all that he says is true, then it would at least explain why the world is so fucked up. It would explain all the unnecessary death, killing and torture as a result of war and unrest around the world.*

"So are you are saying that for the past 12,000 years, the Lemurians have been responsible for every major world event in

127

history?"

Belias smiled. "Oh for far longer than that my friend. Remember, the Lemurians came from the continent of Mu that was established almost 200,000 years ago. Universally, the word Mu means mother. Mu or Lemuria was the original Eden, the true motherland of man. We believe in a higher power, the Creator, call Him what you will, but we believe He created all life on Earth that began with the greatest creation ever. And yes, my forefathers and those before them have also directed the Earth's more recent events in history, following the great deluge and destruction of Mu around 12,000 years ago, as you have just pointed out. Our civilisation has been instrumental in the rise and fall of all the great civilisations in history."

This all sounded like some half-crazed cult that Billy was not sure he wanted to be a part of. He asked the question that he had asked so many times, the question whose clear and distinct answer he had not yet heard. It was a question that deep down he knew the answer to but had to hear it uttered from someone else's mouth - an answer that he could not and would not face himself. There was a mirror in front of him, but he did not have the nerve to look into it.

"So what is my part in all of this?"

Belias's stare drove through Billy like a stake through his heart. "We have been watching you for some time now, biding our time, waiting for the right moment to take you in and introduce you to the organisation. Viktor was the key, Billy. As soon as you got rid of him, everything fell into place. Viktor was offered so much, yet greed and gluttony got the better of him, and he had to go. It was providence that brought you here."

There's that word again.

"And providence that will lead you to even greater things, Billy. Bigger, and better things. More power and control over your life and those that share in it with you. And with the support of your Lemurian family, you have unlimited potential to grow and mature into the warrior that you are destined to

128

be!"

Belias had his arms raised up above his head as he spoke. His eyes were closed, and his voice resounded around the room like it was plugged into a surround sound music system. Kaimi signalled for Billy to close his eyes. A kaleidoscope of colours swam across his vision like an ocean filled with tropical fish. Geometric shapes played shadow puppetry to his senses, and magnificent flickers of light danced across his eyes like he was being allowed to see for the very first time. He felt elated, elevated and exuberant but there was another sensation that he couldn't help feeling and that was indifference. It felt as if his personal space had been violated like he had no choice in all of this. There was something destructive and soul-destroying about that feeling, and he did not like it one bit.

CHAPTER TWENTY-TWO

Connections

For the first time in days, Billy slept uninterrupted. The only thing that hadn't changed was the nauseating, fluorescent light that popped as he walked into the bathroom after he woke. He looked at himself in the mirror, examining his almost fully-grown beard before hopping into the shower. His eyes closed and his mind wandered, sifting through the chain of events that brought him to this underground prison, deep beneath the Earth's surface. Billy wondered if the defensive mechanism that Kaimi activated deep within his cerebral cortex would prevent those with the ability to read his thoughts. He made a mental note to ask Kaimi at their next session.

Another guard in military attire was waiting for him as he opened the door to exit his chamber. With a nod of acknowledgement, the guard turned around to lead the way. Kaimi creased his brow in concern as he was taken down a different path to the usual one. They turned right off the main corridor and then left again until the guard stopped outside a blue door. The guard pressed the index finger of his right hand onto a high-tech, fingerprint recognition system. There was a soft beep and the door clicked open. The guard signalled for Billy to enter the room and then turned and went back the way he came. Billy gingerly stepped towards the door and pushed it open. He was expecting to see Kaimi or even Belias waiting for him on the other side. Instead, Kisha came running over to meet him. She jumped up and into his arms, wrapping her legs around him in a fierce hug.

"Oh Billy!" she cried in disbelief. "I can't believe it's you!" She proceeded to plant about ten firm kisses all over his face.

"Kisha!" Billy responded, equally surprised. "What are you doing here? How did you…"

"I've been searching for you for days on end, been worried sick. I can't believe I've found you. Thank goodness you're alive! Are you OK? Are you hurt? Here let me look at you." Kisha began to look Billy up and down, while running her hands all over his body, checking for signs of injury.

He grabbed her wrists, pulled her close, and then wrapped his hands around her body for another hug of reassurance. "I'm all right Kisha. Relax; these people are not here to hurt us. How'd you get here?"

The words fell out of Kisha's mouth so quickly; Billy struggled to follow her story.

"I called Finn when I couldn't get hold of you. He tracked your cell phone signal to Barbados and then contacted Jo and Maria. They flew out to find you. When I couldn't get hold of Finn, I jumped on a flight to Barbados to find them. Finn gave me a key card, which I swiped inside this diner on the island and then got swallowed into an underground cavern only to wake up in this room! Where the hell are we?"

Billy looked around the room, anxious about who could be listening. "Well, it seems that you know more than me. I knew we were underground, but not that we were in Barbados. I've a lot more to tell you about why we are here, though, and who these people are."

"You said they're not here to hurt us but then why did they kidnap you?" Kisha was perplexed.

Billy reassured her. "They're part of a secret organisation, so I guess they had to make sure that I was genuine. You know - trustworthy, the real deal, before exposing me to their little setup here."

Kisha responded, nodding her head in agreement. "Makes sense, otherwise, why would they have brought you to see me?"

"Quite right. They call themselves the Lemurians, descendants of some ancient mythical civilisation that sank into the Pacific over 12,000 years ago. Viktor used to work for them. He was obviously sworn to secrecy because I've never heard of them."

"The Lemurians…" Kisha pondered over this. "Isn't that part of Atlantis or something?"

"Well, there is some kind of connection, but the Lemurians were around before Atlantis, or so I've been told. They claim to be responsible for all the major historical events of our time - from the pyramids of Giza to the World Wars of the last century."

Kisha widened her eyes in astonishment. "Jeez, really?"

"Yes. I met their leader, Belias. He's one convincing fella. And then there's Kaimi, my instructor." Billy smiled.

"What do you mean instructor?" replied Kisha in surprise. "What has he been teaching you down here? What have they done to you, Billy?" Kisha peered around either side of Billy's head as if she were expecting to find another set of ears or something equally as bizarre.

"Here let me show you. Come. Lie down on the bed. Trust me." Billy led Kisha over to the double bed in the corner of the room. She sat down on the edge of the bed and took off her shoes before lying down with her head on the pillow. "OK. Now close your eyes and relax. I am going to lie down next to you." Billy took off his shoes and lay down on the right side of the bed and then closed his eyes too. His right hand found her left as he slipped it into hers. "You OK?"

"Yeah, fine" responded Kisha. "What you gonna do?"

"I am going to attempt to communicate with you without speaking."

"What do you mean?"

"Just keep your eyes closed and relax. You'll see."

Billy closed his eyes and visualised Kaimi's voice, guiding him.

He began to slow down his breathing, deepening each in and out breath, extending his lungs to their full capacity. He focused on Kisha lying next to him, pictured her beautiful face and pulled his mouth up into a smile that brought tears to his eyes. He experienced a warm, tingling sensation that began in his chest and then traversed throughout his body. He followed this feeling until it reached his fingertips. He focused on his right hand in hers, and, with a bit of effort, nudged the sensation over and into her arm. He glided on a bright, white surfboard across a swiftly moving current. Her hand tensed in his and then relaxed once more. He eased into the current as it traversed her body, before passing through her chest, the thump-thump of her heart, distorting his vision beneath closed eyelids. The pressure boosted him up and away from her chest until he found himself drifting serenely in a tranquil sea. He floated on his back in the water, with only his face protruding, ears submerged, blocking out all sound. He looked up and pictured the night sky, full of twinkling stars on a crisp, clear evening.

Kisha. Can you hear me?

Billy visualised his words, transmitted them into the cavernous space around him and waited for a response.

Kisha thought she was dreaming. She heard Billy, but it was as if he was inside her mind.

Billy? Am I dreaming? How did you?

This is one of the abilities that I have been taught. Kaimi, my instructor, showed me how to communicate telepathically. I can enter your mind and talk to you without speaking. You're able to communicate back to me because I'm inside your head.

But how is this possible? How did they teach you this ability?

Kaimi has been training me to master this skill. There is more that I need to tell you and believe that this is the only way to do so without anyone else finding out. The walls have ears. I told you that I met the leader of this organisation yesterday. He's a madman. He's created some kind of cult following and expects me to follow his lead. We need to escape from here somehow and contact Finn and his team.

But how? This place is heavily guarded and miles underground.

I don't know yet, but we have to find a way. In the meantime, we need to keep up our facade. We need to cooperate with these people and make them think we're on their side.

Billy opened his eyes and turned to face Kisha. A perceptive smile creased his face as he gazed longingly into her hazelnut eyes. She looked back into his, smiled and nodded ever so slightly in acknowledgement. He squeezed her hand and then twisted slowly over onto his side. His arm wrapped around her slim waist, pulling her close. His groin stirred. He cupped both hands tenderly around her cheeks, framing her beautiful face and closed his eyes. He found her soft, delicate lips. They began to part, responding spontaneously to his touch. Their breathing quickened, igniting the flames of passionate desire. They struggled to hold back their carnal desires - a pair of Indians fighting to tame their wild stallions. Tongues connected - an eruption, building into a cascade of mind-blowing ecstasy. Hands - groping, rubbing, embracing. They fumbled with each other's clothes, tearing them off quickly, while barely maintaining mouth contact, yet still kissing relentlessly. Blood pumped intensely into his crotch, fuelling his libido like a tiger on heat. Two writhing bodies glided into a sensual, rhythmic, thrusting dance - up and down, in and out. She shuddered and moaned in anticipation, arching her back in a blissful wave of passion as she sensed his fervour. Her abdominal muscles contracted, shifting control, slowing things down. Faster now, building, pumping, groaning. Almost there. Climax! Billy let out a moan of pleasure and rolled onto his back, closing his eyes to enjoy the last few vestiges of their love-making. Their minds wandered together, through fields of sweet-smelling flowers and long, whispering grass in the summer sun.

CHAPTER TWENTY-THREE

Questions

"Saul my friend!" Josiah stepped up to the manager of Denny's Diner with a big smile on his face; his big hand outstretched in a friendly greeting.

Saul Pilltree jumped in surprise as he turned to find Josiah's big frame taking up most of his view. "Huh! Oh, it's you. Jack, was it?"

Josiah continued to smile graciously. "Yes. Jack Smith at your service."

"Uh, hi. How can I help you?"

"I'm looking for the last waitress we interviewed. Dorothy."

"Um, she's not here at the moment. Is there something that I can assist you with?"

"Hmm, not really. For some reason, my camera only recorded part of the interview with her. We really need to get in touch with Dorothy to complete our documentary. Do you have any idea how I could get in touch with her?"

"I could give you her mobile number."

"Yeah sure, that would be grand. Thanks very much."

Saul pulled out his phone and read out Dorothy's number. Josiah punched it into his device, stepped outside the diner and dialled her number. She answered after three rings. "Hi Dorothy, it's Jack Smith here, from the television channel. Saul from the diner gave me your number."

"Oh, hi." She sounded a little uneasy.

"We need to re-record your interview as my camera, for some reason, didn't capture all of it. I'm truly sorry. Can you meet me at the diner or some other place more convenient as soon as possible?"

"Oh no, I'm thorry to hear that. Um, sure we can meet. How about the Coffee House in Baxter's Road? Do you know where that is?"

Josiah scratched his head. "Baxter's Road...sounds familiar. Isn't that the road with all those restaurants and pubs downtown?"

"Yeah. Thee you there, 2 pm?"

"OK. Sounds fine. Cheers."

Josiah called Finn. "Finn, it's Jo, I've found Dorothy. Meeting her in Baxter's Road. I think I should go alone. Don't wanna scare her off."

"OK. Good. I'll let Maria know. Keep me posted."

Josiah glanced at his watch. 12.47pm. He headed off to Baxter's Road and grabbed some fish and chips from a local eatery called Rod 'n Reel. He sat at the window while he ate, watching the passers-by go about their daily routines. He finished his meal and ambled over to the Coffee House, a brown, two-story building with a wooden, slatted frontage, a little further down the road. He sat down at a two-seater table in the courtyard and ordered a decaf cappuccino. A few moments later, Dorothy arrived. She looked around until she spotted him and then stepped over to his table.

Josiah politely stood up to greet her. "Afternoon Miss Dorothy, thanks for going out of your way to meet with me."

Dorothy smiled in return before sitting down. "No problem Jack." She looked around with a puzzled look on her face. "Where's your camera? I thought you were going to re-record our interview?"

Josiah looked at her and closed his eyes to slits. "This is going to be a very different kind of interview."

Dorothy shifted uneasily in her seat and glanced nervously

around the shop before turning back to Josiah. Her voice had changed. She sounded like a different person, more mature, confident. "What the hell are you talking about?" She stood up to leave.

Josiah quickly grabbed her wrist, twisting it gently, forcing her to remain in her seat. "You aren't going anywhere Miss Dorothy until you tell me what I need to know." Dorothy tugged at her wrist but couldn't budge under Josiah's steel-grip. He slowly twisted her wrist around to reveal the spiral tattoo on the inner side of her arm. "Let's start with this." He looked down at the tattoo then at Dorothy, cocking his head to one side questioningly. Dorothy grimaced and stared back at him mutely. Josiah stared into her eyes, while slowly tightening his grip on her arm.

The staring match continued for a brief moment before Dorothy cried out in pain. "Ugh! OK, OK. What do you want to know?"

Josiah relaxed his grip but still held onto her arm. "We know about you and your kind. The Lemurians." Dorothy flinched when he mentioned the name. Josiah smiled. "I'm looking for my friends, Billy Bayer and Kisha Leeman."

Dorothy's icy stare was focused on Josiah. "Never heard of 'em."

Josiah replied patiently with a smile, "I've got all day Miss Dorothy. I'll ask you again. I'm looking for my two friends that came to Barbados and disappeared inside Denny's Diner. You're part of this secret organisation that has kidnapped them, and I want them back otherwise, heads are gonna roll."

Dorothy smiled sardonically. "You have no idea who you're messing with Jack. You're out of your depth here, private."

Josiah stood up, dragging Dorothy with him. She step-hopped behind him as he walked away from the store. He carried on going around the back of the building, pulling Dorothy with him as he walked. She protested, but he ignored her. He pushed her up against the wall lifting her off her feet, his thick wrist against her throat, suffocating her every breath.

"You're mistaken, Miss Dorothy. It's you who has no idea who you're messing with! Now tell me what I need to know before I snap your scrawny little neck!"

Dorothy writhed beneath his firm grip like a fly caught in a spider's web, her breath rasping in the back of her throat. She waved her hands up and down and forced out the words, "OK. OK. I'll talk." Josiah relaxed his grip. Dorothy brought both hands to her throat and then dropped down onto her haunches, her head hanging on her chest while trying to catch her breath. Suddenly, Josiah experienced a high-pitched ringing in his ears. He brought his hands up to protect them. Dorothy stood up, smiling coldly. The ringing intensified. Josiah closed his eyes. Dorothy was inside his head.

I told you not to mess with us!

A series of random images flashed quickly across his vision. The ringing increased in intensity and then there was darkness. When he opened his eyes again, he found himself alone. Dusk was settling in. There was dried blood in his ears, and his head was pounding like a hammer.

CHAPTER TWENTY-FOUR

Caves

Back at the Bridgetown Inn, Maria wiped Josiah's ears with an antiseptic-soaked cloth, while Finn searched the web for any further clues as to the whereabouts of Dorothy, in the hope that it was at least her real name. "What the fuck are we gonna do now? I cross-questioned our friend Saul at the diner, but he knows nothing. The address that he had for Dorothy is fake, and now she's probably gone underground." Maria had no idea how literal she sounded when she said that.

Finn replied without looking up. "The guy that I obtained this new stuff from," he waved his hand across his new laptop and other digital equipment, "has a shop in town. I showed him the photo of the digital panel in the men's bathroom at the diner, and he said that he'd never seen anything like it. He put me in touch with a guy in Holetown, situated a little further up the coast who, he believes, may have some idea. I'm gonna take the boat from Oistins Bay first thing in the morning. You guys coming?"

Maria and Josiah responded at the same time. "For sure!"

Maria spotted three stars still twinkling in the sky high above the island as they headed out of the hotel at 5.45am, the dawn's early light struggling to find its way into the shadowed crevices between the buildings in the city centre. Finn led them down to the small harbour at Oistins Bay where they found Smithy, the proprietor at *Off the Hook Fishing Charters*, unlocking his office in preparation for the day ahead.

"Morning Smithy!" barked Finn as the small troupe approached him from behind. Smithy visibly jumped up and spun around, ready to clobber whoever had almost frightened him out of his skin. "Sorry Smithy, never meant to startle you so." Smithy was an old sailor, in his late 60's with sparse, grey hair and a matching, bushy grey beard and was the proud owner of several chartered fishing boats. Finn watched him sway ever so gently from side to side. He felt as if he was floating in the deep ocean, rising with the swell and then falling in its wake. Smithy's blue-grey eyes carried with them the history of the briny deep as they looked right through Finn, stirring his soul like a dolphin's echo in the sparkle of the setting sun across the rippling sea.

"Ah, Mr Finnegan. It's you. Never knew ye was coming otherwise I woulda had yer boat ready fer ya a little earlier."

"Not to worry. We'll just wait in your shop until you sort us out, sir."

The three visitors made their way to the tourist shop right next to the charter boat office and sat down in the waiting area. Josiah picked up a promotional leaflet on the table.

Harrison's Cave. Barbados' Number 1 Tourist Attraction. Josiah opened the flyer and continued reading. Visit Harrison's Cave, the greatest natural wonder of Barbados, named after Thomas Harrison who owned much of the land in the area during the 1700's. During the 18th and 19th centuries, there were several expeditions into the caves that never got very far due the many challenges presented by the narrow passageways. The caves were rediscovered and mapped in 1974 by Ole Sorensen, an engineer and cave adventurer from Denmark together with Tony Mason and Allison Thornhill. Enjoy the many naturally beautiful sites deep within the underground caves via a tramway system designed to take you on a remarkable journey through the maze of tunnels beneath the island of Barbados. Let the adventure begin!

Josiah turned the flyer over and found a collage of

photographs displaying the stalagmites and crystal pools inside Harrison's Cave. A single image jumped out at him. It was the same image that flashed inside his head when he was trying to get Dorothy to talk. He closed his eyes, taking his mind back to that painful experience, reaffirming his encounter behind the coffee shop in Baxter's Road. The image was so vivid in his mind's eye that it was like taking a transparency and overlaying it across the copy in front of him. Josiah abruptly jumped up and out of his seat, jabbing his finger into the leaflet that he held out in front of him. "This is it! This is where we have to go!"

Both Finn and Maria looked at him like he was out of his mind. "What you talkin' about Jo?" Maria creased her brow in confusion. "We have to get to Holetown."

"No! We have to go to Harrison's Cave. Trust me; this is where they are." Josiah shouted excitedly.

Finn responded curiously. "Am I dreaming or is Jo going crazy? Enlighten us please, Jo."

"As you know, when I was questioning Dorothy, she somehow generated this high-pitched sound that caused my eardrums to burst. But what I didn't share with you was the image that I saw during this experience."

"What image?" asked Finn.

"This one." Josiah pointed again at the leaflet, this time at a picture of a clump of stalagmites next to a clear pool of water. "This was the identical image that flashed into my head at the time. I thought nothing of it until I saw this picture. I have never seen this image anywhere else before, and yet it's identical to the vision I had when I was cross-questioning Dorothy before she got away." Josiah squeezed his fist and clenched his teeth in anger. "That bitch."

"Let me see that." Maria grabbed the leaflet from Josiah and stepped over to Finn for a closer look.

"Hey! You coulda just asked!"

"It's not far from here, let's go and check it out." Finn had already made up his mind. Josiah smiled. Finn went over to Smithy, dropped him twenty bucks for his time and then the three of them jumped into a taxi and headed over to Harrison's Cave. The drive time was only around ten minutes from Oistins.

The trio joined a group of several other tourists as they made their way into the cave system at the Boyce Tunnel entrance via a tram, built for this very purpose. The group climbed out of the tram several times to examine the caves more closely. The tour guide, Sam, was a local with a friendly face. He began to explain the history of the area and the various rock formations. "Harrison's Cave is a massive stream cave system, at least 1.4 miles long. The interior temperature is an average 80 degrees and its largest cavern, the Great Hall measures 50 feet high. It's an active cave as it carries water with the stalagmites growing by less than the thickness of a piece of paper each year, which is considered fast in geological terms. Who knows what a person who explores caves is called? Anyone? It's a speleologist."

"Excuse me but where is this formation?" Maria approached Sam with the promotional leaflet Josiah had picked up at the fishing charter shop.

"Oh, that's coming up at our next stop," replied Sam with a smile.

He turned back to face the tour group and continued. "Now if you look closely at these stalactites, you'll notice that they are shaped a little different from the last lot we saw…"

Maria walked back to the others waiting by the tram. "One more stop." She sat down next to Josiah as the other tourists stood, transfixed by the guide, listening to him ramble on about the tranquil, glassy pools and the delicate flowstone formations. The tram came to stop alongside a pathway that led around a hidden corner to the right. Finn, Maria and Josiah were off first, fast-pacing it along the narrow path. It wound around the corner, twisted left and then opened out into the cave with a beautiful stalagmite formation alongside a crystal clear pool filled with mineral water. Beams of multi-coloured light filtered through the cave from several spotlights positioned in between the stalagmites and next to the pool, creating a magnificent rainbow effect that took one's breath away.

There was a moment's silence as the trio absorbed the natural wonder and then Josiah broke the silence with a whisper. "This is it. I can't believe it. Now there must be some kind of secret entrance here or something." Just as they began to search the area, the rest of the tour group arrived. Sam broke into a soliloquy once more, about the cave design and natural rock formations surrounding the area. Finn, Maria and Josiah stepped back into the shadows and waited. After a few minutes, Sam allowed the tourists to take some pictures and explore a little further before heading back to the tram. The others stepped forward and continued their search for a clue of some kind. Josiah walked back to the pool and stared at it for a few moments. He dropped to his haunches and looked inside, gazing at the kaleidoscopic effect that the light had as it shone through the clear mountain water.

There has to be something here. Dorothy must have shared this image with me by mistake but why this particular formation? Damn! There has to be more to this conundrum.

Josiah closed his eyes and then took a deep breath. That was when he heard it. The sound. He held his breath this time and strained his ears to listen intently. *Ha! There it is again!* "Finn, Maria, come here," whispered Josiah, louder and with more urgency than before.

"What? What is it?" said Finn, as he bounded over to the pool of water. Maria came running over too.

"Shhh! Listen!" The three of them paused, listened and then waited. "There! Did you hear it?" Josiah spoke excitedly. "It sounds like a whistling sound. Like there was a wind or something."

"But we're deep underground," said Mariah sceptically. "How can there be wind here?"

"My point exactly," said Josiah. "Now, listen again. Close your eyes and listen."

"Hey, you're right," said Maria. "I can definitely hear what sounds like running water." Maria was silent again as she cocked her head to listen once more. "It seems as if it comes every four seconds. Like clockwork."

"Even more curious," said Finn in response. "If this is truly the sound of some kind of water flow and it's a systematic sound, then this indicates that it may not be natural."

"You mean it could be man-made?" Josiah inquired.

"Yes. Man-made," replied Finn. The three of them were silent again, listening to the sound, trying to locate its source.

"Can't make out where it's coming from exactly but it's deeper inside this cave system," said Maria.

"OK. Let's look at this logically," suggested Finn. "The water in this pool must have come from somewhere, right?"

"Right but there's not even a ripple," replied Josiah. "It's like it's trapped in this pool."

"Maybe there's a plug of some sorts?" suggested Maria.

"Now you're thinking!" said Finn.

Josiah, still on his haunches leant further forward to look into the pool. He rolled up the sleeve of his right arm and thrust it carefully into the water, trying to reach the bottom. He dropped his arm down almost to his shoulder. His hand flailed around the water like a blinded eel. It was too deep. He couldn't reach the bottom. He pulled his arm out and stood up, dragging his vest off his huge torso, his enormous muscles rippling and rolling in the process. "I'm going in."

Before the others could stop him, Josiah had climbed into the pool and disappeared beneath the surface. Two minutes passed, and Josiah surfaced again, took a deep breath and dived down into the water once more. With his eyes wide open, he could see quite clearly beneath the watery depths of the pool. He methodically felt his way across the bottom, searching for an anomaly, something unusual, something out of the ordinary. There was a whirring sound as Finn and Maria witnessed the water level begin to drop rapidly, leaving Josiah standing in the pool like a kid in a playpen with a great big grin on his face. He pointed to a tiny stainless steel lever in the far corner of the pool. "I flipped that switch which must have opened some kind of valve." Finn and Maria waited for the water to drop down to ankle level before hopping into the pool with Josiah.

"Now what?" said Maria.

The pool bottom opened up like a trapdoor, without warning, and they slid down a stainless steel shaft and into the darkness below.

CHAPTER TWENTY-FIVE

Great Hall

Billy knew that he had to cooperate to stand a chance of escaping from the underground fortress. He sat with Kisha and Kaimi in the mess hall, eating processed porridge that tasted rather bland, but not too bad, considering. He looked up at Kaimi in-between mouthfuls. "So when do we get out of here?" Kisha carried on eating her food, seemingly oblivious to their conversation.

"Billy, you still have a lot of training ahead of you," said Kaimi. "You need to master some of your skills. Daily practice is the only way."

"I fully understand this but why can't I do this with you on the surface? Why does it have to be here?"

"This is part of our code. We train underground, in secret from the general populace. We cannot be seen to reveal our talents on the surface unless our lives are in danger. Even then, there can be no witnesses." The three of them continued eating in silence.

Kaimi looked up at both Billy and Kisha. "Today the Supreme Master has an announcement to make. We are to assemble in the great hall in an hour. I will collect you from your chambers. Please be ready." With that, Kaimi stood up to leave.

Kisha looked at Billy. "Who is the Supreme Master?"

146

"That can only be Belias Stongrathen, the self-proclaimed leader of the Lemurian people. You finished? Let's go. Come back with me to my room. We'll wait for Kaimi there."

A short while later, Billy and Kisha stepped out and into the main corridor, following Kaimi to the great hall. Billy was unaware that there were so many people in the underground city. He counted at least fifty, all dressed in similar attire, all walking in the same direction. At last, they reached the great hall. The room was around thirty feet high with several entrances. The walls were adorned with long, colourful tapestries covered with abstract designs, interspersed with paintings of scenes from a lush, tropical land. There were beaches lined with palm trees, tempered glass buildings and unusual stone structures. The artist made sure the sun was a prominent feature in every piece, a larger than expected fiery orb, radiating its light over each and every scene. People were streaming into the hall through every entrance, all wearing similar, nondescript, soft, cotton outfits in muted, earthy colours. There must have easily been at least 500 people, with more still arriving. Kaimi stepped into an aisle near the centre of the room and sat down. The others followed - first Billy then Kisha. The hubbub died down as soon as Belias stepped onto the stage. He waited for the remaining people to find their seats before speaking.

"Welcome brothers and sisters. Thank you for taking the time to join me here in the great hall. As most of you already know, the time of reckoning is almost upon us." There was a murmur amongst the crowd. Belias raised his hand, and it quickly died down. "Our extended family at the other clandestine locations around the world are planning to join us here in the coming weeks where we will amass our forces so that we are all prepared for the advent of the Great Prophecy. As you know, the prophecy predicts a significant struggle, the outcome of which will determine a new course for our people. We must be at our strongest to rise triumphant through this challenging period." Again there was a murmur amongst the people in the hall. Belias raised his voice. "But have no fear Lemurians! We have survived every civilisation that has ever come to pass, and we shall survive many more!" The murmur in the crowd became a cheer as hundreds of voices joined in unison to shout their praises.

Billy turned to Kaimi. "What's this Great Prophecy all about?"

"The Great Prophecy was discovered over 50 years ago on Easter Island by Belias Stongrathen himself, etched out in the form of petroglyphs onto ancient Lemurian stone tablets. The prophecy tells of a challenging time in the near future for all mankind. It's told that this adversity will take place when the sun is at its weakest. Following this ordeal, the Lemurian people will be compelled to follow a different path. There's a bit more detail, but that's the just of it."

Belias waited a moment for the din to abate before continuing. "Each and every one of you has been chosen to represent the Lemurian people in one form or another. Now is the time to reflect upon your individual missions here on Earth and commit to fighting for what is yours. Domination, manipulation, subjugation!" There was a combined cheer of agreement from the crowd. "for the prophecy to be fulfilled and for our race to survive, we need to stand together as one, and be sure that nothing stands in the way of our Lemurian birthright!" Cheers and applause. "Be vigilant my friends, take what is yours to take and keep what is yours to keep." Belias punched the air with his fist. "Ad Victorium!"

The crowd bellowed out the same cry in return, "Ad Victorium! Ad Victorium! Ad Victorium!" The cacophony was deafening.

"What does Ad Victorium mean?" enquired Kisha.

Kaimi leant forward in his seat and turned to look at Kisha. "It's a Roman battle cry. It means 'To Victory' in Latin."

Belias stepped down from the stage, and the people began to leave the great hall. Kisha was gazing at Belias like he was a saint come to save her from impending doom.

"Hey! Kisha!" Billy shook Kisha from her stupor as he got up to leave the hall with Kaimi. "Let's go!"

"Huh? Oh, sorry." Kisha stood up, shaking her head from side to side clearing Belias's hypnotic sermon from her mind, and then followed Billy and Kaimi from the great hall and into the main corridor. They walked for five minutes. Kaimi turned left, and they followed the passage as it opened out and into a forest.

How could this be possible? A full-on forest deep underground? Billy looked up and spotted ultra-violet spotlights installed high up in the ceiling. *Ah, OK. Artificial sunlight, so that's how they're doing it.*

"Wow!" exclaimed Kisha. "This is beautiful!"

"How big is this place?" said Billy in awe.

Kaimi turned to Billy. "This fortress is one of the original places of sanctuary. It's believed that when the great motherland of Lemuria sank deep beneath the Pacific many thousands of years ago, Asbeth, our forefather, descended into the bowels of the Earth and established this stronghold as a refuge. It has grown over the centuries into a vast labyrinth of adjoining passageways, halls and rooms, able to accommodate thousands of people."

Kaimi led Billy and Kisha deeper into the forest until they reached a clearing with several low, wooden benches, placed in a semi-circle around a central, slightly higher bench. The benches appeared to be well-worn and were concave-shaped with space for only one person per bench.

"Please take a seat in a cross-legged position on a bench."

When they were comfortable, he produced two smooth, orange-coloured, glassy, translucent stones from his pocket. They were cut into the shape of short, thick pencils with bevelled edges, set in silver clasps and hung from linked chains. "These are carnelian stones. The ancient Lemurians called carnelian 'the setting sun.' They identified its orange hues with the receptive, passive female energy of nature." Kaimi held up the stones as he spoke. They dangled from their chains, reflecting the ambient light around them as they twisted and spun slowly from side to side. "The Egyptians used carnelian in a variety of worshiping ceremonies, connecting to its powerful life force, using it to protect the dead on their journey to the afterlife. Carnelian also stimulates an awareness of the connection between the emotional state and the inner condition of the self. It carries with it the stories and records of the Lemurian people and reflects its light energy back in the colour of the world as we know it. These stones have further been imbued with a powerful spiritual energy that will enhance your psychic abilities, allowing you to advance very quickly in the art of light weaving." Kaimi placed the stones around their necks and then sat down on the central bench, facing them. "Kisha," said Kaimi. "I am going to take you on a rather unusual journey. Don't be alarmed. At no time will you be in any danger. Just imagine that you are a passenger on board a rocket ship to the stars. I am the pilot and Billy is the copilot. All that you have to do is stay with us and enjoy the ride. Billy, take my lead."

Billy turned to look at Kisha, squeezed her hand and smiled a reassuring smile. "Just relax and go with it, you'll be fine." Her heart began to race. A fine bead of perspiration broke out on her forehead. She focused on her breathing and tried as best as she could to regulate it.

Kaimi continued. "OK. Now close your eyes and focus on the sound of my voice. Place your hands on your knees." Kaimi consciously slowed down his speech and deepened his voice. Billy shifted in his seat. "Breathe in, to the count of five. Now, hold your breath for two and then release for five. Repeat." Kaimi allowed Billy and Kisha to fall into a rhythmic flow of breath before advancing to the next stage. "Expand your consciousness beyond your physical bodies and into the forest around us. Experience the living spirits of the ancient trees. Connect to their breathing, their pulse and their souls. You are one of them, a living entity, a part of creation, infused with a life force that is capable of great things."

Billy was surprised at how quickly he advanced into a meditative state of heightened awareness. He felt different, changed somehow. His mind was clearer and sharper. He gained so much control over his emotions that he experienced a level of confidence he had never felt before. Kaimi's energy signature led him deeper into the recesses of his mind. He was stunned beyond belief at the enormity of the experience but then was quickly wrenched back to reality, like a kite being pulled in to stay dry and out of an approaching storm. He felt a throb of energy emanate from the carnelian stone, as it wrapped itself around his head like the smoke from a hookah, drawing him into a steady, purring embrace. And then Kaimi was there, a beacon of light, burning away the strands of smoke, drawing him out and back into the forest. Billy focused his attention on Kisha. He felt her close to him, connected and bound to his energy, enjoying the ride, seeing what he saw and doing what he did. A wave of emotion washed over him, and he knew she felt it too. He smiled inwardly and felt his aura expand and pulse forth like a jellyfish in pursuit of an indistinct object in the distance. It took some time to get used to the powerful, primordial energy of the carnelian stone, to allow it to flow and enhance his body's natural abilities, but Billy seemed to be getting the hang of it, as minutes turned to hours and time became but a river.

At first, there was a gut-wrenching lurch that almost unseated Kisha, followed by a wave of nausea that nearly caused her to heave. She was on a roller-coaster from hell, and her eyes felt like they were going to burn right through her lids. She felt a cool, soothing embrace, Kaimi? Like someone applying an ice pack to her battered body, sending her pockets of fresh, crisp air to breathe, feeding her strength and vitality. Billy was close. She connected to his energy like a magnet that pulled her instinctively towards him. She closed her eyes and held on for the ride of her life.

CHAPTER TWENTY-SIX

Escape

Kaimi sat cross-legged on a zabuton, a Japanese floor cushion, at a low table in the only oval-shaped room in the complex, gently sipping on a cup of perfectly balanced green tea. Most people would simply throw some boiling water into a cup with a teabag, but this tea had that superb balance between the taste and aroma, as a result of the right amount of tea leaves, dissolved in water at the right temperature, for the right amount of time. Belias was on the other side of the room, examining a stone tablet suspended on the wall behind a thick glass frame. The tablet was timeworn but intact. The series of petroglyphs etched into its rough-hewn surface illustrated the fascinating story of a time long forgotten, a time when a vast continent was at the centre of all civilisation, a continent that flourished and thrived.

"They're planning to escape."

Belias replied without turning around. "I know. Let them. It's all part of the plan."

Kaimi placed his teacup down on the table. "Enlighten me."

"It seems that a few more guests have decided to visit. Somehow, Billy's friends have found a way in."

"But how? This has never..."

"Happened before! I know. That's why we need to let him go, make him think that he has escaped. Kaimi, we are so close to the prophecy's fulfilment, that an event of this nature must be left to run its course. If we interfere too much, I fear that we will jeopardise our future and the future of our people. Remember the words of the prophecy?" Belias looked up to the heavens as he spoke, seemingly drawing inspiration from some invisible, spiritual entity. "There will be great adversity for humanity. Kaimi, this part of the prophecy is referring to *us*, the Lemurian people. We represent humanity, as we are the Creator's first people. If there is adversity, we need to do our best to avoid any further confrontation."

Kaimi nodded his head. "But what if we are meant to interfere? What if we are meant to stop Billy from leaving here, from turning against us?"

Belias shook his head slowly from side to side. "This is not the way, Kaimi. We have already invested several years of our time and energy into observing him, and his progress, and then," Belias shook his finger at Kaimi like a schoolteacher scolding his insolent pupil, "just as we find the opportune time to bring him here so that we can convert him, you have your doubts! You of all people should know this man. But perhaps you have come too close, spent too much time with him and his people to see further than what is going on right in front of your nose." Kaimi looked awkwardly away. "He is stubborn and wants things his way, so let's play to his tune. Let's make him think that he's winning and when he comes back; he will bring us adversity as the prophecy states, and we will be prepared Billy is as much a part of this as we are, my friend. I told Billy when I first met him, that we would teach him the path to Providence. This is our mission, your mission, to guide him and show him our way. He may not convert just yet, but we have given him enough ammunition to fight back, and when he does get the opportunity to retaliate, he will either fail miserably or finally ascend to become a true Lemurian."

Kaimi sipped gingerly on his hot green tea before speaking again. "As always, your foresight is flawless, Supreme Master." He bowed his head to his chest in veneration. "What is the next step?"

"Our guests have entered via Harrison's Cave. They should arrive here in about six hours if they travel straight through without rest. I'd give them seven hours, considering their unfamiliarity of the trail. In the meantime, I want you to take Billy, just Billy mind you, to the sparring quarters. I think it's time to unleash his potential before his colleagues arrive and we facilitate his escape."

"Before you go, Kaimi, there is just one more thing I need you to do."

"Yes, and what is that my master?"

Belias looked squarely at Kaimi. "I need you to follow Billy and Kisha back to the surface and then charge them with the Obsidian Assignment."

Kaimi's eyes widened in surprise at this sudden unexpected news. "But I thought you said…"

"No matter, I have changed my mind. I want Billy to complete this assignment. This is my test for him and his Kisha. If he refuses, kill them both immediately. If he accepts, well then, we may have an interesting saga to look forward to. And if he goes further to succeed in this assignment, he will have no choice but to join our ranks. Either that or he will die trying. Win-win for us either way."

CHAPTER TWENTY-SEVEN

Lost

They slid down the shaft for a good five minutes before landing in another pool of far deeper water with a big splash. There was a wan light that eerily lit up the surrounding cavern. The three travellers dragged themselves out of the pool.

Maria was the first to speak, her voice echoing eerily around the cave. "Where the hell are we?"

Finn responded sarcastically. "Umm, deep underground?"

Maria picked up a couple of loose stones and hurled them at Finn. He ducked, and they hit Josiah in the chest.

"Hey! Watch it!" Now it was Josiah's turn to have his voice thrown around the cavern like a boomerang, rebounding like an echo off the walls. Finn pulled his smartphone out of a waterproof bag in his sodden jeans. He was taking no further chances after the last incident.

"Shit!" said Finn, visibly upset. "It's not fucking working!"

"What?" said Maria. "What's not working?"

"The built-in compass on my iPhone."

"But doesn't it work like a normal compass would?" asked Maria.

"Afraid not. A regular compass has a built-in magnet that attracts the dial to the earth's north and south poles. A magnet inside the iPhone would render its cellular capabilities useless. The built-in compass uses a chip inside the phone to pick up an ultra-low radio-frequency signal, broadcast from a radio frequency tower. Not many people know this, but Apple built a Dharma station in the North Pole to transmit such a signal around the world."

"You're kidding!" said Maria, amazed.

"Nope," said Finn. "That's a fact. Together with the built-in accelerometer, the device can calculate its orientation and direction by connecting to the radio frequency signal, instead of to magnetic North."

"OK. But that doesn't exactly help us here does it?"

"No, it does not," replied Finn, clearly upset. "We are so deep underground that the phone cannot pick up the RF signal at all."

"Hey! Shouted Josiah. "I think I've found a path. Looks well-worn."

Finn and Maria hurried over to Josiah to investigate and, sure enough, there was most definitely a path that finally led to an exit. What was most astonishing was a soft glow that seemed to be coming from within the walls themselves, providing just enough ambient light to show them the way. Finn couldn't help but wonder what the scientific explanation for *that* was.

CHAPTER TWENTY-EIGHT

Spar

Billy followed Kaimi, as he led the way through an unfamiliar section of the massive complex. They passed several rooms, guarded by more men in unmarked uniforms, until Kaimi stopped in front of a bearded guard wearing a red beret who suddenly saluted, holding his position like a toy soldier. "At ease private."

The guard relaxed, dropping his hand back down to his side. The door had no visible handle, no evident manner in which to open it, as far as Billy could see. Kaimi extended his right arm towards the door with an open, flat palm facing upwards. He made an anti-clockwise twisting motion in mid-air with his hand. There was an audible click, and the door opened a crack. Kaimi walked towards the door, gave it a light push, and it swung open to reveal a heavily padded, windowless room with a high ceiling. Billy stepped through the door after Kaimi, and it clicked shut, leaving behind a seamless wall of dark, grey cushioning. Billy felt as if he had shrunk like Alice and stepped into a rabbit hole to meet an uncertain fate. He looked around the room and noticed that the cushioning extended beyond the walls and across the full length and breadth of the ceiling. He followed Kaimi into the middle of the room.

Kaimi stopped and turned to face Billy. "Where's your stone?"

Billy reached inside his outlandish cotton tunic and pulled out the orange carnelian stone. He forgot just how much it mesmerised him so, swivelling on its pretty little chain, catching the light and expounding it in a myriad of directions, cutting it up into colourful, gaudy looking fractals. The stone's magnetic, alluring energy drew him into its twinkling depths.

"OK. Good. Leave the stone and come over here." Kaimi was pointing to a large, red, five-pointed star inside a giant circle, which had been painted on the floor in the middle of the room. "You stand on that corner, and I will stand here. OK. Now close your eyes."

Billy did what he was told, regulating his breathing as best as he could under the circumstances. Next, he felt a familiar tingling at the base of his skull and then Kaimi was there.

This is a sparring room. It's where we practice our defensive skills.

Do you have any fencing equipment?

No, Billy, I am going to teach you the Lemurian fighting style. We call it Tinchalo. It's kinda like martial arts, but you use the power of the mind to defend against an attack. Some of us call it psychic martial arts. But first I need to activate your internal vision. Try to relax.

Kaimi probed Billy's mind a little deeper, sifting through a complicated set of neural pathways, searching for the pineal gland, a tiny pine-cone-shaped entity located in the epithalamus, at the very centre of the human brain.

I have found your pineal gland. This gland has long been known by mystics to be the connecting link between the physical and spiritual worlds. This magical gland is believed to be the highest source of ethereal energy known to human beings and was permanently activated inside the brains of the original Lemurians. I'm going to perform a simple psychic operation by connecting the essence of the pineal gland with that of the pituitary gland just below it, allowing your third eye to open.

Billy squeezed his eyes tighter as he experienced a pins and needles tingling sensation inside his head. It felt as though someone had opened a faucet, discharging a waterfall of cosmic energy, raining down on his brain. The pressure was unbearable, and he winced from the exertion. After a couple of minutes, the pressure gradually subsided and Billy was left with a dull throb in the back of his skull. He slowly opened his eyes and quickly closed them again. All that he saw were chunky globules of colourful shapes oozing spectrally around in his periphery vision, much like the stuff inside one of those lava lamps. He wanted to get sick and felt his stomach turn at the thought of it.

"Billy, you OK?" said Kaimi, concern in his voice.

Billy doubled over, waved his right arm in the air while he cradled his belly with his left. "Yeah, I'll be all right, just wish this throbbing in my head would go away." Billy ran his hands through his hair, straightened up and gently opened his eyes. The colourful blobs were gone, but now it seemed that they had been replaced by a fine mist across his vision. Kaimi glowed faintly in front of him, a ghostly silhouette against the dark, cushioned background of the room.

"OK now try and attack me," instructed Kaimi.

Billy took a step towards Kaimi, but before he could even think about connecting with him, he seemed to melt away right in front of him and then magically appear to his left, his fist buried deep in his solar plexus. "Uuh…" Billy doubled over again but this time from having the wind knocked out of him by Kaimi's soft blow to his ribs.

Billy eventually caught his breath. "How did you…?"

"It's called a precognitive attack," replied Kaimi. "I sensed the moment that you were going to attack before you actually moved. Now let me do the same to you and see if you can visualise my attack before I make it."

"You gotta be joking!" exclaimed Billy. "What you're talking about is impossible! How the hell do you expect me to anticipate your attack before you make it?"

"I have just opened your third eye, giving you the ability to see beyond this realm, to visualise what might take place. This gives you the advantage of being able to anticipate my attack. It sounds more complicated than it really is, but the opening of the third eye heightens your supernatural abilities ten-fold and combined with the carnelian stone will make you a force to be reckoned with. Here, let me blindfold you and then we'll give it another try."

Billy cocked his head. *He's serious.*

Kaimi fastened a piece of black cloth around Billy's head and then retreated. "OK, now I am going to make my move, and you're going to defend yourself. Just relax and breathe."

What happened next felt strange, yet wonderful at the same time. Billy sensed a kind of invisible pressure moving towards his head. He instinctively ducked and rolled onto his right shoulder, and then twisted around and stood up, bringing his arms up in a defensive action. He pulled down the blindfold and Kaimi was standing where he had just been, while he was now standing directly opposite Kaimi. He had anticipated a strike and then rolled intuitively out of the way. It was exactly as Kaimi had described. His mind instructed his body to move as soon as his opponent began to conceptualise an attack, just before he made it.

Incredible!

For the next couple of hours, the two of them sparred, punching and kicking, blocking and deflecting until Billy collapsed onto his back from both mental and physical exhaustion. Kaimi smiled and sat down next to him. It looked like he had just woken up as a yawn escaped his mouth.

"How come you're not even out of breath?" asked Billy. "That was exhausting!"

"It's because I regulate my breathing as I practice," replied Kaimi, a smile stretching wide across his face. "You need more time. More time to practice because practice maketh the master. Come, I have one last lesson to teach you." Kaimi gripped Billy's right hand and hoisted him up onto his feet. "OK. Now, try attacking me again."

Billy charged at Kaimi, throwing his full weight into an offensive punch, targeting his chest area. Billy was almost two feet from Kaimi when it felt as if he hit an impenetrable wall of jelly. His punching hand began to quiver and then everything around him slowed down considerably. The speed at which he was travelling diminished so much that he appeared as a choreographed dancer in a slow-motion movie scene. All through this experience, try as he might, he could not penetrate the shield that Kaimi had composed and instead became increasingly trapped in the jelly-like barrier, the harder he struggled. It was almost at the point; that time seemed to stand still, that it happened. Billy's recently activated sixth sense, triggered an impulse, by alerting him to Kaimi's next move, seconds before it was going to take place. The only problem was that Billy was entirely immobile, contained inside an invisible bubble and so could not avoid the inevitable. The best that he could do was twist his face into a look of complete surprise, as a powerful force came shooting out from Kaimi like a water spout, knocking Billy at least five feet backwards and up into the air. He learnt the hard way why there was so much cushioning around the room, as his head bounced off the ceiling followed by the rest of his body against the wall on the far side of the room. He crumpled to the floor, feeling as if a train had hit him.

After a while, Billy regained his composure and sat up. He felt battered and bruised. "What the hell just happened?"

Kaimi came to stand in front of him and began to explain. "The source of this energy burst that you experienced was a result of the release of my internal consciousness. In this process, my energy started mixing with the energy in the immediate environment, and I was able to project an invisible spirit shield within which you became trapped. At the same time, I began tapping into my primal energy reserve, building a ball of exploding energy that I expelled, shooting you up and away from me. I will now begin to teach you not only how to defend yourself against such an attack, but also how to break through the spirit shield that I just conjured."

Several more hours passed as Billy began to unlock pathways to power that would never have been possible if it were not for Kaimi and his guiding principles of light weaving. In the short time that he had been held a prisoner in this underground fortress, Billy had changed. It was like there was another side to him, a dormant energy force that had been awakened and was slowly beginning to manifest itself into something so powerful, that he could feel it beginning to seep into his persona like a virus. He felt different, more confident and more formidable yet there was a part of him that resisted the change, a part of him that wanted to return to the way things were. He realised beyond all doubt that this was not possible, that he had been exposed to the energies contained within the carnelian stone together with the ancient Lemurian blueprints and their raw, unmitigated power and formidable knowledge. He had raised his awareness through the opening of his third eye to levels beyond mere mortal comprehension. Images of Adam eating from the Tree of Knowledge in the Garden of Eden, experiencing a similar feeling of dread and fear by being exposed and laid bare to the true source of intense, brutal power and control over every living thing, came to mind. Billy mulled over these internal deliberations and felt his blood begin to boil.

To think that Belias had the right to force this upon me, to expose me to these forces without my consent. Belias continues with his plans for world domination, and it seems that nothing is going to get in his way to achieve it. I really need to escape but how? First I gotta find Kisha. Can't leave without her. After all, she came here to save me; now it's my turn to do the saving.

Billy made his way back to his chambers and stepped into a cold shower. He closed his eyes, placed his forehead on the wall in front of him and let the water run over his head and across his face. He opened his eyes to slits and watched the water rain down past his face like a torrent of tears, washing away all his frustration, his bitterness. He stepped out of the shower, dried himself off and climbed into the same nondescript clothing. He stepped out of his room and almost walked right into a young guard stationed en route to Kisha's chambers. His telepathic powers instinctively came to life. The carnelian stone beneath his tunic hummed in anticipation, as he focused his attention on the guard, tapping into his cerebral cortex and incapacitating him with a single thought. It was like imprinting a complex maze inside his head and disorientating him for a period, preventing him from finding his way out and back to reality. He followed this up with a quick, hard blow to the guard's left temple, smacking him down and onto the floor in a heap. Billy quickly lifted him up and over his shoulder, pressed his index finger onto the fingerprint security terminal outside Kisha's door, and it opened silently. He knew that time was of the essence, so he dropped the guard to the floor and proceeded to strip off his uniform, all the while ignoring Kisha's look of astonishment. He quickly pulled on the uniform and then pushed the unconscious body under the bed.

"OK, let's go," said Billy. "Follow me." Billy stepped out of Kisha's room, glanced left, right and then turned left, walking at a brisk pace. Kisha followed without saying a word. Billy headed in the direction of the underground forest - this being the furthest place that he had travelled to since his incarceration in the compound. They passed several guards and other individuals along the way without raising any alarm. Billy wondered if they were the only prisoners, as everyone else seemed right at home, smiling and chatting happily amongst themselves. At last, they reached the forest. Billy felt a close connection to the forest with its tall, ancient trees and serene, peaceful atmosphere. They passed the meditation spot and kept on walking. The forest continued for another five minutes or so and then opened out into a large cave, dimly lit from above with a soft, ambient light.

Kisha spoke in awe. "Wow! This is unusual. Very different from the fortress."

Billy agreed, sounding just as surprised. "Yeah. A cave. Wonder where it leads?"

Billy continued walking deeper into the cave, and Kisha followed. The well-worn path narrowed, rounded a corner and then came to a dead end. "That's strange. It can't be. This path looks like it has been used. A lot."

"Wait," said Kisha. "Hear that?"

163

Billy froze, straining his ears to listen. Seconds passed. Nothing. Then he heard it. Muffled voices. Billy whispered. "Don't move a muscle. They may have found us."

The voices disappeared, and then they were back, this time, louder than before. There was a grating sound and then the wall before them began to shudder and shake. Billy and Kisha stepped quickly away and darted back towards the other side of the cave, diving behind a low rock formation. They dropped down onto their haunches; out of sight but still able to keep an eye on the path ahead. Billy could see a couple of flickering shadows, growing larger as they approached the hidden couple. The silhouettes reached colossal proportions, jumping now across the roof of the cave like a horde of shadow puppets at a carnival show. A bulky figure came into view, followed by two others. Billy couldn't make them out in the dim light and decided to wait until they passed so that he could continue to search for a way out of this prison.

"No," Billy whispered out loud. "Jo? Can it be? Oh, my word. It is!" Billy jumped out from behind the rock and ran up to Josiah, wrapping his arms (as far as they could reach) around his big, muscular frame. Kisha followed Billy and came running out towards Finn and Maria, hugging them both at the same time. "Boy, are we glad to see you! How did you find us?"

Maria replied. "It's a long story, but I'm sure yours is far more interesting!"

Billy looked quickly around. "Come, let's get outta here before they find us. No time to lose. We gotta go back the way you came. Finn, lead the way!"

Josiah looked at Billy. "Jeez, boss, where'd you get the uniform? It kinda suits you."

Billy looked up at Josiah. "It's good to see you too my friend, but we don't have time for chit-chat right now. We need to move! I don't wanna end up on the wrong side of this bunch!"

The crew turned and ran back down the path. The path lay open, with a large oval boulder resting on its side near the entrance. Billy noticed a series of pulleys just behind it. They jogged on without saying a word, the path snaking and twisting its way through the underground tunnels. It was only after about fifteen minutes that Billy stopped and sat down on a small rocky outcrop to catch his breath for a few moments. "I don't think anyone's after us yet, but soon they will be," he remarked. "Let's keep moving." The group continued along the path, but this time, slowly and methodically, stopping every few minutes to listen out for signs of any pursuers. After they had relaxed somewhat, Billy and Kisha, began to relate their incredible experiences to Finn, Josiah and Maria as they walked.

The heavily guarded, central command room was located deep inside the complex. Belias wore tight-fitting, black leather pants, boots and a matching jacket with hand-stitched chocolate-coloured detail around the rim. He stood hunched over a 24-inch digital monitor, surveying five little shapes scrambling through the northwestern cave passage like ants en-route to their underground colony. Belias smiled.

Kaimi.

Yes, master.

Everything is going according to plan. They are on their way out. Keep me updated as to the progress of your mission.

Yes, master.

CHAPTER TWENTY-NINE

Top Side

Maria looked up at the dark, vaulted ceiling of the cave and threw her question out and into the blackness around them. "How the fuck are we gonna get outta here?"

The group had reached the point at which Finn, Maria and Josiah had splashed down from Harrison's Cave into the hidden cave system and now were at a loss as to how to return to the surface. Finn began searching the perimeter of the cave. "If there's a way in, there has to be a way out."

"We don't know that for sure Finn," said Maria. "This may be an entry-only point, which means we could all be really screwed." They began to move methodically around the cave, looking for some kind of opening or exit but to no avail. As time ticked by, Maria's words began to eat into their combined consciousness like a naysayer's prediction of impending doom.

Billy sat down on a small flat rock and closed his eyes. He was tired, mentally, physically and emotionally. His mind wandered until a nagging little thought entered his head and began to blossom into something more substantial. Their escape from the fortress seemed too easy. It went far too smoothly considering that the compound was littered with guards and hundreds of people. How could they have just waltzed out of there, unless Belias planned all of this? Billy's head was full of ideas and theories, as he mentally flipped through the chain of events since his capture. He stopped to focus on the training he received from Kaimi and then it dawned on him.

So much time and effort has been invested in me that this all has to be a setup. We're being allowed to escape. I am being allowed to return to the surface, but why? Why not keep me imprisoned? Why allow me to connect with Kisha? If we are being allowed to escape, then there has to be an exit here somewhere otherwise, how could we have travelled all this way uninterrupted?

Billy instinctively began to deepen his breathing until his mind settled on the flow of energy around him. He allowed it to envelop him like a soothing blanket, cradling his worn out body and weary soul. He imagined soft, sensual notes playing to a methodical beat, guiding him on a spiritual journey to a distant land. The notes tickled his earlobes and pulsed through his body as he swayed ever so slightly from left to right, like a cobra to a snake charmer's pungi. He drifted across a vast wilderness, floating just above the ground below, snaking in and out of the crevices and grottos left behind by the winds of time. He realised that the landscape around him was a mirror image of the cave that he sat in, with its jagged, knobbly-knee-shaped rocks and rough, sandy terrain. Intuitively, he opened his third eye and looked about with a fresh, newfound perspective. He drew in the energy of the space around him with an energetic exuberance that he had never felt before. The rocks and sandy landscape pulsed with a heavy, humbling energy that flowed through him, connecting, invigorating. The land spoke to him in a language that was gentle yet intense, a message infused with both purpose and indifference. It was this juxtaposition that allowed him to see beyond the mundane. It was here that he sensed the nuances in the terrain below and around him. It was here that he recognised the flawless rocks, hewn by nature, untouched by human hand. The detail was so intense that he could see between the grains of sand that shaped the very walls of rock that surrounded him. This intense clarity permitted him to perceive the imperfections too. These were evident in the well-worn paths surrounding the area; the rock walls softened by human touch, as well as countless other stains and blemishes on the lower rock formations.

With his eyes still closed, Billy floated across his dream-like wonderland. He rounded a corner and came across a linear tear in the rock. The crack glowed softly in a silky, white haze. He reached down, pulled the crack open, and it expanded into a welcoming haven of light and warmth. Billy slowly stood up in physicality, opened his eyes and made his way up and over to the area where he experienced his third-eye vision. He looked at what appeared to be nothing more than another untarnished rock face. He closed his eyes again and concentrated. This time, the fissure between the rocks glowed softly as in his vision. He reached out both hands, gripped the only available space, about halfway up and pulled. He felt the rock crumbling in his hands, falling away to reveal a black metal lever. He pulled hard on the lever and the very walls began to shake. The other four came running over just as part of the wall shifted away to reveal a long, narrow staircase shooting up and into the darkness beyond.

The five exhausted travellers emerged from the depths of the Earth and into the blinding sunlight. They staggered around like a bunch of inebriated bums, shielding their eyes. They struggled to find their footing, slowly regaining their composure. The group had surfaced in a small glen about 200 yards from the entrance to Harrison's Cave, via a cleverly disguised trapdoor, covered with a large boulder that magically shifted to the side as they reached the top, freeing them from the confines of their underground prison.

The journey back to Bridgetown was a silent one; the travellers lost in thought, as they gazed pensively out at the fleeting Barbados landscape. Back at the hotel, Billy booked flights back to New York for his team and then headed into town with Kisha for an early dinner. Josiah hit the hotel gym with Maria while Finn sat glued to his computer monitor, searching for more information about lost civilisations.

Baxter's Road was filled with the hustle and bustle of both locals and tourists. You could easily tell them apart. The tourists strolled casually up and down, stopping now and again to gaze at the dozens of restaurants and pubs in the area. Some would point and chat excitedly to their partners, while others stood and simply took pictures. The locals looked like they were always in a hurry, snaking expertly through the scattered crowd like they were playing 'dodge the tourist'. Their faces were mostly screwed up in earnest, foreheads down, focused on reaching their destinations ahead of time. Billy and Kisha strolled casually along Baxter's Road, looking for a cosy eatery to appease their hunger. The Duke looked like a nice establishment located between a pizza parlour and a Greek restaurant called Maria's. The Mediterranean-style menu offered a mix of traditional dishes from a range of delicious salads to fish, meat and poultry. Following a scrumptious steak and chips, the waitress delivered a pair of Kahlua Dom-Pedro's for desert. Billy froze. He closed his eyes in anticipation as the back of his head tingled unexpectedly.

Hi, Billy.

Where are you?

Nearby. Don't turn around.

What do you want?

Kisha looked at Billy with his eyes closed and sensed that something was wrong. "Billy?" she said alarm in her voice. "What is it? What's wrong?"

Billy turned to Kisha, opened his eyes and smiled reassuringly. "Don't worry Kish; everything's fine. It's Kaimi. He's here."

Kisha jumped in her seat and looked around the restaurant. She saw no one familiar. "Where?" inquired Kisha, baffled. "How did he find us so quickly? Shit."

That tingling again. Billy winced and squeezed his eyes. He thought he'd never get over that feeling. Even though it was for just a moment, it felt like someone was cheese-grating his brain and there wasn't much he could do about it.

What I want, is for you to take heed. Kaimi's voice boomed inside hi:

169

head. I am not the enemy here, Billy. I am your friend. We have a vested interest in you and Kisha. You are part of a family now; there's no running away.

That felt like an idle threat but it was the truth, and Billy knew it. His life had changed. He had changed, and there was no going back.

OK. What do you want me to do?

Meet me back at Denny's Diner at 8 am tomorrow morning. Don't be late.

Billy felt Kaimi's presence leave, like an exhale of breath out of his body. One moment he was there, the next he was gone.

CHAPTER THIRTY

Obsidian

The lagoon water was cool and refreshing. He dropped beneath the surface, washed his hands over his face and through his hair, brushing away the grit and grime of the day in one quick motion. He pushed his feet down into the soft silt and propelled himself up and out of the water, flopping onto his back to float across the clear, crystal water. Gurgling sounds tickled his ears, as he gazed at the tall, green trees reaching for the bright-blue sky around him.

Billy twisted his body and dived beneath the water again, but this time, when he surfaced, the water had turned to blood. He looked across the lagoon and saw a solitary, naked, female figure, unconscious and strapped to a boulder. He started wading out towards her, calling out to her. No sound came from his mouth. The water started becoming thicker, heavier and deeper as he struggled to reach her. He lost his footing, as the muddy ground dropped away beneath him. He swam towards her, struggling in the dense gore that surrounded him. His muscles strained as he slowly, painstakingly gained ground. He looked up, and it was then that he recognised the girl. Kisha. She turned her head towards him; her hair matted and full of blood. What Billy saw, burned instantly into his psyche like a hot branding iron, searing off his eyelids so that he could not blink or turn away from the grotesque vision before him. Two dark pits where her eyes should have been, peered into his very soul, twisting his heart into a fearful lump, deep within his chest. A foul, blackened liquid poured out of her mouth, and a blood-curdling screech stripped him of any and all defences. He lost control and slipped down into the abyss.

Billy woke in a cold sweat. He lay still for a moment, grounding himself in the present, shifting his mind away from the vivid nightmare that terrorised him through most of the night. After a cold shower and some food in his belly, he headed over to Denny's, on his own, to meet with Kaimi as instructed.

Denny's was pretty quiet this early in the morning. A couple of suits were grabbing a coffee on their way into work and a group of four very young women in brightly coloured leotards were snickering and giggling at a table by the window. Kaimi appeared out of nowhere, sliding down and onto the chair in front of Billy. He smiled, nodded his head and greeted him with enthusiasm. "Good morning Billy! How are you today? I sense a little trepidation."

Billy smiled succinctly, took a deep breath, then looked up at Kaimi. "Let's cut to the chase. What exactly do you want?"

"You are already one of us, my friend. I've told you before that I'm not here to harm you. Instead, I have an assignment for you."

"An assignment? What kind of assignment?"

"It's a very important assignment, but it's also a test," said Kaimi. "If you succeed, then you'll be richly rewarded."

"This has always been part of the plan, hasn't it?" Billy needed to hear the answer, but Kaimi just ignored his question.

"It's called the Obsidian Assignment." Kaimi pushed a narrow, dark wooden box across the table towards Billy. "Go on, don't just stare at it, open it."

Billy reached out toward the box, gripped its sides and pulled it closer. The box was almost the size of a shoebox, narrower, heavier and about half as high. Kaimi lifted the lid to reveal a long, jet-black dagger. The dagger was shiny like it had just been polished. What was strange was that it looked like the handle and blade were one. There was no visible seam or join, and an intricate series of spirals adorned the handle, giving the knife a mystical, supernatural kind of look.

"This is a ceremonial weapon, forged from obsidian, beneath a powerful volcano thousands of years old. Obsidian is naturally occurring volcanic glass, and, despite its age, this blade has never lost its edge. This dagger has also been infused with a powerful energy that was introduced during its crafting aeons ago. You have been charged with its safekeeping and its service in this highly classified assignment for the Lemurian people." Billy stared at the blade, and a perverted reflection glared back at him, mocking and taunting. "The target is The Monarch, and you are charged to kill him with this blade."

Billy sat bolt upright in his chair and, while struggling to contain his anger, blurted out. "Are you fuckin' crazy!? You want me to…" Billy leant forward, glanced around and lowered his voice to a whisper. "Kill The Monarch? And how the hell do you expect me to find him, let alone kill him?"

"Belias himself was going to carry out this assignment. Now he has decided to give it to you to execute. It appears that he believes in you more than you know. This won't be an easy kill, but don't forget Billy; you are different now. You came to us as Billy Bayer and emerged forever changed - aware, astute and enlightened. What you knew then is very different to what you know now. As far as The Monarch goes, we've been tracking him for years, watching him build his empire through drug trafficking among other notorious activities. The time has now come to exterminate him, and we need you to carry out this important charge."

"You mean he's not working for you?" said Billy, surprise in his voice. "He's not a Lemurian?"

Kaimi smiled. "No. He's not. He has become too powerful. Too powerful to convert. He must die instead. Not everyone with power is Lemurian. Over the last twelve months, we have infiltrated his lower ranks, strategically placing our soldiers amongst his men. We know exactly where he is and how to get close to him. The plan is already underway. All that you have to do is follow exactly what we tell you so that you are in the right place at the right time. Providence, Billy."

Billy looked up at Kaimi. "And what if I don't? What if I don't follow orders?"

Kaimi laughed, this time, throwing his head back, his long braids bouncing off the back of his head as he did so. "Billy, Billy, Billy. You still don't understand, do you? If you succeed in this mission, you will take over The Monarch's territory. Belias is giving you an opportunity to earn your keep. This is another test, Billy and if you pass with flying colours, you will truly be rewarded for your efforts. That I can promise you for nothing. You will become a part of the rise of the Lemurian Empire and we will once again rejoice in the spoils of our toils."

Billy was beginning to enjoy the way things were going but if it were not for that madman Belias, he would probably have embraced his responsibilities more. Conflicting opinions wrestled inside his head. He wanted the power and responsibility that came with the success of this assignment but did not wish to be part of Belias's outlandish plans to take over the world. Billy had no choice but to play the game and then wait for the opportunity to usurp Belias's rule somewhere, somehow. He knew that he needed to make some sacrifices to gain Belias's trust in all of this. He needed to show Belias that he had what it took to kill The Monarch. Otherwise, he would just become a useless accessory destined for extermination like so many others before him. Billy blinked hard and then turned to Kaimi, steeling his jaw before responding. "OK. I accept, but I want my people with me."

"Sure, Billy." Said Kaimi. "Like I said, we are on the same team. You'll get what you need to accomplish your task. Now cancel your tickets because we're going to Jalisco."

"Jalisco? In Mexico?"

"Yeah. We'll fly from here via Miami and Dallas before landing in Guadalajara, Jalisco's capital. The Monarch owns a private beach-front villa there, and our informants have advised us that he's in Guadalajara for the National Tequila Fair that takes place in the town of Tequila about 40 miles away. He owns a tequila distillery in the area and likes to support it by attending the fair every year."

The flight out of Barbados was only scheduled for the following day, so Kaimi spent the rest of the afternoon meeting and briefing Billy's crew on the order of events, the goals and objectives and the complete confidentiality of the mission.

"OK. Now listen up!" Kaimi addressed the team. "After landing in Guadalajara, we will make our way to the Riu Plaza Hotel. The following morning, we depart early for the town of Tequila. I have booked us into a tour at Casa Agave de Jalisco, The Monarch's very own private distillery. It's smack-bang in the middle of the Tequila Fair so there are gonna be lotsa tourists which means that we'l blend in nicely. These are the latest photos we have of him." Kaimi handed Billy a manila folder to pass around. "Study them carefully and memorise this man's face like he's family."

Billy opened the folder and began to read out loud. "Diego Marcos Rodriguez, known as The Monarch or El Monarca, in Spanish, is one of the baddest Mexican crime lords of all time. Rodriguez was the leader of the Ropero Cartel, a notorious operation that was formed in the early 80's. The cartel began making a name for itself through its kidnapping and counterfeiting operation. It then built up an international reputation for murder and brutality before expanding into cocaine smuggling from Peru and Colombia. Today, it is believed that Rodriguez is responsible for the smuggling of five times more cocaine to the United States of America than any other trafficker in the world. In the last twenty years, it is believed that Rodriguez amassed a fortune of over thirty billion U.S. He was born in Sinaloa, North-western Mexico in 1964 and grew up an orphan. He was taken in by the Juela Cartel and raised as a son by its late leader Martino Cuarez Bolindas. At the age of 15, Rodriguez is alleged to have killed Bolindas in cold blood, before taking over his step-father's empire." Billy looked around at his comrades. "That's one nasty son-of-a-bitch."

Josiah had his hand up. "Yes, Josiah?" said Kaimi.

"Uh, you can call me Jo." Josiah dropped his hand.

"Sure thing, Jo."

"If we happen to see him, do we take him out there 'n then?"

"No. We are just there to scope the place out, get familiar with the environment."

"And have some tequila," Josiah grinned.

"Good plan Jo," said Finn. "First round's on me."

"Hey people, it's gonna be early in the morning!" Said Maria, scrunching up her face in distaste. "You guys are crazy!"

"We'll be on a tequila tour," said Josiah. "So we gotta at least taste the tequila! Hey, have you guys heard the tequila joke?"

"No, pray, please tell us Mr Tequila," replied Maria, mockingly.

Josiah winked at Maria. "Why did Mexicans create tequila?" He looked around before answering. "So ugly people could have a chance at getting a fuck!"

Everyone broke out into fits of laughter. Even Maria giggled. Kaimi silenced them. "OK. Enough. We'll have plenty of time for fun and games later. Right now, we have a serious mission ahead of us."

Billy had his hand up this time. "Yes, Billy?" said Kaimi.

"Firstly, I agree with Jo. We need to drink some tequila. I've never had the opportunity to be at a tequila fair in the town of tequila while drinking tequila. That's three tequila's in once sentence!" Said Billy grinning from ear to ear. "Secondly, on a more serious note, I agree with Kaimi - this is a serious mission, and we can't afford to fuck it up. I don't wanna be stuck behind bars in a filthy Mexican jail somewhere, while some greasy gringo decides to make me his bitch."

Kaimi nodded. "Right. So, as I was saying, later that evening, there's a big party in town, hosted by Rodriguez himself." Kaimi looked across at Josiah. "This is not another opportunity to take him out. Instead, following the tequila tour, we will split up.

Finn and Jo will head over to Rodriguez's private villa on the Jalisco beach-front, break in, and extract his offshore banking account details, while Maria and I will remain behind to keep an eye on him at his tequila party."

"What about us?" asked Kisha.

"I haven't forgotten about the two of you," replied Kaimi. "You and Billy will head on back to Guadalajara, to the UAG School of Medicine, where you'll collect The Monarch's daughter, Elena Katerina, and take her back to our hotel where she will be used as collateral, if necessary."

"What about weapons?" enquired Maria. "Where do I get me some?"

"Don't worry about weapons and supplies," said Kaimi. "I've got all of that covered. I'll take each of you through the rest of the mission objective details en route to Mexico. We have a couple of transfers to make and plenty of time to talk and strategise."

CHAPTER THIRTY-ONE

Danse II

Billy sat at the edge of his bed later that evening, holding the ebony-coloured dagger in his hands, rolling it left and then right, testing its weight and getting used to the grip of the handle.

I wonder how many lives this weapon had taken over the centuries. Can it really be that old?

"What's troubling you, my love? You can talk to me, you know?"

Billy turned to Kisha, her dark brown eyes mirroring concern for him. He gazed at them affectionately. "I'm so proud of you, my darling. You've been very brave. I'm just sorry about this big fuckin' mess." He hung his head.

"Don't be sorry; it's not your fault. I'm just glad we found each other again. I was so worried about you when you just disappeared."

"Yeah. Sure." Billy nodded and then smiled.

"Let's just get through this mission and it'll all be over soon," said Kisha, reassuringly. "I'm also struggling with this. I mean, are these people - the Lemurians - for real?"

"Well, they believe themselves they're legit. Let's just say for a moment that they are. This means that every religion, every modern belief system is flawed. Most modern theories hold that creation began with Adam and Eve in the Garden of Eden about 6,000 years ago. Darwin theorised that, before this time, there were Neanderthals and before that apes and modern man evolved naturally. Science seems to corroborate both religion and Darwin's theory of evolution but until now, I've never heard mention of civilisations that spanned hundreds of thousands of years before the story of creation as we know it. It does sound like a far-fetched fairytale, like the story of Atlantis. I do remember, though, Kaimi telling me that there was scientific proof of the existence of the Lemurian people and the mounting evidence that I've personally experienced over the past few weeks has shifted my perspective on things, that's for damn sure. Listen, I know that we haven't had much time to talk since we were underground, but…"

Kisha placed her index finger over Billy's lips. "Shhh. No more talking. Not now. We've had a long and eventful couple of days. Time to relax."

Kisha increased the pressure of her finger, gradually pushing him down onto the bed. She nimbly hopped over his body and straddled him across his pelvis. He turned his mouth up into a smile when he realised what she was up to and shifted silently into the centre of the bed. She gently leant forward, bringing her face close to his and pecked him tenderly from the base of his neck up towards his ears, first one side and then the other. She continued, delicately sucking his right earlobe and then darted her tongue around and inside his ear, causing him to squirm and then moan with pleasure. She moved across to his other ear, tightening her thighs around his, anticipating his moves like an expert rodeo rider. She closed her eyes and slid her wet tongue across his cheek, found his expectant mouth and dove straight in. Heated passion exploded inside her head as she lost complete control - her tongue thrusting and groping around his, their bodies locked in a crushing embrace.

Billy loosened his jeans while trying to maintain their connection, awkwardly kicking his legs to get them off. She reached down to assist and then abruptly sat up, pulling her dress up and over her head. Her firm, tanned boobs bounced out, liberated from their unnatural confinement. He reached up to cup them gently in his hands. She threw her head back and moaned with pleasure as he started massaging them gently at first and then more assertively. She increased her rhythmic, rolling hip thrusts over his hardened groin and then dropped forward and down onto her hands, lifting her hips just enough to allow him entry. She threw her head back again and then dropped forward onto her elbows, finding his mouth with hers, licking, sucking and moaning with brutal indulgence. The bed began to protest, and the headboard started knocking steadily against the wall as the lovers increased their vigour. A solitary rivulet of sweat trickled steadily down Kisha's spine as Billy pumped his hips to her dance, building into a formidable, explosive climax. They reluctantly separated, Kisha rolling over and onto her back, exhausted from the hot-blooded ordeal. Billy closed his eyes and smiled, his chest still heaving from the physical exertion.

"Wow! That was incredible," said Billy as he turned to face her.

Kisha smiled and gripped his hand, squeezing it reassuringly. "I love you," she replied with the most beautiful of smiles.

CHAPTER THIRTY-TWO

Diego

The sun began to melt into the horizon, sliding languidly into the ocean like a dying phoenix, eloquently submitting to the cold, forgiving waters before rising again, rejuvenated and restored into the birth of a new day filled with promise and anticipation. Wraith-like spirals of circular smoke drifted up and into the dusk sky before dissipating and disintegrating into a gentle ocean breeze, as a solitary figure puffed on a chunky Don Jose Correa. He was a middle-aged Mexican, born and bred. He lay on a lounger on his balcony in a pair of orange and muddy-brown striped swimming trunks, gazing idly out across Bahía de Banderas. A half-full glass of premium, single malt scotch on ice sat on a side table, while blissful beats drifted out of the living room, caressing his ears like the waves of the ocean. The exclusive, beach-front resort on the Jalisco Riviera, consisting of the main flagship casona and four luxury ocean-side villas, shared the facilities available to Puerto Vallarta Beach Club members and was valued at over US$20 Million.

Diego Marcos Rodriguez was happy. He closed his eyes and a smile stretched across his face, his cheeks pushing his eye-slits into two mini smiles of their own. He was looking forward to the National Tequila Fair, an annual highlight in his calendar and the one week of the year that he felt like he was really at home. Diego's life was complicated. He very seldom got to have time out from his busy schedule. He spent most of his time keeping tabs on the dozens of shipments between Mexico and the U.S., managing the bribes, deals and unfortunate exterminations that were all part and parcel of the life of a Mexican drug lord.

There was a knock at the door. He opened his eyes and lifted his head in response to the disturbance. It was Carmen, one of the villa's live-in maidservants. "So sorry, Señor, but Carlito Escapor is here to see you."

"Good, good. Send him in."

Diego stepped off the lounger and walked into the living room, ducking slightly as he stepped through the door. He was tall for a Mexican. His 6'2 frame towered above most of his contemporaries, making him an imposing and commanding character. He was a Mexican of European descent with fairer skin and more slender features than the indigenous type. He had dark, thick, wavy hair with a moustache to match and sported several tattoos on his arms, chest and back. He grabbed his vest, threw it over his head and then proceeded to sit down on a large white leather divan in the centre of the room. A moment later, the door opened, and a young man entered. He was visibly nervous, clutching his Stetson too tightly, the whites of his knuckles blanching from the effort.

"Carlito my friend!" Said Diego, beaming. "Come inside and make yourself at home." Diego gestured for Carlito to sit down opposite him.

"El Monarca," said Carlito, dipping his head in acknowledgement. He slowly made his way to sit down in front of Diego, placed his hat down on the table and then sat back tentatively into the couch. A look of unease etched its way into his creased brow. He seemed concerned that the divan would suck him in and swallow him up whole if he sat back too far.

"So, how did it go? Where's the dough?"

Carlito quickly looked away and then ran a trembling hand through his hair. "Um, er, it's gone."

Diego jumped up off the divan. "WHAT?! Whadjoumean gone!? What the fuck you talking about? That was a two-bar deal, and you say the cash is gone! What the fuck went down?!"

Carlito was hyperventilating. He struggled to get the words out. "We were hit. It… it was definitely an inside job. They knew that w…w…we were coming. There was nothing I could do." He hung his head between his hands and looked down at the floor.

"Bullshit!" Diego shouted. "There was plenty you could do. Too bad you didn't take the opportunity because now there is nothing you can do."

Diego reached his hand behind the cushion of the couch and pulled out a Beretta M92 with an ECO-9 silencer. A subtle *thwwwt, thwwwt* was all that was heard. The first bullet went in through Carlito's solar plexus, exploding his insides out of his back and onto the couch in a messy, red splodge, while the second entered the top of his skull. The force of the impact at close range, lifted him up and back into the white leather couch with a thud, so that it looked as if the divan really was a colossal mouth trying to eat him, blood dripping down its sides in satisfaction.

CHAPTER THIRTY-THREE

Mexico

Thirteen and a half hours and two transit stops later, American Airlines Flight number 2314 touched down at Guadalajara International Airport in Mexico. Guadalajara, Mexico's second largest city, sits on a high plateau of more than 15,000 feet above sea level and is often called "The Pearl of the West" by locals. The city was founded in 1542 by the Spanish conquistador, Nuno de Guzmán and is named after the Arabic word, "Wad-al-jidara" which means "river of stones".

Six travellers disembarked and hung loosely together, before crossing the jetway bridge and into the airport terminal, together with the other passengers. At first glance, it was hard to imagine that they were connected at all. Instead, they looked like three sets of detached couples, standing around in the baggage claim area. Kaimi, with his red shades and conspicuous dreadlocks hanging halfway down his back, stood next to Maria, who was equally as striking, with her tall frame, high cheekbones and dark hair tied back tightly behind her head. She wore a pair of black, tight-fitting leggings and a red and white striped vest, exposing her assets in a low-cut cleavage that caused every male in the room to stare yearningly before quickly turning away self-consciously. Finn with his Leprechaun looks and sprightly disposition, next to Josiah's bulky physique looked equally as extraordinary. It was only Billy and Kisha who appeared to be a conventional couple. Billy wore a pair of navy-blue G-Star's with a crisp, white collared shirt and hung languidly over his luggage trolley. Kisha wore a knee-length, sleeveless, black dress with matching black cardigan draped over her shoulders. She stood casually by Billy's side, her arm resting peacefully on his shoulder.

The travellers made their way to the Rui Plaza Hotel, an elegant, classy establishment in Guadalajara, with elements of the visually frenetic architecture known as Mexican Churrigueresque, so named after the Spanish architect and sculptor, José Benito de Churriguera. This was evident in the design of the main entrance with expressive, decorative detailing, together with lavish, bright red tiles. There was also a collection of Talavera pottery on display that included a series of beautiful, ornate plates and bowls suspended on the walls around the hotel.

The six exhausted guests crashed in their hotel rooms as the sun began to dip below the horizon. Most of them simply ordered room service and went straight to sleep in anticipation of the big day ahead. Finally, by around midnight, it was only Kaimi still wide-awake. He selected two of the firmest cushions in the room and placed them on the floor in front of his bed, showered and dressed in a comfortable, pale-orange gown, with a black embroidered dragon that wrapped itself around his body, its ruby-red eyes twinkling on his back as he glided across the room. He settled into the cushions on the floor in a half-lotus position, his left foot pulled up and on top of his right thigh. He reached inside his robe and pulled out a pyrite crystal that was suspended around his neck. He used this powerful crystal to draw energy from the Earth through his physical body and into his aura, creating a shield against undesirable forces that may seek to harm him. The stone glittered in the soft light of the room, as Kaimi focused on its mirrored, golden surface, much like the native Indian tribes of America who used it as a healing stone of magic, by polishing it into mirrors for divination. Pyrite, often called "Fools Gold", is often mistaken for real gold but has a slightly darker golden colour and far more brittle consistency. It was popular in the Victorian era when it was crafted into marcasite jewellery, often set in silver. It was also popular in the 16th and 17th centuries as a source of ignition for some of the first firearms of that period.

Kaimi released the crystal, closed his eyes and relaxed his hands on his knees. He immediately went into a deep trance, his eyelids fluttering briefly, as he felt himself leave the confines of his physical body to rise up and away from the hotel. The sensation was familiar, like so many times before, and yet it still felt new in some way. He enjoyed that feeling and tried to hold onto it, but it was fleeting. He shifted his gaze up and into the heavens above, to marvel at the design of the universe and its splendour. In his supernatural form, the skies above looked very different. Instead of bright pinholes in the dark fabric of space, the stars appeared to be indistinct and blurry, their constellations seemingly connected by faint blue lines of energy. Kaimi could easily make out the pictograms of each and every constellation. He could see the shimmering connection between stars that made up the Southern Cross, Orion the Hunter and the Scorpio from the Scorpius constellation. He learnt that this was how the ancient Lemurians saw the constellations in plain sight and could travel directly to each of them at the drop of a hat. Belias said that following the fulfilment of the prophecy, the Lemurian people would rise again to see this day.

The crystal gave Kaimi intent and purpose, grounding him, guiding him toward his destination as he traversed the landscape in an instant, speeding East across the continent until he reached the island of Barbados. He twisted and rolled, as a spirit-being of light and dropped down and into Mother Earth, diving deep beneath her surface. Belias was waiting for him in his chamber as he glided down from above, hovering spectrally in front of his master. Belias was also in a meditative state, resting on his knees on a dais in the centre of his room. He met Kaimi beyond the physical realm.

Kaimi, I trust you bring with you positive news?

Yes, Master, everything is in place. We visit the tequila festival tomorrow and then we split up to complete the individual assignments. Billy has the dagger, but I am yet to charge him with the time and place of the actual extermination.

Wait until Diego is back at his private villa following the festival, then send Billy to complete the mission, while Kisha holds Elena. Make sure that he finishes the job. I want no loose ends.

That's the plan. Don't worry; I have everything under control.

It's my job to worry. Just don't fuck this up. Our combined futures count on your success. How are the others? Have they put up any resistance?

No. They follow Billy's lead. As long as Billy cooperates, the mission is safe. He trusts me and is beginning to believe in his newfound abilities.

Good. Soon he will truly be one of us.

Yes, Master.

You haven't told Billy about Diego, have you?

No. He knows nothing.

Good, keep it that way.

Belias smiled sardonically before retreating into physicality.

Kaimi rose quickly out of the underground city and up to the surface again, focused on the pyrite stone suspended around his neck back in the hotel in Mexico and willed himself across the continent to reunite with his physical self. The journey back was always much easier, much quicker. It was like the force of two magnets being pulled apart and then reunited once more. That tug of resistance, letting go and then connecting, two opposing sides determined to stay bound to each other, always. The experience of sound was always the first sign that the spiritual body had reunited with the physical again. There was a soft ringing in his ears, as Kaimi started connecting to his senses like he was just waking up from a long and peaceful slumber. The ringing became more distinct and began to shape itself into the ambient sound of the environment. He listened intently, as sounds from the city mingled with the sound of the wind through the trees and the hoot of an owl on the hunt in the deep of the night. Kaimi gently rubbed his hands together and then placed his palms over his shut eyes for a moment, applying some pressure as warm, invigorating energy flowed into and around his eye-sockets and then through his motionless body once again.

CHAPTER THIRTY-FOUR

Tequila

It was early in the morning when the travellers boarded a tour bus that took them roughly forty miles from Guadalajara to the small village of Santiago de Tequila, famous for its blue agave and the alcoholic beverage produced from this plant. En-route. Josiah read out loud from a promotional pamphlet he found on board. "Tequila is actually a variety of mescal, the original name for the alcohol fermented from the blue agave by the indigenous people. When the Spanish built a distillery in the town of Tequila in 1600, mescal was distilled to create Mezcal Wine and then only renamed to Tequila in 1873 to distinguish it from other Mezcal spirits produced in other regions of Mexico. Today, the town of Tequila and the agave fields around it are a World Heritage Site and as such, attract thousands of tourists."

"Hmm. That's interesting. Never knew that. Thanks mister tour guide," said Kisha. Josiah grinned. She gazed out of the window as they drove past Volcan de Tequila, a huge dormant volcanic peak dominating the landscape with its unusual central spine known as la tetilla (the nipple) that had solidified and pushed itself up and out of the crater from immense pressure thousands of years ago. "Wow…" she said, her mouth agape. "That's incredible."

Maria stared introspectively at the volcano, thinking back to a time when she was hired to assassinate Dakai Tujo, a Yakuza boss on the island of Honshu in Japan, home to famous Mount Fuji with its prominent symmetrical cone. She spent several months there, getting close to her mark, learning all she could about the organisation before finally completing the mission. A sudden pang tore across her heart, as images of Ichiro flashed before her eyes. She had grown too close to him and had allowed her feelings to get in the way of her job. She had to leave without saying goodbye. It was one of the hardest things she had ever done.

"Ha! Told you so!" cried Josiah excitedly. "We're gonna drink some tequila!" The tour guide demonstrated how to drink tequila the Mexican way. He took the group of around sixteen visitors through the distillery, educating them on tequila's history and production process, before ending up in a small room set up for tastings. He stood behind a table laden with a variety of tequila bottles and glasses of different sizes. He wore a guayabera, a typical white cotton shirt that originated in Mexico, together with a red scarf around his neck. A badge pinned to his right shirt pocket displayed the name Pablo in gold letters, and a black and gold sombrero was perched amicably on his head.

"OK. Everybody please, you leesen now. OK?" Pablo's Mexican accent was typical of the region. "Thees eez very important information for you to hear from me," Pablo smiled a toothy grin. "In Méjico, you sip the tequila leetle by leetle to savour the taste." Pablo demonstrated by selecting what looked like a brandy glass but with a chubbier base. He then selected one of the tequila bottles and poured a small amount into the glass. "OK. Now you must swirl the tequila like so." Pablo began to twist the glass, making the clear liquid swish around like he was swirling a glass of fine wine. "Next, we close the eyes and breathe in the magical aromas of the blue agave coming with the drink. Finally, we have a sip." Pablo, still with his eyes closed, brought the glass to his lips and tapped a small amount into his mouth, swirling it around to enjoy the full bodied taste before swallowing. He opened his eyes. "We continue to sip the drink slowly, enjoying the aroma and exceptional taste. In Méjico we do not down thee tequila in one go. No. This is impolite, and you do not get proper taste. OK. Thank you for your patience. I am glad that you enjoyed the tour. Who's first for some tequila?"

Josiah bolted eagerly to the front of the crowd with the biggest of smiles. "Yes, me please," grabbing one of the brandy-looking glasses and thrusting it forward towards Pablo. "And can you make that a double?"

"Sure, big man," said Pablo. He continued his speech while he poured. "Did joo know that the most commercially available tequila brands mix their tequila with cane spirits and only the ones whose labels state they were distilled from 100% pure blue agave are of thee very best quality? Also, there are over 300 million blue agave plants that are harvested in Jalisco region every year."

"What about the tequila worm?" asked Maria. "Where can I buy a bottle?"

"Unfortunately, you cannot" replied Pablo. "Only a few mezcals, usually from thee state of Oaxaca, are sold with worm inside. The worm is actually the larvae of moth that is found on the agave plant and is considered a contamination, therefore this type of mezcal is usually much cheaper than anything else." Pablo waved his finger from left to right in front of Maria. "Not healthy. Don't buy."

There was a loud bang outside, followed by several more, even louder than the first. Josiah's voice boomed through the room. "Everybody down! NOW!" he bellowed, pulling Kisha and Finn to the floor in a heap. The others turned and dropped down onto their bellies, twisting to look up and in the direction of the sound. Some of the other visitors dropped with Josiah and his team while others panicked and screamed in fright.

An outlandish cackle broke through the pandemonium that turned into a great belly laugh, echoing mockingly through the room. It was Pablo. Just as quickly as they had appeared, the explosions ceased. Josiah frowned hard and carefully stood up to peek through the window at the commotion outside. There was plenty of smoke that was slowly beginning to clear. What he saw next slowly began to make sense as he started to join Pablo in laughing out hard and loud. The explosions were a result of a group of kids lighting fireworks in the streets. Next to them were a group of musicians playing instruments and singing traditional Mexican songs. The group of visitors to the Casa Agave de Jalisco distillery spilt out onto the street to join in the festivities of the Tequila Festival, clapping their hands in time to the music like those traditional wind-up circus clowns with symbols sown into their hands. Kaimi and his crew stood back to allow the other tourists to move ahead of them.

"There!" Billy whispered hard so that his voice could just be heard by his team through the din. "It's him! Rodriguez!"

The flat, primaeval blade pressed into his lower back felt very heavy now as he watched Rodriguez just a few feet away from him. He was wearing a blue and red hat that was flamboyantly decorated in honour of the festival. His dark glasses hid his eyes, but his face was twisted up into a smile as he danced in front of the musicians together with a striking brunette who was snaking her body provocatively. Left, right, forward and back, repeat, twist, jive and grind. Kaimi signalled for the others to keep their distance by raising his right hand discreetly by his side. The group stood and watched him unassumingly for a while before moving off to the side after another signal from Kaimi.

"OK. We all know what we have to do" said Kaimi to the group. "It's time to go now. Let's all synchronise our watches. We check in on the hour, every hour, from 2 pm. Got it?" Everyone nodded his or her heads.

"OK let's do this," said Kaimi, clenching his fist and punching the air with a short jab. With that, he and Maria turned and walked casually back to the crowd of dancing people that had gradually begun to swell in numbers. Finn, Jo, Billy and Kisha made their way to the bus that took them back to their hotel in Guadalajara where they stocked up with ammunition and other military gear before embarking on their individual missions.

It was 3.14 pm when Billy and Kisha arrived at the UAG School of Medicine in Guadalajara. They sat in the parking area, waiting for a silver-blue Mercedes, license plate JHX-87-99. A few moments later, it arrived and pulled into a bay about six cars away. Billy stepped out and advanced towards the vehicle just as the driver opened the door. He quickly slammed the door shut, connecting the driver with the door in the head with a *bang*. He yanked the door open again and punched him in the face, knocking him out cold. He quickly bound his wrists together with cord and pushed him into the back seat of the car. He fished the driver's cell-phone out of his pocket, smashed it into the tarmac and then threw it back in the car. He closed the door and walked casually back to his vehicle. Kisha made her way inside the university to find Elena. The campus wasn't very busy as she arrived in the student cafeteria. She immediately recognised Elena from photos Kaimi had shown her. She was sitting by herself in the corner, engrossed in a book entitled The Republic by Plato.

Kisha sat down opposite Elena with a smile. "Hi, Elena."

Elena lowered her book and looked at Kisha with a puzzled look on her face. She was an attractive looking girl with long, dark hair and dark brown eyes. "Hello. Do I know you?"

"No. But I know you. I am your ride home today" said Kisha.

Elena hastily sat up and looked around suspiciously. "Where's Carlos?" she asked.

"Oh, he's off sick today. Has a tummy bug or something. Asked me to help out. Name's Kisha." She extended her hand towards Elena and smiled graciously.

"Uh, hello. Pleased to meet you." She ignored the handshake and looked around guardedly again. She wasn't quite convinced. She pulled out her cell-phone. "Mind if I make a quick call?"

"Sure," said Kisha. "No problem."

Elena dialled Carlos's number. It went straight to voicemail. "Hmm. Seems Carlos's phone is off."

"Yes. I dropped him off at the doctors on my way over here. He wasn't looking good at all. I'm sure he'll turn his phone on again later."

Elena closed her book and put it in her bag. She stood up. "OK. Let's go. You know where to take me?"

Kisha smiled. "Yes of course. To Villa Sobre las Nubes, just above the Puerto Vallarta Beach Club."

"Yes, that's my home. Thanks. I do hope Carlos is going to be all right."

"I'm sure he's just knocked out right now," replied Kisha. Elena looked at her enquiringly. "I mean from all the meds."

Kisha walked to the parking lot with Elena in tow. They approached a silver Volvo. Kisha opened the back door; Elena climbed in, and Kisha quickly followed.

Billy turned around and smiled at Elena.

"Who the hell are you?" enquired Elena, disdain in her voice.

Kisha pressed a Smith & Wesson pocket pistol into her ribs. "This is Billy and he's the driver."

CHAPTER THIRTY-FIVE
Villa

It had just turned 4 pm, as Finn typed out a message to Kaimi on his phone.

>*Just arrived at the Villa. All on schedule.*

Josiah peered through a pair of Steiner military-grade binoculars as Finn tucked his phone away.

"What do you see?" asked Finn.

"We have two tango's at 3 o'clock, just beyond those trees and one more behind them in the security cabin."

"OK. Let's do this," said Finn. "Just as we planned. Go." Josiah crouched down low and disappeared into the bushes, making his way stealthily around the perimeter of the property.

Finn stepped out from behind the trees and onto the road that led up towards the estate. "Good afternoon. Buenas tardes," said Finn with a grin on his face. "I'm lost. Please, can you show me the path down to the beach?"

A burly Mexican brute, wearing a pair of dark green pants and a burnt-orange blazer, approached Finn while his colleague looked on with interest. His over-sized biceps strained through his blazer as he walked. "This is private property," he said in a high-pitched voice that belied his size. "And so is the beach below."

"Oh, I'm sorry. I was told that there was a pathway down to the beach from here somewhere," replied Finn, scratching his head.

Josiah had made his way to alongside the security cabin. The guard inside was munching on a big, salted beef sandwich. He crept as close as he could and then pulled out his Glock. It had been fitted with a titanium silencer that glinted in the late afternoon sunlight. He waited.

"I have a map here," said Finn as he reached his right hand into the inside left pocket of his jacket. The guard reacted by moving quickly towards Finn while reaching his right hand behind his back for his weapon. That was the sign. Josiah aimed his gun at the guard in the cabin. *Thwwwt!* Finn pulled out his gun and shot the approaching guard in the chest before he could draw his weapon. He collapsed in a heap at his feet. Blood oozed into his blazer, turning it an even darker orange and then finally red. Josiah moved quickly out of the shrubs and took the third guard out by shooting him in the back of the head. They quickly dragged the three corpses out of sight, into the bushes and then threw sand over the long trail of blood, covering the evidence.

Finn signalled for Josiah to head around the back of the main house, as they approached the property, while he sprinted across the front lawn and into the safety of the porch area. Josiah jumped over a low wall at the back of the house and into a courtyard. A monstrous rottweiler pounced out of the shadows, snarling viciously. Josiah crouched down in anticipation. The dog launched into the air, mouth wide open, rows of razor-sharp teeth ready to do some serious damage. Josiah moved instinctively. He swung his right hand around in a hook, connecting the dog in the side of the head, causing it to fly across to the other side of the courtyard. The Rottweiler whimpered for a moment, vigorously shook its head from side to side and turned for a second attack. Josiah hastily looked around for a weapon. He spied a wooden mop propped up against the corner of the courtyard. He dived over to grab it, rolled onto his back, pushing the stick around and up just in time. The dog was already in the air, mouth agape, teeth flashing. The solid jaw of the dog clamped around the stick, and it began to splinter. Josiah pulled the stick close to his chest and then pushed it away with all his strength. The dog flew into the air and landed on all fours just a short distance away. Josiah took the opportunity to jump up and bolt for the kitchen door, slamming it closed behind him, just in the knick of time.

"What took you so fuckin' long?" said Finn as Josiah opened the front door allowing him into the foyer of the mansion.

"I was distracted by the nice doggie they had out back," said Josiah with a smirk. "We played fetch and then I got kinda bored."

"OK then, let's do a quick recon of the place to make sure there are no more guards. Then we need to get to the study."

Josiah walked into a maidservant in one of the bathrooms, who directed him to the maidservants' quarters where he found two more staff members. After locking them all in the room, he made his way over to the study to meet Finn. "Most of El Monarca's posse must still be with him in Tequila. Couldn't find any more guards, just a few servants that I managed to detain."

"I think you're right," said Finn, nodding his head in agreement. "I couldn't find any more either." Finn and Josiah looked around in fascination. The study was a mini-library with mahogany bookshelves extending from floor to ceiling, filled with rows upon rows of books. There was even one of those characteristic, mobile, wooden step ladders hitched onto the highest shelf so that you could get to the book you were looking for with ease.

"There's the painting," said Finn. "Let's use the ladder to climb there."

Suspended high on the wall between all the books was a magnificent painting of a herd of wild stallions running through the surf on a long stretch of beach. Finn climbed halfway up the ladder, and Josiah pushed it across until it was positioned right next to the painting. Finn carefully felt around the edge of the picture frame until he felt a small latch. "Click." The painting swung open to reveal a combination safe. Finn had memorised the numbers obtained from one of Kaimi's agents in Rodriguez's organisation. Right 28, left 134, right 45. Finn gripped the stainless steel door handle and yanked it down. The safe opened to reveal a single, A4 plastic folder. Finn reached out to grab it and then climbed back down the ladder.

The study door burst open to one of Rodriguez's henchmen. "Hey!" He opened fire with an Uzi-Pro submachine gun, spraying bullets all over the place. Finn dived off the ladder just as the alarm began to screech through the villa like a banshee on the loose. He went into a roll beneath a table to the side of the room. Josiah reached over to grip the table and pulled it back over Finn and himself to act as a provisional shield from the lethal onslaught. Josiah had his weapon out and began firing back at the attacker as he crouched down behind the table. The dim-witted goon suddenly decided to charge them. He came running at the table and managed to leap right over it, just as Josiah was getting ready to open fire. Before he knew it, Josiah had 250 pounds come crashing down on top of him. With his gun knocked out of his grip, Josiah was left to defend himself with his hands. His assailant bore down on him with a twelve-inch military commando knife, slashing at his face with all of his strength. Josiah managed to block the first strike but the second one was poorly deflected, and the heavy blade ended up sliding into his left shoulder, right up to the hilt. With a roar of anger, mingled with pain and anguish, Josiah's powerful muscles flexed. He punched the guard hard in the face, sending him down onto the floor. He stood up and faced Josiah again. Josiah was bigger and stronger than his assailant, but he was injured. Blood ran down his arm. It dripped off his fingers and onto the floor forming a dark, wet patch beneath his feet. The guard looked down at the blood and smiled contemptuously. Josiah edged closer to his enemy, the long blade protruding garishly out the back of his shoulder.

"You will die now," said his attacker with conviction.

He ran towards Josiah, aiming to impede his advancements further by connecting with his injured shoulder. This time,

Josiah stepped his right foot forward, twisting his body around and spinning left. He kept twisting and turning. The rolling action was timed perfectly as it caused the blade protruding from his back to connect with the right eye of his attacker, slipping gently into the socket and tearing it open like a soft-boiled egg. Blood spurted out of his eye in a fountain, as his assailant clamped his hand over his face, dropped to his knees and howled in pain. This gave Josiah time to grab his gun and fire off two shots, silencing the guard for good. Josiah gritted his teeth in discomfort. His shoulder was on fire.

He turned towards Finn lying on his side a few feet away. "Finn! Hey, Finn! You OK?"

Josiah pulled Carl Finnegan over onto his back. His left hand was on his chest. Blood oozed through his fingers and gurgled out of his mouth. He looked at Josiah and lifted his right hand. He was holding the plastic folder. "Here. Take this," said Finn with difficulty. "Take it and get out of here. I'm done for." Finn coughed, and more blood oozed from his mouth. His breathing was laboured.

"Don't worry Finn; I'll get you outta here and fixed up in no time." Josiah made to scoop Finn up off the ground.

Finn gripped Josiah's arm with what little strength he had left. "Jo. No. Don't. I'm not gonna make it. You gotta go. They're coming. The alarm…"

Finn's grip softened. He coughed again, wheezed and then went silent. His eyes remained open, and his head dropped to the side.

Josiah wiped his hand over Finn's face closing his vacant eyelids, knowing full well that they would gradually open again as rigor-mortis set in, but he still felt compelled to do the honourable thing. With another grimace, Josiah took the plastic folder, stood up and left the building, jogging over the front lawn and back into the surrounding woods.

CHAPTER THIRTY-SIX

Showdown

Kaimi and Maria had spent almost two hours keeping track of Rodriguez and his crew of abhorrent hoodlums as they moved through the festivities along the streets of Tequila, enjoying the parades, the dancing and the charreadas (Mexican rodeos) that took place across the little town. Many bottles of tequila later, the gang became overly untoward with a couple of young locals. Rodriguez himself had to step in to sort out their inappropriate behaviour. About half and hour later, they were at it again. This time, they were so drunk, that the women themselves managed to beat off their attackers with sticks and stones.

"Look. Something is wrong," said Maria. "He seems pretty upset."

Rodriguez was talking animatedly to an out-of-breath messenger that handed him a note to read. He crumpled up the note and smacked the messenger across the head, cursing profusely. He rounded up his team and headed off towards the vehicles. Kaimi checked his phone. There was a message from Josiah.

Got the documents. Finn was shot dead.

"Shit," said Kaimi out loud.

"What is it?" said Maria.

"Finn was killed, which means Rodriguez must know about

the break-in. We have to follow him."

Four black Range Rovers sped off in the direction of Rodriguez's Villa. Kaimi and Maria followed. Kaimi closed his eyes.

"Hey, now is not the time to sleep, buddy," said Maria.

"He's in the second last vehicle," said Kaimi, opening his eyes. "See if you can take out the rear vehicle and then I'll do the rest." Kaimi closed his eyes again.

Maria pressed down the accelerator. The red Audi S5 leapt forward like a racehorse in motion, gradually catching up to the black Range Rover, as they bolted across the winding, hazardous roads in the Jalisco Province. Maria expertly manoeuvred the vehicle alongside the other car, swerved out in a wide arc and then came back in, slamming hard into the left side of the black car. It swerved across the road but regained control and then rammed into the Audi with a bang. Maria pulled the car back to connect with the Range Rover again, sending it spinning out of control, off the road and into a ditch. Kaimi's eyes were still closed. He sent his thoughts forth and into the mind of the driver of the next car, causing him to slam on breaks. The vehicle, travelling at over 120 miles per hour, skidded sideways, flipped over onto its side and rolled several times across the tarmac. Maria came to a stop alongside the vehicle and both she and Kaimi stepped out to investigate. They approached the vehicle cautiously and watched as one of the hoodlums dragged himself out of the passenger window. He lifted his gun to fire off a shot, but Maria was first with her shotgun, obliterating his arm and sending his weapon flying into the air.

Rodriguez dragged himself out of the vehicle. He was battered and bruised but looked like he was prepared to defend himself as he slowly stood up. "Master Kaimi! It's been a long time. How's my friend Belias?"

Maria looked at Kaimi in surprise. "He knows you?"

Kaimi replied without turning to look at Maria. "It's a long story, but the short of it is Diego over here used to be with us. He had an altercation with Belias and decided to go his way."

Rodriguez laughed wickedly. "You Lemurians. Always getting in my way."

Kaimi smiled. "Diego, always the cynical one. Your time is up old man."

"No, Kaimi. It's you who is going to die today." Suddenly, there was a loud screech as a silver Volvo pulled up behind Kaimi. Kisha climbed out with Elena, her Smith & Wesson pressed hard to the side of her head.

Diego baulked, his face ashen. "Elena," he said in an anguished voice. "Let her go; she has nothing to do with this. With us."

Billy climbed out of the driver's seat and walked over to Kaimi. "Got your message. Sorry, I'm a little late. Maria." He nodded in Maria's direction.

"Good to see you, boss."

Kaimi smiled. "You're right on time, Billy. Right on time."

The very air between Billy and Kaimi began to shimmer and distort like there was an instant heatwave yet without any heat. Billy felt a tingle at the base of his skull again and then Belias magically stepped out of thin air. He smiled at Billy and nodded at Kaimi; then his attention turned towards Rodriguez.

"Diego," said Belias. "We meet again, after all, these years. It's been too long, old comrade."

"I'm no comrade of yours!" shouted Rodriguez in reply and then he spat on the ground beside him. "You miserable piece of scum! Me cago en la madre que te parió!" (I shit on the mother who gave birth to you.) And with that he raised both arms into the sky, his fingers spread wide like a pair of fans. Through some kind of invisible force, Belias lifted up to around fifteen feet into the air and flipped upside down, his long grey hair covering most of his face. Rodriguez brought both arms down, slapping them against the sides of his legs and Belias shot down to the earth again like a bullet. Just as he was about to hit the ground, he slowed down, twisted around in mid-air and landed softly back on his feet with a smile.

"Nice trick Diego, but I have grown much stronger since we

last met."

Now it was Belias's turn. He pointed at the ground in front of Rodriguez and closed his eyes. Billy felt an immense pressure in his eardrums as if they were going to burst and then the ground rumbled and split wide open to reveal a gaping hole, about ten feet in diameter. Belias moved his other arm over his head in an arc and Rodriguez was flung down inside the hole which miraculously closed up after him.

"There we go." Said Belias. "That was easy enough."

A few moments later, both Kisha and Maria screamed and dropped to their knees, their hands pressed against their ears. Billy saw Elena turn and run into the arms of her father, Diego! *What? But how?*

Kaimi shouted across to Billy. "The dagger, get the dagger, it will protect you!"

Billy reached the Volvo in a few steps, yanked open the door and reached inside for the jet-black dagger. He grabbed the dark wooden box lying on the seat and pulled off the lid. A searing pain erupted abruptly inside his head. He fought back, struggling to focus. The dagger looked like it was underwater as he reached down for it. It felt like he was moving inside a giant tub of jello that was burning his flesh as he tried to move painstakingly through it. His hand finally closed around the hilt of the blade, and the jello instantly turned to gas, melting quickly away. His vision returned to normal, and the painful burning sensation subsided. Tightening his grip on the ancient weapon, Billy stepped away from the car. He turned to face Rodriguez who looked flummoxed, as he stared at the dagger in Billy's hand, the source of his protection against his powers.

He quickly pushed Elena behind him, gritted his teeth and bellowed out loud. "Get out of my way gilipollas!"

"No." replied Billy. "I'm going to take you down, you rotten Mexican piece-a-shit!" He felt formidable, mighty even, as he stood in front of Rodriguez holding the ancient weapon before him.

Diego made the first move. Billy's instinctive reflexes came into play. He dodged a strike, blocked a kick to his groin with the flat side of the blade and then retaliated with a jab and a spinning slice that carved a large gash into Diego's left tricep, as he raised his arm to protect the dagger from cutting into his face. Blood ran down his sleeve, soaking his shirt in a deep, red stain. He staggered back, snarled and then attacked again. This time, he feigned a strike and dropped down to slide on his right side, kicking his legs up and into Billy's leg, crushing his knee in the process. Billy crumpled to the ground, rolled onto his side, holding onto his knee in visible agony. Diego sprang up and onto Billy, both hands going for his neck. Billy rolled away just in time but not enough to avoid Diego from gripping his neck from the back with his left hand and then using all of his weight to pin him down. Billy still held onto the dagger with his right hand, extending it out at a right angle away from his body, just out of Diego's reach. Diego stretched across, trying to reach the blade to wrench it from his grip. He shifted his weight across Billy's back and onto his right arm, pressing it even harder into the ground. With some of the weight off his left side, Billy was able to grab a fistful of sand with his left hand and throw it back, over his head, and into Diego's face. Diego shouted more profanity and the pair began scuffling around in the dirt, twisting and rolling from side to side, throwing up more sand and dust in the process. Billy roared loudly, gripped the dagger with both hands, twisted it around, and thrust it deep into the side of Diego's neck. Arteries and vessels severed, blood sprayed out and into the air haphazardly. It was all over. He pushed Diego's limp body off his legs and lay down on his back in the blood-dirt, catching his breath.

"Well done, Billy!" said Kaimi. "It's finally over."

"No, it's not," said Belias wryly. "It's only just begun."

Billy pulled himself up and limped over to Kisha who was still lying motionless on the ground next to the Volvo. He looked across at Maria who also lay unmoving. Her legs were twisted at a crooked angle. He rolled Kisha over and onto her back. "Kisha! Kisha!" Billy shook her body vociferously. "Wake up! Come on Kisha!" He put his ear to her chest and held his breath for a moment, listening intently for a heartbeat. "Kishaaaaaaaa!!! Nooooooo!!!" Billy snapped. He stood up, dashed over to Diego's lifeless body and tore the black blade from his neck. Pieces of flesh and bone came with it, flying up into the air. Billy turned and charged at Belias, weapon extended over his head in a murderous death cry that could be heard for miles. "Aaaaaaaaaaahhhhhh!!!" Belias, powerless against the primordial weapon, jumped back but not far enough to escape injury. Billy brought the blade down, burying it deep inside his thigh. Belias collapsed onto his back, maimed from the savage blade. Billy picked up a rock the size of his head and lifted it up, high over his head and prepared to smash it down on top of Belias.

"No Billy!" cried Kaimi. "Don't!" Billy carried on walking, carrying the large stone over to where Belias was lying. The rock grew heavier and heavier until he couldn't carry it any longer. His muscles began to burn; his arms began to shake, and he was forced to discard the rock that had suddenly become as heavy as a tonne of bricks.

You have no chance against me, Billy. Come, join us.

Nooooooooo! Neverrrrrrr! Get out of my head!

You have completed your mission. You passed your test. You are now one of us, Billy. You are a true Lemurian.

Grief overcame Billy; anger and complete rage all at once. "Nooooooo!" he shouted, running and diving onto Belias with the intention of crushing him into the ground. Belias reached down, pulled the black dagger out from inside his leg and twisted it around all in one motion. Billy landed with his chest directly on the blade as it sliced right through his ribs, ripping a bloody cavity through to the other side of his body. He wheezed once and then stopped breathing, his life taken from him in an instant.

Two more black Range Rovers pulled up on the other side of the road. Several of Rodriguez's men ran over to find out what had happened to their boss. The first three on the scene could have sworn that the very air in front of them rippled like glass, but when they looked again, all that they saw was the clear blue sky above four dead bodies and a young girl sobbing over one of them.

Part 3

The world cares very little about what a man or woman knows;
it is what a man or woman is able to do that counts.

- Virgil

CHAPTER THIRTY-SEVEN

Reset

There was no place for physicality here. This was an otherworldly place. It was not here nor there nor anywhere. It just was. There was no sense of time or measure, nor were there any borders or boundaries. This place was concealed to all but those that knew the way and could navigate between those that didn't. It was a place of sanctuary and a place of revelation. It was a place of desolation, and yet it was also a place of salvation. Those that came to this place did so in search of something. Something remarkable. Something extraordinary. They were guided by extra-dimensional beings, taking them on their personal journeys of spiritual enlightenment, searching for answers to questions that plagued their waking lives. Some delved deep, while others simply brushed the surface of the surreal, dreamlike landscape, stirring and awakening the unconscious mind on its inquisitive and interminable voyage.

There were a few moments of lucidity but otherwise the surroundings were blurry and indistinct. A thick, dense fog over a shifting landscape, concealing and confusing the mind from its fantastic journey of self-discovery and introspection. Each rational moment was one filled with wonder and astonishment as individuals were led to experience their destinies along their paths of fate. Disciples were exposed to the unlimited potential of the spirit and yet there was always a threshold, a limit to the lessons learnt. Only by returning to this place of sanctity, were participants able to navigate swiftly across the familiar terrain and explore the next level of intellect. With each return, came a deeper understanding of the truth. A teacher with infinite lessons to teach. It was a journey experienced by few, but those that chose to open their minds to this higher calling became changed forever.

There were many spiritual entities in this place. Some were helpful guides while others were reflections of the physical world; tree spirits and animal spectres imparting their eternal knowledge of the ancient world. Visitors to this place did so at their own risk and were fully aware of the dangers. Others sat serenely meditating, equally aware of their physical environment as well as their spiritual pathways into the ether. In this state, the objective was simply to disconnect from the physical and then reconnect with the mystical and divine. To rewire the brain into a state of exchange with the tree of knowledge, a transcendent experience that was unique for each and every explorer.

This session had almost expired. A ripple of chords between the physical body and its spirit, quivered in the space between spaces; a sign that the reunification of body and spirit had begun its course, the effects of the potion beginning to wear thin, gradually bringing the five senses back to the body. The return was always juxtaposed between feelings of elation and desolation. Elation because the spirit began to feel the bond with the physical body and longed to be reunited with it. Desolation because the spirit was forced to leave a world of bliss and enlightenment, a place of discovery and adventure, only to return to a more mundane state of existence.

Just as mud is washed away after a heavy downpour, the spiritual web began to melt into the green of the forest. Sparkling sunlight flashed through the trees above, revealing a solitary figure lying motionless on the ground below, lethargically absorbing the energy of his surroundings like a newborn baby into the world. The man felt as if he was experiencing things for the first time, the flit of a bird through the treetops, the call of a monkey not too far away. The colours of the forest were as vivid as an oil painting in bright sunlight. They melted into one another, bringing streaming tears of joy to his eyes. He smiled and began to feel his body as it came to life, albeit sluggishly. He rolled over onto his belly and then pushed himself up against a tall, sturdy tree, dropping his head back to look up at the canopy above.

Doctor David Steel felt aware. And he felt good about it. He thought not to question whether what he did was good or bad; he just felt that the awareness he experienced was an extension of goodness, nothing more, nothing less. There was simply no room for anything else other than goodness. He felt calm with this awareness, a serenity and peace of mind which further led him to believe, with his deepest faith, that what he felt was good and that he was only capable of projecting goodness in this state. This newfound awareness brought with it a reflection of character like a mirror of acceptance that allowed him to see his faults, accept them and then watch them simply melt away. He felt transformed, reborn, where each waking moment was like an eternity of bliss. He couldn't imagine anything else. There was no room for doubt or self-pity, no time for burden or encumbrance on this journey, in this new world of wonder and appreciation for life.

There was movement in the dense jungle where there shouldn't have been. Silhouettes against the trees shifted from beyond into the dimension of now. The invisible tribe magically materialised from a place in between the shadows and the bands of light filtering down through the vast canopy above. They were Yusca, a secret tribe of Indians living deep in the Colombian rainforest. They were the unseen, blending into the environment like camouflaged chameleons, stealing through the greenery like slithering snakes, undetected and enigmatic. David looked up and into the painted face of Guru-Ak, the leader of the tribe. He smiled and touched his index and middle fingers to his lips, indicating that it was time to eat. David nodded his head, returned the smile and stood up to follow Guru-Ak and the rest of the group through the forest and back to camp.

CHAPTER THIRTY-EIGHT

Yusca

It was almost a year ago that David had decided to go on an expedition that would take him through the Río Puré National Park in Colombia and on to the rain-forests of Brazil. It was a journey that had begun with his fascination of people and cultures that had led him to complete his doctorate in anthropology at the Michigan State University. He became fascinated with the work of controversial anthropologist, Doctor Bruce Carli, an alumni of the University, graduating in the 60's, under the tutelage of Leslie Black. Carli was famous for his fieldwork with the Aoti, a tribe of indigenous Amazonians living in the Brazilian rainforest. He spent several years living with these people, learning about their customs, beliefs and social behaviour. His findings were published in an ethnography entitled Aoti, The Noble Savages that is still in use today as part of the Anthropology syllabus in many universities around the world.

The Río Puré National Park in Colombia was where David was first introduced to the Colombian National Parks service, a conservation group working to safeguard the indigenous tribes in the area. The Rio Puré protects a million hectares of unspoilt rainforest between the Caquetá and Putumayo River basins along the Brazilian border. The park was set up by the Colombian government to protect these isolated tribes. It is suspected that there are only a handful of tribes still living in this area that have never been exposed to life outside of the forest. David's first field survey took him deep into the park, where he spent three months with the Yusca tribe. The Yuca were a group of previously undiscovered Indians that were exposed to the world by the National Park Service in a series of photographs designed to alert the Colombian government to boost their protection from armed guerrilla groups and illegal tree fellers in the area.

It was here that David learnt about the spiritual connection that the Yusca had with the forest and the life that it contained. Just six weeks into his field survey and he found himself being swathed in the thick brown mud of the river bordering their village. He closed his eyes as he stood knee-deep in the water while a young female tribe member covered his body until he was completely concealed beneath the oozing sludge. The soggy mud was heavy and uncomfortable but was also a cool and relaxing respite from the humidity of the forest. The girl began painting his face red with urucum dye from the achiote tree, humming a sweet melody as she worked. The small red seeds from the fruit of the tree were crushed into a powder and then mixed with a little water to form a thick, red paste. The body paint was a mandatory undertaking for the spirits of the rainforest forest first to recognise and then protect the initiate during the awakening ceremony. Even before the commencement of the ceremony, David felt detached and isolated, concealed beneath the body paint, as it dried to form an outer, protective layer.

Guru-Ak, a friendly, congenial tribe member, with a rudimentary command of the English language, had taken upon himself to teach David the tribal customs and ancient traditions of the Yusca. Thwack, thwack. He hit his left forearm with two fingers of his right. "Paint like protective armour of armadillo," he said. "It symbolise shield, barrier, created to protect inner being." He pounded his chest like an ape. "On its journey through spirit world."

Guru-Ak was a disciple of the great shaman of the Yusca tribe. He was a typical Amazonian Indian with thick, black hair, cut short into a straight line, high across his forehead. His skin was an olive brown, and he was scantily clad in a thong just covering his genitals. At just under five foot in height, Guru-Ak was short in stature compared to most Europeans, but pretty average compared to the rest of his tribe. He carried a big smile whenever he saw David, in awe of his bodily hair and towering frame. This time, though, Guru-Ak approached David with a sombre look on his face. He signalled for David to follow him into the forest where the initiation ceremony was scheduled to take place. Guru-Ak walked up to a huge tree in the middle of a clearing about two miles from the village. He stopped, turned around and came to sit at the foot of the tree, the broad trunk expanding out like a giant wall of bark behind him. David looked up and marvelled at the height of the tree, its branches towering high above the other trees in the area, creating a green, protective blanket overhead. Guru-Ak extended his left hand, beckoning David to sit down in front of him.

As David closed his eyes, he remembered the story of the Dreaming Tree, recounted to him by one of his university professors who had first introduced him to the Yusca. The story told of a young boy called Ptelomi from the Yusca tribe that stumbled upon an ancient tree in the jungle while he was hunting one day. He found a spider monkey, an anaconda and even a jaguar fast asleep at its base. As he approached the tree, stepping carefully between the animals, he began to feel drowsy. He fought to keep his eyes open and then before he knew it, he had collapsed in a heap, sound asleep beneath the massive trunk. He began to dream. He dreamt of the forest and the big tree beneath which he slept. He watched from above as he left his body to rise into the boughs of the tree, soaring up through its branches, breaking out of the canopy of the forest and up into the night sky. The moon was full and on display for the world to see, generously lighting the sky with her brilliance. Ptelomi looked down on the forest below, the light from the moon illuminating the tops of the trees as far as the eye could see. He felt like a night owl, drawn to the light of the mesmerising celestial orb in the evening sky. He graciously sailed down and back through the forest canopy, to land softly on a branch of the Dreaming Tree. He gazed inquisitively at his body lying motionless below.

A man appeared next to him. He wore the skin of a jaguar, black as silk. "My name is Sonei-Ra, the Jaguar Man." Ptelomi listened to him as he spoke, his mesmerising words spinning stories of forgotten lands and magical creatures. When he awoke, the sun was rising, and all the animals were gone. He ran back to his village, wolfed down some hot broth before returning to the tree for another session of dreamlike bliss and philosophical teachings. This went on for a few weeks until Jaguar Man spoke to him with concern in his voice. "If you continue to visit me as frequently as you have done, you will damage your physical body, lose yourself altogether and never be able to return to the world of the living. You must resist the tree's spellbinding influence," he told Ptelomi. "And take care of your body lying asleep under the tree, by building up your strength, before returning to the world of the spirits." Ptelomi had to exercise all of his resolve to resist the calling of the tree. A siren singing a hypnotic melody, pulling him into the very deepest of sleeps.

One day while wandering through the lands of the Dreaming Tree, Ptelomi spotted a young man covered in blood and crawling painstakingly on his hands and knees. The man was very ill and malnourished. Ptelomi ran over to assist him, recognising him as Mokolai, from his tribe. He quickly pulled him up, threw one arm over his shoulder and helped him back to the village. He lay Mokolai down in his hut and then began touching him all over his body, breaking out into a rhythmic chanting song as taught to him by the Jaguar Man. Within moments, scores of tribesmen had surrounded them to see what the commotion was all about. The young afflicted man sat bolt-upright, let out a wail of intense agony and then collapsed

215

back down onto his bed. He slept through the rest of the night before waking in the morning completely healed and full of vigour. News of this incident spread and ailing tribes-people began arriving at Ptelomi's doorstep demanding treatment. He cured them simply through touch, quickly earning the reputation as one of the greatest shamans that ever lived.

Time passed, and news of the shaman's powers spread far and wide. One day, the Yusca village was attacked by a neighbouring tribe who grew jealous of Ptelomi's power. They came running into his tent, ready to kill him but instead, they found themselves in the midst of hundreds of snakes that tried to attack them. Ptelomi had predicted the incursion and had returned to the spirit world to seek solace with Jaguar Man away from the evils of humanity. He had become a very powerful magician and could move between the physical world and the spirit world with ease. Jaguar Man was pleased to see Ptelomi again after so many years. He told Ptelomi that he was happy he had used his powers in the interest of others and their challenges. He bestowed goodness upon Ptelomi and his people and told him to go back to his tribe and continue the good work that he was doing. Ptelomi returned to his village and began making beautiful ornaments and charms based on the fantastic visions he experienced in his dreams. He gave these creations to his patients and those that sought out his aid. The time came again when some of the members of his tribe grew jealous of his abilities and the things he made and plotted to kill him. Again, he predicted the strike and in an instant he had vanished into thin air, leaving his bewildered attackers with nothing but a deserted hut and a smoking hearth. The tribe's elders became very angry with the Yusca that had tried to slay Ptelomi. They relied on Ptelomi's healing powers to take care of the tribe's health and well-being and now he was gone. They banished the usurpers from the tribe, sending them into the forest to fend for themselves, never allowed to return again.

Today the Yusca believe that Ptelomi, the great and powerful shaman can still be found in the spirit world but only if a person with an honest heart seeks him out, filled with an abundance of love and gratitude. This story reminds members of the tribe to remain humble and free of ego and self-worth, to care for their fellow members and practice peaceful relations with other tribes they come into contact with. Many shamans have reported having met Jaguar Man in the spirit world after ingesting what they call teaching plants and then going to sleep under a large tree. Often it's with the intention of connecting to their ancestors and the animals of the forest to solve a problem or heal a cursed tribe member.

David opened his eyes as Guru-Ak handed him a smoking, sweet-smelling brew in a wooden goblet. "You must drink. Drink!"

The potion tasted bitter and slightly burnt and left a nauseating sensation in the back of his throat. It was ayahuasca, a powerful medicinal brew that had its origins in the Peruvian Amazon. David remembered studying this mystical potion. Ayahuasca has been in use for thousands of years, known to be administered by Amazonian shamans in over seventy tribes across the continent. "Aya" means spirit or ancestor in the indigenous Quechua language of South American Indians, while "Huesca" means vine or rope, indicating the spiritual, hallucinogenic properties of this ancient medicinal concoction.

David closed his eyes again as Guru-Ak began to chant softly, his hypnotic voice filling the silence like water rushing to fill an empty riverbed. David felt his body sway left to right like a snake, charmed by the song of its master. A tingling sensation began at the back of his skull and traversed down his spine. The thought of the snake gained substance in his mind until it came to life. He was a cobra, shedding its skin, the husk of his body melting away, his spine twisting and writhing, finally breaking free, extending up and twisting around the tree in front of him. The tree began to move, shifting, bending. He felt the entirety of the tree - he was fully aware of the organism, from the tips of its branches down to the ends of its roots, deep underground. He touched every fibre of the tree, feeling it gripping the earth to support its massive bulk above ground. He rippled down to its base and felt the earth open up like a yawning leviathan, swallowing him whole and spitting him out the other side. He had breached the spirit realm, riding the currents through the corridors of time and space like a swashbuckling pirate on a voyage of incredible discovery and extraordinary adventure.

The bile in his throat burned like a dollop of Tobasco. David tried to sit up, but his head reeled, and he collapsed onto the ground in a heap, his right cheek pressed into the soft soil of the earth. The side angle of the forest was surreal and fuzzy as he struggled to focus his gaze. His insides shifted. He arched his back and then heaved, spewing his guts out in front of him. His stomach muscles burned from the convulsions. He lost count as to how many times he had erupted since returning to the now. He never thought it would end until he was led groggily to the river and shoved into its depths. The river waters closed over his head and then there was silence. The voices in his head stopped and the sounds of the forest dissipated. It was, in an instant, a most unexpected event. David smiled. Refreshing water washed over him, cleansing and restoring his energy, clearing his bleary head from the haze of his dreamlike state. His body felt heavy and fatigued from his ordeal, as he dragged himself from the river. Despite the lethargy, he felt more aware and conscious than ever before. His blue eyes absorbed his surroundings like a sponge. Colours appeared more vibrant, and his ears pricked to sounds that were clearer than ever before. He understood the language of the forest - the wind rustling the leaves and bending the boughs of the trees. Conversations between monkeys interspersed with singing birds; a synchronised current of energy coursing through the Amazonian air. Everything was balanced, and he was part of nature's harmony. Sparkling stars fizzled in his periphery vision as he looked around; the last vestiges of his out-of-body experience fading into the beams of morning sunlight that pierced through the canopy of the forest around him.

As days turned to weeks and weeks to months, David became more and more accustomed to life in the Amazon rain-forest, his life in the concrete jungle a distant, almost forgotten memory. He took notes, daily, of his experiences with the Yusca, marvelling at their natural survival instincts in the dense, hostile jungle. He was particularly amazed at their resourcefulness in their ability to utilise everything around them to their advantage, leaving nothing to waste, preserving and conserving as much as they could as they lived their lives, hunting and foraging for food and sustenance. Despite the fact that the Yusca lived, for the most part, undisturbed in the jungle, there was still a feeling of apprehension and ambivalence in the air. David knew that it was natural for him to feel this way because he was far more aware of the potential threat of modern man on the Amazon and its plethora of life. However, there were times that he thought he could see fear in their eyes, fear of the unknown, fear of his mysterious world outside the forest.

"Guru-Ak," said David one day. "What is your understanding of the tribes in the big cities where I come from?"

Guru-Ak answered him most profoundly as he sat comfortably on his haunches, gazing up into the trees above. "Some time ago, Yusca shaman eat strong herbs then went to sleep under great tree for three days and three nights. He ate and drank nothing during this time. Nothing." He waved his hands as he spoke. "He woke from long, deep sleep and spoke to Yusca. He tell Yusca must talk to tribes in cities. He tell Yusca that Yusca must tell men to help Yusca protect forest and life in forest. Some men did listen and helped Yusca."

David realised that this was how the Colombian National Parks service was formed.

CHAPTER THIRTY-NINE

Aoti

"David! Camila!" shouted José. "Over here!"

José Parabalos was a member of FUNAI, the National Indian Foundation, the Brazilian government body that established and carried out policies relating to indigenous people in the Amazon. David turned and followed the sound of José's voice, as he hacked away at the jungle with his blade, carving a path towards him.

"What is it?" asked David. He stepped up to José and looked down at the ground for some kind of sign. Camila came running close behind him. José pointed at a feathered shaft of an arrow protruding from the side of a tree. David looked furtively around for some kind of activity, but José quickly reassured him.

"Don't worry; it's been here for some time. The sap around it has hardened. Look."

Sure enough, there was a hard, yellow, honeycomb-looking substance around the base of the arrow that was stuck in the tree.

"This must be their hunting ground," Camila said as she looked up into the treetops above them. Camila Ortiz was another agent of the FUNAI foundation. She was attractive, with long, dark hair, matching hazelnut eyes and bronze-coloured skin, typical of the native Brazilians. David often found himself mesmerised by her hair as it shimmered in the sun like liquid chocolate.

After another hour of trekking through the dense jungle, David looked up and rubbed his eyes. *Can't be. Those trees.* "Guys. Wait. Stop. The trees. Look."

The three travellers stopped and stared. At first, it looked as if a group of trees ahead shifted to the left until it became clear that a group of painted Indians had silently stepped out from behind them. Aoti warriors. They had peach-palm bows raised and stretched back, taut against sharp, dangerous-looking arrows ready to be fired. David threw his arms up into the air above his head and dropped down to his knees in a typically submissive gesture. José and Camila followed. One of the Aoti stepped forward and began to bind their hands behind their backs with a thick-looking type of vine. They were then marched on to the village and presented before the leader of the tribe. David breathed a sigh of relief when José started speaking Tupian, the native tongue of the Aoti, saving them from an early retirement. The Warriors started lowering their bows and arrows as he spoke and then the tribal leader approached José, placed one hand on his head and said a few words so that all could hear. José slowly reached inside his shirt pocket and produced a sugar coated fruit stick that he handed to the leader who gingerly took it from him. He peered at it, sniffed it hard and then took a menacing bite. He wolfed down the rest in a heartbeat, hardly chewing the sweet, fruity surprise. He turned to look at José with a grin and slapped him on the back, shouting something that sounded as if he were amused. The rest of the tribe erupted in response, laughing and cajoling with each other excitedly. There was a bit of banter back and forth and then the tribe began to sing, rocking in unison to their own staccato beat, the sound of a drum beating out a methodical thud that reverberated through the forest like a wave. *Boom, boom, boom!*

David, Camila and José remained with the Aoti for several

months, learning about their culture, habits and belief system. At first, they were the centre of attention - the Aoti prodded and poked them, fascinated by their pale skin and unusual body hair. As time wore on, they were left alone to fend for themselves, forage for food or join the men on a hunt. David and José sat back-to-back while the women painted their bodies in a ritual that was practised by the Indians ahead of each and every hunt. The warriors' bodies were painted so that the jungle should protect and conceal them from being seen by their prey. They also believed that to become the hunter; each warrior had to be transformed through ceremonial body paint into a creature of the forest, identifying and then actually connecting with the flow of energy inherent in every living thing. As they left the village to go on their first hunt, David couldn't help but notice how the Aoti could perfectly mimic the sound of the jungle animals. At first, he thought that his ears were playing tricks on him until he realised that the Indians were trying to elicit a response from the animals that they were hunting.

The troupe of hunters picked up the pace, running through the forest, sidestepping trees and brushing away vines as they ran. David looked down and at his bare feet and then across at José running alongside him and smiled, feeling exhilarated and energised as he ran carefree through the jungle. He looked ahead and realised they were beginning to lose ground to the smaller, more agile warriors. He squinted his eyes, trying to follow them as they darted between the trees ahead like a school of dolphin, riding the forest currents that only they could feel. David almost collided with one of the warriors as he ducked under a low-hanging branch. The Aoti was crouching low, bow and arrow at the ready while making soft grunting sounds in the direction of a group of wild boars gathered in a small clearing ahead. As quickly as they had all been running, the group had become completely silent, squatting down and slowly taking aim with their bows and arrows. The pungent waft of animal faeces hit David's nostrils. He blanched, struggling to hold back his breakfast.

Thwwwt! Thwwwt! Thwwwt! The Warriors let their arrows fly. It all happened so quickly. The boar began honking loudly as their fear turned to panic when the arrows found their mark. This sent the rest of the herd stampeding into the forest in a multitude of directions. The warriors let out a victorious battle cry and charged into the forest after them. David was holding a long Aoti spear aloft, shouting at the top of his lungs as he ran vigorously into the forest, chasing down one of the boars.

It was just a short while later that David was out of breath. The adrenalin rush of the hunt had taken him on a powerful chase through the jungle until it was his body that told him that it could go no further. His lungs burned. He stood, bent over, hands resting on his thighs, arms locked straight for support, head hanging, vigorously sucking in the forest air. He slowly straightened and looked around. Rivulets of perspiration rolled begrudgingly across his forehead and down to the tip of his nose. The sounds of the forest echoed around him. The boars were nowhere in sight. He heard a wail and then another shout somewhere to his left. He began walking vigilantly ahead, looking out for signs of movement from the bushes around him. He looked up instinctively, and a pair of yellow glowing eyes stared straight back at him. He froze. An uncomfortable tingling sensation bristled across his scalp. A black jaguar was perched precariously on a tree branch about eight feet above him. He looked quickly away, for fear of startling this magnificent creature. He had heard of several stories where Jaguars had killed for less.

His heart beat like a drum through his chest, calling all the forest animals to action. His fear caused him to look up again at the menacing animal. It bared its razor-sharp teeth in a ferocious grin. He began slowly edging backwards while maintaining eye contact with the wild creature. The jaguar moved. David turned and ran without looking back. There was a loud snarl and the hair at the back of his neck stood up.

This is it. I'm done for.

Visions of being mauled by the black cat deep in the forest

flashed through his mind. He heard a yelp and turned back to witness a black shape gliding through the air with the tip of an arrow shaft protruding from its side. A small and sprightly Aoti hunter came skipping animatedly through the bush, stealing a glance at David before running over to his kill. Within moments, he had cut the creature open, spilt its guts and hoisted the carcas over his shoulders.

He approached David, looking up into his eyes with a grin. He beat his chest with his left hand. "Turu,Turu..."

CHAPTER FORTY

Camilla

It was nearing the end of their sixth month with the Aoti Things were going well. The trio felt very much a part of their culture. Their command of the Aoti language was proficient enough that they could hold a conversation with them quite easily, as long as they spoke slowly and used their hands to explain further what it was they were trying to elucidate. As the days and weeks passed, they began to feel that they contributed to the tribe and its welfare, taking part in the hunting and gathering process on a daily basis. And then one morning Camila woke with a fever.

"Good grief, Camila! You look dreadful," said José, greatly concerned.

Camila had rings around her eyes, and her face was pale as a sheet. "Yeah, not feeling that well. My head feels like it wants to explode and my vision is blurry."

"Maybe you were bitten by something?" suggested David, scanning her body, grabbing her arms, twisting them out, looking at her legs and around the base of her neck.

"Or it could have been something you ate?" said José.

"I'm going to call Turu," said David. He dashed out of the hut to find him. Within moments, Turu arrived. The tribal leader wore a leather thong and carried a quiver with several fletched arrows on his back. He approached Camila and did another physical examination, looking into her eyes and pinching her a couple of times. He grabbed her wrist and pulled her out of the hut in a hurry.

"Hey!" shouted David as he ran after them. "Where are you taking her? What's wrong with her?" Turu just ignored him as he dragged Camila up and away from their hut. David and José ran after them, shouting on deaf ears. Turu marched up the path towards the shaman's hut. José and David looked at each other. It had to be serious otherwise why the shaman? By the time that they reached the hut, Camila had been placed on a low, narrow bed with an animal skin stretched taut over its frame. She seemed to be in a daze, muttering incoherently and rolling her head from side to side. David turned to Turu and asked again. "What's wrong with her?"

Turu looked up at David this time and replied. "Jungle fever. Shaman will fix." He pointed at the solitary figure sitting silently in the corner. The shaman was a reclusive character who seldom left the confines of his hut. He was both feared and revered by the members of the tribe who solicited his services for healing as well as for dark magic, required to fight enemies and those that sought to do the tribe harm. He stood up and came over to look at Camila. He turned to Turu and whispered something in his ear. "Come," Turu said sternly. "We must leave hut so shaman can work magic." Turu walked out of the hut, beckoning the others to follow. José and David followed him out but not before David turned back to catch a glimpse at Camila still writhing in agony. José kept trying to illicit some kind of coherent response from Turu as they walked back down to the tribe's central area but he just shook his head and waved his arms about, shooing José away as if he were an irksome mosquito.

"She looks dangerously ill," said José.

David nodded his head in agreement. "I think we need to get outside help. Like a western doctor or something."

"Yes. I'll go."

"I'll come with you."

"No. You need to stay with Camila in case she wakes up. I don't want her left here alone." José began packing his bag, grabbing necessities for his journey back to civilisation. The nearest town was over thirty miles away so he threw in a water-skin and enough food for a few days travel.

"Safe journey my friend," David said as he embraced José. They gave each other a firm hug and a pat on each other's backs. The children from the village followed José all the way into the jungle even after he disappeared and only came running back much later that afternoon.

David sat gazing out at the river, contemplating Camila's uncertain fate. He prayed that she'd recover from her malady. She was young, just 26 years old, and came from the small town of Embu in the state of São Paulo. Her family was tragically killed eight years back by a militant gang. They were on a family camping weekend, on the outskirts of the Amazon, just south of Manaus. Camila was only 18 when she and her older brother, Bruno, decided to go down to the nearby river for a swim early one morning. They returned to shouts and screams from their camp, only to find everything burning and both their parents and younger sister dead. The surviving members told of a gang of soldiers that stormed through their campsite, shouting and shooting their guns into the air. One of the gang members grabbed a jerry can of gasoline and began dumping it on the smouldering fire. Soon, the fire spread to Camila's family tent. Larissa, Camila's younger sister, came running out of the tent, screaming at the top of her lungs. She stabbed the soldier in the leg with a small, sharp hunting knife. He retaliated, by opening fire with his machine gun, instantly killing her at his feet. Bullets sprayed into the tent where her parents lay fast asleep. The tent continued to burn. No one came out. The soldiers ran off into the jungle, never to be seen again. Days later, there was a report of an Indian hunting party of seven that were brutally murdered in the same area. The authorities found evidence of guerrilla activity. Camila knew that it was the same group that killed her family. She vowed to find them one day and make them pay for what they had done. It was then that she decided to devote her life to protecting the Amazon from these and other groups that threatened to destroy it and all that it represented.

David walked back up to the shaman's hut to check on Camila. The shaman shook a handful of smoking reeds over Camila's head, filling the hut with thick, clogging smoke. He chanted loudly and swayed his body from side to side, shuffling around her still figure. David's eyes started burning from the smoke so he stepped outside and took a deep breath of fresh air. Turu was there to meet him.

"We must prepare," he said, pointing to the shaman's hut.

"Prepare for what?" enquired David, frowning.

"The journey down and battle to follow. We must fight. Fight bad spells, fight sickness," replied Turu with a serious look on his face.

David wasn't quite sure what Turu meant. He sensed David's confusion so he began to explain further.

"We take medicine." He pointed at David then at himself. "We go down." He pointed down into the ground. "We find poison and fight back." He repeated a flicking motion several times with his hands, twisting them out and then away from his body as if he was expelling a foul energy. David felt a nauseatingly anxious feeling wash over him as he began to understand what it was Turu was trying to say. David's first spiritual experience with the Yusca tribe was a personal, introspective journey of self-discovery. The mission that Turu described was very different and something that David had read about but never experienced. David was to join Turu, Camila and the shaman in a spiritual practice designed to find the source of the illness inflicting Camila and eliminate it in the spiritual realm through the administration of Ayahuasca. David had learnt that shamans often used Ayahuasca to heal or cure their patients of physical, mental or spiritual disease.

228

Experienced shamans were able to journey with their patients into the spiritual realm to find the cause or root of an illness to cleanse the soul and rid it of the malady. In other instances, shamans communicated with the spirits of the forest to find answers to tribal disputes or solve more intricate problems for their patients.

"Come," Turu said. "We go."

Turu entered the hut. David followed. The smoke had dissipated somewhat, but it was still quite thick, hanging in the ceiling like a coagulating cloud of vapour, threatening to drop down and engulf its prey without warning. The shaman was mixing the Ayahuasca brew over a fire in the corner. Turu signalled for David to sit on a wooden bench next to Camila. Turu sat next to him, closed his eyes and began to chant. There must have been a mild stimulant in the smoke because as soon as David closed his eyes, his head began to spin. Soon he heard the shaman join in on the chanting, which went on for some time. Camila was still moaning as she lay on the skin-covered bed. The chanting stopped, and David opened his eyes. He watched as the shaman propped Camila up with his left hand and then began feeding her the Ayahuasca concoction from a wooden beaker. She started drinking, albeit slowly, until she finished her share. He gently lowered her back down onto the bed. The shaman refilled the beaker from the pot and passed it on to Turu who in turn passed it to David. The brew was thick and grainy and tasted pungently bitter like burnt bile. He gulped it down, trying not to gag. He passed the beaker back to Turu who went over to the pot to refill it for himself before passing it on to the shaman.

David closed his eyes again while the shaman began shaking his leaf rattle and singing spirit songs. Minutes passed, and nothing happened. Then it started. Geometric shapes began oozing into his vision. He opened his eyes, and the shapes were still there. They were all over the hut, shifting silently across the walls and all over the ceiling like an army of ants in search of food to feed their colony. This first vision signalled the opening of his third eye and the connection to a multitude of dimensional realities. The geometric shapes began to glow and change colour. A flood of emotion washed over him as the colours became more vivid, glowing brightly, pulsing like a heartbeat in a magnificent rainbow arcing through the heavens. Tears streamed from his eyes as the sheer beauty of the experience caused his senses to overflow with intensity.

A warm tingling sensation began to build in his feet. He looked down and watched, as a shimmering green vine began to wrap itself gradually around his ankles, moving up and around both his legs, pinning them tightly together. It felt as if his legs had fused together into one solid mass like the trunk of a sturdy oak tree. The sensation extended up into his arms that became boughs and branches and spread back down through his legs and into the ground that became roots to support his colossal trunk. He became the tree, stretching up towards the light and down into the dank, damp, darkness. Swelling, swallowing, subjugating. A magnetic force pulled him down through the tree until he shot through and out its very roots, deep beneath the earth. Faster and faster he descended, darker and more oppressive became the blackness. And then from out of the darkness, it came, and he was vulnerable. His worst nightmares come to life. No matter how hard he tried, he could not shut his eyes to the barrage of horrific images that threatened to tear his eyes from their sockets. His eardrums exploded in excruciating pain, to a high-pitched scream that came from his mouth. Spineless serpents with enormous fork-tipped tongues lashed his back, drawing blood and sinew, spraying it across his face and blurring his vision, causing him to stumble around blindly in pain and agony.

And then he felt a swelling pressure beneath him that pushed him up and away from the darkness and pain. He instinctively knew that Turu and the shaman were there, guiding his uninitiated spirit to a place of solace and safety. The pressure subsided. He looked around, and he found himself floating in a surrealistic, dream-like bubble. The very air around him felt weird, different, like it was alive and moving, flowing in and out of his body of its own accord. At first, it felt like someone was tickling his eyelids. This was followed by the sensation of a torch being waved across his face. Tiny beams of light struggled to tear open his eyes as his feet touched down on a solid surface. He strained to open his eyes, bringing his hand up to protect them from the sudden brightness that ensued. He looked around. Turu and the Shaman were standing in front of him, smiling cheerfully. They were glowing as if they had immersed themselves in a pool of luminous liquid. They signalled for David to follow, as they turned and began moving ahead. Their glowing auras rearranged themselves, tapering off behind them, to form a radiant vapour trail that melted into the cloudy surroundings as they moved. David glided along behind them, watching the silhouettes of gigantic serpent-like shapes, writhe and slither beyond the hazy veil, threatening to breach the insubstantial barrier that divided them.

David looked ahead and caught a glimpse of an orange, glowing light on the horizon. Everything appeared to be moving in slow motion, and yet the time it took for them to reach the light source, seemed unusually quick. He noticed a solitary figure lying in a horizontal position. It was Camila. She was resting at waist height, on a glowing, spongy surface. Hues of orange light throbbed eerily through the sponge, lighting up the surroundings in warm, welcoming waves of colour. The orange light reflected off the enveloping fog, cocooning them inside like a group of caterpillars, getting ready for a symbolic metamorphosis into creatures of beauty. David glimpsed something stir on her chest, so he moved in for a closer inspection. Hundreds of long, black wispy tendrils protruded from her body, waving through the air like seaweed in an underwater current. They spread from the top of her chest down, across her trunk, all the way to her lower abdomen. Her skin had a translucent, insubstantial appearance as if only part of her was present. She lay still, her eyes closed, her chest rising and falling peacefully.

David turned to look at Turu; consternation etched into his face. There was no speech in this spirit world, no way to shout across this misty, foreign landscape. Instead, there was a form of telepathy that could be described as something more than a feeling in your gut. It was an understanding that could not be put into words but rather an innate knowledge of the truth communicated and interpreted through an emotional response. Turu's mouth turned up into a smile in slow motion. He started making those flicking movements once again with his hands, but it looked like his hands were moving through water, much slower and somewhat distorted at the same time. And that was when it dawned on David. He knew about this type of treatment and how it worked. The tendrils represented the disease or sickness, embedded in the victim that had to be removed. The shaman's job was to source the root of the disease or affliction that often came in the form of a curse placed on the victim by an enemy. The shaman acted as a spiritual warrior, by removing the evil curse and shooting it in the form of darts or arrows back to its source. Unfortunately, there was no guarantee that this treatment would work. It was the shaman's magic against the power of the curse or ailment and sometimes the disease was stronger.

The shaman moved forward, placing both hands about two feet directly above Camila's chest, one on top of the other. The sinister tendrils responded to a magnetic current, all straining together in the direction of his hands. Turu placed his hands next to the Shaman's, cupping them together over the supernatural twisting strands protruding from Camila's body. David followed suit and watched as the tendrils began fusing together to form a thick column of dark, hideous matter, straining to reach the three pairs of hands hovering just above it. The Shaman began gradually lifting his hands up and away from Camila. David and Turu moved with him and the glistening column of pulsing dark energy followed. Camila's body began to lift up into the air, curving into an arc as resisting the extraction by the intrepid trio. She opened her mouth to scream, but nothing came out. Instead, David experienced a soft buzzing sound that began to build in volume and pressure the harder they pulled. The shaman looked at Turu and David and nodded. They all twisted their hands, flicking them out and away at the same time. The solid column of black energy surged and then exploded outward, transforming back into dozens of long tentacle-tendrils, shooting out and into the fog. The fog parted, shifting aside like a curtain, drawing back and away from the poisoned tendrils, allowing them to pass before floating back into place, closing the cocoon-like construction around its occupants once more.

David turned back to look at Camila. She lay still, her eyes closed, the spongy base beneath her still glowing softly, hues of orange light shifting and pulsing gently. Her body abruptly convulsed out of control, writhing around like a serpent. Turu and the Shaman moved in quickly to hold her down. They grabbed her limbs, but she continued to twist and shake around violently. The air around them started to crackle, and the light began to dim. Large, bulging shapes moved around just outside the cocoon and an uncomfortable pressure pressed in from all sides. Camila opened her eyes wide, and more black tendrils shot out of them, groping and probing the air for something to latch on to. It was obvious that the disease had not been completely expelled from her body. David moved forward to help Turu hold Camila's legs down. As soon as he touched her, there was a blinding flash, and then they were falling into a deep, dark chasm. The fog was gone. The orange light beneath Camila had faded. Dark shapes brushed past them as they fell, testing, nudging. David felt their cold, lifeless presence. It was as if he had stepped into a freezer, the coldness triggering a bone-chilling sensation that ran deep inside his body. He felt a sense of overwhelming despair as the darkness increased in density. His eyesight began to fade and panic set in. The ominous shapes brushed past him more frequently now as he lost sight of Turu and the Shaman. He opened his mouth to shout, but nothing came out. He could just make out Camila, but she looked lifeless and unmoving on the platform in front of him. The writhing tentacles were now sliding like slippery eels out of her eye-sockets and into her mouth, out of her nostrils and back into her eyes. She didn't budge. David grabbed her and shook her aggressively. Her head rolled to the side. She appeared to be completely lifeless.

David felt his back begin to burn. He guessed that the evil creatures beyond the barrier had broken through and were now carving him up into little digestible pieces. The burning started to warm his body. He turned to face his adversaries, accepting his death before it was too late to do so. He opened his eyes and experienced a powerful, glaring white light shining upon him from afar, projecting a warm and tender energy as it approached. The dark shapes began to retreat as the orb of glowing light floated closer, melting away the menacing clouds as it moved. He experienced a sense of incredible peace and love. He felt like a child, being embraced by its mother, secure and safe in her arms. He watched the light as it grew even brighter, searing his vision. Just before he closed his eyes to protect them from being blinded by the brilliant white light, he saw the shape of a solitary figure inside it. He felt another entity, and it wasn't Turu or the Shaman. A being of pure love and light entered his body and connected with his spirit in a very deep way, speaking to him inside his mind, reassuring him, comforting his thoughts, spreading positivity and warmth that radiated through every pore. He was guided by this entity, towards Camila, as she lay motionless on the slab right next to him. Even with his eyes closed, he could see and feel the entity leave his body and enter Camila's, radiating through her core, washing through her like molten lava, flowing up and down her arms and legs, back up into her chest and then her face, illuminating it for an instant with a soft glowing pulse of light. Turu and the Shaman appeared from the gloom. They looked weary and drained, their usual smiles replaced by deep-set frowns upon heavy, pallid faces. David imagined that they had returned from battling the spirits intent on harming Camila.

They looked down at her, their smiles returning to their faces when they saw that she was resting peacefully, free from the dark infection that threatened to take over her body just moments ago.

His knuckles were white as they gripped the edge of the bucket. Vomit spewed out of his mouth like it was under pressure, burning his throat as it discharged. Just when he thought there was nothing left but bile, he threw up again. Most ayahuasca experiences end in retching, a side effect that shamans believe is the final physical cleansing of the body after a soul-purifying hallucinogenic experience. David heard of reports of the spiritual malady expelling itself in the physical form of dead black worms or snakes. David rolled onto his back and lay there, staring up at the roof of the hut as the journey ended the way it started with kaleidoscopic, geometric patterns fading into the walls. He lay there for at least another half an hour before sitting up. He was parched. After a long, much-needed thirst-quencher, he slowly stood and made his way over to where Turu and the Shaman were tending to Camila. They had moved her to a more comfortable bed, and she appeared to be sleeping. The Shaman was shaking his rattle again and chanting his spirit songs. Turu stood close by, observing Camila's sleeping form. He had a curious look on his face, but David brushed it off as remnants of the trip he had just experienced. David was so exhausted; he couldn't even open his mouth to talk. He stumbled down to his hut, collapsed on top of his bed and passed out.

CHAPTER FORTY-ONE

Dream

It was midnight when David slowly opened his eyes from a deep, dreamless sleep. He was completely disorientated. He lay still on the bed for a few moments and allowed his thoughts to gradually clear and piece back together. He slowly sat up and went to get some water, before climbing back into his bed with a smile on his face.

The ground was soft. He was in a forest clearing that was different to any other he had experienced. He was trying to work out what made it different. It was a subtle distinction, yet it was there. He heard movement to his left and turned to see a rabbit in the grass. Wait. No. It wasn't a rabbit. It looked like a rabbit, but it had a long tail and tiny ears. It looked more like a cross between a rabbit and a baby kangaroo. It bounced away from David as he turned his head towards a steady breeze that brought with it the smell of the ocean. He closed his eyes and took a long, deep breath, drawing in the salty energy of the sea. It was a wild, sparkling energy that gave him a sense of freedom. He calmed his breathing to listen to the sound of waves crashing into the rocks somewhere down below. He filled his lungs again, held his breath, dropped his shoulders and then relaxed completely, sighing out in relief. He opened his eyes to a creature of beauty standing before him, her long chestnut hair blowing in the breeze and her bright green eyes sparkling like

236

the sun's setting light reflecting off the ocean, as it sank beneath the distant horizon. Her smile burned into his heart with a yearning so powerful that he gasped, more surprised at his instinctive reaction than anything else. She turned slowly, her hair flowing around her like the mane of a stallion, and started running towards the sun. David began running after her but for every step he took, it seemed that she took five. He traversed a rise and stopped to take in the magnificent view before him. He was standing on top of a mountain. Rolling grasslands interspersed with shrubbery and small trees covered the side of the mountain that dropped down for about three miles until it met the edge of an ocean that continued for as far as the eye could see. The girl was far away now. She glided over the ground as if she were flying. She reached the sea and then mysteriously disappeared.

David woke to the sound of a baby crying. He rubbed his eyes and it came back to him in a flash.

Those green eyes. Who was she? Where was that place?

After eating some fresh fruit, he made his way up to the Shaman's hut to check on Camila. Turu was there too.

"We give her sleeping medicine," said Turu. "She sleep now. She tired from fighting. Need energy for strength."

David nodded his head and walked down to the river. It was his favourite spot, a small, grassy knoll under the canopy of a beautiful tree. He sat down, closed his eyes and began consciously breathing, deeper and deeper with every breath. After twenty, slow, well-regulated breaths, he slowly stood up, straightened his legs, and reached his arms up high above his head. He spread out his fingers and stretched his entire frame up as hard as he could. He felt his shoulders lift up, and his spine extend, pulling his torso up and out of his hips. He brought his hands back together at his heart centre and slowly rolled forward and down to touch his toes. He placed his hands flat on the ground, lifted his left leg, stepped it back and then did the same with his right so that he was in an upright push-up position. He remained in this pose for a few moments longer before gently pushing back into a downward dog. He slowly peddled out his feet, one at a time, stretching his aching calves and taught hamstrings. The painful release felt good. He relaxed his head, closed his eyelids and pictured the sparkling green eyes of the girl with the chestnut hair and magical smile.

Following his yoga routine, David dived headfirst into the refreshing waters of the river. He floated on his back, gazing up at the sky beyond the canopy of trees alongside it and wondered when José would return with the doctor. He smiled when he imagined the look of surprise on José's face after seeing Camila healed and healthy. After a leisurely swim up and down the river a couple of times, David made his way back to the village and the Shaman's hut to check on Camila once more. She was awake.

"Camila, you don't know how happy I am to see that you've recovered," said David, beaming. "It's a miracle!"

Camila looked at David and smiled. She slowly sat upright on the bed inside the Shaman's hut.

Wow. She looks so incredibly beautiful. "How're you feeling?" asked David, concern mirrored his face.

Camila just looked at him and continued to smile.

"Camila? Are you OK? Can you hear me?"

For a moment she just sat there and stared. David thought she must still be in a daze from the sleeping potion, but then she nodded slowly in acknowledgement. "Oh thank goodness!" said David, relieved. He gave her a hug. She reciprocated but hesitatingly so. David released his hug and stepped back. "Do you remember anything that happened last night?" he said inquiringly.

She gazed back into his eyes, and he had a strange bilious sensation. A bright white light, a misty landscape, the feeling of falling... *Damn. That shit was strong.* He shook his head to clear the images from his mind. He stared at Camila. She smiled again and then lay down on the bed, closed her eyes and went back to sleep.

David spent the rest of the day making notes of his

ayahuasca experience. He kept going back to the girl in his dreams, closing his eyes to glimpse her golden hair blowing in the breeze and those eyes. He couldn't help but think that there was something very familiar about her - the way she looked right through him, touching his soul, stirring his heart in a strange, affectionate kind of way. Even though he kept telling himself that it was just a dream, probably the after-effects of his hallucinogenic experience, he imagined it to be real, reliving the fantasy over and over again. Later that evening, David lay alone in his hut, wondering when José would return. Meanwhile, Camila still lay in the Shaman's hut, building her energy and regaining her strength. Turu said that she would be better in the morning and strong enough to return to the village.

David stood beneath a huge volcanic peak. He looked up, and he was reminded of Mount Fuji with its telltale, lenticular cloud formation hovering directly above it. He slowly turned around and saw her again, just standing there on her own, her chestnut hair blowing freely in the breeze. His heart skipped a beat as he gazed into her piercing, green eyes. He opened his mouth to speak, but there were no words. He imagined the question in his mind.

Who are you?

I'm Mala.

Why are you here?

I have always been here. Gaia is my home. Come with me.

She turned and ran down the side of the mountain and into the forest below.

David started following her and then felt the very air around him start to vibrate like it was being compressed. His ears popped and this time, the ground itself shook beneath his feet. He turned to look back at the volcano as he ran. A plume of liquid lava erupted from inside the huge crater, cutting through the white circular cloud concealing its peak like it was melted butter. He lost sight of Mala as he ran blindly into the forest below the mountain. The air around him grew hot, as fiery raindrops began to fall from above, annihilating everything they touched, burning whole trees to cinder in a matter of moments.

Just as the sun's light graced the tops of the trees in the Aoti village, David awoke, drenched in sweat. He stood up and threw water on his face, before making his way back up to the Shaman's hut to check on Camila. To his surprise, there was no one there. He made his way down to the communal eating area and found Turu helping Camila to a breakfast of fruit and berries. Camila looked up at David and smiled.

"Good morning!" David smiled warmly. "You look great, Camila. How are you feeling?" Camila nodded her head. David's brow creased in confusion. "Turu, what's wrong with her? She hasn't said a word in two days?"

I'm fine. The words sounded like a whispering breeze, tickling the finest of hairs on his earlobes.

David's jaw dropped as he turned back to look at Camila. "How did you..." he faltered. "Who are..."

David's mind was racing. It cannot be. He closed his eyes, dropped his chin to his chest and exhaled deeply. *The dream. Mala.*

Yes. It is me.

"But how...?" David spoke out loud as he looked back up at Camila.

I am Mala. Camila is gone.

David froze for few moments, staring at Camila-Mala as if she was an apparition.

The bright white light. Who are you?

I am Lemurian.

Camila-Mala took David's hand in hers and began to walk out of the village and towards the river below.

David hadn't quite registered that he was conversing telepathically. He looked at Camila-Mala as they walked. *You're real.*

She smiled that magnificent smile. They continued walking through the forest without speaking, without thinking. As they neared the river, David noticed his spot and led Camila-Mala over to sit down under the trees overlooking the beautiful

240

waters below.

Can you talk? David brought his hand to his lips.

Not yet. I am still learning your language.

How is this possible? What is a Lemurian? Who are you? Why are you here?

David's anthropologist logic gave him a rear-ended wallop. He was confused, excited and flabbergasted all at the same time. He looked at his arm and pinched himself. The pain was real. He heard himself chuckle hysterically.

I am here because of you.

The words formed inside his head. He cast himself back to the ayahuasca experience. He went under to help Camila, to save her from the disease that was afflicting her, to rid her of the black poison that was implanted inside of her. He watched through closed eyes how the sickness was alive in her. How it took control and would not let go. He watched as he saw the virus writhe through her, breaking her, killing her. He watched as her head rolled to one side. He watched as she died there in that place. Her lifeless body cold and heavy. And then there was the heat, that warmth that came from behind him, feeding him, giving him hope, giving him strength. Did he will Camila to live by somehow summoning this entity? Was it he that motivated the spirit that was Mala to revive Camila? Is that what she was saying?

Close your eyes.

Camila-Mala stroked her hand over David's eyes. She kept her hand delicately touching his face and then the visions began without warning. He saw a tribe of people gathered around a towering stone pillar in an oval space amidst a lush, tropical forest. It felt like he was flying as the trip took him west across pristine white sandy beaches and over the shimmering deep blue sea. Then he was back, touching the treetops of the green forest below before climbing up and over a colossal volcanic peak. David smiled. It felt like he was really there, the sun on his back and the wind in his face.

David opened his eyes; his smile still glued to his face.

Lemuria.

Camila-Mala returned the smile and nodded in acknowledgement.

This was my home. Her face dropped. But it's gone. It's been long gone. Over 12,000 years ago we were a flourishing nation. My father, King Andor, ruled the seven lands. And my mother...

Camila-Mala looked up into the treetops above them, her face ashen. Tears began streaming out of her beautiful big brown eyes. David felt her pain, her anguish. He moved closer and wrapped his arm around her slender frame, hugging her reassuringly. She gently rested her head on his shoulder as they gazed out across the gently flowing river, losing themselves to the sound of water lapping against the sandy shore.

CHAPTER FORTY-TWO

Prophecy

David felt as though he was seeing the world anew. The more time that he spent with Camila-Mala, the more naive and guileless he became. It was like peeling back layer after layer of time and experience until he was but a child, ready to learn again, to absorb the lessons of life but from a far more radical and advanced perspective. He felt vulnerable, yet at the same time protected, like a hatchling by its mother, getting ready to fly from its nest into the great unknown. He gazed at Camila-Mala as she prepared a meal with the female members of the Aoti tribe, mesmerised by her mere existence right here, right now. He contemplated the significance of this manifestation, this visit by a 12,000-year-old spirit, from a world that she claimed had thrived and prospered for thousands of years before it sank beneath the watery depths of the Pacific so very long ago. Whatever this was and the significance thereof, it was a first as far as he knew. There was no doubt that she was genuine, of that he was certain. Her telepathic and clairvoyant abilities were so incredibly advanced, and she connected with David on a level so pure and genuine that her truth immortalised deep inside his very soul. He smiled as he watched her at work. She turned to look at him returning the smile as if she was reading his very thoughts.

Later that afternoon, David and Camila-Mala returned to sit

on the bank of the river below the village.

Where is Camila?

David looked at Camila-Mala as he transmitted his thoughts. He was still unsure how he was able to perform this ability. It felt like a flower was beginning to bloom inside his mind. He attributed this to Camila-Mala's facilitation as the task became easier each time he conversed with her this way.

She turned to gaze up into the clear blue sky before answering him.

She has left us. She has returned to the Creator to begin her journey again. She turned to face David. I have come here in her place to teach you.

To teach me what? Responded David, puzzled.

Her piercing brown eyes twinkled as he became captivated by their infinite profundity.

The truth, she replied, with a smile on her face.

David turned away thought back to the time before Camila became ill. She was a determined young lady, focused on her work and hardened by her tragic experience in the jungle. There had been a couple of times that David had been turned on by her physical attributes, but they had been fleeting experiences that were eclipsed by her indifferent and hard-hearted attitude to almost everything she did. Camila was gone, replaced by a very different entity altogether. He closed his eyes and David visualised the girl with the sparkling green eyes and chestnut hair in his dreams. He opened his eyes and looked at the body that was Camila but the spirit that was Mala.

Mala. She turned instinctively to look at David in acknowledgement. *"You are so beautiful. Inside and out."*

Mala smiled. *Thank you.* As her words formed in his mind, he felt a warm sensation wash over him that flowed up and into his cheeks. He clasped her hand in his and returned the feeling, imagining the flow of energy shift back into her body. It tickled the tips of his fingers and sent a quiver through his body. He was troubled by an anxious feeling that came over him. It was a desire to protect this exquisite creature from the scrutinising that would come from the real world, from society and

244

especially his ilk – the anthropologists and his professors back home. The logical part of him knew that this discovery was a groundbreaking find that just had to be shared with the scientific community, and yet he found himself emotionally caught up in his desire to safeguard Mala from invariably being turned into a laboratory experiment. David resolved to find out more about Mala and the secrets she harboured before making any rash decisions about her future. He brushed these thoughts from his mind as he took in her presence, allowing himself to bathe in her golden aura.

Feelings of contentment and happiness pulsed through his body as he sat with her, still holding her hand in his, alongside the gently flowing river. He watched as an Oropendola bird flew across the river and into its nest, a hanging construction of twigs and leaves suspended from a nearby tree. The crested Oropendola, a striking creature, with a pitch-black plumage and contrasting bright yellow beak and tail feathers, let out a high-pitched rasping call, as it settled into its home. And then Mala started to hum, softly at first, and then louder, as she settled into a delightful rhythm. She began to sway gently, left to right and David found himself joining in as they sat cross-legged on the soft, smooth earth. They turned to look at each other, smiling warmly. She shifted around to face him, taking his other hand in hers. She pulled herself up until she was standing on her knees. David followed. They looked into each other's eyes as they edged closer together until their noses were almost touching. He closed his eyes and slowly rolled his head to the right, moving even closer. He could feel her breath brush across his face like the breeze from the river below, soft and gentle. His lips found hers, and he felt his whole body tremble with trepidation. He was a teenager again, taking his first kiss. He gently pushed his tongue into her mouth as they connected. She tasted sweet and juicy like a watermelon. His head felt like it was going to explode with pleasure as the tender kiss sent a ripple of delight down into the pit of his stomach. It felt like it was going to last forever until Mala slowly dropped down onto her haunches, gently severing the connection between them. She grinned sheepishly, still holding David's hands in her own. David also dropped back, letting go of her hands and smiling hard in return.

That was incredible. Wow!

Mala's smile broadened. *We are connected, you and I. In the spirit realm, I saw you, I felt you, I entered you.*

Yes. I remember. I felt you too. Why…how did you find me?

I was summoned, woken from my slumber. The prophecy is almost upon us.

Prophecy?

The Lemurian Prophecy. It's an era that was preordained long before I was born; a sacred chronicle that was compiled at the dawn of time.

David's mind began to spin. *What's it all about?*

It tells of a time of great adversity for mankind. It also tells of the Lemurian people playing a role in overcoming this adversity to follow a different path that will bring the nations of the world together.

But the Lemurian people are no more.

Yes. The Lemurians perished during the great cataclysm but then the question beleaguers me — why am I here? I have been summoned by my ancestors, called forth to play a role in concluding this unfulfilled prophecy. My first task is to follow the path that will lead us to the Lemurian people.

OK. Where do we start?

Every moment has a purpose. The Creator's will makes it so. We start with you. You are very much a part of my purpose here as you were the conduit, my channel into this world. David was silent, too stunned to respond. *If it were not for you, I would not be here. Don't you see that the fate of this world rests on the fulfilment of the Prophecy of which you play an integral part?*

Yes, but… I am just a man…

Yes. A man who bravely fought to bring me into this world. A man who will lead me forth from this place to help me find my people and fulfil the Prophecy. This is your destiny, David Steel.

David contemplated her words burning into his mind like hot lava. *How could this be happening?* He was stunned by this disconcerting revelation. His scientific mind demanded proof, some kind of physical evidence, and yet he felt her words ring true, echoing across the echelons of time, reverberating with the sound of her voice chanting that ancient melody, sealing their fate together, forever. David tried to rationalise this narrative that swirled around in his mind. He felt as if he was alone on a vessel lost at sea, holding on for dear life as the wind buffeted the fragile craft this way and that. Mala took David's hand in hers, and he instantly felt the turmoil inside his head subside. The sun's rays broke through the dark grey clouds that began to clear, and the sea became calm and tranquil. He closed his eyes and experienced the same warmth he felt when Mala first appeared to him in the spirit world. He felt a calmness, a peaceful exuberance wash over him and everything became clear.

I have much to teach you. We will start at the beginning. Close your eyes and relax.

David closed his eyes, took a deep breath and exhaled forcefully through his mouth.

Now lie down.

Mala, still holding his hand, lay down next to David, the two of them stretched out on the grassy knoll next to the river. At first, it felt as though he was having another ayahuasca experience as speckled shapes drifted in and out of his vision and then he was standing in front of the giant volcanic peak he saw in his dreams with Mala by his side.

This is Mount Vexus. For time immemorial, this volcanic peak was a source of power for our tribe, the Lumniites and for many more Lemurian visitors to our village. Mount Vexus was one of the by-products of creation, a living, breathing life force that we Lemurians could tap into, allowing us to enhance our powers and extend the life of our physical bodies. Upon reaching adulthood, we ascended, coming into the full extent of our powers by immersing ourselves in the raw energy that flowed deep inside its core.

What was it like, this Ascension?

I don't really know. I only reached sixteen summers during my Lemurian lifetime and so did not have the opportunity to make Ascension.

The scene changed, and they were standing in a tribal village. In front of them was an imposing stone column that shot up into the sky.

This was our ceremony oval.

David picked up a hint of sorrow as Mala's words entered his mind. He turned to look at her standing next to him. A tear ran down her cheek as she looked up at the towering column in front of them.

We gathered here each morning to pay tribute to the creative forces that shaped our universe. I can still hear the beating drums that guided us on our journey into the heavens.

David stared at the stone column, picturing the Lumni tribe encircling the oval space in praise of the Creator. And then he saw them albeit briefly like a flash of light, a proud people, chins lifted, all eyes transfixed at the stone pillar in front of them. His head spun until he found himself standing on a beach in the moonlight, while a group of unusual looking people sang and danced around a fire.

This is the eve of the Lumniart Festival, one of my favourite events, held each year on Baybol Beach. Watch how my people dance around the fire and sing songs of love, joy and happiness.

As he studied the movements of these indigenous people, David observed many similarities to the Polynesian dancers of Hawaii. The multiple scenes that he experienced were so vivid that he felt he was truly there, living out these visions as if he had travelled back in time. He returned to the space beneath the tree by the river. Mala sat up and turned onto her side to face him.

Now keep still. Close your eyes. Relax.

She placed the fingers of her right hand against his left temple, opening her hand so that her thumb stretched across his face and over his nose until it came to rest on his opposite cheek. *Breathe,* she commanded softly.

I am opening your third eye. This is the first step of the Lemurian Awakening process.

When was your third eye opened?

248

All Lemurians were born with their third eyes already open to the world. Over time, this ability was apparently suppressed, and now I see you and your people have a very limited spiritual connection to the source of all things. You may feel some discomfort, but I will dampen this feeling as best as I can.

Mala began to access the inactive regions of David's brain, stimulating the synapses into action, connecting nerve endings and jolting the dormant areas like she was a doctor with a defibrillator. He could sense her probing, as he lay on the soft jungle earth. A pins-and-needles feeling tingled down one side of his face and continued all the way down his body until it reached the tips of his toes before flowing up again on the other side. He felt alive for the first time in his life as the sounds of the forest echoed inside his ears and the smells around him exploded inside his head like overpowering perfume. With heightened senses, he drank in the life around him like a parched tree in the Gobi desert. He felt a pressure inside his head like someone was pressing on his skull and then it was gone. He opened his eyes.

How are you feeling?

Fine.

He sat up and looked around. Everything seemed brighter and more vivid. The trees swaying in the breeze seemed to jump out at him like he was watching a 3D movie.

Great. Now I want you to sit up into a seated position.

David crossed his left leg over his right in half-lotus.

That's right. Now close your eyes.

Mala sat cross-legged directly opposite David. She took both his hands in hers.

The next lesson is going to be fun. Stay with me. Whatever you do, don't let go of my hands.

David felt a warm energy flow into his hands. Whatever Mala did, had made him hyper-aware of the energy not only inside him but also in the surrounding jungle and the life it contained. It felt like he was wearing a pair of infra-red night goggles. Even with his eyes closed he could see the auras of the trees and animals throbbing like orange glow sticks in a steamy New York night club. Mala's luminescent glow was bright and sparkly. It reminded him of the time he had first seen her in the spirit realm. She gripped his hands tightly and his stomach lurched as he was dragged rapidly up and away from the ground. He felt his inner spirit soar up and out of his body as it sat rooted to the earth below. He imagined his spirit as a magnificent kite flying high up into the heavens, attached by a golden thread to his body on the earth beneath him. He was free and unrestricted, soaring above the clouds like an eagle. Countless stars twinkled and flickered in the sky above, like a fleet of candles shining their lights across an endless sea. He journeyed with Mala on an interstellar voyage through space and time, across countless stars, galaxies and worlds of every size, shape and glorious colour, marvelling in their beauty and splendour as he passed them by.

This is how we pay homage to the Creator and His work.

They reached a powerful source of energy. A seething, churning thing of fire that was frightening yet wonderful at the same time.

The Sun, our Sun. The constant flow of energy for our planet and the life it contains. Come with me David and drink from the source.

Mala pulled David to her side as they floated in a dreamlike state in front of the fiery ball of energy. David felt Mala tense as he witnessed an arc of blue light shoot into the top of her head from the direction of the fiery body in front of them. He closed his eyes in anticipation of something momentous. The blue-light energy seeped gently into David's fingertips at first and then came in a torrent like a tidal wave of emotion, drowning out everything in its path. He felt like he had just tapped into an endless current of electricity that recharged every cell of his being. He laughed out loud, delighted with this new and exciting sensation.

Mala gave an instruction to the kite flyer to reel them back in. David felt a tug on the invisible thread, signalling an end to the awe-inspiring expedition into space. He was drawn reluctantly back to his physical body like a magnet.

Very good. You have mastered this part of the lesson, elucidated Mala.

David spent the rest of the afternoon becoming familiar with the universal life force energy and how it flowed and interacted with the plant and animal life of the forest. Mala taught him how to manipulate the energy, bending it to his will and cause it to manifest in the physical world after drawing it out of the spiritual. This was the hardest thing he had ever done. It took all of his concentration to get a leaf to lift up and float into the air. He watched it rise as if it were being supported by an invisible breeze before landing in the river and floating away. Perspiration radiated out of the pores on his forehead as he focused his intent and concentrated on the task at hand.

Mala was humming that familiar tune again, her angelic voice rising above the trickle of the river as David relaxed into a meditative state, breathing deeply, restoring his energy and the beat of his heart in his chest after the vigorous exercise. He blinked his eyes open as the light began to fade into dusk. He rolled onto his side and found that Mala had disappeared. He sat up slowly, rubbing his eyes, looking around for some sign of her until he spied her clothes lying by the side of the river. He cast his gaze up and caught her slender frame silhouetted against the glistening water in the sun's waning light. David felt his breath quicken, and his heart skip a beat as she turned and silently beckoned for him to join her. David looked around self-consciously for a moment before removing his clothes and stepping into the cool water. The soft mud beneath his feet oozed between his toes as he waded out towards her. Her long, dark hair hung loose and half-floated around her head as she watched David approach. She quickly and unexpectedly dipped below the surface for a moment before reappearing with closed eyes, her hands sweeping over her face and back over her head.

David moved slowly now, closer and closer. Time seemed to stand still as he hovered just inches away from Mala's face, examining her exquisite facial features, the cut of her jawline, the curve of her petite nose and the mesmerising intensity of her dark brown eyes boring into his very soul. She moved forward this time and found his mouth. He closed his eyes and delicately felt his way around her luscious lips, exploring their soft and delectable texture, his tongue connecting with hers in ecstatic pleasure. He felt himself back in the vastness of space, flying and soaring through the heavens with Mala by his side, as the stars flickered in recognition of his revelation. He felt a surge of energy as their kissing became more intense. He lifted his hands out of the water, gripping her shoulders, as a continuous flow of energy exchanged between them. Hands wrapped around his body, and she pulled him closer until they became intertwined like a pair of coupling dolphins frolicking in the ocean. David felt himself let go of all inhibition. Nothing else mattered. Two souls bonding as one, connecting on every level, uniting in harmony. David felt vulnerable as he let go, yet at the same time, safe and protected. He was at peace, happy and content. A permanent smile stretched across his face that shone like a beacon all the way through his body, warming it up from the inside out. He questioned this feeling, probing its purity, pushing against its outer layer, testing its resilience and authenticity, until he realised that he was falling in love.

CHAPTER FORTY-THREE

José

"David, David."

The voice was familiar. It came to him from afar, calling his name out, over and over again. He ran towards it, eager to hear what more it had to say. And then he woke, rubbing his eyes, struggling to open them after a long night's sleep.

"José! You made it back!" exclaimed David. He swung his legs off the bed and ran his hand through his hair.

"Yes, here I am, safe and sound!" said José. "David, this is Doctor Larisa Castro. She comes from the small town of Novo Airao."

"Hi, Larisa. David Steel. Pleased to meet you." David held out his hand, and Larisa reached out to shake it.

"Hello. Nice to meet you. Sorry for waking you." Larisa smiled warmly. She had olive skin and short-cropped auburn hair with soft grey streaks across her temples. "Where's Camila? How is she?"

"You won't believe it, but she is healed!"

"What? How?" said José in disbelief.

"It was the Shaman. He...he..." David was at a loss for words. "I don't know what he did, but he healed her." David's head was swimming. "Uh, but she's kinda lost her memory. And her speech."

"You mean she can't talk?" asked José. David nodded quickly.

"Does she know who you are?" asked Larisa.

"Um, yes but it took her some time to work this out." David was winging it. He hoped they were buying his story.

"Where is she?" asked José.

David looked at his bed and flashes of the evening's events moved through his mind caused him to falter. "Um, I…I'm not sure. Maybe she went to bathe in the river." He quickly turned away, his face hot and flushed. David stood up and pulled on his tunic. "Why don't you meet me in the village centre while I go and see if I can find her?"

"Sure no problem," replied José. "Come, Larisa, let me introduce you to the rest of the tribe. I'd also love some food. I'm starving!"

David marched quickly down to the river. "Mala!, Mala!"

Over here. Mala's voice was strong and direct, cutting through the clutter threatening to engulf David's head. She sensed his panic. *Relax. Breathe.* David opened his mouth to speak. "Shhhhh…" Mala place her finger on his lips. *I know. We must depart soon.*

Yes, but I told them that you lost your memory and could not speak. José has brought a doctor with him. Her name is Larisa Castro. She will need to examine you - you know, check your health. Don't resist this examination otherwise, things will just get more complicated. David saw a look of concern etch itself across Mala's face. *Don't worry; she's not going to hurt you.*

"I can speak now," said Mala. Her accent was odd. It sounded Portuguese but far more guttural than previously.

David's eyes widened in surprise. "You said you were learning our language, but I never knew that you'd grasp it so quickly!"

"Well, I've been practising."

"So how does the Lemurian language sound anyway?"

"Well, it sounds very different to English or any of the other modern languages you speak. It has thirty-six characters with a subset of another eighteen. When spoken properly, it is combined with telepathy to produce a form of communication that incorporates sound as well as spiritual intellect. Kind of like a double-layered language. Here let me show you... Griuk dormengo pristileos."

David couldn't understand the language but instantly felt the words begin to form images in his mind. He closed his eyes to see the imagery more clearly. "Food! You want food! You're hungry!"

"Correct!" replied Mala, excited at David's quick interpretation.

"Wow, that was freaky," said David. "I couldn't understand what you were actually saying, yet images of food formed in my mind and I felt my stomach ache in response. Incredible!"

"Yes," confirmed Mala. "We combine a visual, telepathic aspect together with the spoken word. This combination elucidates what we are trying to convey more clearly to the receiver."

"Amazing."

"During the Lemurian age, babies began communicating their needs at a very young age," continued Mala. "In fact, Lemurian mothers were able to understand what their babies wanted soon after they were born. The telepathy was always rudimental and their needs simple, but the imagery was there, and there was implicit understanding. So the telepathic communication always came first, followed by speech when they learnt to form words."

"And then they combined the two and voila!" David threw his hands in the air.

Mala smiled. "Yes. Exactly."

"This is remarkable. It's nothing like I've ever seen or heard of before, and I'm an anthropologist! This is the most phenomenal thing I've ever experienced. Ever! We are going to have to document this somehow. You must teach me this language. Imagine if we could re-establish it, bring it back. Oh my goodness." David's head spun. "Come, let's go and meet José and Camila. To avoid any confusion, let's stick to the story that you are Camila and you were healed by the Shaman of the Aoti."

"Camila! It's so good to see that you are well," said José as David and Mala arrived. "This is Doctor Larisa Castro. I travelled all the way to Novo Airao to find her. I was so worried about you. You were so sick."

Larisa stepped forward, extended her arm and smiled. "Lovely to meet you, Camila. Do you mind if I take a quick look at you, check your vitals and that sort of thing, you know…?"

"Sure, no problem, go right ahead," replied Mala. "It's good to see you too José; I'm feeling much better."

"You can talk?" said José, surprise in his voice. He turned to look at David, lifting his eyebrows and furrowing his brow questioningly. David shrugged his shoulders.

"Well, yes, I did lose my voice for some time, but now it's back! Thanks to David and the Shaman for taking care of me. I don't know what I would have done without them." She looked across at David, turning her mouth up into a warm smile.

"It really is incredible," said José "that you recovered so quickly. I was worried for your safety."

"Breathe in," instructed Larisa. She lifted the right side of Mala's top and pressed her stethoscope against her ribs.

"Yes. If it were not for the Shaman…" Mala's voice trailed off as she breathed in and at the same time, contemplated the harrowing experience she had to endure while attempting to enter back into physicality.

"Breathe out." Larisa had moved across to the other side of her body now.

"What exactly did the Shaman do to cure you of this dreadful malady?" asked José with intrigue.

"He used his power to wipe out the malicious virus that was attacking my body."

"Wow. That's incredible!" exclaimed José. "You know what this means, right? You experienced a healing ritual by a tribal shaman and you were cured! We have to document this and present our findings to FUNAI. I'd love to hear about your experience in more detail."

Mala glanced at David quickly before responding. "Well, yes, sure." Larisa was checking Mala's glands now, pressing gently into them as she moved from her neck, down and through the rest of her body.

"She's right, José," confirmed the Doc. "She's as fit as a fiddle. Whatever was affecting her must have been a virus because now there's no trace of it or whatever was troubling her. Stick out your tongue and say aaaahh!"

"Aaaaaaahhhhhh!"

Larisa peered down Mala's throat and examined her mouth. "All looks good to me," she said with a smile. "How do you feel, Camila?"

"Still a bit weak and groggy, but much better thanks."

"I'd like to check you again at the end of the day, just to be sure if that's OK?" asked Larisa.

"Yeah fine, no worries," replied Mala.

"David, I think it's time to head back to Meireles," said José. "We have been here long enough, and Camila's experience is a breakthrough that I'd like to document properly and investigate further. This can only be done back at the FUNAI head office. What do you think?"

David nodded his head. "Yes, I agree. Let's start getting our things together. I think we should leave at dawn tomorrow morning."

CHAPTER FORTY-FOUR

Pacific

Turu was visibly upset when he found out that the visitors were leaving the forest to go back to the big city. He hugged them over and over and shed tears of sorrow. He insisted that they stay for a feast in their honour and quickly coordinated the festivities with his tribe. A warrior party went out to hunt for surplus food, and the women of the tribe began preparing skirts made out of reeds and colourful flowers. The children collected the ingredients needed to mix different coloured paints that would be applied later that afternoon. Their youthful cries could be heard echoing around the perimeter of the village as they foraged for berries and plants in the forest. José and Larisa took an afternoon nap, leaving David and Mala alone to stroll through the forest.

"David, I need to ask you something," said Mala.

"Sure. What is it?"

"Is there anything left of Lemuria?"

"Um...no, I don't think so. You told me yourself that it sank beneath the sea over 12,000 years ago. What do you mean? Why are you asking me this?"

"Well, you see, I need to ascend. I need to enter inside a volcanic peak and come fully into my powers. I was only sixteen summers when I lost my life to the destruction of my home - not old enough to take Ascension yet."

"I see. There are many volcanic peaks all over the world. I'm sure we can find one for you." David smiled reassuringly.

"No," said Mala emphatically. "It needs to be Lemurian."

"I'm sorry. Don't think I can help you there, I'm afraid." David scratched his head. "Didn't you say Lemuria was in the Pacific Ocean?"

"Yes."

"Well, there's Easter Island. It has three volcanoes, and it's in the Pacific. Do you think that it could be a remnant of your lost continent?"

"Yes! Let's go there!" said Mala, pulling David's hand enthusiastically.

"Come to think of it; I don't think you can go inside them. They're all extinct. All that's left are craters and hard rock." A light flicked on inside David's head. *Hawaii. Yes, of course.*

"What's Hawaii?"

"Hawaii is a group of islands in the Northern Pacific Ocean with several active volcanos!"

We have to go there.

Yes, we will, he responded, visualising images of the islands as he transmitted his thoughts to Mala. She jumped into his arms, wrapped her legs around his torso and threw her head back laughing out loud in delight. David staggered backwards as he steadied himself, trying to keep his balance. He laughed with her, hugging her tightly as he did so.

That's uncanny, thought David quietly to himself. *Both Easter Island and Hawaii contain volcanoes, and both are in the Pacific. And then there's also the Ring of Fire, an area in the basin of the Pacific Ocean where a large number of earthquakes and volcanic eruptions take place.*

It felt like one of those times where the facts seemed just too indisputable to be coincidental.

The map was grubby but legible. David smoothed it out on the soft earth beneath the tree next to the river. The afternoon sun glinted across the water, reflecting its light on the beautiful creature lying next to him. He watched her, seeing beyond her physical body. There was a golden glow, an aura that shimmered around her as the sun's rays mingled with her energy, flowing in-between strands of gleaming, colourful hues. Mala carefully scrutinised the map, tracing her index finger carefully around the edge of each continent.

"This is where we are." David pointed at Brazil on the map. "And this is the Pacific Ocean and here is Hawaii."

"I can't believe that it's gone. All gone," she said with sadness in her voice.

"It just occurred to me that everything is going to be very foreign to you here, in this time," said David. "A lot has changed in 12,000 years. We have technology."

"What is technology?" asked Mala enquiringly.

"Well, basically it's the application of modern science in everyday life, and it's been advancing pretty quickly over the past couple of hundred years."

"OK. So gimme some examples? Why haven't I seen this technology?"

"Because we are in the jungle," replied David, "where tribes like the Aoti are cut off from society, from the rest of the world. There are over eight billion people on this planet right now."

"Whoa! Eight billion!?"

"Yes. And they live in colossal cities filled with tall buildings shooting up into the sky," said David, waving his hands about. "We travel by land, sea and air in great big machines and at super high speeds. We have conquered all the known lands across the world and even been to the moon." He pointed into the sky, and Mala smiled.

"But I have already taken you to see the stars and to bathe in the sun's powerful light," she retorted.

David turned to her and smiled. "Yes, you most certainly have, but we call that kind of travelling astral projection - when our spirits temporarily leave our physical bodies. But our kind of space travel is a little different. There are people we call astronauts that journey in big rocket ships out of the Earth's atmosphere and into deep space. Some have physically landed on the moon."

"Ah, OK, but for what purpose?" enquired Mala. "Why build these ships with rockets when you can just visit the moon and the stars from Earth like we did?"

David smiled. "Because modern man does not have the ability to do so. We do not have the powerful, extra-sensory abilities that you possess. It seems they were lost along with your continent so many years ago. Instead, man's innate desire to explore and progress turned us to science, the practical use of physical elements around us, as a means to conquer the known world."

"So out of these eight billion people on planet Earth, there is no one that can communicate the way I do?" asked Mala. "No one that can visit the stars and pay homage to the Creator of all living things?"

"There have been claims by some people over the years, but extra sensory perception is still a widely disputed phenomenon..."

Mala looked down, dejected. "Well, that's disappointing."

"The reason that I'm telling you all of this is because we're going to be leaving here soon. You're going to be exposed to modern society, and I need to prepare you for it. We're going to have to board an aeroplane, a great big metal flying ship with wings, to reach the islands of Hawaii." David turned the map over and pointed to an image of an aeroplane in the top corner, part of a travel logo printed on the map.

"We fly inside that?"

"Yeah. All the way across the ocean," said David.

"There's something else that I can do," said Mala. And with that, she quite simply disappeared.

David sat bolt upright. "Mala!" he cried. "Mala?"

"I'm over here!" she called. David stood up and looked around. Mala stepped out from behind a tree at least 150 feet away, waving both arms in the air.

"How the heck did you get over there?"

"I'm able to shorten the distance between two points and step through a kind of doorway to reach the other side," replied Mala, as she jogged back towards David.

David shook his head from side to side in disbelief. His mouth dropped open in astonishment. "But that's...that's impossible!"

Mala laughed out loud. "Nothing's impossible if you set your mind to it, David Steel."

David smiled. "So why can't we just step through a doorway to Hawaii?"

"Because I haven't been there before. You see, it's only accurate if I've visited a place before. Otherwise, we may just end up landing in the Ocean!"

"Mala, you cannot show anyone else these abilities," said David, his brow creased in concern. "Please, promise me. If you do, you will be in danger. People will want to exploit you. They will use science to find a way to extract your powers and duplicate them. You will be seriously harmed in the process, maybe even killed. You need to keep this a secret."

"But why would your people do such things to me? I wish them no harm."

"My people live in fear of the unknown. They have been using science for thousands of years to find ways to justify this fear. Every conceivable experiment has been made in the name of science. The end result is always the betterment of the human race, but this is a fallacy. Science and technology have been responsible for polluting the environment and the imbalance of nature. The world is sick and clogged up with the by-product of science. From plastics choking life in the sea to chemicals thinning the Earth's ozone layer, modern man is his own worst enemy. In the pursuit of progress and evolution, man is slowly destroying himself and everything around him."

"The Prophecy..." Mala whispered. "This is the great adversity that it speaks of. This is why I am here, David." She grabbed his hands and looked deep into his eyes. "We need to save this world. We need to restore the planet to its former beauty. This is the Creator's will and it is up to us to see it through."

Just then, a shrill sound echoed through the Jungle. "That's the signal for the start of the feast," said David, looking up towards the village. "Come let's go."

The Aoti pulled out all the stops. A great big fire was burning in the centre of the tribal enclave. Turu ushered David, Mala, José and Larisa to have their faces painted by the women of the tribe. Elaborate, feathered headdresses were attached to their heads and colourful beads around their necks. The drums beat a steady rhythm, and the Indians started singing. They stomped their feet in time to the beat, bobbing their heads in unison. Row upon row of Aoti warriors stepped forward, spears in their right hands and orange and yellow-striped shields in their left. They joined in the chanting, deliberately moving around the fire, shuffling their feet left, forward, right, then left, forward and right again like a giant centipede moving to a spellbinding beat. The women began singing in time to the drums' rhythm until all the sounds merged into a trance-like tune. David watched, as the flames leapt higher, crackling into the night sky like a blanket of orange and yellow silk, rippling in a ferocious wind, threatening to tear loose from its base. The children also painted with colourful designs, handed out wonderfully prepared platters of fresh fruit, vegetables and fish.

As the night wore on, the intensity of the rhythmic dance increased in tempo. The warriors pounded the earth with greater force that caused the dust beneath their feet to stir and rise into the clear night sky like an enchanted wanderlust veil, threatening to envelop the village and carry it away to some distant nirvana. A pipe was passed around the enclave. David took one hit and was instantly catapulted into a trance-induced utopia where he found himself gliding through the air like a bird, riding ballooning currents of warm air in an azure sky. The rest of the evening was a blur of dance, fire and chanting.

David's only vivid memory was seeing Mala's beautiful face, her radiating smile and her eyes. They flashed bright green in the light of the fire just as he saw them in his first dream of ancient Lemuria.

"David, David…" A voice pulled him from his deep slumber like an anchor being dragged from the ocean bottom, churning up the sediment, slowly cutting through the water like a heavy paperweight. He could feel the clunk-clunk of the heavy metal chain reverberating inside his head as he opened his eyes, the after effects of the evening's celebrations contributing, without remorse, to his throbbing headache. "Here, drink this." Mala fed him a sweet, hot brew that tasted like chai tea. He sipped it slowly, being careful not to burn his tongue. His stomach warmed up almost immediately, relaxing his tense muscles and softening his creased brow. He closed his eyes and lay down again for a few moments.

"Good morning! How's my Aoti warrior!?" bellowed José as he came marching into the hut.

"Uuuhh. You don't have to shout," replied David, clamping his hands to his ears.

José laughed out loud. "You were on top form last night, my man! You must've had three or four hits of that pipe. At one stage I thought that you were going to dive straight into the fire. I wouldn't be surprised if you singed every hair on your body!"

Mala laughed too. "At one point, I had to hold you down. You had so much energy!"

"I don't remember a thing," said David. "All I know is, my head hurts." He squeezed his eyes shut and rubbed them vigorously as if to wipe away the evening's series of events.

"I think we all have sore heads," said José. "But I guess yours is a little worse. Heh, heh. While you've been dozing, mister sleepyhead, we've been packing. Once that brew sorts you out, we can get going."

After saying their goodbyes, the four travellers set off into the dense jungle. A group of children, this time with several Aoti warriors in tow, walked with them for a few miles before turning back to disappear into the Amazon forest wilderness. After almost two days of trekking through the jungle, they arrived in Novo Airao, a small town of just over 15,000 inhabitants, located alongside the Rio Negro River, about 100 miles north-west of Manaus and home to Doctor Larisa Castro. The Novo Airao hospital was where they said their goodbyes to Larisa before catching a riverboat down to Manaus, the capital city of the state of Amazonas, with a population of almost two million people.

David found Mala sitting at the back of the boat staring mesmerisingly at the motors churning through the river water.

"How does this work?" she asked, clearly stunned by the powerful engines fuelling the vessel.

"This is part of science just as I told you," said David. "These are man-made devices called motors that power this craft through the water. Very strong metallic blades twist at high speeds pushing the water away from the boat, thereby creating a strong thrusting motion. The faster the blades spin, the faster the water is displaced and thrust out behind the boat."

"But what is their power source?"

"An oil called petroleum that is found underground. It is mined and then refined into a fuel that is ignited under pressure to produce energy," replied David. "This is how most modern engines work. Similar engines are used in ground vehicles or cars that you saw in Novo Airao. The flying ships that I spoke of, also use this kind of fuel, but it is used to power motors known as jet propulsion engines."

"This is wonderful!" said Mala beaming. "I love your world David Steel. It's so magical and enchanting!"

David regarded Mala and smiled. She was like a child in a fantasy world surrounded by a plethora of baffling phenomena that most people took for granted.

CHAPTER FORTY-FIVE

Airborne

The three and a half hour flight from Manaus to Fortaleza, home to the headquarters of the FUNAI Foundation, was not without incident. Mala, David and José were comfortably seated in the emergency exit row, when the air hostess came around to inform them about the emergency evacuation procedures. Mala clearly misunderstood her instructions because, at around ten minutes into the flight, the emergency seatbelt lights went out, she unclipped her belt, stood up and tried to open the door. José was sitting on the aisle, eyes closed and resting. David was reading the in-flight magazine. He almost jumped out of his seat when a woman behind him let out a panic-stricken shriek. "Aieee! ela abrir a porta!" (She's opening the door!)

David dropped the magazine and yanked Mala back down into her seat. José almost jumped out of his seat from the frightful yell. "What the hell are you doing?" said David in a tight-lipped whisper.

"She said I must open the door," replied Mala.

"Only in an emergency!" said David.

The air hostess appeared. "Is there a problem here sir? Madam?"

"No ma'am, no problem," said David. "My colleague here just thought that the door handle was loose."

The air hostess leant over the three of them and pushed on

the door handle lever to make sure it was secure.

"It seems fine, sir, don't worry," said the air hostess, loud enough for some of the other passengers to hear. "It's impossible to open an emergency door hatch during flight because the cabin pressure will not allow it." She turned back to Mala. "Please refrain from touching this door handle madam. Thank you."

The Boeing 747 touched down at the Pinto Martins–Fortaleza International Airport, amidst cold, wet conditions. Fortaleza is the capital of the state of Ceará and is situated in the North-east of Brazil alongside the Atlantic Ocean. The grey skies created a gloomy, melancholic atmosphere as the trio made their way to the FUNAI headquarters in Meireles, a suburb in Fortaleza along a beach-strip popular with tourists. José ordered a burger from the local eatery around the corner before meeting David and Mala in his office.

"Camila, how're you feeling?" enquired José. "You seem a little distant."

"I'm still a little a bit groggy, and my memory hasn't fully returned," replied Mala. "Even this place is unfamiliar like I'm in some sort of fog."

"Don't worry," said José. "I'm sure all you need is some R 'n R."

Mala looked at David quizzically.

"Yes, some rest and relaxation will do you wonders," piped David.

"OK now tell me," said José, "what you experienced in every sordid detail. I mean how did the Shaman cure you? What did he do to you?" José was excited as he leant forward eagerly, ready to hear Mala's intriguing story.

Mala looked across at David again and smiled. "Well, what I didn't tell you was that David played a part in saving me, rescuing me from the illness that threatened to take my life. It was surreal, the whole experience."

"What do you mean?"

"I mean we were all under the influence of ayahuasca so

things weren't as they seemed. The Shaman, together with Turu, the leader of the Aoti tribe, courageously battled the demons that sought to take me into the next world. And then David was there. He brought me back into the light. He saved me from the darkness that was intent on destroying my soul. I opened my eyes and immediately I knew that something was different. It was like I had woken up reborn. Somehow it felt as though I had a new purpose in this life and David was very much a part of it."

"Interesting," said José, making some notes in his book. David was surprised. Mala had pretty much stuck to the truth although there were many more hidden truths that she dare not share.

"David and I are going to Hawaii," said Maria matter-of-factly.

"Whaaat?" said José perplexed. "Whatever for? What about your work at FUNAI?"

"Like I said, I now have a new path to follow and it leads me across the Pacific Ocean." She looked at David, and he winked.

"OK, whatever you say, Miss Ortiz," replied José. "But before you leave, I want to hear all about the two of you."

David's mouth dropped open. "Wha…" Mala's face flushed a deep red.

"I'm not stupid. I have been watching the way you two have been looking at each other." Mala looked at David and smiled.

CHAPTER FORTY-SIX

Hawaii

David and Mala arrived exhausted at Hilo International Airport in Hawaii, after a long transit flight via Los Angeles. Hilo Airport is situated on the east side of the big island of Hawaii. It is one of two major airports on the island and one of five major airports across the state. They checked into the Hilo Bay Hotel at around lunchtime and, after a quick snack, collapsed onto their king-size bed together and passed out for several hours. David woke first and ran a steaming hot bath. He found a complimentary bottle of Hawaiian Red bath salt and scrutinised the label.

Also known as Alaea sea salt, this Hawaiian Red bath salt is a naturally unprocessed salt. It gets its distinctive colour from purified red volcanic Hawaiian clay, rich in iron oxide. Hawaiian Red salt is recommended in your bath for healing body aches and muscle sprains. It draws toxins from overworked muscle tissue. Mix Hawaiian Red salt with one of our other bath salts for an aesthetically soothing combination.

David poured about a quarter of the bottle into the jacuzzi bath. The water began to turn pink in colour and an aromatic aroma filled the room. He switched on the jets and turned around to look for the towels. Mala stood at the entrance, watching David with interest, her long, dark brown hair hanging loosely over her shoulders. He stopped and smiled to admire her natural beauty and sultry looks, watching her as she began to

269

undress, first dropping her jeans to her ankles and then lifting her top up and over her head. The most perfectly sized, well-rounded breasts were perched above her slender frame. His eyes gazed over her bronze-coloured skin, tracing her figure from top to bottom. Blood flowed to his face and then his crotch. It ached with desire. She stepped out of her jeans and glided silently up to the edge of the bath. Taking his hand, she stepped slowly down into the bubbling water. He threw his clothes aside and climbed in after her, waiting briefly for his body to adjust to the temperature before submerging himself fully into the warm, soapy water. He closed his eyes to savour the moment, as mini-jets massaged his aching muscles from the long flight.

The couple sat unmoving for a while as the jacuzzi jets pulsed through the tub, the sound of the motor coupled with the gushing water louder than expected. David hit the jets and then there was silence. He breathed deeply, drawing in the hot, steamy, aromatic air like it was an elixir, cleansing him of his exhaustion and recharging him with warm, soothing energy. He lay deep inside the bath, his eyes almost level with the water's surface. The steam clouds rising into the air were so thick that Mala's face on the other end of the bath resembled an indistinct shape. He felt her smooth legs pressed up against his outer ribs on either side of his body. He reached his hands further down and found her soft fingers. He interlaced his hands into hers and pulled gently until they both rose up together. He let go of her hands and found her face, pulling it towards his for a tender kiss that became a passionate embrace. More steam rose from their bodies, fogging up the bathroom mirror. He pulled her closer, feeling the silky touch of her tender breasts against his chest. She moaned softly as her nipples began to harden from the intimate contact. He felt her body tremble with anticipation as he reached down into the water, gently feeling his way around her erogenous zone, stimulating her until she became completely aroused. She began moaning louder, squirming around, causing the water to splash about the tub. Her increased groaning caused David to become hard and erect. He

270

instinctively reached forward, lifted her up and then gradually placed her down on top of his lap. Mala, using her left hand as a guide, and her right to grip the side of the bath for support, lowered herself down until David was deep inside of her. She placed her left hand on the other side of the bath and then began pushing both hands down to lift herself up and then lower herself again, at the same time initiating small, yet vigorous thrusting movements with her hips. The bath water began to swish from side to side, this time splashing right over the edge of the tub and wetting the floor. Mala's moans increased in tempo, as did the intensity of the churning water around them. It was like a mini-tsunami had found its way into the bathroom, churning through the bath water, injecting it with energy. David groaned as he began to reach a crescendo. Their lovemaking erupted like a volcano spewing forth its hot, molten lava up into the air.

After a peaceful, dreamless sleep David awoke to the dawn's early light, ordered a light breakfast from room service, switched on the kettle and then flipped open his laptop to search for more information about the closest active volcano in the area. Mala peered over his shoulder.

"What's that?" She pointed at the laptop.

"It's called a laptop computer, another marvel of science."

Mala reached out to touch the screen as some content started loading. She pulled her hand back instinctively. "It's a magic window!" she said, enthralled by the images loading onto the screen. "How'd you open it?"

David smiled. "The window is open. It lets you see into the world of information called the internet that is shared by people all over the planet. There is an almost endless stream of information about everything you need to know stored in this space that has been growing exponentially ever since it was started around thirty years ago. There are tools that have been created to make searching for specific information quite easy to find. Here, watch."

David typed *Hawaii volcanoes* into the Google search bar and hit enter. A list of search results popped up. David clicked on a link entitled *Mauna Loa volcano - Hawaii Island,* and a website opened on his screen with detailed information about the volcano. He read the content out loud. "Mauna Loa means Long Mountain, so named due to its sheer size. Although its peak is only 120 feet high, its cubic volume is 18,000 miles, which makes it the largest active volcano on planet Earth. Mauna Loa is classified as a shield volcano, the most common out of the four different types of volcanoes. These types of volcanoes resemble a shield lying on the ground and always have gentle slopes."

"Oh wow!' said Mala. "Where is this volcano?"

David skimmed through the copy. "Um. It says here that it's not far from Hilo. About 30 miles."

David opened up a few more sites with imagery and additional information.

"OK. We are going to have to drive there." David pointed out the location of the Mauna Loa Weather Observatory. "We can then take the Observatory Trail to reach the summit. It says here that the round trip on foot is 12,4 miles. We can also stay overnight at the Mauna Loa cabin situated at the summit if you wish?"

"Hey that sounds like fun!" said Mala excitedly as she jumped up and out of bed. "When can we get going?"

"Well, we just need to stop by a store in town to get some gear and supplies and then we can head out," replied David. He felt some trepidation but also excitement for the journey ahead as he gazed out of the window at the sea crashing on the rocks below.

CHAPTER FORTY-SEVEN

Volcano

David found himself out of breath, soon after they started hiking from the observatory. He realised when his head began feeling light headed at over 11,000 feet above sea level; he was suffering from a mild bout of altitude sickness. The temperature was much higher up on the peak as a result of the dark, volcanic terrain and exposed environment. Mala seemed unconcerned. She marched on in front of David as if she had been to the site before, determined to reach the summit. David was still unsure what her Ascension entailed or where and when it was supposed to take place and then Mala abruptly stopped.

"Did you feel that?" she said, turning towards David with a great big grin on her face.

"Uh, no…"

Mala went down on one knee, turned her right ear to the ground and closed her eyes. Her smile widened. She jumped up, clearly elated.

"What is it?" asked David.

"The energy, its everywhere! Flowing, surging beneath us like a river!"

Mala turned back to David and grabbed his hand. It felt like she injected an electric current into his arm. He pulled back impulsively, but Mala held on. His entire arm started tingling with pins and needles, and then he felt it. It came to his ears at first; a soft hum like an electric motor. Then it extended with a quiver through his body that seemed to come from under his feet. It felt as if the sand beneath his shoes was sifting, vibrating ever so gently. "Breathe it in," said Mala in a soothing whisper.

David closed his eyes and took a deep breath. He could feel the energy now. It flowed inside him, drawing into his body as he breathed. Visions of deep red colour flashed beneath his eyelids. It was the lava flowing deep inside the mountain, and it was alive. He opened his eyes, and the world had changed. He had changed. He was supercharged with a raw, visceral energy. His laboured breathing had become one with the flow of energy inside the mountain. He walked effortlessly without having to think about breathing. In fact, it felt as if the earth's energy had taken control of his breath, as it coursed like a raging inferno through his body. He looked around and saw through new eyes. The landscape was different, brighter, more vibrant. He laughed out loud and felt exalted as he ran easily with Mala up the steep mountain path.

Mala slowed down as they approached a peculiar looking volcanic rock on the side of the path on the way to the summit. It was about ten feet high and shaped like a mini volcano with a tiny little crater scooped out of its top. It consisted of the same volcanic rock of the surrounding landscape, yet it was different; it appeared to be lighter and seemed to have been formed more recently than anything else in the area.

"What is it?" asked David.

Mala didn't answer. Instead, she approached the rock and placed both hands on it. David stood still. The seconds ticked by. Mala was unmoving. There was a humming in his ears again. This time, it grew more powerful than before. He thought the sound was coming from Mala herself, but he wasn't sure. He couldn't think now with the sound inside his head. He wanted to shut it out, but he didn't know how. It grew even louder, building in timbre and resonance until his ears began to throb like he was standing inside the bass bin of a nightclub speaker.

"Mala." He called her name, but he didn't even hear the

sound of his own voice. "Maaalaaa!!" he shouted with all his might.

There was a boom that reverberated like a jet breaking through the sound barrier. What happened next was just inexplicable. First, it felt like an avalanche had hit. The ground began to shake, and the air became clammy. David watched with eyes like saucers as the curious rock in front of him split in two. The crack extended down the rock, between Mala's legs and then began to creep towards where he was standing. He ran towards her, intent on pulling her to safety but instead, felt himself falling, as the ground opened up and swallowed them both. A sand-slide carried them about thirty feet through a narrow vent and into the depths of the earth. The volcanic rock collapsed in on itself, plugging the hole from the top like a cork and trapping the couple inside. Miraculously they were unharmed as they ended up coming to rest in a tiny cavern underground. Very little light penetrated the gloom. David squinted his eyes, trying to make out Mala's vague silhouette nearby.

"You OK?" asked David, deeply concerned.

Yes, I'm fine. How about you?" replied Mala.

"Thank goodness, alright. This must be a volcanic fissure," said David.

"What's a fissure?"

"It's a side vent of a volcano. When a volcano erupts, there is immense pressure that builds up beneath it. Some of this pressure forces lava to spew out through the softer earth near the surface to create several fissures," explained David.

"Excellent, we need to get close to the lava," said Mala. "The closer we are, the more powerful the Ascension."

"But this appears to be an old fissure," said David. "It's all dried up."

"But I felt the lava, the energy flow when we were on the surface," said Mala in consternation.

A speck of bluish light appeared that instantly lit up her face. The glowing light looked like it was coming from her hands. It increased in intensity.

"What's that?"

"It's called a marker light," replied Mala in a whisper.

"It looks like it's coming from inside your hands. What are you holding?"

"I am the source of the light," said Mala. "The light comes from within me."

David was silent, in awe of the miracles that Mala seemed to produce effortlessly. She moved to the edge of the small cave, placed her hands on the wall and closed her eyes. The light left her hands and disappeared into the earth. Darkness settled in on them again. Seconds ticked by and then David heard a grumbling sound. He imagined it was his procrastinating stomach until the ground began to shake. The wall of the cavern caved in to reveal a narrow corridor small enough to crawl through. Mala went down onto her haunches and began crawling through the newly formed passageway. David followed. They crawled in the darkness for a while and then out into another open space. An orange glow came from the far left corner of the cave. David followed Mala towards the source of the light in the distance. He felt a hot wave of sulphur-scented air wash over him as they rounded the corner to find a narrow stream of molten lava flowing lazily across their path.

Mala turned to David and jumped into his arms, giving him a great big hug of excitement. "This is it!" she said enthusiastically. "This is where it happens."

Mala let go of David and stepped back, looking at him with a frown.

"What is it?" asked David.

"We'll do this together."

"What do you mean?"

"Ascension," she said, quite frankly.

"Um, OK. So how do we do this?" asked David hesitantly.

"All you have to do is follow my lead. Just stay with me and everything will be all right. Your third eye is already open, so think of this as the very next step." Mala sat down cross-legged on the hard, packed earth. "Please, sit down facing me," she said, looking up at David imploringly. "Now close your eyes and focus on your breath."

The softly flowing, red-hot gloop, let out a gurgling sound as it passed by the couple, oblivious to their mundane activity. David closed his eyes and immediately experienced a heightened sense of awareness that came to him stronger than ever before. His eyelids were closed yet he could still see Mala, but it was as if he was looking at a photographic negative of her. The glow from her aura burnt into his vision like the flame from a blowtorch. He concentrated on his breathing and felt the atmosphere constrict like he was sucking in the very matter that surrounded him. He reached the limit of his intake and then slowly breathed out, feeling his breath expand his conscious environment like a helium balloon. And then he was with Mala, somehow joined to her side like a magnet, as her spiritual body floated up into the air and down into the stream of molten lava below. He cringed, trying to shut his eyes until he realised that they were already closed.

What at first felt like a painful burning of his flesh was replaced by a warm and refreshing feeling on his body, as if he were detached and floating in a hot bubble-bath, soaking in the rejuvenating heat and oozing out all of his untimely stress and discomforts. Just as he began settling into this feeling, Mala was there again, taking him deeper into the hot river of lava. He tried to grasp the magnitude of the stream but then realised that he was moving beyond the corporeal and into a cosmos of infinite proportion, the lava merely a conduit to this deeper, more unlimited state of existence. It was here, in this place, that he knew was the source of the raw, unmitigated power that he felt bristling all around him like electrically charged particles. He felt overwhelmed and infinitesimal in the wake of this supernatural force, until a wave of calm, collective energy washed over him, as Mala guided him through the turmoil and chaos that had begun to wrap its tendrils around his naivety.

He let go of his fear and succumbed to the thick, gelatinous earth energy that flowed around him. It oozed through his nonphysical self as it journeyed through the underground caverns formed aeons ago. Like a reverse-river, the lava flowed up from deep within the Earth's core, spitting its liquid mass forth like some giant, wrathful, terrestrial fire-dragon. He sensed Mala again, come to rescue him from the fiery flames licking at the edge of his vision. This time, she opened her arms as if to fly, embracing the flames like a phoenix accepting her fate. The heat grew in intensity, or was it heat? David couldn't quite confirm that feeling any longer. It was a constant burning, and it was turning white. And bright. Brighter. Searing through his eyelids and into his very soul. Burning, yet cleansing. Stripping, tearing, ripping, healing, mending, bonding. He felt like a piece of clay being reshaped into something new, moulded into a being of light and energy. It was all-new, this feeling, this experience. He could feel himself begin to change, and he allowed it to pass.

David opened his eyes, and everything looked over-exposed. Even the darkest corners of his vision were bright and alive. He stumbled out of the side of the mountain with Mala at his side, supporting him as best as she could. He dropped to his knees and gazed across at the setting sun on the horizon. It regarded him with its mighty power and he simply stared back. He was able to somehow, inexplicably neutralise the sun's powerful rays that threatened to burn through his retinas and instead absorb them into his essence like a dry sponge in a bowl of hot, churning water. He turned to look at Mala and saw that she also had changed. He felt a powerful energy connection ripple between them, a perpetual wave, a double-helix bond of intuitive, super-charged, life force energy that carried with it an instruction that was beginning to blossom into a flower of heightened consciousness in their combined psyches.

The Mauna Loa cabin beckoned to them like a beacon in the dwindling light of the day as they stumbled inside to collapse, exhausted, on the thin, hard-packed mattresses, only too grateful for a place to rest their weary bodies after the gruelling tribulation.

Part 4

The whole course of human history
may depend on a change of heart
in one solitary and even humble individual
- for it is in the solitary mind and soul of the individual
that the battle between good and evil is waged
and ultimately won or lost.

- M. Scott Peck

CHAPTER FORTY-EIGHT

Frenchman

Saul Piltree washed his hands, splashed water on his face and then peered into the mirror. "C'mon Saul, pull yourself together," he whispered urgently to himself as he gritted his teeth and pursed his lips together in a grimace.

An unusual influx of patrons came through diner these past few days, and the numbers weren't letting up. He wasn't complaining as business had never been so good but what was most unusual was how people went to the toilet but then never came out again. He turned around and checked the single window again. It was closed and locked from the inside. He made sure of it the last time he was in here, and the time before that. At first, he hadn't noticed anything until too many people asked him where the toilet was. He began watching people walk in and then never come out. The first few times it happened, he just disregarded it as his eyes playing tricks, until he decided to sit down at the table closest to the toilet after directing a middle-aged Frenchman in jeans and a yellow jacket to relieve himself. He checked his watch. Five minutes... nothing. Six, Seven. He stood up and approached the door.

Knock, knock, knock. "Hello. You in there?" Nothing. He pushed open the door and stepped inside. The Frenchman had inexplicably disappeared.

This can't be happening. I must be going mad. There has to be a logical explanation for this.

He ran out into the diner and looked frantically around, trying to spot the colour yellow as if it was going to save his sanity.

Dorothy came up to him; concern mirrored on her face. "Saul, Saul! You all right?"

He turned to Dorothy, realising that he must have looked quite anxious. "Uh, yes, yes, I'm fine. Why do you ask?" He forced a smile.

"You look like you've seen a ghost." She couldn't have been closer to the truth. Saul felt his stomach turn. "Who are you looking for?" asked Dorothy.

"The Frenchman," he muttered, without even realising he spoke out loud.

He began to feel light-headed. He looked at Dorothy. She spoke, but it sounded like she was positioned at the end of a long corridor, her voice was so indistinct. He heard himself say Whaaat? But it, too, sounded peculiar, like an echo inside a large, cavernous chamber. Dorothy led him to a table, pushed him down into a seat and handed him a glass of water. Dorothy whispered into his ear, but when he turned to look at her, she wasn't there. He looked down at the water and watched his reflection wobble hazily across the surface. He took another long sip and then placed the glass down on the table once more. He looked up and then scratched his head, wondering for a moment why he was seated at a table all by himself when his diner was so damn busy.

CHAPTER FORTY-NINE

Reception

The hot shower washed away a layer of grime and grit that had collected on his body like seeds from a dandelion. His glistening skin shone surreally in the artificial light as a steady pool of water formed around his feet, dripping steadily from dreadlocks that hung long and heavy, halfway down his back. Kaimi towel-dried his body and then his braids, being careful not to rub them too hard, as he stepped from the bathroom and into his living chamber, deep inside the hidden city. It didn't seem that hidden of late, with all the visitors pouring in. Kaimi headed up the reception committee. He had to make sure that each and every visitor was not only accounted for but that they also had food and lodging during their visit. He had already registered 312 foreigners, and there were at least another 50 expected over the next few days. These members came from groups located all over the world. There was the Larson family from Sweden, the Ojukwu's from Nigeria, the Korchagin's from Russia and the Watson's from the United Kingdom. Unlike the giant, clandestine, underground city in Barbados, the other Lemurians around the world lived above ground, secretly hiding their origins and cautiously practising their arts.

It was almost time for the next meeting in the great hall. Belias instructed Kaimi to let him know as soon as the balance of the guests had arrived so that he could address the populace.

Kaimi got dressed, sat down on the carpet in front of his bed and closed his eyes. He gently placed his hands on his knees for a few moments before turning them to face palms-up. He touched the tip of each thumb to the tip of each corresponding index finger and splayed out the remaining three fingers of each hand. This was considered to be an ancient gesture or mudra, designed to stimulate knowledge and ability, while at the same time, instil a sense of calmness and receptiveness. His third eye opened, giving him the ability to sense his fellow Lemurians as if he were seeing them through night vision lenses. They were scattered all over the compound like hundreds of bugs going about their daily duties, attending to the colony and foraging for food. He zeroed in on the elevator that was transporting visitors from the surface, down into the bowels of the Earth.

Kaimi.

Your grace.

Are we on track? How many more are expected?

No less than fifty.

Where's Belengera?

She has not yet arrived.

Good, let me know when she gets here so that we can begin.

Very well, my lord.

Belengera Duarte was the acknowledged leader of the European descendants of Lemuria. She lived in Bilbao, the capital of Biscay, a province of Northern Spain, just south of the Bay of Biscay. Biscay is one of three provinces in Spain that form part of an autonomous community that was granted its own nationality within the country of Spain by the government of Spain in 1978. This was done to preserve the Basque culture and language of the region.

Kaimi had accompanied Belias to visit Belengera in Bilbao several years ago. It was a trip that he'd never forget. Kaimi was adopted by Belias when he was just a boy, following the unfortunate death of both of his parents in a plane crash. He was forever indebted to Belias for raising him as his own, caring for him and providing him with a life worth living. He never doubted his guardian's legitimacy, despite the many rumours that followed him around like the long shadows cast by the setting sun. So when, during the long flight to Spain, Belias began relating his story to Kaimi, it only served to strengthen his loyalty to Belias and the cause. They had just finished their meal when Belias turned to Kaimi, smiled and then asked rhetorically.

"Have you any idea why we are going to Spain?" He paused for a moment before continuing. "Our extended Lemurian family has made a very important discovery. They have found a lodestone."

"I've heard of a lodestone, but I'm not sure what it is exactly," said Kaimi, creasing his brow in thought.

"A lodestone is a naturally occurring magnetic rock. But this is no ordinary lodestone. This lodestone is large - about the size of a book and has inscriptions carved into it. Very old inscriptions - about 20,000 years old."

Kaimi's eyes widened. "Wow! So this, lodestone, is kinda like a stone tablet?"

"Exactly. Belengera says it's Lemurian. We're going to assist her in deciphering its meaning," continued Belias with anticipation in his voice. "Kaimi, there is more that I must share with you, more about our forefather Asbeth and his great legacy. Belengera is my sister. We were born in Bilbao, Spain, to where we are now headed. Our parents and those before them are direct descendants of Asbeth. This information has been passed down from generation to generation since his very first arrival in Spain."

"But I thought that Asbeth escaped from the destruction of Lemuria to land in Barbados where he established the great underground city," said a confused Kaimi.

"Ah yes, but he did, he did," said Belias, nodding his head in confirmation. "But, before this time, he settled in Spain. You've heard of the Basque language, no doubt?"

"Yes, it's spoken in Spain, I think?"

"It's only spoken in a tiny area of Northern Spain, in the

province of Biscay. Did you know that the Basque language is unique in that it's been found to have no connection to any other European language? In fact, scientists and anthropologists have still, to this day, found no conclusive evidence proving its true etymology. Instead, a number of hypotheses exist, linking the language to the Iberian Peninsula, Celtic and Kartvelian languages. Interesting, is it not?" Kaimi nodded. "Basque, or a form of it, is the language of the old world, the language of Lemuria," said Belias matter-of-factly. "It represents evidence of Asbeth and his establishment of a settlement there."

Kaimi looked up at the aircraft's seatbelt light on the panel above him in thought. "But I'm still confused. When did Asbeth come to Barbados and why did he leave Spain to do so when he had already established a settlement there?"

"When Asbeth and his followers escaped the devastation of Lemuria, they fled north-west, sailing towards present day China. They continued travelling until they reached the Middle East and established a settlement that flourished and grew to become the Egyptian Empire eventually several centuries later. They travelled from there to Morocco and crossed over into Spain where they settled in the Bay of Biscay. The land was uninhabited at the time and only became populated with Europeans hundreds of years later. Asbeth spent the rest of his life searching for remnants of his lost land. He crossed the Atlantic to the West, landing in the America's, before travelling south to establish another colony that built temples in Peru, led to the rise of the Aztecs, Incas and other civilisations that have since all but disappeared. His journey ended in Barbados, with the establishment of this great underground city, designed to preserve the Lemurian heritage and keep it hidden from those that wished to steal its secrets. It was from this underground city that he controlled the world, influencing Kings and rulers with his unlimited power and consummate supremacy. If it were not for Asbeth, we would not be here to continue his legacy and fulfil the Lemurian Prophecy."

Belengera was waiting in the arrivals hall of Bilbao airport as Belias and Kaimi stepped through the doors. She opened her arms wide in a warm welcome. "Aaah, my brother! So good to see you!" she said, hugging him fiercely. "And Kaimi, I've heard so much about you! Here, let me look at you!"

Belengera was a very loud woman, both in spirit and appearance. She was also quite rotund. She had dyed her naturally blonde hair a soft pink and wore a long, colourful silk gown that billowed around her like a fluttering flag on a royal turret. She didn't stop talking from the moment they left the airport until they reached their hotel. Kaimi felt more tired from her babbling than from his long flight across the Atlantic. Soon after arriving in his room, he stepped out onto the balcony to admire the view. He imagined walking in Asbeth's shoes as he witnessed the magnificent view of the Bay of Biscay upon his first arrival to this land. The sun's golden rays turned the sky multi-coloured hues of orange, red and yellow as it dipped into the distant horizon. The sea glistened like a blanket of sequenced fabric, rippling in the spotlight of a spectacular sunset.

The following morning, Belias and Kaimi joined Belengera and her team on a journey into the famous cave of Altamira.

"Wow! This is incredible!" exclaimed Kaimi, as he studied the rock-art inside the cave. "This looks like a Bison."

"That is correct," said Belengera. "That particular Bison image is estimated to be over 30,000 years old."

"Incredible. How is the age determined?"

"Scientists use something called uranium-thorium dating on the paint. Apparently, it's pretty accurate. No! Don't touch it! We are cky to have even been granted access to this cave. It has been closed to the public since 2010 because the carbon dioxide discharge from the many visitors has, over time, eroded the artwork."

"When was the cave discovered?" enquired Kaimi.

"In 1880. It is believed to have been sealed for over 12,000 years."

"Around the same time that Asbeth arrived here?"

"Exactly! We believe that he hid the lodestone here before sealing the cave himself."

"So how did you find it?" asked Belias.

"One of my people was working with the university's archaeology team. He was measuring the level of air pollution with a nitrogen laser. It began to malfunction but only in one particular area of the cave. After spending some time searching the area, he came across a pile of loose stones beneath which he found the lodestone. He deduced that the magnetic qualities of the stone interfered with the electromagnetic calibration of the laser, causing it to malfunction."

Belengera lifted a black briefcase and placed it down on a large flat rock in the cave. She tapped a code into an electronic panel, and the case unlocked with a beep. She opened the case to reveal the stone. It was silvery-grey in colour. Even in the wan light of the cave, it glistened as if it were alive and pulsing with some kind of alien energy. A series of intricately carved shapes and lines crisscrossed its surface, weaving a secret message, just waiting to be deciphered. Belias's eyes lit up like a starving child seeing food for the first time in days. "Aaaah. The lodestone!" Belias ran his fingers across the ancient talisman, tenderly stroking the intricate patterns etched across its surface. His mouth turned up into an impish grin as he caressed the stone like it was a new-born puppy.

"So, dear brother, what does it say? Is it Lemurian?"

"Yesss of courses." Belias dropped his voice to a hiss that echoed through the cave like the flutter of a bat's wings. "It represents further substantiation of our heritage, our lineage. Asbeth was here. He hid this lodestone for his descendants - for us to find. Look here and here." Belias pointed at a recurring pattern of squiggly lines on the lodestone. "These represent waves. The very waves that destroyed our ancestors' motherland. Then see this." Belias touched another symbol that was shaped like an oval with a line cutting it diagonally. "This is a boat. It represents the people that escaped the destruction of

Lemuria. It depicts Belias and his followers."

"How do you know all of this?" enquired Belengera of her brother.

"A lifetime of study and dedication. The question is, why a lodestone? Why would Asbeth use a lodestone to create these messages?" Belias asked out loud.

"Maybe it's some kind of beacon used to call aliens!" said Kaimi.

"Interesting hypothesis, but the Lemurians do not believe in aliens," replied Belias matter-of-factly. "Instead, we believe in our destiny here on Earth - a planet created by a higher power so that He could share His goodness with us mere mortals, giving us the free will to rule this world. No. I think that it has something to do with navigation. I believe that Asbeth brought this stone here from Lemuria and used the magnetic powers of the lodestone to help him, and his followers navigate across the great oceans and traverse the continents until he arrived here in Biscay. The energy contained within this stone guided him here. I can feel it."

CHAPTER FIFTY

Angel

The SSHF headquarters was situated on the corner of 3rd Avenue and East 75th Street, New York. The building was nondescript - a grey, double-storied structure with a small, faded brass plaque at the entrance. Mary-Jane Fontaine, the founder in chief, was busy compiling her latest e-mailer for the organisation. It was nearing the Summer Solstice, and the unification of the group and its activities was vital to the strengthening of the awareness surrounding the crystalline matrix. She proof-read her work one last time before distributing the message to over 5,000 active lightworkers positioned all over the globe.

Sun Salutation Humanitarian Foundation – Newsletter #273

Dear fellow light worker,

As you are well aware, tomorrow is the Summer Solstice. As an awakened group consciousness, it is our duty to take advantage of this significant incident by coming together as one focused alliance to open the portals of light to those that are blinded by the truth of creation. As always, this is a plea for you to join us in active service, in offering yourself up as a conduit for world transmission designed to illuminate Humanity's higher consciousness on a metaphysical level.

To maximise the potency of this transmission, we urge you to focus on the following key locations around the globe as part of the crystalline grid: Giza, Greenland, Mexico City, the Persian Gulf, Atlantis, Nepal, Hawaii, Venezuela, Peru, Lemuria, Scandinavia, Japan, and Australia. The crystalline grid is a network of energy that surrounds and permeates the Earth. It consists of 12 main points and 144 secondary points of energy that come from crystals located deep inside the Earth's core. These energy points can also be found in and beneath many ancient temples, monuments and pyramids. Spread the word to get your fellow light workers on board and part of this momentous activation.

We look forward to welcoming you on our journey to raise world consciousness through the power of the Summer Solstice. Our intention is to create a mass domino effect across the crystalline grid matrix, awakening the global elite. Our goal is to direct our consciousness into one or more of the key locations worldwide, to create an impenetrable pattern of pure light energy that will reflect our intention of love, peace and divine compassion.

Yours, in Love and Light,

Mary-Jane Fontaine

A smiling portrait of Mary-Jane was placed below her signature. An image of planet Earth, surrounded by a glowing matrix of light, formed part of the mailer-header, with several more rainbow-coloured kaleidoscopic images gracing the footer. She sent the newsletter via MailChimp and then opened Outlook and clicked on her calendar. It opened up into the weekly default view. A number of highlighted, orange blocks indicated the several meetings she had planned over the coming week. She checked the event titled, Summer Solstice meeting. It was scheduled to start at 12 pm, Tuesday, in Central Park. Mary-Jane sighed deeply.

Everything was falling into place just as it was meant to be.

She habitually fingered a small pendant in the shape of an angel that hung around her neck on a thin golden chain - a gift from her mother that she inherited following her passing so long ago.

Mary-Jane was the only daughter in a family of three siblings. She grew up with the knowledge that she was different to her peers. She struggled to fit in, to follow rules and instructions from her teachers and especially her parents. She was a strong-willed, headstrong child, labelled as having ADHD. One day, just before her seventh birthday, she picked up the telephone in the study while her mother was on the other line.

"...the colour indigo? What do you mean?" It was Aunty Sally on the other end. Mary-Jane began to replace the receiver when she heard her mother's voice in response. She gently lifted the phone back up to her ear.

"Well, apparently an indigo child is stubborn, tenacious and rebellious, just like my Mary-Jane." Her voice sounded so pitiful that Mary-Jane's heart sank like a stone into the bottom of her belly.

"Really? But surely that's not enough to just label a child like that?" Aunty Sally's voice squeaked like a mouse. Mary-Jane clamped her hand over the receiver to muffle the sound.

"Well, that's not all. She challenges us all the time. She never listens to anything we say and has this air of absolute authority that resists the notion of punishment and reward. It's even becoming a problem at school. I don't know what to do anymore."

"Lulu, have you considered medication?"

"Well, Stephan keeps wanting to but I'm dead against it. I believe that she's inherited my grandmother's genes. She reminds me so much of her; it's frightening. You know, the other night she told me that she couldn't sleep because she kept seeing Wenona."

"Who's Wenona?"

"Exactly what I asked myself. It was only the next morning that it dawned on me. Wenona was my grandmother. I called her

Wenny for short. She's been dead for over ten years."

"Wasn't she a priest or something?"

"She was a seer. And a shaman. From the Apache tribe in Arizona."

"Oh…"

"I don't talk about her much because she was so weird. I mean, I hardly ever saw her, but when I did, she always placed her hands on my head and mumbled some kind of incantation. My father called her a witch. He despised her much to my mother's regret. Anyway, the point I'm making is that Indigo children can also see and communicate with spirits, and I've never told Mary-Jane, the full name of my grandmother. I may have mentioned great-granny Wenny but never Wenona. The name Wenona means first-born daughter in the Native American Indian language. And did you know that Lulu is also Indian? It means rabbit."

"Hee hee hee!" Aunty Sally's piercing laughter exploded through the cracks in Mary-Jane's hand over the receiver like laser beams of piercing light. "You know you do remind me of a rabbit!"

"Very funny Sal," said Lulu. "I don't want to medicate her because if she can see spirits then I believe that this is a gift that needs to manifest itself without being stymied by some kind of medical treatment that will probably do her more harm than good."

"Lu, are you sure about this? I mean shouldn't you seek professional help?"

"No. I've made up my mind. I'm going to give her this angel pendant I got from Wenny before she died. She told me that I would know what to do with it when the time came. And I think the time has come."

CHAPTER FIFTY-ONE

Sun

It was a mild, summer's day in New York City. Central Park was a moderate 77 degrees, as Mary-Jane walked briskly, mat in hand, down East 66th Street and into the cluster of trees at its perimeter. She glanced at her watch. 10h25.

Perfect. An hour and a half to settle in.

She walked on until she arrived at The Dairy, Central Park's very first visitor information and gift shop. The Dairy was originally built as a Victorian cottage, designed to serve as a peaceful sanctuary for children. Later, it served fresh milk and cookies to families that came to visit the nearby pond to the south. Mary-Jane favoured this venue for her gatherings and often walked by the Dairy on her many strolls through the Park. She stepped out beyond the structure and onto the grass area in front. The fresh-cut smell of grass permeated her nostrils as she dropped her yoga mat, placed her hands on her hips and drew in a deep, satisfying breath of fresh Park air. Skyscrapers rose into the sky just beyond the trees like misshapen Jenga blocks and the steady hum of the city reverberated through the air like the drone of a thousand bumblebees in flight.

Mary-Jane rolled out her mat on the soft grass, smiled to herself and slowly dropped down into Balasana, or more commonly referred to as Child's Pose. She sat down on her knees with her feet tucked away beneath her. She widened her knees and bent down to touch her forehead to the earth, extending her hands out in front of her. She pushed her hands further forward, lifting them up onto her fingertips and felt the muscles in her back and shoulder girdles ease into a gratifying stretch. She closed her eyes and continued to focus on her breath, deepening each inhale and exhale like the ebb and flow of the tide, slowing down her breathing. Meditating, sinking, releasing.

Mary-Jane glided gracefully into a seated position, lifting her feet, one at a time, into a full lotus pose. She brought her hands together in prayer in front of her chest and focused on maintaining her posture. She began to become aware of her body and the way it was positioned on her mat, from her legs twisted into place to her elongated spine and slightly tucked chin. She began to visualise her happy place. Images of Silver Island filtered into her consciousness. She smiled as her memory of this beautiful Greek sanctuary and the yoga retreat that she attended there last summer, brought feelings of joy and abundance to her present state of mind. She coaxed her smile inward, feeling it melt into her inner being. A golden thread of energy, expanding and intensifying throughout her body.

MJ.

Mother, is that you?

No. I'm Mala.

Where...how are we communicating?

Open your eyes.

Mary-Jane's face tingled. Her breathing quickened. She felt uneasy; fearful of what she might see when she opened her eyes. A wave of calm, soothing energy washed over her, dissipating her fears instantly. She smiled and then opened her eyes. Kneeling in front of her was a beautiful creature, a young girl in her twenties with long, dark hair and matching brown eyes. She smiled, revealing a perfect set of teeth. Mary-Jane looked into her eyes and saw a flicker of something that was enough to tell her that she was much more than what she seemed. Just behind her, stood a dishevelled-looking, handsome young man wearing glasses. He had his hands folded casually and was smiling too.

"Mala?"

"Yes." She turned to the man behind her. "And this is David."

He waved. "Hi."

"What...just happened?" Mary-Jane was confused. *Am I dreaming?*

Mala smiled again. "We are here to join you in your ceremony."

"Who are you? Have we met before? Did you receive my mail?" Her mind spun. *OK. OK. Breathe, breathe.*

"Yes, we received your...message," said Mala.

Whew. Thank goodness. I'm not going crazy. "Good! Well then, welcome to the tenth annual Sun Salutation Summer Solstice Ceremony." Mary-Jane smiled and opened her arms in a warm welcome, visibly relaxing as she lost herself in the excitement of her event.

Mala and David continued to smile, nodding their heads in acknowledgement. "Thank you," they said in unison.

"We generally host around fifty members at most of our gatherings. Have you ever been to one of our events?"

Mala looked at Mary-Jane and smiled. "No. This is our first."

"OK. Then allow me to introduce you to the order of events."

"Sure. Of course."

"Right, so everyone sits in two concentric circles. You can join me in the inner circle if you wish. Then, once everyone is ready, we hold hands and close our eyes. I then guide everyone through the session. All you need to do is listen to my voice as we prepare to honour the longest day of the year and the celestial body that provides life and sustenance to every living being here on planet Earth." Mala looked up into the sky. Shafts of sunlight pierced the canopy of trees, as the fiery orb that was the sun lay partially concealed before its full reveal, closer to its noon zenith. Mary-Jane followed Mala's gaze, instinctively bringing her hand up to shield her eyes from the blinding beams of light. They found each other's eyes again.

Who are you? Really? Mary-Jane stared questioningly at the young girl. Mala moved forward, taking hold of Mary-Jane's hands in hers. She gazed into her eyes. Mary-Jane stared straight back. She felt light-headed and then blinked. What's happening?

I am from Lemuria, brought back from the spirit world to save humanity.

Mary-Jane felt woozy. *What?* Mary-Jane opened her mouth to speak but instead tears bulged and then trickled out of her eyes like brimming pools of mountain water. She felt an overwhelming abundance of feelings all mushed together like silly-putty. *Is this really happening?*

"Yes. It is." This time, it was David that spoke. "We are here to help you and others like you save planet Earth from being destroyed by humanity itself."

"But wha... how?" Mary-Jane was at a loss for words.

"I know that this is a lot to take in at once, but we have recognised the work that you do here and it is perfectly aligned with our intentions," continued David. "We are fortunate to have found you and your organisation. The effort that you put into encouraging other light workers around the world to raise global consciousness is admirable. It is also an important endeavour in the process of universal transformation, the object of which is to heal the planet through enlightened awareness."

Mary-Jane realised that she was still sitting in lotus position. She slowly pulled her feet out, one at a time and brought her hands to her face, washing them over eyes and forehead. She took a few long, deep breaths. Her head still felt light and dizzy. "I don't know how you are able to communicate with me like that, but you have my attention. You say that you are here to save planet Earth. Have you seen the into the future? What's going to happen?"

Mala turned back to look at David and then clasped Mary-Jane's hands in hers again. "No. I can't tell you what will happen as I cannot see into the future." Mala closed her eyes, and a vision of her father flashed before her. "But what I can tell you is that humanity was once wiped off the face of this planet, and I'm not going to let it happen again."

Mary-Jane's head was spinning.

"Have you heard of Lemuria?"

"Yes. It's a mythical land like Atlantis that disappeared in the ocean somewhere, right?"

"Right. That was over 12,000 years ago. I know because I was there."

"What? Now you're talking complete nonsense. I bet the next thing you're going to tell me is that you're a time traveller or something. How can you expect me to believe a word you say?"

"I know it's hard to believe so let me show you rather." Mala moved closer to Mary-Jane. She instinctively pulled away.

"What are you doing?"

"Relax. Trust me. I'm not going to hurt you. Just close your eyes for a moment and all will be revealed."

Mala gently placed her hand on the right side of Mary-Jane's face. Mary-Jane closed her eyes, and the visions began. She stood high on top of a mountain, overlooking a lush, tropical land. Magnificent, glass-like structures below, reflected rainbow-coloured light. A volcanic peak, sheathed in a thick, grey cloud loomed ominously on the horizon. The scene changed. She was flying high above an unusual city made of stone. She swooped down into an enclave where a group of people were busy tending to some animals. Sheep? They all turned at once to look in her direction. Their expectant faces all smiled at once, and their eyes bore right into her soul. Mala lifted her hand off Mary-Jane's face. She opened her eyes and gazed in awe at Mala.

"But if you are from Lemuria, then you must be over 12,000 years old. How is this possible?"

"This is a body of the current time and place. It's my spirit that's from Lemuria."

Mary-Jane looked at David expectantly.

David smiled. "No. I'm not Lemurian."

Mala bowed her head. "I know that you have many more questions, but right now, we would really like to join you in the

298

ceremony of praising the sun and its abundant life-giving energy."

Mala and David sat on the grass opposite Mary-Jane with the inner circle of members. Many more members arrived and took their places amongst the crowd, some as part of the inner circle while others, part of the outer. Almost all of the visitors approached Mary-Jane and paid their respects, some simply with nods and handshakes while others with great big hugs and happy smiles. David glanced at his watch. 11h48. The sun was almost at its apex. It shone now, directly through an opening in the trees and down onto the group of light workers. He felt its heat on his head like a blowtorch. A small crowd of onlookers had gathered around the assemblage, looking on with interest Some were taking photographs with their smartphones while others just stood and stared in awe. The group of members chose to ignore them as they gradually settled into a quiet meditative space, seemingly oblivious to the world beyond their double-circle.

Mala gracefully stood up and walked over to Mary-Jane. "This crystal," Mala opened her palm to reveal a smooth, red stone. "must be placed in the centre of the circle. It will enhance the group's efforts and facilitate the opening of the portals of light." Mary-Jane nodded her head and smiled in acknowledgement. Mala placed the crystal in the centre of the inner circle on her way back to her seated position across from Mary-Jane.

Mary-Jane looked around her, making sure that everyone was ready before speaking. "Welcome everyone, to the tenth annual Summer Solstice Ceremony. Please turn to the person to the left of you and introduce yourself and then do the same with the person to your right." There was a murmuring hum from the group. "Good. Now hold your neighbour's hands in yours and close your eyes. Is everyone comfortable?"

There was a combined "Yes!" from the crowd.

"Excellent. Now all that you have to do is listen to my voice as we focus on the global transmission of love, peace and divine light at this auspicious time of the Summer Solstice when the sun is at its strongest and days are at their longest. Our intention is to create a mass domino effect across Earth's crystalline grid matrix. Our connection here today must be unified into a powerful force, targeted at the spiritual centres positioned all over the globe. To increase the potency of this transmission, we need to focus on the sun's powerful energy that will fuel our intention to raise the level of global consciousness, opening up new light portals and expanding those that are already open." More onlookers and tourists gathered around the group as the participants sat completely still with their eyes closed, holding each other's hands, their faces turned partially up towards the heavens. Smiles graced their faces as the sun shone its light down on the participants.

"We are now going to hum a collective Om, so that we align our combined consciousness, leading to the expression of the infinite within each and every one of us. Please contemplate the meaning of Om, as the primordial seed of the universe, and, in this way, we will enhance the experience and spread the divine across planet Earth to where it is needed most." Mary-Jane shifted ever so slightly in her posture. "OK. Now take a deep breath in, to my count. One, two, three, four, five, six and then out again; six, five, four, three, two, one." The combined breathing of the group could be heard as a deep, rasping sound. "Now take a deep breath in. And we begin." A whooshing intake of breath could be heard, and then a loud and united "Auuuuuuuuuuuuuummmmm" vibrated through the air like the sound of a motorboat passing by. It lasted roughly ten seconds and then faded gradually away until silence prevailed.

Mary-Jane felt that familiar presence again that she identified as Mala, but this time there was another entity with her...David. She more than sensed their glowing aura's. She saw them in her periphery vision, but each time she moved her eyes to bring them into her line of sight, they jumped away just out of reach. She started feeling a strange lethargic sensation come over her, and then, without warning, she began to speak to her tribe. Her tribe? Her lips started moving, but on their own accord. She felt like she was being manipulated like a marionette on strings. It felt strange, yet oddly comforting at the same time. "A red crystal has been placed in the centre of our circle by an anonymous benefactor. I want each and every one of you to focus your intent on this stone. Once we have a single vision and our focus absolute, the power of the crystal will be activated, and your level of consciousness will expand and grow. Above all, stay grounded and connected to the group, so that we can successfully activate the portals of light across Gaia."

Mary-Jane felt Mala's energy recede, leaving her alone and floating in a sea of serendipity. And then it came out of nowhere like a tornado, whisking the group up and away on a tumultuous roller-coaster ride across a surreal landscape of broken colour and jagged terrain that seemed to distend the mind as if it were being torn apart. She felt the strain of the rest of the group as it fought to hold on to the crystal's red energy trail, tearing across the spiritual divide like a celestial comet hurled into space by an astronomical anomaly. "Stay with me." Mala was back, communicating through Mary-Jane. "We need to focus our energy on awakening the unenlightened, through the activation of the crystalline grid matrix."

The group moved as one, connecting their combined consciousness to crystals buried deep within the Earth's mantle. They followed Mala through Mary-Jane as she traversed the web of energy that crisscrossed the planet, awakening, reconnecting, energising. Some pushed, others were pulled; yet all were unified and focused on a single directive. A flock of swiftly swooping swallows, diving together as one and then rising again.

They began to return to the now, their enlightened selves still in a state of complete bliss and harmony, free from physicality and its heavy burden. Beams of white light radiated out of their spiritual bodies, connecting to the powerful solstice sun energy, beaming down from above.

Three members of the outer circle slowly opened their eyes

together and gazed intently at Mary-Jane, as she sat serenely in the middle of the group. They turned to look at each other, nodded, slowly stood up and began to walk away. One of the three was a portly woman with a head of pink hair that bounced off her shoulders as she marched across the grass clearing towards The Dairy. Mala opened her eyes to watch them leave.

David! Let's go! Follow me!

David sprang up in response to Mala's urgent demand, following her as she jogged to catch up with the three individuals that hastily decided to leave the ceremony.

CHAPTER FIFTY-TWO

Chase

"How do you know that they're going to the airport?" said David. The cab swerved to avoid a cyclist coming in the other direction. The Armenian driver cursed loudly out of his window while waving his free arm wildly about.

"I can hear them. Here." Mala's eyes were closed as she tapped her forehead with her right index finger.

"I can sense them, but..." David screwed up his eyes, trying to interpret what Mala was hearing but all he got was a kind of static energy.

Mala smiled. "It comes with training and experience. I have much to teach you."

"Who are they?"

"They're like me, but different." Mala creased her forehead. "They have the sight but their knowledge is limited."

"Jet Blue, flight 342 to Barbados is now ready for boarding. Will passengers kindly report to departure gate number twenty-four."

The first boarding announcement echoed shrilly through the airport speakers as Mala and David stepped out of the taxi. They followed the three suspicious characters to JFK's terminal number five. David spotted the mop of pink hair at the Jet Blue Airlines ticket counter.

"Hi, we need to go where they are going, please," said David with a smile. He pointed in the direction of the three travellers, watching them make their way to the security check.

"That's Grantley Adams airport in Barbados, sir," replied a very friendly looking ticket counter clerk.

"Thanks. Two one-way tickets please."

"Any luggage to check in, sir?"

"Uh, No." David was carrying both of their passports. He placed them on the check-in desk. "Here you go."

"Thank you, sir. Please make your way to the boarding gate immediately. The gate is already open for boarding."

The four hour, forty minute flight was uneventful. David and Mala sat in row number sixteen, four rows behind the three protagonists. David managed to get a glimpse of the other two characters, as he walked past them to his seat. They sat either side of the large woman. They were both talking excitedly and gesturing animatedly with their hands. He picked up a strange guttural language that sounded like Spanish but with distinct differences he had never heard before. The two men had dark skin and strong facial features that marked them as European.

David turned to Mala soon after takeoff. "So any more clues as to who they are?"

Mala looked at David, her dark brown eyes melting his resolve like hot butter. "We're too close. They'll know if I start probing." Mala closed her eyes and dropped her head back into the seat cushion.

"Follow that cab!" David imagined he was in a movie, as he barked out the command to the taxi driver. The ride from the airport took just fifteen minutes. Before they knew it, they were weaving through traffic in Bridgetown, Barbados' capital. Rivulets of sweat trickled down David's neck, as he stepped out of the cab and into the island's stifling humidity. The cab driver had smartly pulled over a block away from the other cab. David and Mala watched, as the rotund woman and her cohorts stepped out of their cab and into a diner. David paid the driver and then jogged to catch up with Mala who was already halfway there. They stepped inside and quickly scanned the room. There was no sign of the three travellers. No pink hair, no peculiar looking Europeans, just a few people drinking coffee and reading the afternoon paper. David and Mala looked at each other and then headed for the toilets. David stepped into the Men's, and Mala the Ladies'. They both stepped out together with exasperated looks on their faces.

Wait.

What is it?

Mala closed her eyes. *There is something.*

David closed his eyes and tried to connect. He found Mala. Her aura burned into his subconscious like the orange flames of the setting sun. He took in a deep breath and then breathed out again, visualising the very air leaving his body come alive like a vaporous serpent, wrapping its tendrils around Mala's spiritual body, enveloping, binding, merging. The parallel landscape of the diner glowed like a photographic negative as David and Mala floated eerily between spaces, probing and scanning for signs of the three mysterious individuals.

There. See?

David felt Mala pull their combined consciousness towards the Men's. A soft, turquoise luminescence glowed from the hand-drier. It pulsed as if it had a life of its own.

What is it?

It's the faint trail of energy left behind by others, built up over time due to unusually high activity in this area.

But it's a hand-drier.

I'm sorry, but I don't know what that is.

David forgot for a moment that Mala was an ancient being with no real understanding of modern technology. He realised just then how quickly she had learnt to adapt, thinking that there must have been many instances where she just went along with things without question.

It's a machine that's used to dry your hands if they are wet. It's normally used a lot.

David floated closer to the drier for further inspection. There was something odd about it. It didn't look quite right. The glow seemed to be coming from the side of the drier, but it was hard to determine this accurately in a sepia-infused environment. He glided back to his body outside the toilets and then together with Mala, physically stepped back into the Men's. David instantly realised the oddity. There was what looked like a credit card slot attached to the side of the drier, that he had never seen before on a unit like this. It didn't quite make any sense. Mala stepped forward and silently placed both of her hands over the machine. She closed her eyes. Seconds passed and then David felt his legs buckle as if the room shifted. *Impossible.*

"What the?" David felt the ground shift beneath his feet. He put his hand against the wall to steady himself and then felt a blast of air swirl around the small room as it dropped down without warning into the bowels of the Earth.

CHAPTER FIFTY-THREE

Announcement

She has arrived, your Grace.

Excellent! Seal all access to the city and make the announcement.

Kaimi went to personally meet Belengera and her colleagues. "Good evening Belengera and welcome to the great underground city of Lemuria."

"Kaimi! It's so good to see you! Oh my, but it's been a long journey. Where *is* my darling brother?" Belengera was as gregarious as ever. Her colleagues hovered like mere shadows at her side, slinking back even further the louder she bellowed.

"He's preparing for a gathering in the great hall. Come, I will show you to your chambers and then we are to join him and the rest of our brothers and sisters."

"No. I need to see him now. I have important news. It cannot wait." Belengera was adamant.

Kaimi raised his eyebrows. "Very well. Follow me."

The elevator room slowed and then stopped with a slight shudder. The door opened, and a soldier in a grey, unmarked uniform with a red beret stepped inside. "Welcome comrades. Please state your business."

David opened his mouth to speak, but Mala quickly interjected. "We have come in response to the invitation from

the great Belias Stongrathen, leader of the Lemurian people."
Mala bowed her head slightly.

The soldier stepped aside. "Please exit through here," he said,
pointing at the door, "and follow me to your chambers."

How did you?

Mala turned her head to wink at David as they followed the
soldier into the compound.

He led them down a long, narrow corridor and stopped
outside a green door. "You're just in time for the next gathering
in the great hall, where our esteemed leader will be making a
very important announcement. Please make your way there as
soon as possible."

"We've been waiting for you, sister. Where've you been?"

"Belias, you never cease to amaze me."

"Whatever are you talking about?"

"You are so caught up in your prophecy shmophecy, that you
don't even have the decency to greet me. Your own sister! Bah!"

Belias took a step back. "It's just that…"

"Blah, blah, blah. Whatever it is, it's yet another excuse."

"It's no excuse, it's the future, Bel. The time has come. This
gathering signals the fulfilment of the Great Prophecy that will
set us all free!"

"Belias! You are missing the point as usual. Ah, no matter, I
have something more important to share with you anyway."

"Can't this wait until after the Gathering in the great hall?"

"No! This is important."

"OK. OK. So, what is it?"

"Have you heard of the SSHF?"

Kaimi spoke. "The Sun Salutation Humanitarian Foundation.
A group of light workers intent on revitalising the crystalline
grid matrix."

Belias smiled. "Yes. Of course. One of those group
consciousness organisations. But they're infinitesimal and have
never amounted to much. We monitor most of their
activities…"

"Well, that's what I was doing. We attended their summer solstice event in Central Park yesterday."

"And?" said Belias.

"And, we were taken by complete surprise! I mean we had an interstellar out-of-body experience, led by the group's leader Mary-Jane Fontaine."

"Interstellar? Impossible."

"That's what I thought. But it totally happened. At the start of the session, she introduced us to a powerful, red crystal placed in the centre of the group by one of its members; that enhanced the intensity of the experience at least tenfold."

Kaimi put his hand into his pocket and pulled it out again. "Like this one?"

Belengera leant forward for a closer look. "Yes! Same deep, red colour but easily double in size."

Kaimi looked toward Belias for guidance. "This is concerning. Could this member be one of ours?"

"Could be, but where and how would they have sourced such a powerful crystal without our knowledge? No. Whoever it is, he or she must be working alone. I wouldn't worry too much about it, my sister."

"Belias, you are too impetuous, dammit!" Belengera threw her arms up into the air, clearly agitated by his arrogance. "This group was guided by a very powerful force that was able to use the crystal as a conduit. I was pulled along with the group, unable to tear myself from its powerful trajectory across the Earth. I experienced powerful crystals hidden deep within the Earth come to life as we passed over them. I was blinded by a light so strong, that I almost lost myself to its mighty, magnetic force. It was only at the last moment that I managed to escape."

Belias raised his eyebrows. "And you have no idea who was responsible?"

"Well, at first, I thought it was Mary-Jane, the group's leader. But then it seemed that the source of the power and control was coming from somewhere else as if Mary-Jane was being used as a channel for the crystal by another powerful entity. It doesn't seem possible, but that's the only way I can explain it."

"Hmmm. Interesting. Kaimi?"

"Yes, Master."

"After the Gathering, I want you to investigate this Foundation and find out more about this Mary-Jane. Maybe pay her a visit. Let's get to the bottom of this."

"Yes, sir."

"But right now, my people are waiting!"

The great hall was filled to capacity. Over 2,000 people were packed into the large room. The chairs had all been removed to accommodate the increase in numbers and there was a loud buzzing that came from the hundreds of voices all talking at once. Kaimi stepped up onto the stage, and the noise dropped to a low hum. David and Mala joined the throng of people as they gathered in anticipation of seeing their great leader and hearing his important announcement. The air was electric, bristling with a supercharged energy.

Kaimi stepped to the front of the stage, looked out over the crowd in front of him and smiled. "Welcome, fellow Lemurians, to the great underground city of Barbados. Few people know the true origin of the name given to this sacred island we call home. It comes from the Portuguese Los Barbados which means the bearded ones, thought to be named after the long, hanging roots of the bearded fig tree, indigenous to this place. But, in truth, it comes from our ancestor, Asbeth and his devout followers who landed here to establish this stronghold thousands of years ago." A few shouts of praise burst from the crowd. "And here we still stand, united together as one, ready to accept what is rightfully ours to receive." More shouts and fist pumps from the crowd. "I give you the one man who has the power and authority to deliver us into the new age. The one man who will open the door to a new world. The one man who is going to save us all! I give you Belias Stongrathen!" Kaimi stepped backwards, extending his right hand out in a welcoming gesture as Belias stepped up and onto the stage, to a tumultuous roar from the enthusiastic crowd.

Belias was wearing a long, white flowing robe that dragged on the floor behind him. His white, wavy hair had been straightened, and his black, beady eyes shone out of his narrow skull like a raven's. He smiled as he took Kaimi's place on the stage and extended both hands out in front of him, signalling the crowd to become silent. He turned to Kaimi and bowed his head. He turned back to the crowd of people before him and began to speak, his magically amplified voice booming across the sea of expectant faces.

"The time has finally come, my brothers and sisters. The time of the Great Prophecy!" Another eruption from the crowd. "The prophecy tells us that there will be great adversity for humanity when the sun is at its weakest. This will take place at the next solar eclipse, in less than two days time. Mankind will convert to follow a new path - the path of Lemuria. The time has come for us to expose ourselves fully to the human race, establishing our leaders as the destined rulers of this world, so that the path of Lemuria can be resurrected in the name of Prince Asbeth and his people!" The thunderous roar was deafening. "My people. I stand before you, ready to lead you into a new and exciting future. A future where you need hide no longer. A future where you will be able to practice your arts without fear or prejudice. A future filled with promise and potential." Belias had the crowd hanging onto every word. "The fulfilment of The Lemurian Prophecy will herald a time of freedom and autonomy, but also a time of power and control. The world will see us for who we really are. We will step from out of the shadows and join our governors, prime ministers and presidents to rule this world. We will be revered as gods among men. This will be a new age. Our age. The age of Lemuria returned. And our great forefather, Asbeth's dream finally fulfilled!" Belias stood back and took in the wave of applause that hit him like a blast of hot air. He smiled wickedly, admiring the hundreds of followers that surrounded him in the Great Hall.

Belengera stepped up onto the stage in all her splendour. She resembled the lead in an opera performance with her bright, pink voluminous dress that swayed around her as she walked. There was another round of applause as she waved to the crowd before her. Belias extended his arm in greeting. "For those of you who have not met her, this is my sister Belengera Duarte from Spain and leader of the European movement." Belengera glowered menacingly at Belias. "Oh. Excuse me. Belengera comes from the Basque Province, a unique part of the world that was also founded by our ancestors, many thousands of years ago." Belias tilted his head with a smile and shrugged his shoulders in compunction. "It has been her guidance and leadership that has kept the organisation alive and prosperous over the years. I welcome all our brothers and sisters from our extended European family, who have joined us here at this time." A roar from the crowd. "We extend our hospitality to you and look forward to sharing in the riches that the prophecy has ordained for us and our kind."

"Thank you dear brother." Belengera nodded her head in Belias's direction and then stepped forward to the edge of the stage. She cast her gaze across the room. "My fellow Lemurians, we have a busy agenda over the next few days." Her voice sounded deeper than usual as it boomed out across the eager crowd. "This afternoon and into tomorrow, we are hosting a series of workshops, designed around the successful coordination and implementation of Operation Liberty. You should all have received your programmes. You have been split up into groups with an appointed team leader. Please report to your designated training room, situated in the complex and identified by your respective group's colour. The day after tomorrow we will depart the city and travel for several hours underground before climbing to the surface. We will emerge near Harrison's Cave where we will witness the solar eclipse and the fulfilment of the Great Prophecy." Belengera thrust her fist into the air. "Ad Victorium!"

Over 2,000 voices erupted in response. "Ad Victorium! Ad

Victorium! Ad Victorium!" The walls reverberated with the sound.

David grabbed Mala's hand in his and pulled her away in a hurry. His mind was racing. Gotta get outta here. Can't breathe. He pushed through the crowd, straining his neck, searching for one of the exits between the closely crammed bodies. There. David increased his pace. It felt like he was climbing uphill. The sea of bodies around him became a mudslide; that threatened to carry him down to the bottom of a dark, gaping pit. He finally squeezed himself through an opening, stumbled into open space and then dropped, out of breath, onto the floor. Mala sat down with him. There was a concern on her face.

"David. You OK?"

David took in a deep breath. "Yes, I'll be fine." He reached forward to give Mala a hug. "Come. Let's go." They made their way back through the maze of corridors to their chambers. David closed the door behind him and then ran his hands through his hair. "We're doomed! What're we gonna do?" He looked at Mala. She was beaming. "How can you be happy at a time like this?" He threw his hands down in frustration and then waved them about as he paced up and down the room. "There's this madman talking about taking over the world, and you just stand there and smile?"

"It's a miracle."

"A miracle? Is that what you call it? I'd say it's a nightmare. Mala! What're we to do?"

"He mentioned Prince Asbeth."

"Who?"

"Asbeth. He was my brother. He must've escaped. Over 12,000 years ago. And this is his legacy." She looked up and around her, opening her palms in acquiescence.

"OK. But did you hear what this Belias said? He spoke about a prophecy. Is it the same one that you mentioned? Sounds similar but your version says nothing about a race of angry Lemurians attempting to take over the world!"

"Yes, that is troubling. We have to stop him."

313

"Ha! Easier said than done. He's powerful, as is his sister - that woman we followed here. What if he's right? What if the prophecy means that he will see your brother's vision come true? What if it means that these self-proclaimed Lemurians will take over the world?"

Mala closed her eyes. "Asbeth was different. He always got up to no good. Father would never have wanted this."

"Your father?"

"Yes, he was King. He had the gift of sight. He taught me that the Great Prophecy spoke of a time of peace, where the nations of the world would be brought together as one. I must speak with Belias. I must convince him otherwise."

"No. I won't let you. Didn't you hear him? He's a crazy person. There'll be no reasoning with him."

"I must at least try."

"But…"

"I'll converse with him from here."

"You mean telepathically?"

Mala nodded her head in affirmation.

CHAPTER FIFTY-FOUR

Darkness

It was just a few days ago that she remembered opening her eyes to an intense pain inside her head and a loud ringing in her ears that made her feel nauseous. Everything was a blur. She lifted her head and grimaced, just making out the outline of a girl with long, dark hair crouching down in front of her, hunched over something. Or someone. Elena. She dropped her head back down onto the ground and rolled it slowly to the right. Her vision began to clear. She saw a body. There was blood. A lot of blood. She lay there, unmoving, for a while longer and then slowly, painstakingly, pushed herself up into a seated position and turned to look at the body again. Tears welled up in her eyes. *Billy. No.* Her heart ached with despair. Her senses tingled as she turned to glimpse something come swinging towards her head and then everything went black.

The small, confined space was dark, except for the outline of wan light that framed the door. A musty smell permeated the air, as she lay on the single bed in the far corner of the room. She heard voices just outside the door. Mexican voices. A key rattled in the door. She shielded her eyes as the door opened to a bright light that silhouetted a solitary figure.

"Kisha."

She recognised the voice. It was Elena. She slowly sat up in bed to get a better look at the girl, her eyes gradually adjusting

315

to the light.

"Finally, you waken. Your boyfriend killed my father. And now you're gonna pay. But first, tell me where my father's documents are." Elena sounded very different to the sweet little girl that Kisha met in the cafeteria.

"I dunno what you're talking about." Kisha's throat was dry. Her voice rasped like she was talking through a sieve.

"Don't lie you fucking bitch! Where are they?"

"I told you, I don't know!"

The muscles in Kisha's neck contracted involuntarily. Elena slapped her hard across the face, throwing her back into the headboard. Her cheek went numb with a stinging pain, and her eye began to water.

"Someone broke into the Villa and emptied my father's safe. If you don't confess, I'll personally have you killed!"

"I was with you and Billy." Kisha dropped her head and tears welled up in her eyes. *I can't believe he's gone.*

Elena smiled sarcastically. "Ha. Belias made a meal of him."

Kisha looked up in alarm. "Belias?"

"Yes. After Billy had killed my father, Belias killed Billy. Billy went on a rampage when he thought you dead. He must have loved you so…"

"Fuck you."

"Ooh. Temper, temper. Remember who's in control here. Now tell me what I need to know or else…"

Kisha stood up and shouted, slowly enunciating her words. "I already told you, I do-not-know-what-you-are-talking-about!"

"OK. Two can play that game. I'll give you some time to think about your options. Life or death. When I return, you had better give me what I need to know." And with that, she turned and marched out of the room, slamming the door shut behind her.

Kisha dropped her head into her hands and slowly slid down the wall onto her haunches, her body shaking in despair.

CHAPTER FIFTY-FIVE

Truth

"I'll join you."

"No. I must do this alone. He may be too powerful for you."

"But what if he is too powerful for you?"

Mala smiled. "I am over 12,000 years old. I think I have the advantage of age, wisdom and experience."

David held her hand in his. "OK. I'll be right here."

Mala looked into David's eyes, moved forward and kissed him on the lips. "I'll be fine. Don't you worry."

David stood up and checked that the door to their room was locked. Mala sat down cross-legged, placed her hands on her knees and closed her eyes.

Belias.

Kaimi?

No. My name is Mala.

How…who are you? What do you want?

I am Lemurian. Like you.

Why have I never heard of you? Met you? Are you one of my sister's people?

No. I know that this is going to be hard for you to believe but I am an original Lemurian. I have come to warn you.

Haha. Is that a threat? How dare you.

The Prophecy is not what you think it is. The Great Prophecy predicts a time of peace and love, not conflict and subjugation. Your plans can only

317

end in disaster for you and your people.

You lied. You said that you were Lemurian, and yet you speak of my people. Are they not yours too?

I said I was an original Lemurian, born in Lemuria.

You are a charlatan. If you were an original Lemurian, you would be over 12,000 years old. Who are you? Where are you? Why do you not face me? What are you afraid of?

I am not afraid. I wanted to face you this way, to show you, that like you, I have telepathic abilities and that I speak the truth.

Truth? You speak of truth? The only truth is in the here and now. I am the ruler of the Lemurian people, charged with fulfilling the Great Prophecy. We have been hiding from the world for thousands of years, waiting in anticipation for this moment. And now it has come. We will rise to show the world who we truly are. We will expose our power and spread our regime across the planet, taking control of what is rightfully ours. Nothing can stop us because it is preordained.

Don't you see that your plan will only cause chaos and destruction? The governments of this world won't just relinquish control to you and your kind. They will resist. There will be war. There will be fighting. There will be death.

I tire of this charade and your idle threats. Face me now so that I can crush you. Coward.

Belias focused his intent on the strange visitor and, with some effort, followed the thread of energy that emanated from the source of the communiqué. Instead of the typical result, he would have expected from this endeavour; he experienced a pang of unease as he faced a foreign obstacle in his path - a forcefield, preventing him from probing any further. It was then that he realised the threat was very real.

This has to be a group of Bel's people that have ideas of their own. There's no way that an individual could block me by herself.

He decided to gather his resolve for one final attempt at breaking through his adversary's barricade. He pulled back, all but severing the connection between them, creating a mini-shield of his own to disguise his mustering of energy, his building of reserve power to strike back with enough force to overwhelm this threat, this thorn in his side. Now. Belias attacked. His feigned retreat worked, to some degree at least. The forcefield had shrunk as he pushed through it, following the trail of energy that would lead him to his challenger. He was almost there; he could feel it. He knew that he was close because he could sense the source emanating from within the compound.

Just a moment more and then I will know who it is...

But then the impossible happened. It was like he had stuck his entire arm into an electric socket. The shock-wave sent a reverberation through the spiritual realm. He was catapulted right back to his quarters, physically lifted up into the air and then dropped down on the floor like a puppet. His entire arm felt like it was on fire and his head felt like it was going to explode from the pain. "Aaaaaaahhhhh!!!" Belias tried to lift his arm, but it was completely immobile. He looked at it disdainfully. It may as well have been a prosthetic limb. A pins-and-needles feeling started manifesting itself in his fingertips. His fingers felt like they were swollen sausages at the end of his wrist. Try as he might he could barely get them to move.

Mala opened her eyes. They were filled with tears.

"Mala. You OK? What happened?"

Mala shook her head slowly from side to side. "So much anger and hatred. He is blind. There is no use. We have to leave. We must get out of here and somehow warn the rest of the world before it's too late. We must prevent these people from carrying out Operation Liberty. It is our duty to save the planet from this impending catastrophic event."

"But how? How are we going to stand up to these people? They are too strong. There are too many. And how are we going to warn the world? These people already control things out there."

"I don't know yet. But what I do know is that we have to get out of here. We have a better chance of defeating this threat once we are on the surface."

"OK. But how do we get out of here? Where do we go?"

"Belengera spoke of an underground route to Harrison's Cave. I know where that is. Remember that soldier we encountered when we first arrived?"

"Yes. The one that you told, we were invited by Belias?"

"Yes. I read his mind. He also had a map of the complex." Mala tapped the side of her head. "There is an underground forest here. That's where we need to go. Now," she said with urgency in her voice.

CHAPTER FIFTY-SIX

Break In

"Here, let me look at that. Hmmm. Not too bad, big boy Looks like the Doc did a good job." The nurse cleaned the wound on both sides with antiseptic before applying a fresh set of gauze and bandages to the region so as to prevent further infection. "Come back in five days so that I can change the bandages." She was wearing a short, white skirt. Her slender legs were a soft, brown and appeared longer than usual. He stared at them as she turned to wash her hands in the basin on the other side of the room.

"So, Sofia, was it? Are you free this evening? I think I might need some after-hours medical attention."

She replied without turning around. He knew she was smiling by the tone of her voice. "Mr Ligman, are you hitting on me?"

"Um, no, just need your help to change these bandages. You did such a good job. Besides, I can't reach the other side on my own."

She turned around to face him. "Well, you won't need to change them until you see me again to have the stitches out."

"Well, I don't think I can wait that long. I mean I might just rip off this bandage tonight so that I can call you to come and put on a new one."

"OK. I'll tell you what. If you can wait until tomorrow night when I'm free, then just maybe…Now go on, get out of here."

Josiah hopped into a cab and headed back to the Rui Plaza Hotel in Guadalajara. He looked at his reflection in the twelve-inch blade that they had let him keep as a memento, cleaned to a shine by nurse Sofia. Back at the hotel, there was no sign of Kaimi, Maria, Billy or Kisha. Finn's equipment was still set up in his room, where Josiah spent some time trying in vain to contact his companions before crashing for the night. He woke the next morning and switched on the television. He flipped through the channels until he reached CNN. He hopped onto the web again, leaving the television playing in the background.

Where is everyone? Come on Jo, think. He looked up from the laptop when he heard the word Mexico on the news.

"Our correspondent in Guadalajara, Casey Tiguan is on the scene right now with this report. Casey."

The picture changed to a blond reporter holding a CNN-branded mic with a highway behind her. She was wearing too much red lipstick that reminded Josiah of a plastic Barbie doll. There were police moving around in the background amidst a lot of yellow tape that appeared to be cordoning off a crime scene. A red banner with bold yellow text flashed onto the screen. Mexican drug lord murdered. Josiah sat up in earnest.

"Good morning." The doll could talk. "I am standing alongside the highway on the outskirts of the city of Guadalajara, here in Mexico. Behind me is what could be a scene out of a movie, involving a car chase, a shootout, drugs and cold-blooded murder. The infamous Mexican drug lord, Diego Marcos Rodriguez or more commonly known as The Monarch, was murdered here last night, along with what is believed to be three other high-ranking officials in his organisation. Rodriguez was the leader of the Ropero Cartel, a well-known association responsible for large quantities of cocaine being smuggled into the U.S.A. He was fatally stabbed with an unidentified weapon. It is believed that he was killed by another cartel intent on taking over his territory."

"Thank you, Casey for that report. Well, you know what they say, live by the sword, die by the sword…"

Josiah jumped up. He had to get back to the villa. If Diego was dead, then perhaps his daughter Elena was still alive. She would know something at least. He caught a cab, climbed out two miles away and ducked into the bushes. He trekked to the road leading in and out of the villa, staked out the property for just short of five hours and watched as a white, Tacos Company branded van made two return visits. He followed the van back to a food delivery company in the city, hot-wired the van very early the next morning and drove it straight back up to the villa.

"Donde está Carlos?" The security guard peered into the van.

"Uh, Carlos is sick. He has a tummy bug or something."

"Abierto." The guard waved his hand, signalling for Josiah to open the van.

"Sure. No problemo." Josiah stepped out of the van, walked around the back and opened the doors. The van was filled with a mix of groceries and foodstuffs. The guard had a quick look inside and then gave Josiah the thumbs up. He climbed back inside and made his way up the driveway to the rear of the villa. He knocked on the door that led into the courtyard he scaled not so long ago. After a few minutes, a maidservant opened up to let him in. The Rottweiler that attacked him was nowhere to be seen. Fortunately, the servant wasn't one of the ones that he locked up on his last visit. He figured the staff were all replaced after the recent break-in. Josiah started off-loading goods from the van into the kitchen. Halfway through the job, he turned to the servant assisting him. "I need to go to the toilet. Al Bano." The servant nodded and led him down the passage.

Josiah peeped out the door and saw a security guard approaching. He stepped out of the toilet. "Buenos días."

"Buenos días," replied the guard.

Josiah brought his left arm up at lightning speed and connected the guard in the throat with the side of his hand. The guard's tongue shot out of his mouth, and he clutched at his throat with both hands, choking on his crushed windpipe. Josiah swung his right hand around in an arc, connected with the side of the guard's neck, instantly putting him out of his misery. He

323

quickly dragged the guard into the toilet, undressed him and lifted him up and into the bath. His clothes were pretty tight, and the shoes didn't fit, so Josiah left his sneakers on. He stepped out of the toilet and proceeded to move stealthily down the corridor. He opened doors to empty rooms until the corridor turned to the right. Another guard was standing outside a door. It looked like he had been positioned there.

He turned as Josiah approached. He creased his brow. "Quién es usted?"

"Huh?" replied Josiah. The guard looked down at his shoes, lifted his head, surprise etched on his face and reached for his weapon. Josiah grabbed the guard's wrist and twisted the gun out of his hand before he could raise it to shoot. He dispatched the guard with a series of blows, first to the solar plexus, followed by a knee to his face as he doubled over, and then finished him off with another punch to the face. He turned to open the door. It was locked. He took a step back, raised his foot and booted the door, smashing the lock. He stepped inside, his eyes adjusting to the gloom.

"Kisha!"

"Jo! Is that you!?" Kisha ran and jumped up into his arms, giving him a huge hug. She burst into tears.

Josiah consoled her for a moment before letting her down. "Miss K. We have to get out of here before someone realises that I've broken in for a second time." Josiah dragged the guard into the room, took his gun and then pulled the broken door closed as best as he could. They made their way back to the kitchen as quickly as possible. A surprised servant jumped in alarm as Josiah rounded the corner with Kisha in tow. He had the gun pointed at the servant as he passed him. "Shhhh, sí?" The servant nodded, his eyes wide. He put his hands up and backed away as Josiah and Kisha made their way out the kitchen door. They turned and ran to the van. A siren sounded, followed by shouts from around the villa. Elena came running out and jumped onto the back of the van, grabbing the door handle just as Josiah pulled away. She pulled the door open and jumped inside. Kisha climbed over her seat to face Elena in the back of the van.

"You bitch!" cried Elena. "You won't get away with this!" She dived at Kisha who nimbly sidestepped the young girl. Elena crashed onto the floor of the van. She jumped up and turned to face Kisha who was now standing with her back to the open door that was swinging wildly as Josiah swerved across the villa's grounds. The van swerved left, and the girls were thrown right. Elena kicked her legs out and into Kisha's right shoulder, forcing her out the back of the van. She grabbed onto the handle of the swinging door as it was closing. Her weight and momentum swung the door open, and she went with it, her legs flailing out of the van, as she held on in desperation. She bent her knees, lifted her torso and swung back towards the van, driving the door closed again. She kicked out her feet and connected Elena in the chest, catapulting her into the front of the van. She let the door go in the nick of time, saving her fingers from getting crushed, and dive-rolled inside. Elena stood up and charged at Kisha with a loud yell. She deftly sidestepped Elena again and then it was her turn to fly out the back of the van. Her yell turned to a panic-stricken scream as she struggled in vain to reach for something to hold onto on the way out. Kisha watched Elena hit the ground in a cloud of dust with a thump and a wheeze, before quickly moving to the rear of the van to pull the door closed.

Josiah approached the closed white, metal gates at the entrance to the property. He pushed his foot flat on the accelerator, punching the van through the gates with a bang. The wheels spun on the gravel road, gained traction and then pulled the vehicle away from the villa, under a rain of bullets and foul curses.

CHAPTER FIFTY-SEVEN

Lies

"Oh, my goodness." David was admiring the vast canopy of trees that spanned above them. "This is a botanist's dream. These trees look really old."

Mala followed his gaze. She smiled, walked up to the nearest tree and carefully dropped her head forward until her forehead was touching the trunk. She closed her eyes and stood completely still. David stopped to watch her. She turned her head, opened her eyes and signalled for him to join her on the other side. David walked towards the tree and followed suit.

Focus on the energy here.

Mala's instruction came to him like a whisper.

David felt his eyes begin to tingle behind his closed lids. Ghostly shades of light played across the screen by an absconded projectionist. He focused his attention on the things around him; the things in the here and now. It was easy to become distracted. The tingling in his eyes intensified and attracted the light like a magnetic beacon, as it grew brighter and brighter, enveloping him in its cocoon-like embrace. The light swallowed his body, and his spiritual entity toppled forward and into the tree. There was an immediate sense of peace and quiet like a weight had been lifted from his shoulders. David felt the dense pressure of the tree. It was a claustrophobic experience, bringing a sample of burning bile up from his insides. He swallowed. Twice.

David thought he heard a faint melodic sound as he concentrated his breath on the life flowing through the tree. He moved deeper inside the tree as his conscious breath left him and became involuntary. He felt the tickle of golden light against his lids again. He opened his eyes, and there was Mala, beaming in front of him like an angel in heaven. Mala held out her arms and the two beings of light energy embraced each other inside the tree. David felt an overwhelming sense of connectedness like he was part of everything around him, of a greater organism, an ongoing process of creation. Life.

David opened his eyes and found himself hugging the tree, his right cheek pressed up and into the bark. He let go and stood back, surprised to feel quite fresh and rejuvenated. He heard that sound again. This time, it sounded like a whisper, rustling through the treetops high above him. He looked at Mala and together they walked past the edge of the forest and into the set of caves beyond, making their way towards the exit several miles on.

Why are there people leaving the city via the caves? Belias sounded agitated.

I do not know, your eminence.

Follow them and bring them back for questioning.

Yes, my lord.

Kaimi wondered why Belias didn't ask him who they were and then he realised that he already knew.

Kisha felt the heat from the hot bath soothe her aching muscles and stiff joints. She felt wave after wave of tension lift up and melt off her body like an invisible hand was sponging her. She sank deeper into the bath, closing her eyes, trying to block out the maelstrom of prodigious images and sensations that coursed through her mind. She felt alone, yet she also felt charged with a sense of awareness of her mission, her duty - to avenge Billy's death. She replaced her feelings of sorrow with anger and animosity. She climbed out of the bath, dried herself and then looked into the mirror at her reflection. "I will take revenge Billy if it's the last thing I do."

She met Josiah at the hotel bar. He was sitting alone, cradling a scotch on the rocks.

"What's a good looking guy like you doing all alone in a place like this?"

Josiah turned and smiled. "I'm glad to see that you're all right. Miss Kisha."

"Yeah, I guess I'll be OK. Gotta carry on, you know?"

"Yeah. I know." Josiah dropped his head. "I know. Whatcha drinking?"

"Uh, a gin and tonic, I guess."

"You heard her, barmen. And throw in a slice of lemon."

"Thanks, Jo. For being there, for saving my ass." Kisha squeezed his hand.

Josiah shrugged his big shoulders. "Juss doin' my job, ma'am."

Kisha sipped her drink, savouring the tingling sensation. Her taste buds came alive to the alcohol as it washed all the hurt and pain down her throat.

"So you're telling me this Belias character killed Billy?" Josiah said.

"That's what Elena told me."

"OK. So let's pay him a visit and punish him." Josiah deepened his voice so that it sounded like the voice-over in the Mortal Kombat computer game fighting sequence.

"That's exactly what I wanna do, but he has a city full of worshippers. How we gonna even get close? We can't exactly arrive unannounced in that elevator in the diner."

Josiah's teeth flashed as he grinned. "Harrison's Cave."

The bus filled with Chinese tourists pulled into the parking area outside the Boyce Tunnel entrance to Harrison's Cave. A solitary ticket office poked out of the mountainside like an indignant alien structure, white and exposed. Josiah stepped off the bus and into a sea of five foot Chinamen, his bulky frame towering above them like a giant. Kisha followed, the two of them making their way inside the cave and onto a tram that took them into the bowels of the Earth. They climbed out of the tram, breaking away from the tourists to find the area filled with stalagmites adjacent to the pool.

"Come, this way, it's just around the corner. Shit." The path was blocked by red barrier tape. They could go no further.

Kisha rounded the corner. "Oh no. What now?"

"Let's have a look." Josiah lifted the tape, climbed underneath and made his way towards the rock pool. His shoulders visibly slumped. The pool was filled with rocks. It looked like they had broken away from the wall next to the pool from some sort of disturbance. "Damn. This was our way in," said Josiah. "We're gonna have to double back and take the longer route. I just hope that it's still open cos I have no idea how to get through from this end if it happens to be closed."

David followed Mala up a very long, narrow staircase hewn directly into the rock surrounding them. A grating sound echoed down, through the stairwell as they reached the top. A large rock mysteriously shifted to one side and shafts of morning sunlight filtered in, blinding the two travellers as they emerged into the daylight beyond.

"Don't move." Josiah's deep voice stopped Mala and David in their tracks. "Who are you and what are you doing here?"

"David stepped up to the imposing Josiah. "Um, we were just exploring the caves."

"Bullshit. You've come from the city. This is a secret exit from that damned place." He pointed down the steps from whence they came.

David looked at Mala. "Look, we don't know what you are talking about. Just let us pass and we'll do you no harm."

"Ha, ha!" Josiah glanced at Kisha standing just behind him and grinned." You promise you'll do me no harm? Now that's a joke if I've ever heard one. Look, don't fuck with me. I know

329

where this tunnel comes from. If you aren't straight with me, then you're the one that's going to get harmed."

"OK. Yes," said David. "You're right. We have come from the underground city."

"Great, then you're going to take us back inside." Josiah stepped up to David and then reached out to grab him by the scruff of his neck. His muscles just froze. They were working to move, but they had simply locked into position on their own accord. He looked at David with disdain. "What have you done to me? Let me go. Now!"

"Calm down. We're not going back inside. There is a madman down there who wants to take over the world. We plan to stop him."

Kisha stepped forward. "Belias."

Mala looked at Kisha. "Yes. Belias. You know him?"

"He killed my boyfriend. We're on our way to find him and make him pay."

"Well, it seems that we have something in common. I'm Mala."

"Kisha." They shook hands.

"Are you gonna let me go now?" said Josiah.

"Sure. Just promise not to touch me." David looked up at Josiah's daunting frame.

Josiah felt control to his movements return. "How the hell did you do that?"

Kisha looked at David. "He has powers, like Kaimi."

"Hi. I'm David."

"Kisha. And this is my friend Josiah."

"Call me Jo."

"So, why are you leaving if Belias is still down there?" Kisha enquired.

"We tried to talk to him, to convince him that what he is doing is wrong, but he is blinded by mistruths and fabricated lies. He's coming here with his people. Thousands of them. They will arrive very soon, right from this tunnel."

"I'm confused," said Kisha. She impulsively brushed her long, brown hair from her face. "You say that you're also against this Belias, but then why is it that you have powers like him and his people? Whose side are you on?"

"We are on the good side," said Mala with a gentle smile.

"So how'd you plan to stop him?" Josiah asked. "I mean it's just us versus a couple of thousand. I wouldn't call that the best of odds."

"Well, we could ask you the same question," said David. "How were you planning to stop him?" He looked around. "Where's your army? He'll crush you in a heartbeat."

Josiah shifted on his feet, and his muscles flexed. "Well, the plan was to sneak in and attack him unawares."

"He won't paralyse you the way I just did; he'll kill you. He has no remorse. We also happen to have a plan." David looked at Mala and shrugged his shoulders. "Well, kinda. We know that the Lemurians are going to be coming out of this exit. That's an advantage right there. We also know that the staircase is only wide enough for people to walk single file, which means of course, that only one person can exit at a time. We expect Belias and his sister to be stationed in front, so we'll surprise them as they appear and then seal the exit so that no one else can leave. This will allow us to deal with them individually."

"And just how're you going to do that?" Kisha said. "I've seen Belias. He's far stronger than the both of you put together. He can do things."

Mala smiled and took a deep breath. "Belias has power. Yes, he is strong, but he still has much to learn."

Kisha looked at Mala suspiciously as if she was scanning her, trying to read her thoughts. "Who are you really and why do you want to stop Belias? What has he done to you?"

"It's not what he has done; it's what he will do. He plans to take over the world. He must be stopped at all costs. Otherwise, chaos and destruction will follow."

Josiah looked over David's shoulder as a solitary figure with long, braided hair stepped out from below ground. "Kaimi!" The others turned around.

"Jo, my friend," said Kaimi. "It's good to see you. And Kisha!" Kaimi smiled.

"You! This is all your fault! You made us do this, and now Billy is dead!" Kisha ran up to Kaimi and started banging her fists against his chest in frustration. Tears flowed down her cheeks.

Kaimi grabbed her wrists. She eventually calmed down and took a step back. "I'm sorry, Kisha, but Billy attacked Belias. He defended himself and then, unfortunately, Billy was killed."

"Billy only attacked Belias because he thought he killed me!" wailed Kisha.

"That was Rodriguez. He was the one that attacked you so that he could free his daughter, Elena from your custody."

"I don't care! It doesn't matter anymore, does it!? Billy's dead, and he's not coming back. If you hadn't made him carry out that stupid fuckin' assignment, he'd still be alive."

"What were you doing in the tunnels, in the city?" asked Kaimi.

"It wasn't us," said Josiah. "It was them." He pointed at David and Mala.

"Hi, I'm Kaimi." He extended his arm.

"David." They shook hands.

Mala smiled and reached out her hand to Kaimi. Mala closed her eyes as her hand gently settled into his. Kaimi's face widened in awe. "Who?"

I'm Mala.

Where are you from? You have so much power, so much energy. I can feel it.

I am an original Lemurian, come back to save humanity.

Come back?

Kaimi's jaw dropped as he closed his eyes. Mala's eyes were still closed, and her hand still rested in Kaimi's.

I can see. Beautiful. Mountains. Sea. And a village. Where is this?

It was my home. A very long time ago.

Who is that? Looks like a King.

My father. Yes. He was King. That's my brother Cuthru next to him.

They're looking at something. Can't see what it is. Oh, there. Another man. Training. Fighting.

That's my other brother, Asbeth.

Kaimi flashed open his eyes, jerked his hand away from Mala's and jumped back in alarm. He brought up his hands; ready to defend himself from an invisible assailant. "Who are you! What lies have you placed in my head?"

"Not lies. The truth. I am Lemurian, summoned back to help fulfil an ancient prophecy." Mala continued to smile.

"Impossible! Belias will fulfil the prophecy. He is on his way here to see that it is done. How could you? No. It cannot be." Kaimi had a look of horror on his face. The kind of look that you see when someone's beliefs are challenged. David saw fear.

"Belias thinks that the prophecy is going to give him the opportunity to expose himself to the world. To seize power and take control of the governments, its leaders. This is misinterpreted, misguided. Yes, your secret society already has power and control over many, and has been instrumental in building the world into what it is today - a corrupt, sinful and egotistical expression of Asbeth and his cruel personality. I can see that now." Mala's voice was calm and assertive.

"No! Lies!" Kaimi raised his hands and grimaced. Kisha and Josiah lifted up into the air like puppets and were dumped about ten meters away. Mala and David remained. "How?" said Kaimi, perplexed. He began to walk toward Mala and David and then slowed down, moving like he was wading through a torrential river, struggling against its powerful current.

Don't fight it, let go. You have skill, but you are doing it all wrong.

Kaimi's face blanched with the effort. He visibly relaxed, and his movements sped up.

You see?

Kaimi reached Mala and David but then suddenly they weren't there. He turned around. They had both reappeared behind him. *Hmmf.* He steeled himself and lifted both hands again. This time, he turned his hands inwards, so that his palms faced each other. The wind whipped itself up out of nowhere and began to swirl around Mala and David, building in strength. Dust and sand began to fly up and into the air around them until they disappeared from view behind a spinning, hazy vortex. The vortex seemed contained but then it expanded, much to Kaimi's dismay, until the very edge of the wall of dirt reached him. His eyes widened in alarm. He clenched his jaw and stiffened his arms. The spinning tornado stopped advancing for a moment but then expanded again, swallowing Kaimi into its depths. The outer wall passed over him. He opened his eyes and found himself weightless and floating in what felt like the eye of the storm. Mala and David were also floating just in front of him. They were smiling. The swirling matter around the three of them looked like the perimeter of a sandstorm held at bay by unknown forces. For the first time in many years, Kaimi felt powerless.

We don't want to hurt you, Kaimi. Just calm down and everything will be all right.

No! It won't be. You cannot disrupt the order of events. You cannot interfere with the prophecy. Our prophecy, our birthright! It shall be fulfilled, and we will all be free!

No Kaimi, you will all become slaves. Slaves to a new system. The bad news is that most people won't like this system. They will rebel. There will be war. I have seen the future, and it's not pleasant.

David watched as Kaimi brought his hands up to either side of his head and closed his eyes. "No! No! No! Get out of my head! Damn you!" Kaimi shook his head vociferously from side to side, his dreadlocks swinging through the air, slapping against his face. *Thwack, thwack, thwack.* Kaimi dropped his hands to his sides, as Mala began to initiate the transfer of an irrefutable truth - a more detailed account of her history on planet Earth and her mission to save the world from imminent destruction.

Kaimi, I know that you have an unassailable loyalty to Belias. It is this loyalty that has clouded your judgement of this man and the atrocities that he wishes to inflict upon the human race. Deep down, you are a good person. I know this. I can feel it. We can help you face and overcome the fear that you have lived with for so long. It is time for you to join us and confront Belias.

Just then there was a flicker in the fabric of space from within the swirling vortex. Mala whispered to David. "He's coming." Mala began to calm the swirling sand, and dust and its three occupants were placed gently down onto the Earth. Kaimi appeared rather dazed, as he surveyed his surroundings; eyes wide like a schoolboy in a museum. David watched the very air around them begin to vibrate, twisting reality like a reflection from a convex mirror and then Belias and Belengera stepped out of the distortion.

CHAPTER FIFTY-EIGHT

Confrontation

Josiah helped Kisha up onto her feet. "You OK?"

"Yeah. Just a shoulder graze. I'll be fine." Kisha looked towards David, Mala, Kaimi and two more people standing at the exit to the underground city. "That's him! That's Belias." She pointed at the white-haired character that had mysteriously appeared out of thin air. Josiah reached into his jacket and pulled out a Desert Eagle pistol. He stepped ahead of Kisha, raised the .357 calibre weapon and marched steadily towards the group.

"Kaimi! Why have you not responded to my request?" said Belias. He was livid. He ignored the others as if they weren't even there.

"I'm sorry, master, but I haven't received any requests. What is it you wanted me to do?"

"Stop being impudent. It was a simple task - follow the two infidels and bring them back to me. I see that you've caught up with them." He glanced at David and Mala. "So why haven't you apprehended them as I asked?"

"I tried."

"You tried!?"

"Yes, your grace. I tried to bring them back as you requested, but they resisted."

"What do you mean resisted? They are no match for you.

Who came to their aid?"

"We can speak for ourselves," said David stepping forward. "My name is Doctor David Steel, and this is Mala."

"They aren't mine," said Belengera.

"They aren't yours?" Belias turned to his sister and creased his brow. He turned back to look at Mala. "So, you're Mala," said Belias with a wicked grin. "Mala who dared threaten me. You're Brazilian. Let me guess. Rio?"

"No. I'm from Embu, in the state of São Paulo."

"So you did lie to me earlier. Why?"

"I did not lie. This body is 26 years old, but my spirit is that of Princess Mala of the Lumni Tribe, daughter to King Andor, Monarch of the Seven Kingdoms of Lemuria. David brought me here from the spirit world to fulfil the Great Prophecy of Lemuria."

Belias roared with laughter. He doubled over and continued to laugh some more. "Who are you working with? How did you manage to block me earlier?" His voice sounded ominous.

"Belias!" Josiah's deep voice interrupted the banter.

"Yes? That's me. Who are you?"

"Name's Jo and this here's Kisha."

Kisha stepped forward with her hands on her hips. "You murderer! You killed Billy. Now it's time to pay!"

Belias laughed. "Billy deserved to die. He tried to kill me."

"Don't move a muscle, pal or I'll shoot," said Josiah menacingly.

Belias turned to the round woman with the pink hair by his side, winked once and then moved, much to Josiah's dismay. *Blam! Blam!* He pulled the trigger, into nothing. Josiah looked quickly around. "What the fuck?"

"Jo! Help!" Belias had inexplicably materialised behind Kisha and had his arm wrapped securely around her neck. Josiah spun around.

"Don't try it, Jo. Put the gun down. Otherwise, she dies," said Belias in a threatening voice.

"Let her go! Otherwise, you die," said Josiah with all the

337

intent he could muster.

Belias tightened his grip around Kisha's neck until her face began to turn red. "Nnnnaahh," she gagged.

"OK. OK." Josiah carefully placed the weapon down at his feet and lifted his arms into the air.

"Now kick it over here," instructed Belias.

"No. Wait," said Mala. "Let her go, Belias!" She raised her right hand, and Belias's arm involuntarily relaxed its grip around Kisha's neck. His eyes widened in alarm. He felt as helpless as a stuffed animal.

It's not possible. How are you doing that?

You are no match for me, Belias. It's time you put an end to this charade.

Kisha pulled away from Belias and ran towards Josiah.

"Belengera! Stop her!" shouted Belias.

Despite her girth, Belengera moved quickly to intercept Kisha. "Oh no, you don't!" She grabbed Kisha's wrist and pulled. David stepped in and grabbed Kisha's other arm.

"Enough of this! No more games!" shouted Belias. "Kaimi, apprehend Mala. Now!" Kaimi hesitated. He looked at Mala and then back toward Belias. "Kaimi! You with me?"

Kaimi stepped forward. "This ends now." He bent down on one knee, touched his fingers to the earth, looked up and closed his eyes. The air compressed and then expanded in a wave of energy that shot outward like a series of ripples from a stone being thrown into a pool. Everyone was lifted up and hurled backwards with the force of the energy discharge. Belias twisted in the air and landed in a forward roll, successfully protecting his body from the impact. He turned and ran towards Belengera, who wasn't thrown very far due to her size. He grabbed her hand, and the two of them stepped through a shimmering slither of an opening that materialised out of thin air.

Mala stood up and dusted herself off. She reached out her hand to David. "Come. We follow."

She pulled him through the split after the nefarious couple.

David's insides lurched on a roller-coaster ride in distorted space-time. His senses were enhanced, and his breathing laboured. A kaleidoscope of colours flashed before him like stained glass. A white light burned away the colour and his vision cleared. He looked around and found himself standing with Mala, in a space of infinite proportions. The walls spread out and away from them in never-ending straight lines of brick and mortar. There was no ceiling, just dark, emptiness above.

Belias and Belengera appeared, first as hazy, indistinguishable figures in the distance and then became more distinct as they moved towards Mala and David.

Belias. Stop, said Mala. We don't want to fight. Let's talk this through. There's no need for violence.

You're starting to annoy me, interfering in matters beyond your control. The Prophecy will be fulfilled with or without you. And if this is where you choose to die, then so be it.

Belias and Belengera pulled out a pair of dark purple crystals the size of golf balls and pointed them directly at David and Mala. Two fiery bolts of lightning erupted in unison from the crystals with a loud crack, connecting their targets in a flash of light, catapulting them back into the darkness. A putrid, burning scent filled the air. Belias and Belengera advanced on the unmoving couple. They raised their crystals for another attack. Belias pulled his face into an evil grin as purple lightning cracked out of the stones once more. This time, an impenetrable force-field surrounding David and Mala protected them from the fateful strike. The purple energy dissipated instantly. Mala was on her knees. Her palms face-up, pressed together at their base, in a full lotus mudra. Her thumbs and little fingers were touching, while the three other fingers of each hand were spread open as wide as possible. Hovering between her palms was a large, red, glowing crystal, the source of the force-field's power. David opened his eyes. His chest was on fire. He rolled over and lifted himself up onto all fours.

Push through the pain said Mala.

I can't move.

Focus on the crystal. I'll feed your body with its energy.

David closed his eyes and focused on the red crystal in Mala's hands. He felt its warmth seep into his weakened body, charging it with fresh, revitalising energy. He turned around and came to kneel next to her, closing his eyes again. He sensed Belias and Belengera attempting to break through the energy field that protected them.

Focus on the crystal again. Can you feel how I am using it to protect us?

Yes. I sense the flow of energy.

Good. Now let's expand this energy.

David joined Mala, connecting to the crystal's power, expanding the force-field outward, slowly at first, creating enough space for both of them to stand and confront Belias and Belengera on the other side. Jagged, purple energy continued to fire from their attackers' crystals, pounding relentlessly against the red energy field, trying in vain to break through. Together, Mala and David repelled the destructive energy, eventually forcing it back and into the crystals. The purple crystals began to heat up and then imploded in a gigantic pulse of energy, engulfing both Belias and Belengera in a strange, purple fire that fizzled and sparked as it burned. They disappeared in the angry flames, the echo of their screams heard in this world and the next.

The air shimmered and Mala and David stepped back into reality. They joined Kaimi, Josiah and Kisha to gaze mesmerisingly at the moon, as it began to slide into place, blocking out the sun's light in a total eclipse that lasted for several minutes.

EPILOGUE

Josiah handed an envelope to Mary-Jane.

"What's this?"

"It's the future."

Mary-Jane carefully opened the envelope. "A cheque?"

"This is our gift to you," said Kisha. "It's for the Foundation."

"What? There must be some mistake. It says here one million. No. Wait. *Ten* million dollars?" Mary-Jane was perplexed.

"No mistake," said Josiah. "And there's plenty more where *that* came from."

"But I can't accept this. How did you come by so much money and why do you want to give it to me? To the Foundation?"

"Think of it as a gift from Mexico," Josiah replied, winking at Kisha.

"You must use these funds to expose your message to the world," said Mala. "We will help teach you and your members to open your minds to a higher form of energy that will be used to heal the world and spread the message of hope, love and peace. It's prophesied that the world will be redeemed from the evils that have reigned over it for so long. The time has come to raise the level of global consciousness, to awaken the full healing power of the Earth's crystalline matrix in a universal, transformative process that will be led by you and the Sun Salutation Humanitarian Foundation. This gift will help turn the foundation into a new movement, a new way of thinking, a global shift into a new age of peace, love and happiness."

David took hold of Mala's hand. They looked into each other's eyes and smiled.

Captain Pierre Houline looked out over the starboard side of *La Dauphin*. He could still see the speck that was Easter Island on the horizon. The French captain was an explorer and environmentalist. He had been paid handsomely by an unknown benefactor to spend the last two weeks combing this remote stretch of ocean for 'anomalies' on the seabed. The instructions were quite specific. He had to stay within ten square nautical miles of Easter Island; he was to keep his mission top secret, and he was to ask no questions.

"Mon Capitaine!"

"Yes. What is it?"

"Look! Look what we've found!" Frans had been working with the Captain for just short of five years. He was a quiet, solitary soul, so it was quite a surprise to see him so excited. "Just look at this." Frans pointed to a grainy image that he had just printed.

Captain Houline put on his spectacles and peered at the printout in front of him. "Good grief! And that's at 5,000 feet below?"

"Yessir!"

The Captain scrutinised the page more closely. "These look like pyramids."

"Yes, and these," Frans pointed at the page, "look like a series of monolithic blocks that are clearly not a natural phenomenon."

"It seems that we're looking at an ancient, submerged city," said the Captain. "And if that's the case, then we are going to

342

have to rewrite history!"

I really hope you enjoyed reading my book. Thank you for reading it! Reviews are very important for authors. If you enjoyed the book, please consider posting a review on Amazon.com.

Please visit my website, richardgradner.com for more information about my other novels, *Unicorn, Servant of Memory* and *Acoustic Alchemy*.

Thanks in advance for your support!

Richard

CHAPTER FIFTY-NINE
Untitled

ACOUSTIC ALCHEMY

Richard Gradner

CHAPTER SIXTY

1 ~ Naming Rights

The sound of silence consumed her like a suffocating shroud. It was all around her and deep inside her head, buzzing inside her ears from both the inside and out. She squeezed her eyes tight to banish the maelstrom and clear her mind from its scrutiny. An inquisition by the psyche. That's what it was. An inquisition. Why *was* she so inquisitive? She couldn't help feeling this way.

It's in my nature; she said to her mother when she scolded her for asking too many questions.

Tracy blinked her eyes open in the darkness. She massaged away the sleep with the knuckles of her left hand and then pushed her right arm out from beneath her, reaching for her phone on the bedside table. Her fingers tingled with a mild bout of pins and needles as her thumb found the home button. The LCD screen sprang to life, blasting the blackness away, along with the pressing silence of her thoughts. She squinted. 4.33am. She took a deep breath, sighed it out, and turned over in her bed. She was wide awake. There was no way she was going back to sleep. It was the fourth time this week that she woke up before the crack of dawn. It was as if there was a nagging feeling tugging at her mind, pulling her to do something, always just beyond her grasp like the tendrils of a dream that faded into memory as soon as she opened her eyes. She closed her eyes once more, trying in vain to see the visions, straining her mind, stretching it taut like a rubber band that came back to snap at her, leaving nothing but a welt of frustration deep inside the synapses of her brain.

The buzzing from her phone startled her. A wave of apprehension that threatened to engulf her like a restless spirit washed over her entire body, sending jittery tingles down her spine.

Why's my alarm going off so damn early?

Tracy twisted around in her bed, reaching for her mobile again. She tapped the red, blinking snooze button, killing the annoying sound and checked the time. 6.45am. She closed her eyes and smiled, relieved that she had somehow managed to succumb to the elusive succour of sleep. Today was going to be a good day. She sighed out heavily, and the stifling wave receded, leaving her exposed in the warm sunlight on a sandy atoll. She stretched out her body beneath the covers and yawned, enjoying the feeling of her muscles tensing from her fingers all the way down to her toes. Her foot popped out of bed, and she quickly pulled it back beneath the duvet as the wintry air in the room stung her toes with an icy kiss. She curled into a foetal position, pressing her head into her soft pillow, savouring the warmth beneath the covers. Thoughts of the day ahead flooded through her mind like a relentless torrent.

Friday.

Two more days until my seventeenth birthday.

She tensed her body in anticipation of the exciting occasion and then realised that she was still holding her phone. She pressed the Home button and opened Instagram, quickly scrolling through her feed, absorbing the content, getting lost in the pretty images and the fascination of the lives of others.

"Good morning," whispered Tracy. She closed her eyes and breathed in her mother's familiar, reassuring scent. She wrapped her arm around her mother's waist and shifted her body closer beside her, snuggling into a comfortable spooning position.

"Morning, angel," whispered her mother. "How did you sleep?"

"Much better, thanks."

"Good."

"Mom." She kept her voice to a whisper. "I love you."

"Love you too, baby."

Tracy hugged her mother affectionately and smiled deeply. She felt safe. Safe from the world and its complications. Safe from the anxiety she experienced when she spoke to Josh. Safe from that weird-looking homeless man who sat on the corner of Pine and Grove watching Tracy as she drove past him in the mornings. Safe from Veronica Lipman, that bitch who just wouldn't leave her alone, even when her bestie, Lisa, told her off several times. Stupid cow. Tracy sucked in a deep breath.

Focus on this moment, the here and now. Free your mind from the shackles of the past. Stop worrying about the future. Breathe in all those memories. Breathe in all those feelings that are making you tense and just let them go. I want to hear your breathing. I want to hear the sound of your breath as you breathe.

The soothing voice of Denise, her yoga instructor, echoed inside her head as she pulled herself away from her racing thoughts and focused on the present. She took pleasure in her mother's scent and the rise and fall of her ribcage as she breathed, the softness of the pillow beneath her face and the warmth she felt as she cuddled in the safety of her embrace.

"Can I make you some coffee?" whispered Tracy into her mother's ear.

Her mother nodded. "Thank you."

Tracy squeezed her mother one last time before letting her go. She rolled out of the bed and tiptoed into her own room, pulled on her slippers and threw her gown over her shoulders, shivering as she made her way into the kitchen. She peered out of the window, gazing up at the morning sky as she brewed two mugs of piping hot coffee, savouring the aroma that filled the air. It was a clear winter's day with not a cloud in sight. Morning sunlight streamed into the kitchen, bouncing off the counter-top in a bright, white light without much warmth.

"Here you go," said Tracy placing the hot mug on her mother's bedside table. She propped a cushion up against the headboard and climbed back into bed beside her, sitting up to sip gingerly at her hot coffee, enjoying the feeling as it warmed her body up from the inside. She turned on her phone in her free hand and opened Whatsapp. Her class group chat was out of control again. 147 messages. She scanned through the conversation. Mrs. Perkins was seen at a nightclub again. Oh, the drama! Avril Perkins was a fifty-three-year-old English teacher at Milwaukee High. Brenda Descartes always said that she was a twenty-one-year-old trapped in an older body. She had her boobs done. More than once. It was likely the only reason that she was hired by Dean Anderson. That perve. She always wore short skirts and low-cut tops, shamelessly showing off her heavy assets, and spent more money bleaching her hair to maintain its white-blond look than Veronica did on her highlights for an entire year! Tracy smiled. She was still trying to understand who saw Mrs. Perkins at the club. It could only have been Paul Williams. He always boasted that he used his fake ID to get into clubs. To his credit, he did look way older than twenty-one.

Camilla slowly pulled herself into an upright position. She brushed her dusty-blond hair away from her face, the same dusty-blond colour as Tracy's, only a little shorter, and picked up the mug of hot coffee from her bedside table. "Hmmm, this smells good," she said with her eyes closed, as she breathed in the aroma. "Thanks, Trace. Dylan still asleep?"

"Must be," replied Tracy without looking away from her screen.

"Trace, please go and wake him. You know how he is in the mornings. He needs time to wake up and get ready for school. I don't want to have to rush to get him ready again."

"Yes, but you know that no matter what time we wake him up, he still manages to do everything last minute."

"Just go and wake him, please. And bring me his phone. That's the reason he is late, actually. He lies in his bed playing games and watching videos before getting ready. And put yours down too, please. As the older sister, you need to set an example, little lady."

Tracy sighed. "Yes, mother." She stretched out her words, lacing them with enough sarcasm to cause her mother's eyebrows to rise in alarm. She took another sip of coffee before throwing her legs out of bed.

"Dylan, Dylan!" Tracy shook her brother awake.

He turned over with a groan. "Uhhh."

"It's time to wake up, little bro. Come on. Don't make us late again, okay?"

Dylan groaned again. His eyes were still closed. They looked as if they were glued shut. He screwed up his face as if he had just eaten a bitter lemon and then rolled over, away from his sister.

"Oh, no, you don't," said Tracy, pulling her brother over again.

This time, Dylan opened his eyes. "What?! Leave me alone! I'll get up, just leave me alone."

"Okay, okay. Calm the fudge down." Tracy unplugged her brother's phone and left the room.

"Here," she said, handing the phone to her mother.

"Thanks, Trace," said Camilla. "These electronics," she murmured. "They're gonna drive me to drink."

"Don't drink and drive, mom."

"Ha-ha. Very funny."

Tracy smiled. "Speaking of which, I'm driving to school today."

"Okay," said Camilla with a smile. "Just make sure Dylan gets to class. I don't want another call from the school asking if he's sick at home." She looked at Tracy askance. "Can't believe that you're seventeen come Sunday. Where have all the years gone? Come sit here so that I can brush your hair." Camilla patted the bed. "You know," said Camilla, as she pulled the brush through

Tracy's long, blond hair, "my mother used to brush my hair just like this before I went to school."

Tracy sighed. "I know, mom. You've told me this story hundreds of times."

"There *is* one story that I've never told you about."

"Which one?"

"It concerns your second name."

"Sybil? I know that you named me Sybil after Granny Sybs."

"Yes," whispered Camilla. She was silent for some time, deep in thought. The steady raking sound of the bristles through Tracy's hair filled the room.

"And so? What's the story?" Tracy was intrigued. She'd never really cared much for her second name.

"Do you know *why* your grandmother was given the name Sybs?"

Tracy scratched her head. The bristles tickled her scalp. "No. What's the significance?"

"It's a Greek name."

"Greek? Now that's something I never knew. Really?"

"Yes. Her mother - your great-grandmother - was Greek."

"She came from Greece?"

Camilla smiled. "Yes, Trace. Greeks come from Greece."

"Duh-uh. Obviously. I was just surprised because you never told me any of this before."

"Sybs, short for Sybil, comes from the Greek, Sibylla, meaning prophetess. Your grandmother's name was passed down a long lineage of women dating back thousands of years."

Tracy turned to look at her mother. "Interesting. So, the first Sybil was a kind of seer or something? In Greece?"

"Something like that." Camilla smiled.

"How come *you* don't carry some form of the name?"

"The naming skips a generation."

"Why?"

"I'm not really sure. What I do know is that the first Sybil was a powerful oracle. She could see the future. Through prophecy. There were others too. Angels communicated through them, predicting great events like famines, the outcome of great battles and the fate of men. Some regarded them as deities themselves."

"What's a deity?"

"A divine or supernatural being."

"Wow. What about Granny Sybs? Can she see into the future?"

Camilla placed her hands on Tracy's shoulders and whispered, "Yes. And you will too."

Camilla's words created a strange, tight feeling in the pit of Tracy's stomach twisting her insides like a knot.

"What do you mean?"

"As I said, it skips a generation."

"Why… haven't you told me this before?"

"Because you're not seventeen yet."

"What's that got to do with it? You still could have told me. When? how do I?…"

"Trace. Relax. Everything will be fine. You're not the first and certainly won't be the last."

"Granny Sybs? Really?"

"Yep. She's been able to foretell the future since she was seventeen. That's when it starts happening."

"So *you* can't? It skips a generation?"

"Uh-huh." Camilla nodded.

"And it's been like this for thousands of years?"

"Exactly."

Tracy's mind raced. "Geez. I have so many questions. Ha-ha-ha." Tracy laughed out loud.

"What's so funny?"

"Now that I think about it, every single time that I visit Granny Sybs unannounced, she has tea and cookies ready and waiting like she's expecting me! And remember that time we couldn't visit her because she said it was dangerous? You just agreed with her but when I asked you why, you just said, 'Granny Sybs knows best.' It made absolutely no sense to me. Then that very evening, there was that shooting at Dixon High, right near where she lives." Tracy felt a cold shiver run down her spine. "So weird."

"We must pay her a visit," said Camilla. "Tomorrow. We'll leave early. Spend the day there."

A look of distress crossed Tracy's face.

"Don't worry; I'll make sure we're back in time for your party."

"Yessss!" Tracy fist-pumped the air. "Can we go to Navy Pier? Please?"

"Sure. We can take Granny Sybs there for lunch."

"What about Dylan?"

"He can join us unless he wants to go to a friend."

"I'm sure he'll stay. He hates driving to Chicago. He always says it's boring."

"We'll see. In the meantime, you'd better get ready for school, young lady. You're going to be late. And get that brother of yours out of bed. Otherwise he'll soon be at another detention."

"Yes, ma'am!" Tracy stood up and saluted. "Love you, mom," she said, giving her a squeeze.

"Love you too, baby." She kissed Tracy on the cheek.

The End!

www.ingramcontent.com/pod-product-compliance
Lightning Source LLC
Chambersburg PA
CBHW050543260626
47157CB00002B/412

* 9 7 8 0 6 2 0 6 2 2 6 5 3 *